Taproot

A STORY ABOUT A GARDENER AND A GHOST
Keezy Young

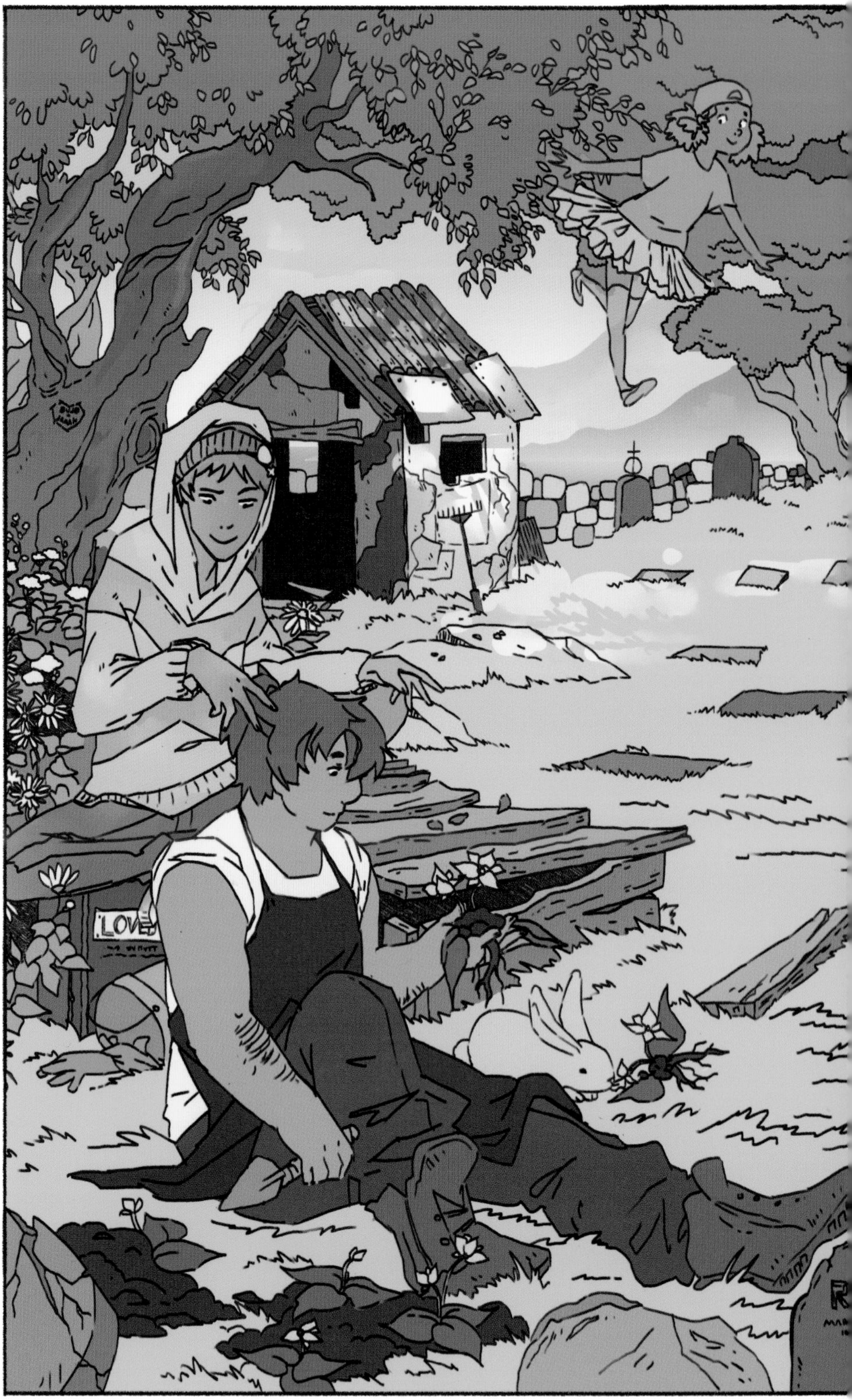
LOVE

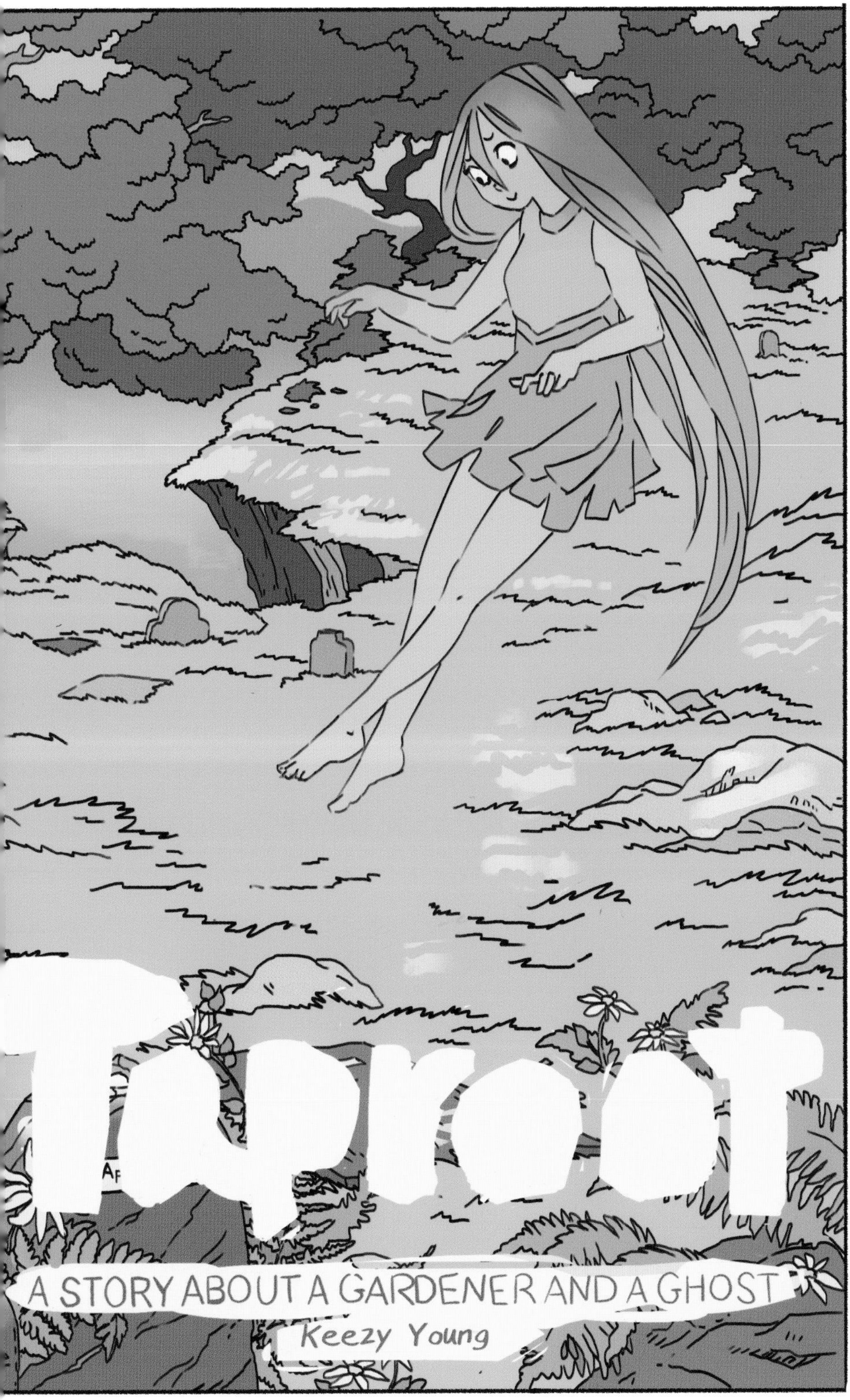
Taproot
A STORY ABOUT A GARDENER AND A GHOST
Keezy Young

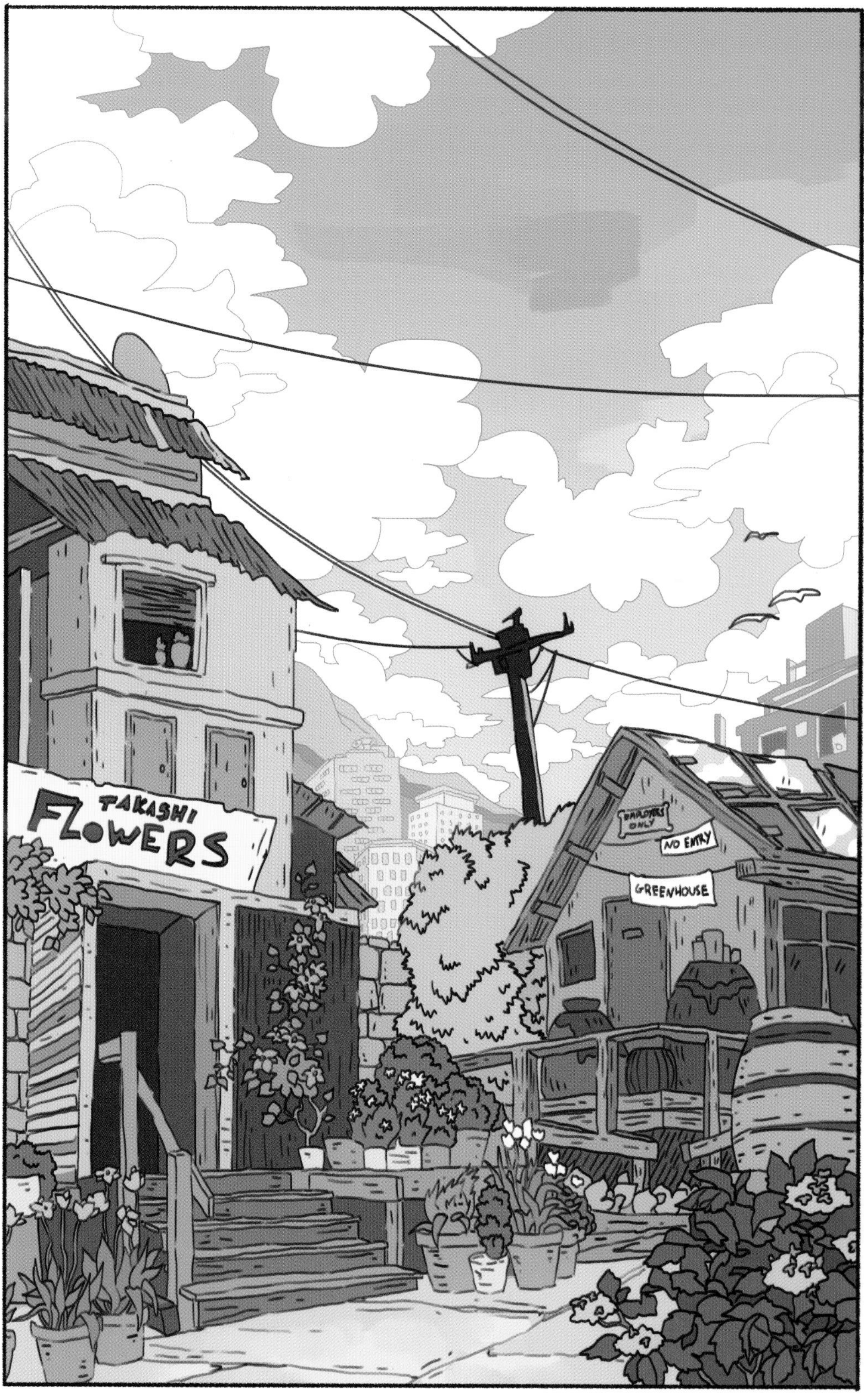
TAKASHI
FLOWERS
NO ENTRY
GREENHOUSE

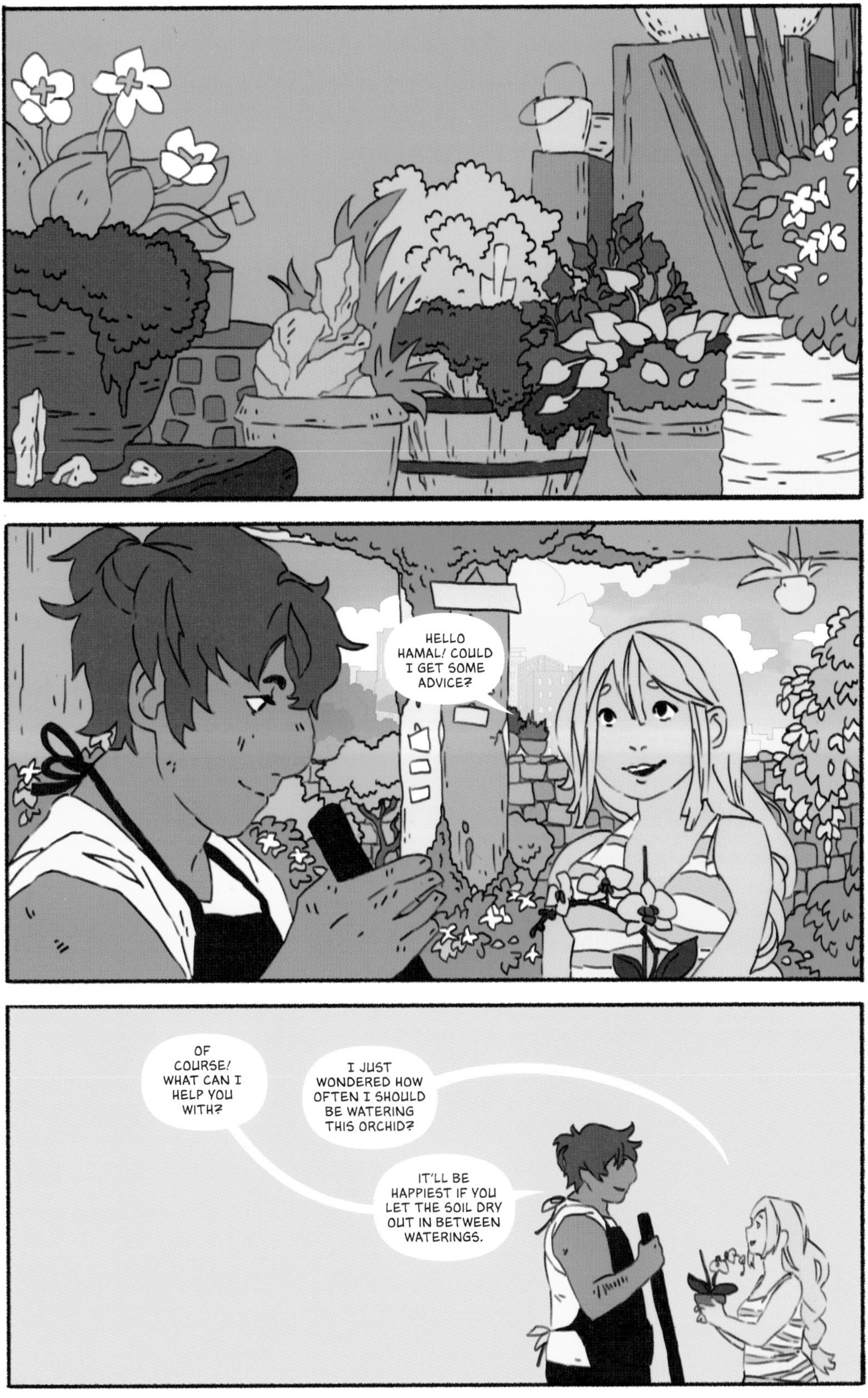

HELLO HAMAL! COULD I GET SOME ADVICE?
OF COURSE! WHAT CAN I HELP YOU WITH?
I JUST WONDERED HOW OFTEN I SHOULD BE WATERING THIS ORCHID?
IT'LL BE HAPPIEST IF YOU LET THE SOIL DRY OUT IN BETWEEN WATERINGS.

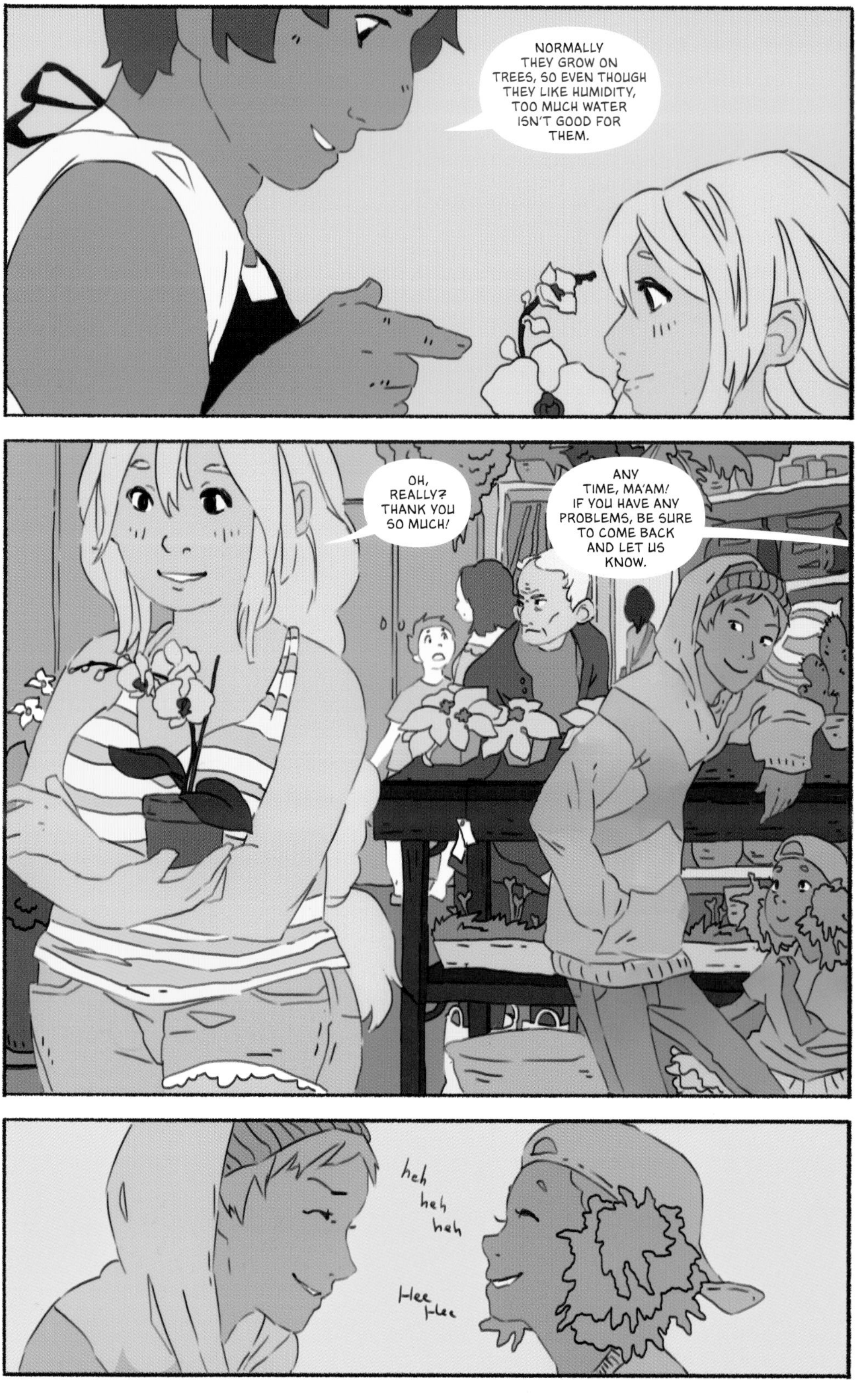
NORMALLY THEY GROW ON TREES, SO EVEN THOUGH THEY LIKE HUMIDITY, TOO MUCH WATER ISN'T GOOD FOR THEM.
OH, REALLY? THANK YOU SO MUCH!
ANY TIME, MA'AM! IF YOU HAVE ANY PROBLEMS, BE SURE TO COME BACK AND LET US KNOW.
heh heh heh
Hee Hee

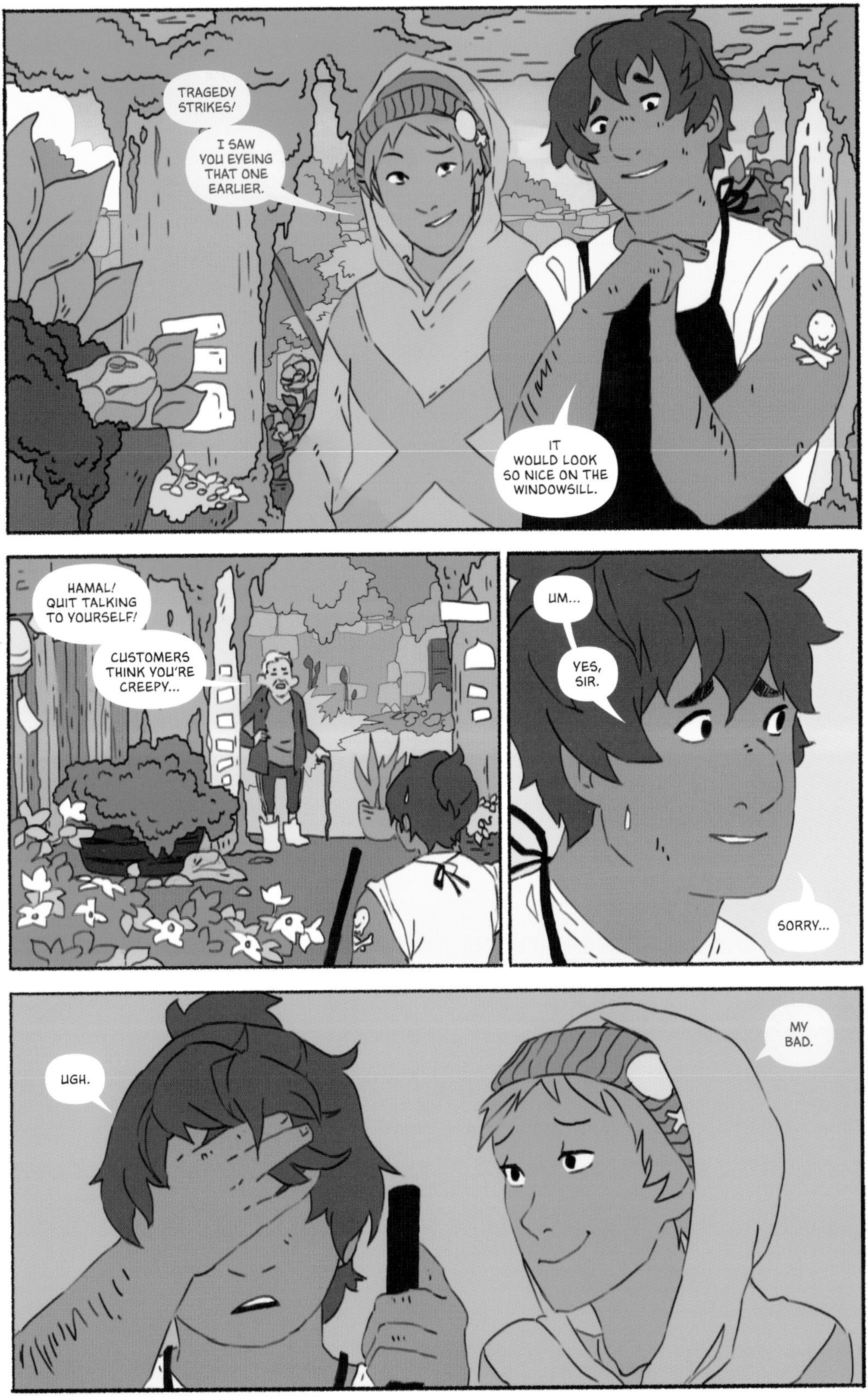
TRAGEDY STRIKES!
I SAW YOU EYEING THAT ONE EARLIER.
IT WOULD LOOK SO NICE ON THE WINDOWSILL.
HAMAL! QUIT TALKING TO YOURSELF!
CUSTOMERS THINK YOU'RE CREEPY...
UM...
YES, SIR.
SORRY...
UGH.
MY BAD.

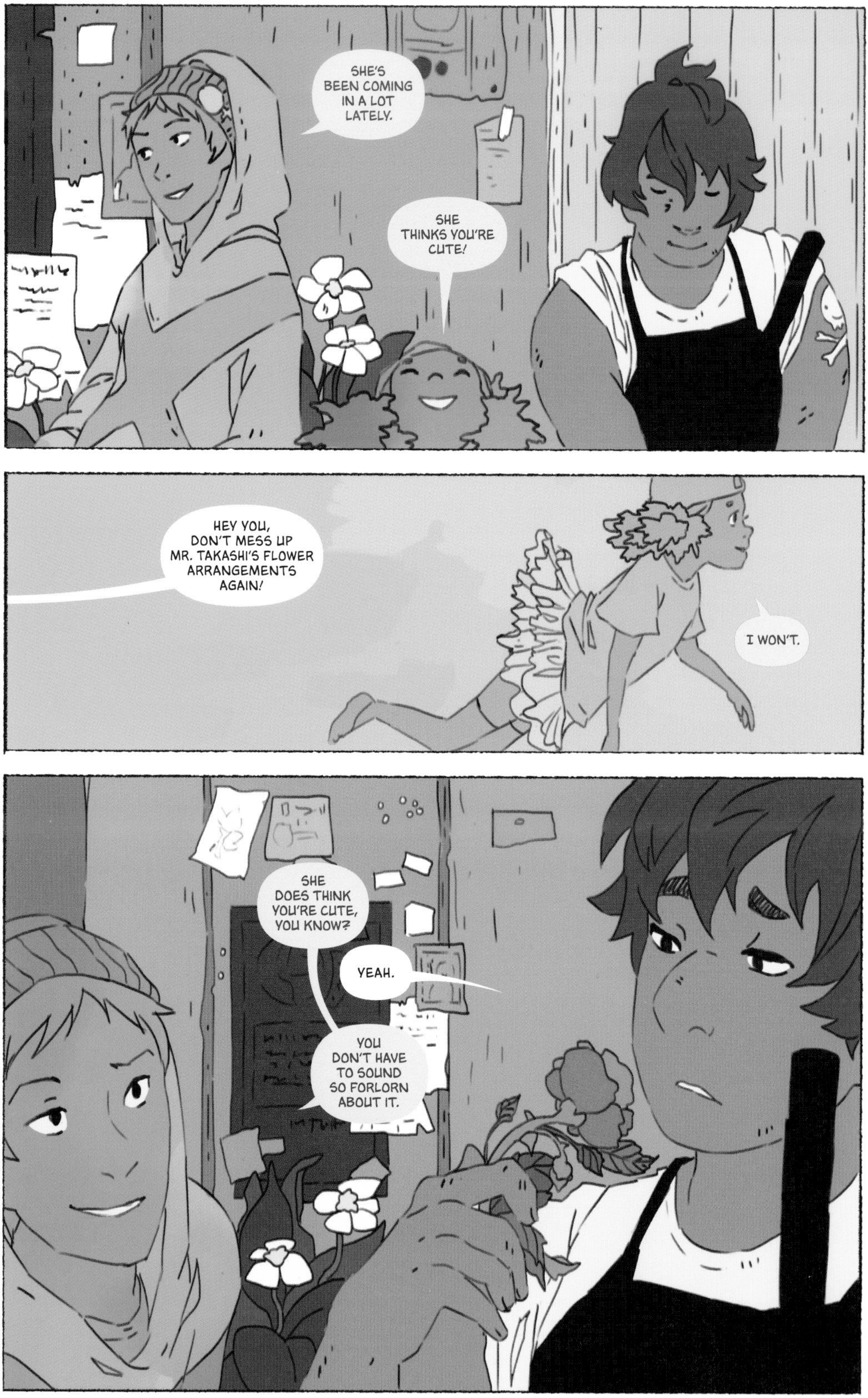
SHE'S BEEN COMING IN A LOT LATELY.
SHE THINKS YOU'RE CUTE!
HEY YOU, DON'T MESS UP MR. TAKASHI'S FLOWER ARRANGEMENTS AGAIN!
I WON'T.
SHE DOES THINK YOU'RE CUTE, YOU KNOW?
YEAH.
YOU DON'T HAVE TO SOUND SO FORLORN ABOUT IT.

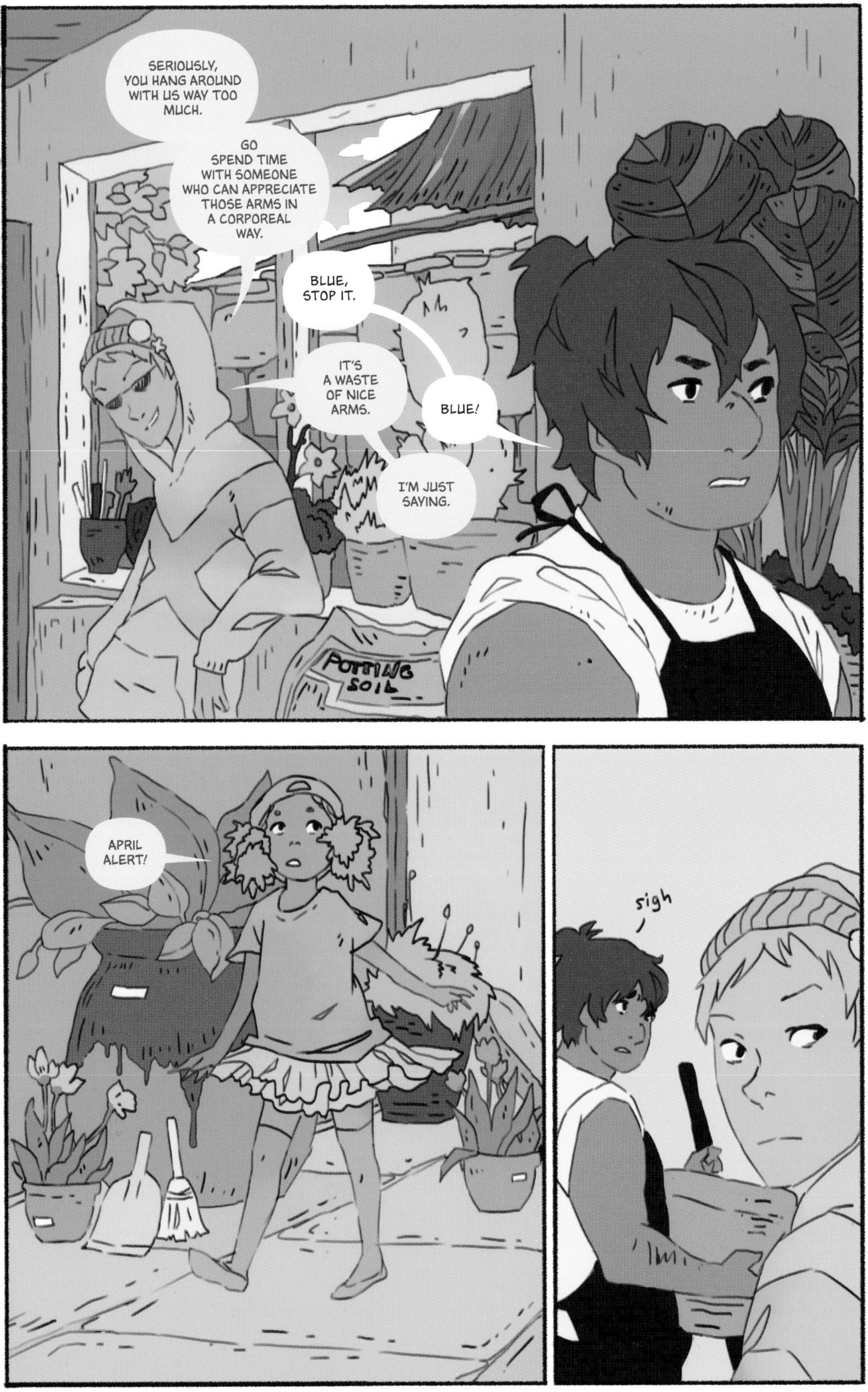

SERIOUSLY, YOU HANG AROUND WITH US WAY TOO MUCH.
GO SPEND TIME WITH SOMEONE WHO CAN APPRECIATE THOSE ARMS IN A CORPOREAL WAY.
BLUE, STOP IT.
IT'S A WASTE OF NICE ARMS.
BLUE!
I'M JUST SAYING.
POTTING SOIL
APRIL ALERT!
sigh

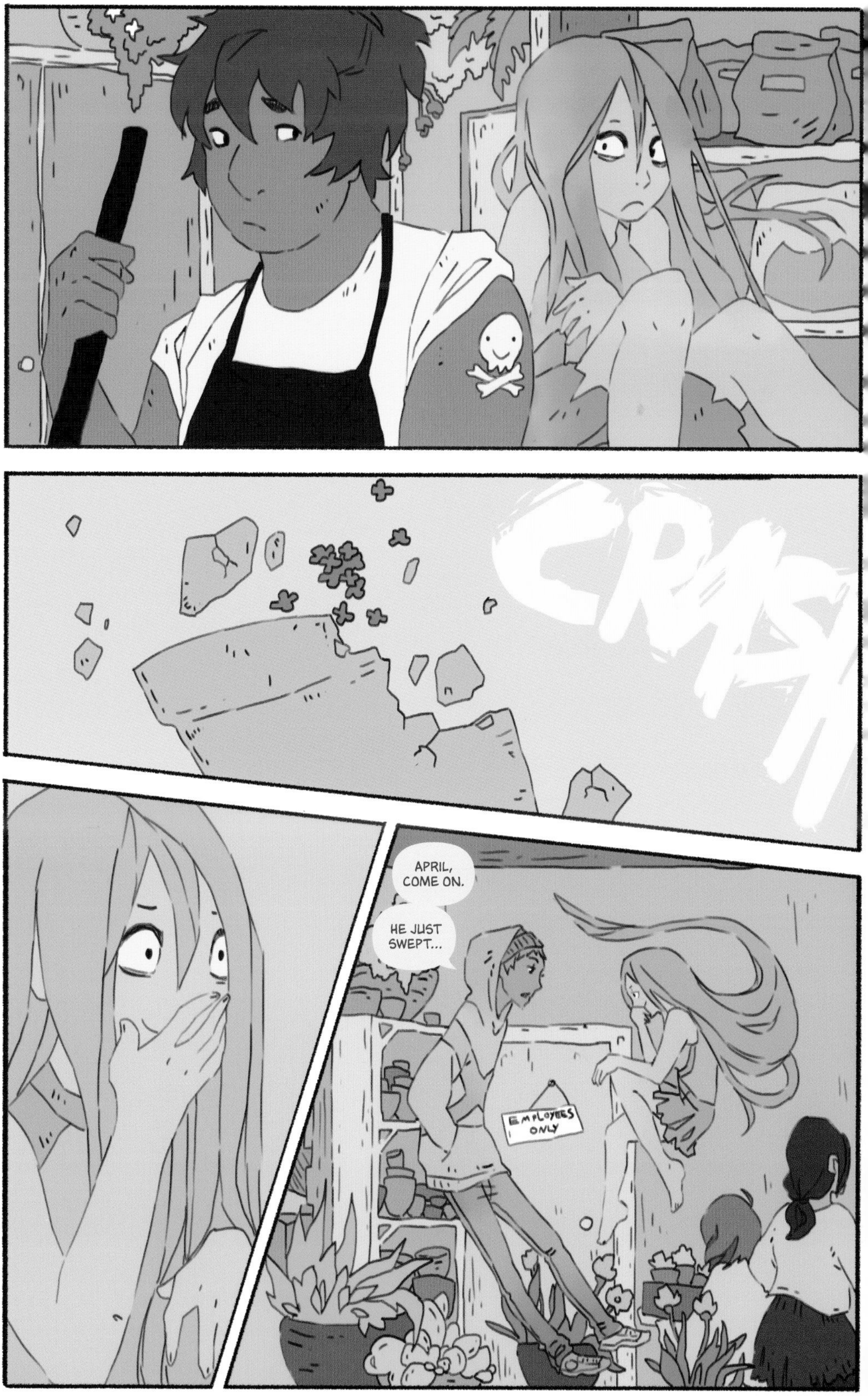
CRASH
APRIL, COME ON.
HE JUST SWEPT...
EMPLOYEES ONLY

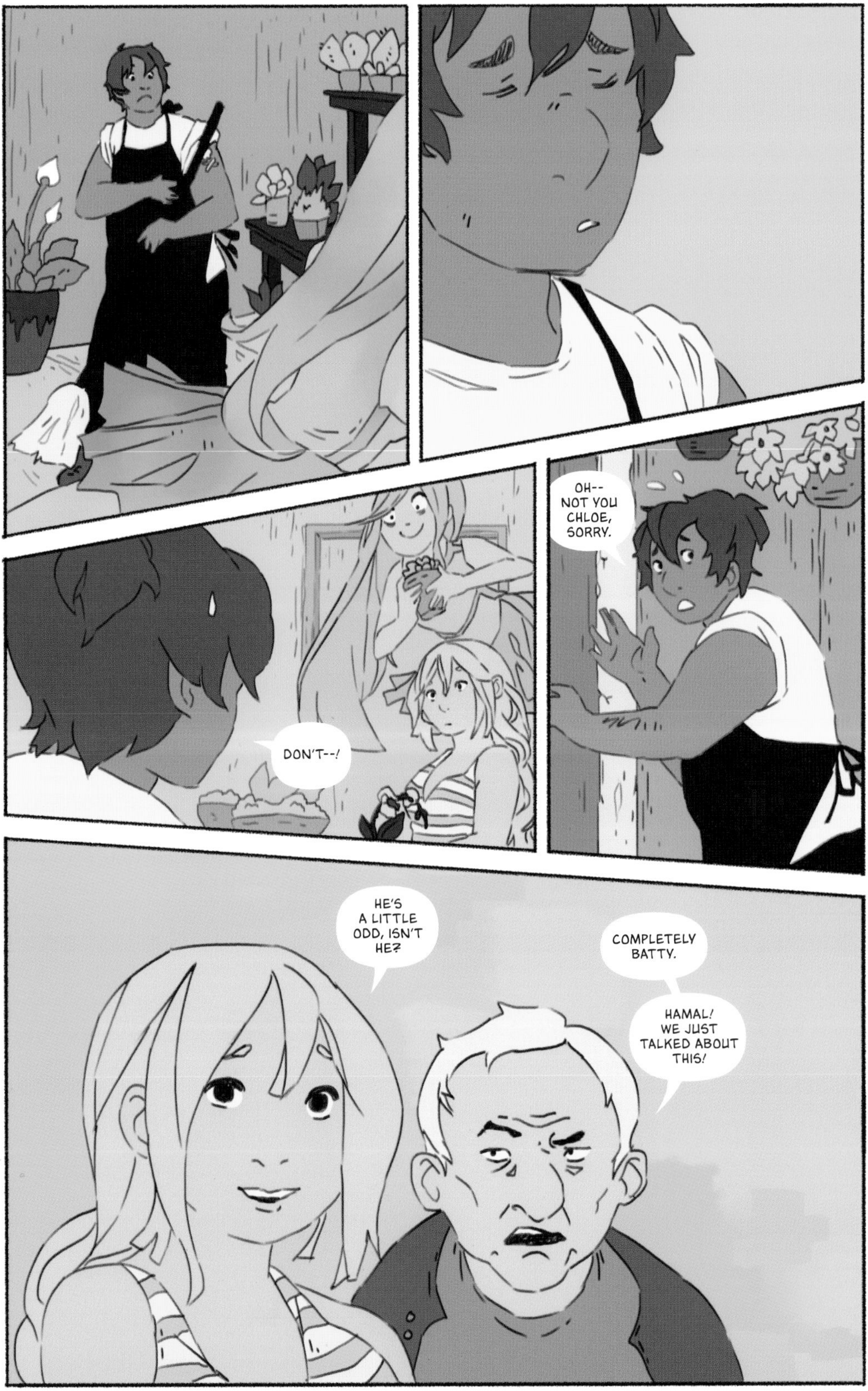
DON'T--!
OH--
NOT YOU
CHLOE,
SORRY.
HE'S
A LITTLE
ODD, ISN'T
HE?
COMPLETELY
BATTY.
HAMAL!
WE JUST
TALKED ABOUT
THIS!

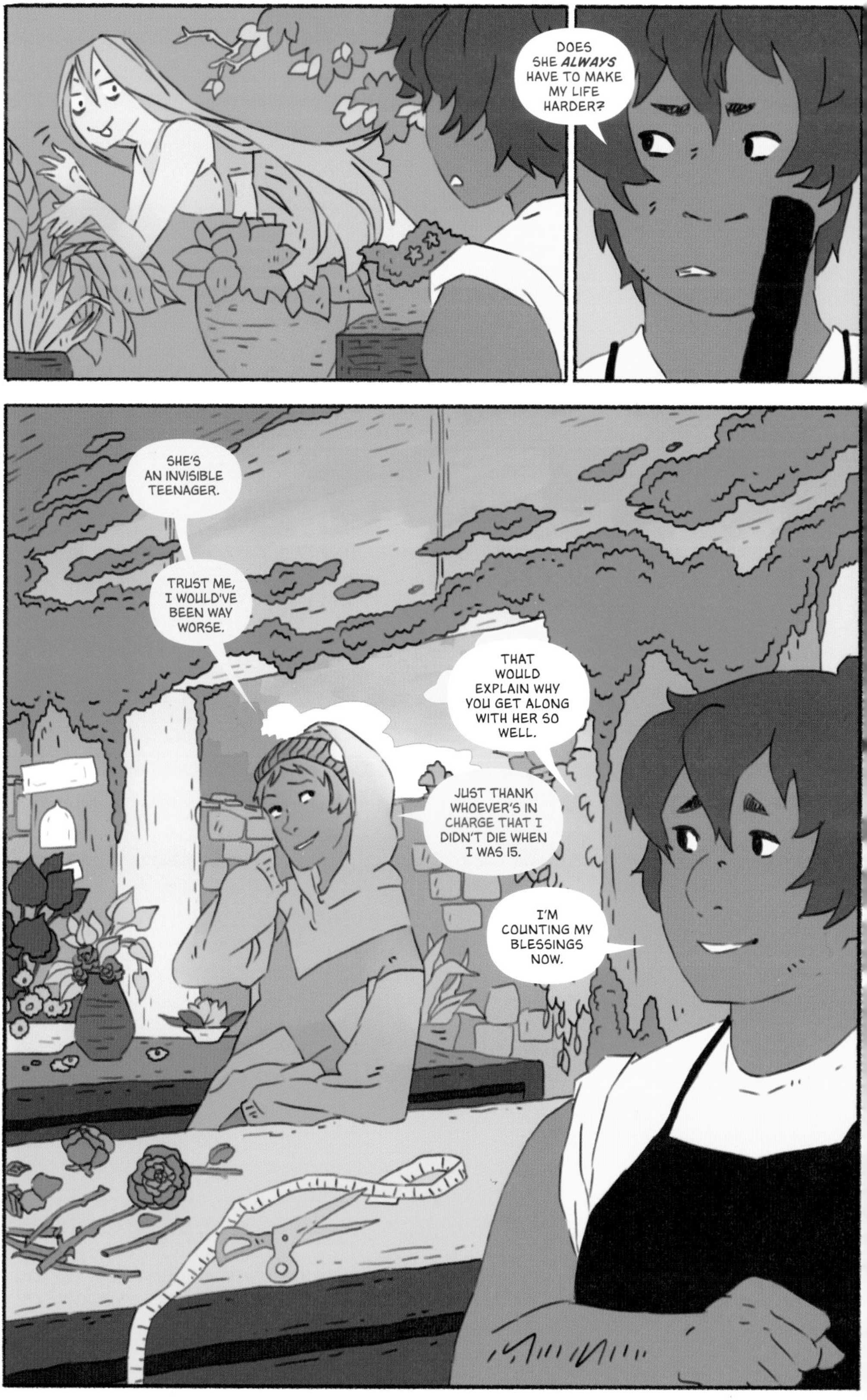
DOES SHE *ALWAYS* HAVE TO MAKE MY LIFE HARDER?
SHE'S AN INVISIBLE TEENAGER.
TRUST ME, I WOULD'VE BEEN WAY WORSE.
THAT WOULD EXPLAIN WHY YOU GET ALONG WITH HER SO WELL.
JUST THANK WHOEVER'S IN CHARGE THAT I DIDN'T DIE WHEN I WAS 15.
I'M COUNTING MY BLESSINGS NOW.

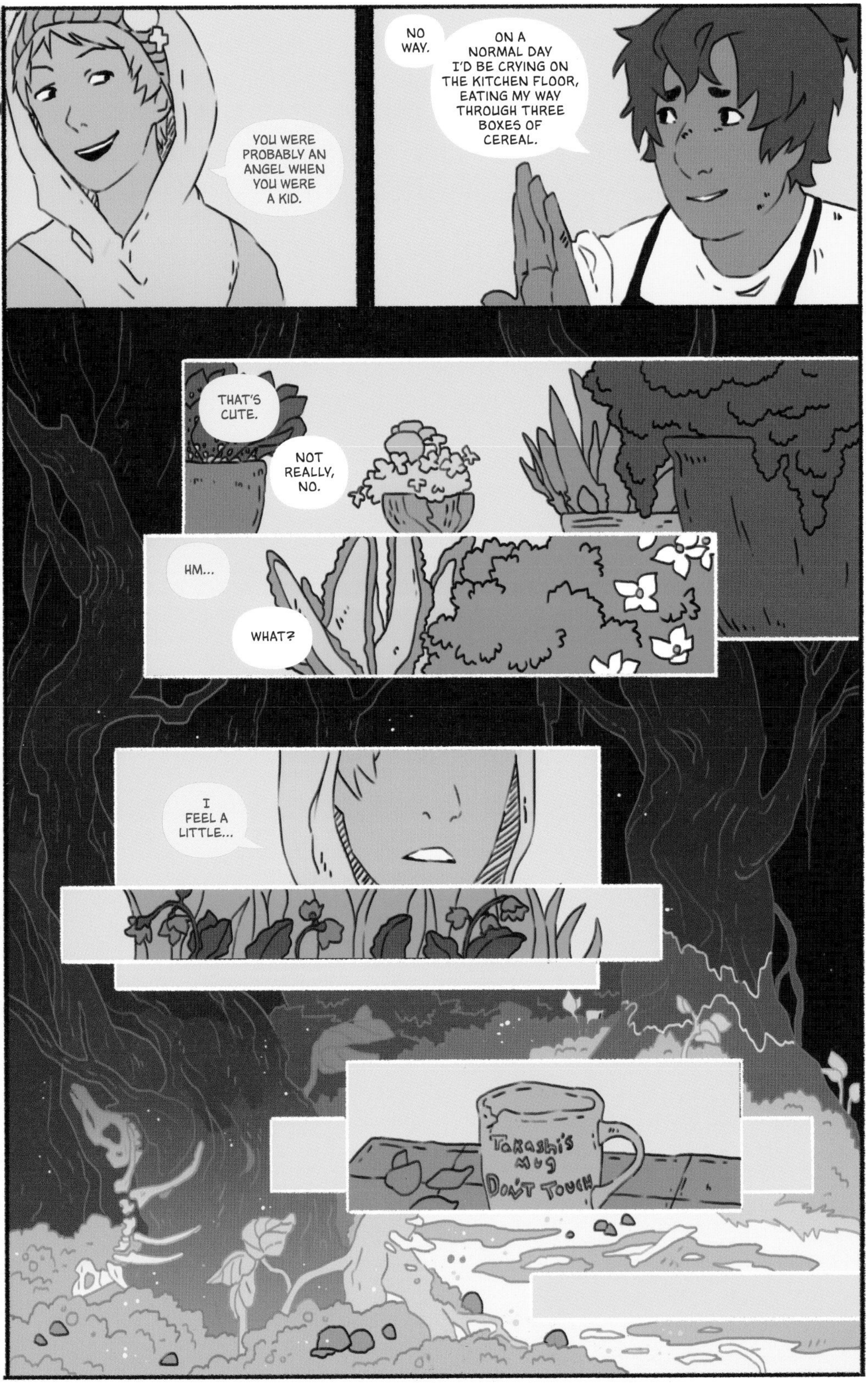
YOU WERE PROBABLY AN ANGEL WHEN YOU WERE A KID.
NO WAY.
ON A NORMAL DAY I'D BE CRYING ON THE KITCHEN FLOOR, EATING MY WAY THROUGH THREE BOXES OF CEREAL.
THAT'S CUTE.
NOT REALLY, NO.
HM...
WHAT?
I FEEL A LITTLE...
Takashi's Mug DON'T TOUCH

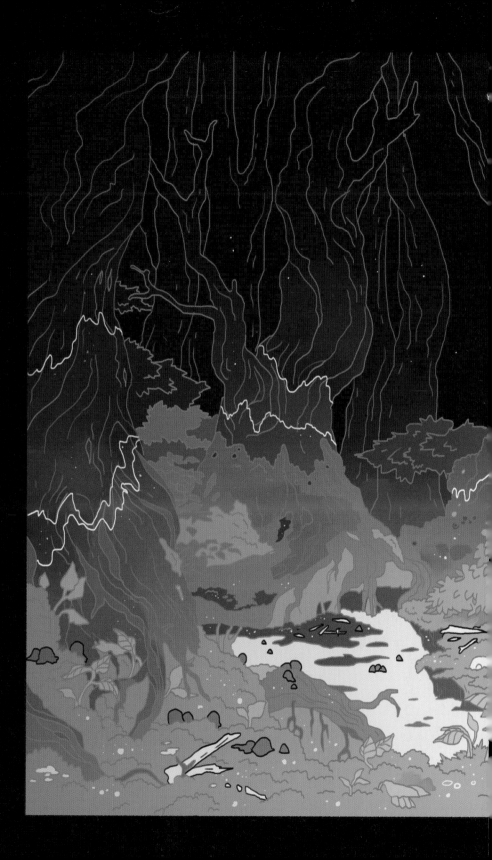

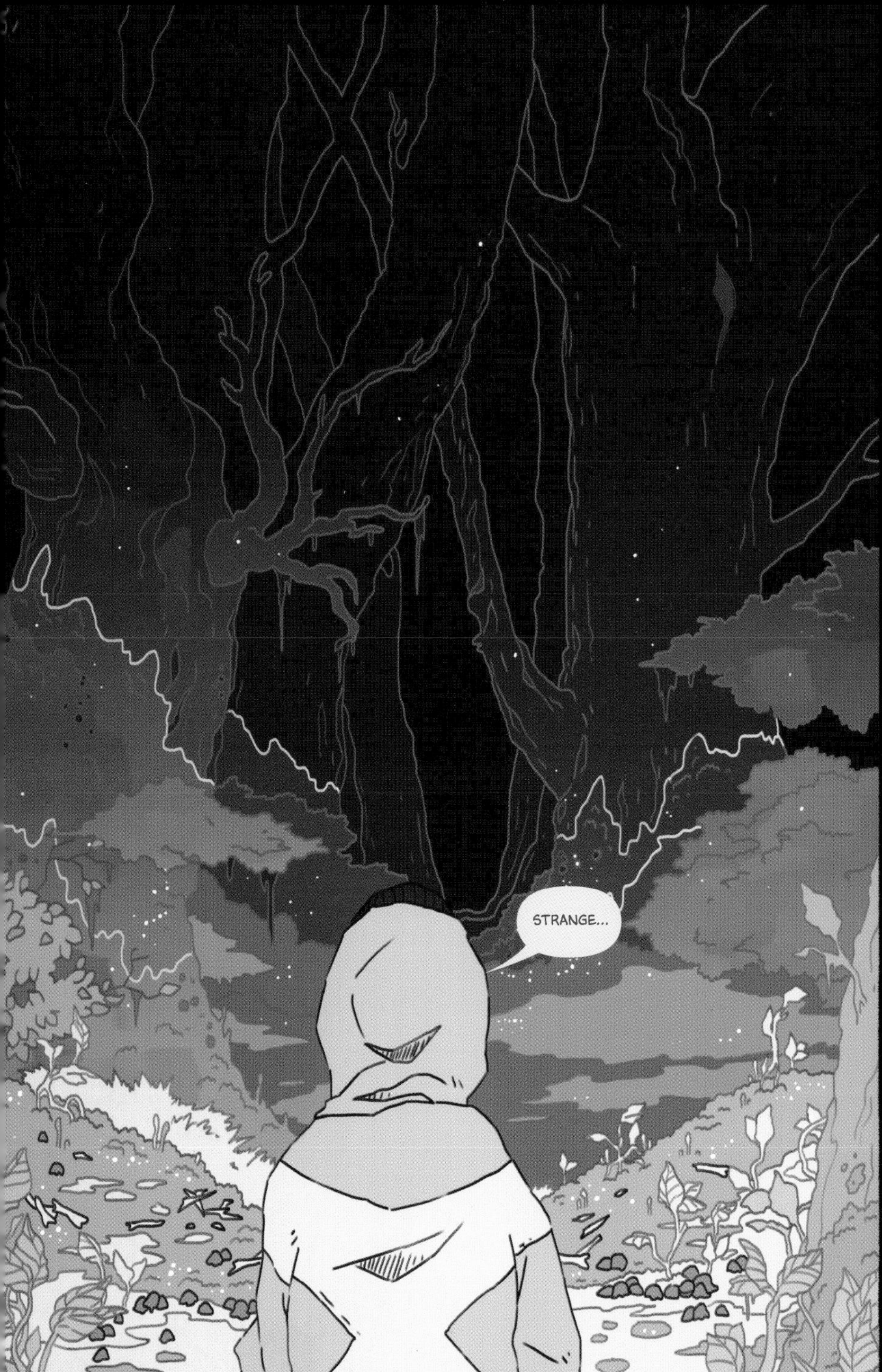
STRANGE...

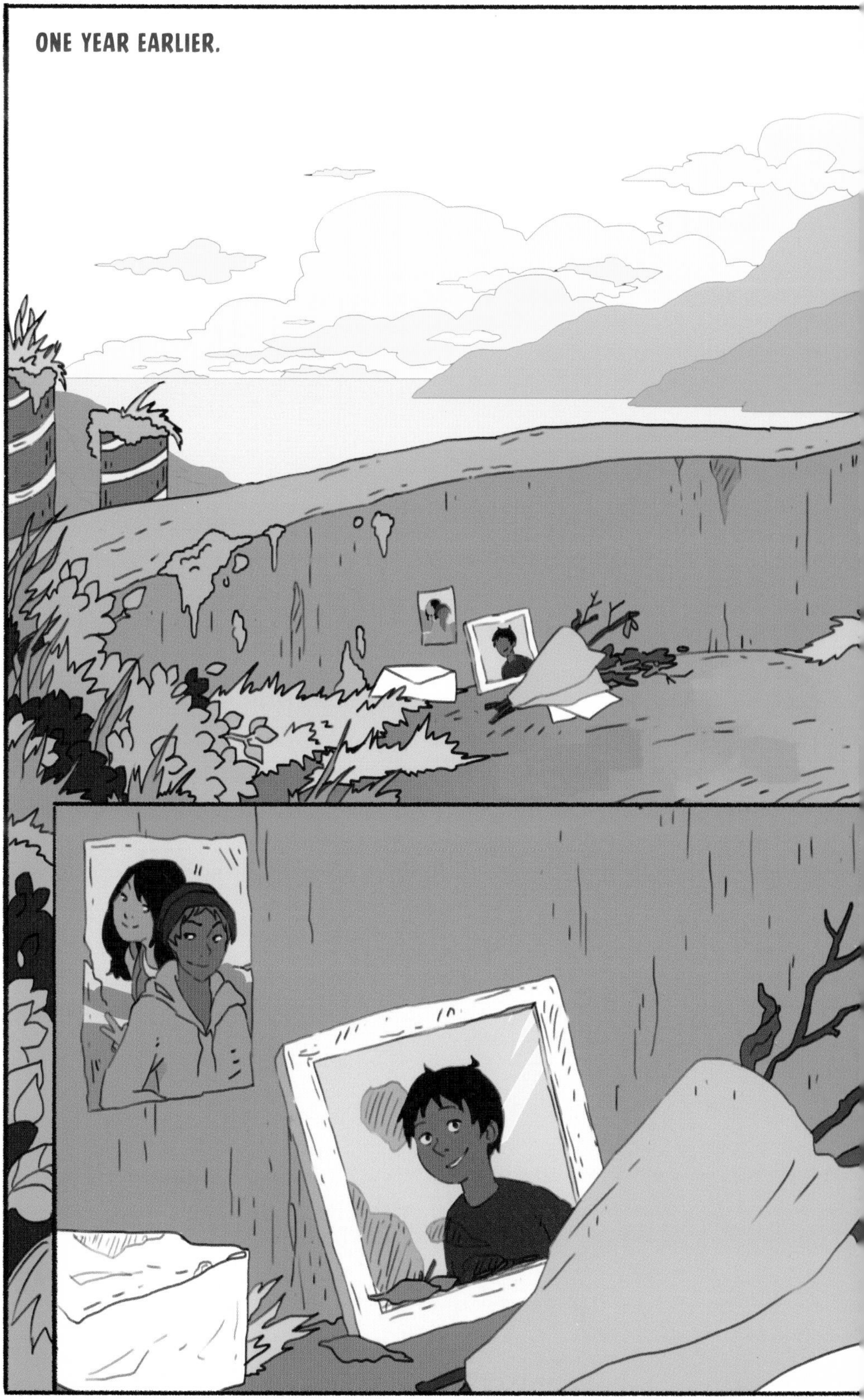
ONE YEAR EARLIER.

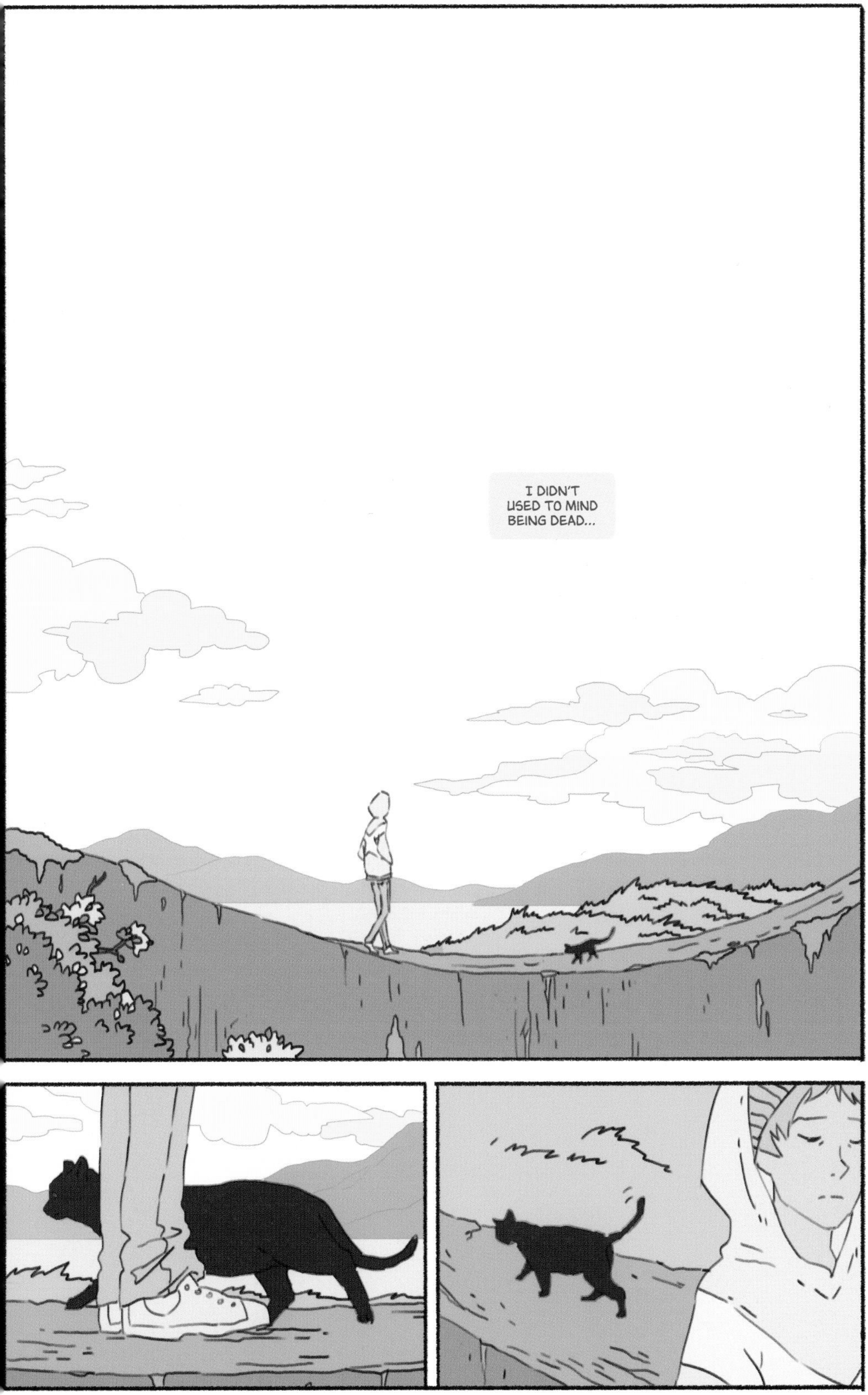
I DIDN'T USED TO MIND BEING DEAD...

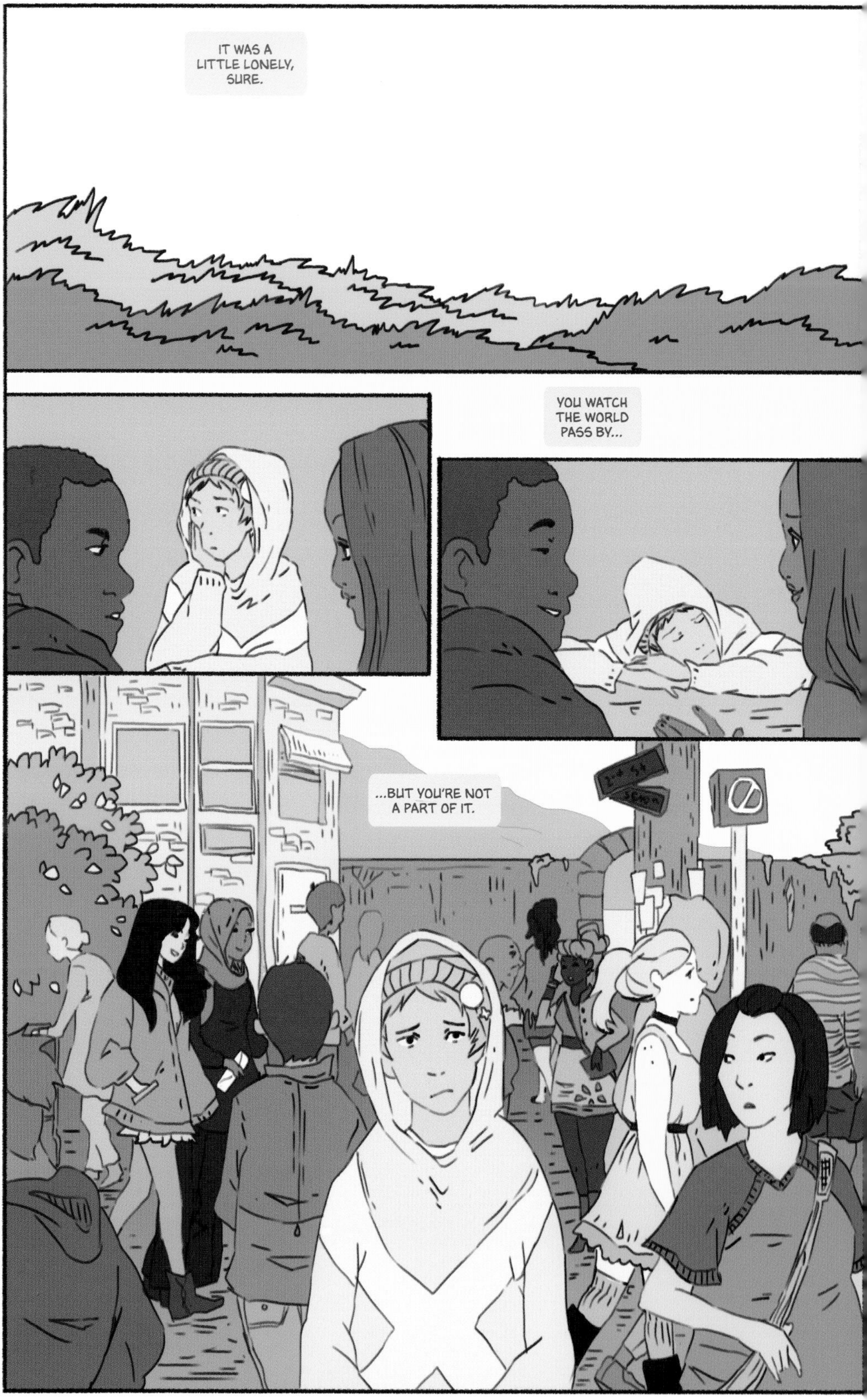
IT WAS A LITTLE LONELY, SURE.
YOU WATCH THE WORLD PASS BY...
...BUT YOU'RE NOT A PART OF IT.

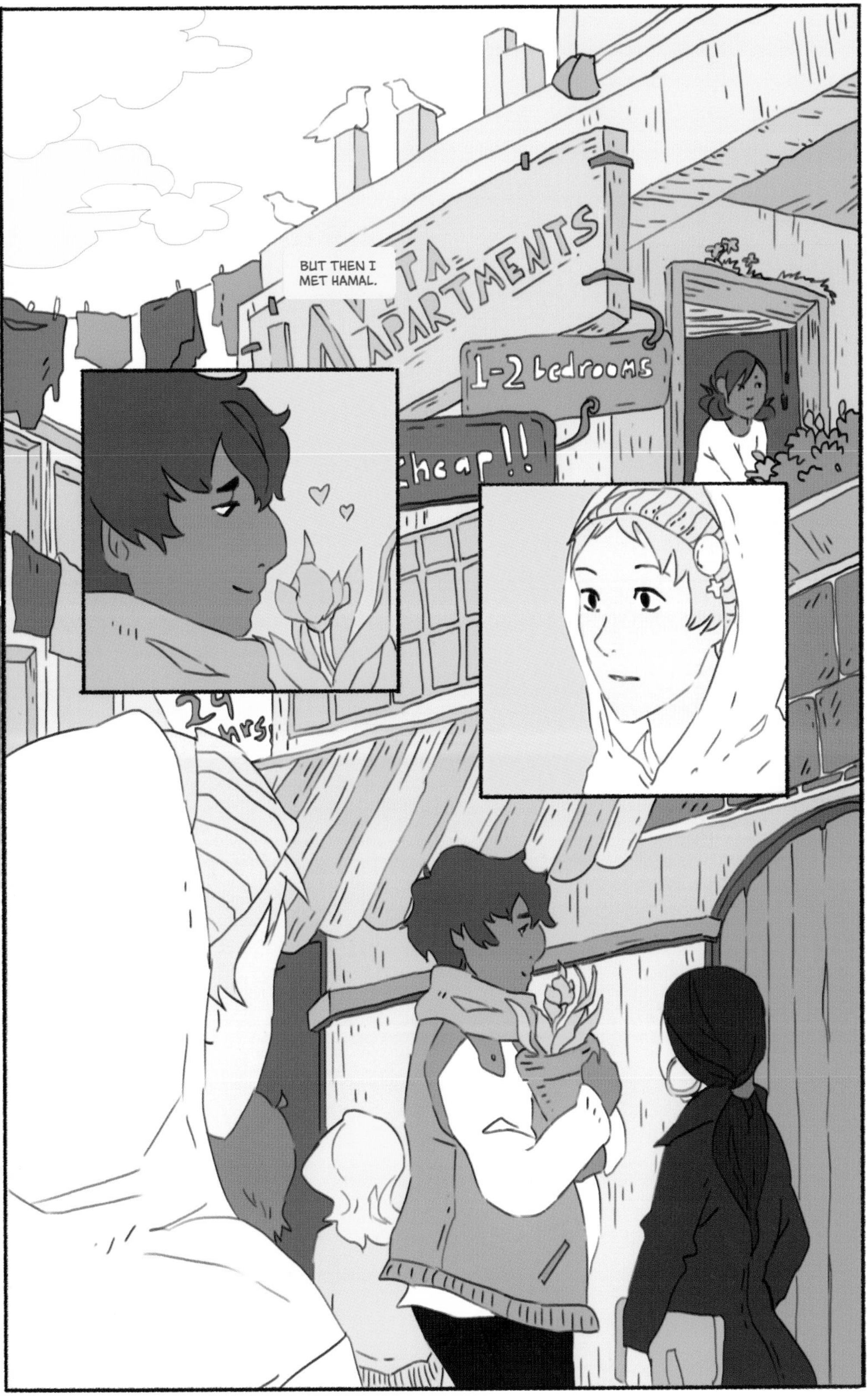
BUT THEN I MET HAMAL.
APARTMENTS
1-2 bedrooms
cheap!!
24 hrs

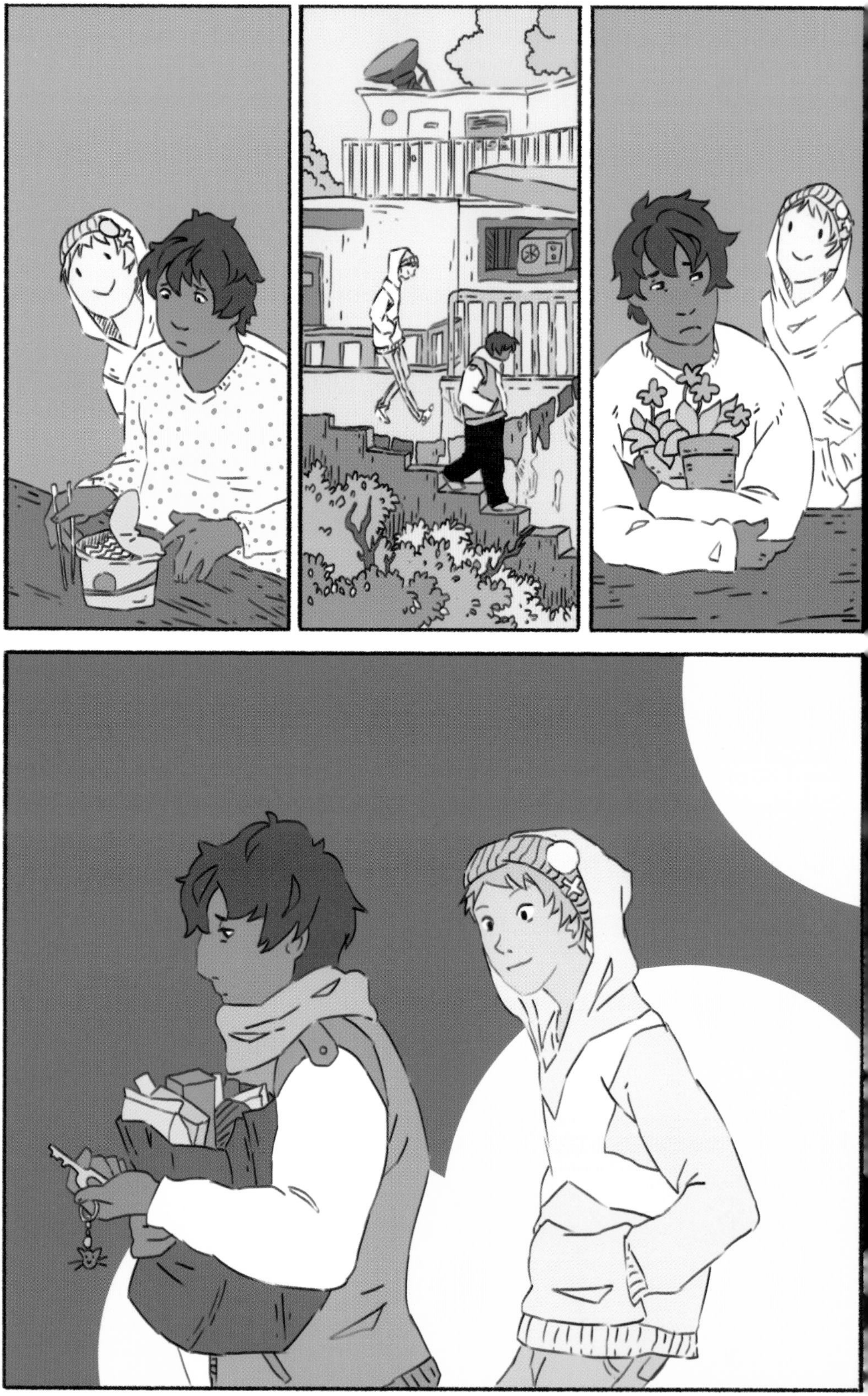

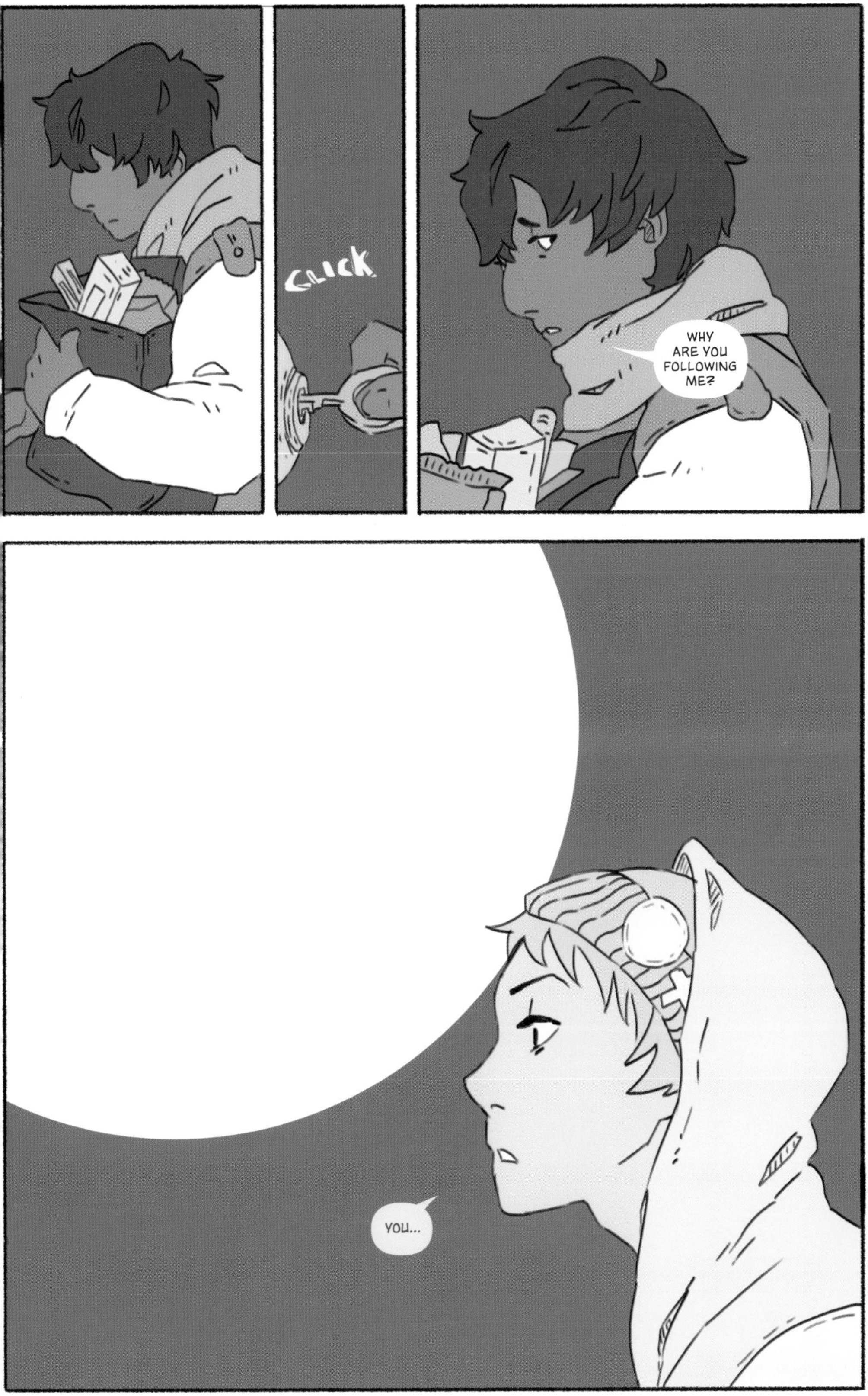
CLICK
WHY ARE YOU FOLLOWING ME?
YOU...

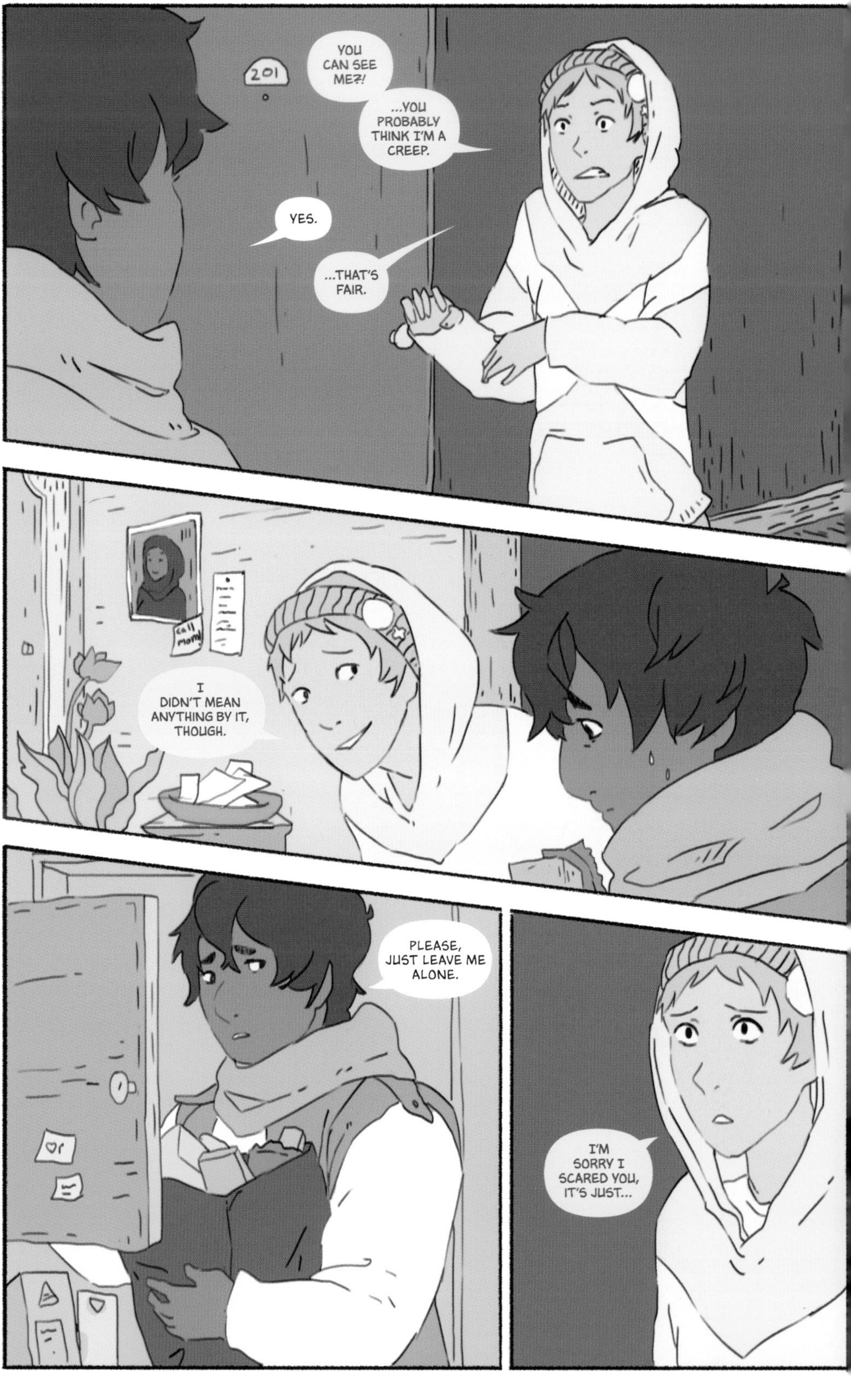

201
YOU CAN SEE ME?!
...YOU PROBABLY THINK I'M A CREEP.
YES.
...THAT'S FAIR.
call mom!
I DIDN'T MEAN ANYTHING BY IT, THOUGH.
PLEASE, JUST LEAVE ME ALONE.
I'M SORRY I SCARED YOU, IT'S JUST...

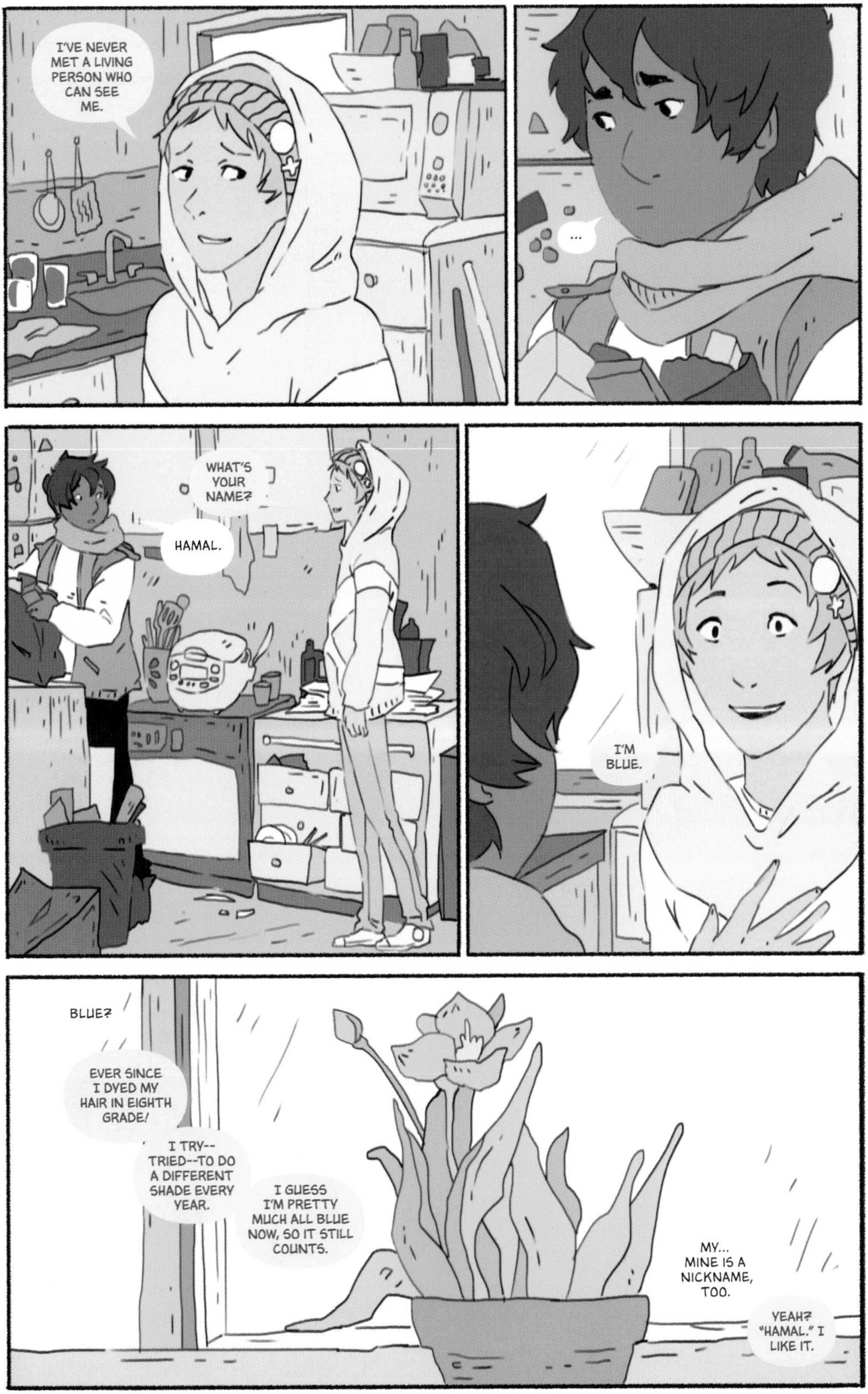
I'VE NEVER MET A LIVING PERSON WHO CAN SEE ME.
...
WHAT'S YOUR NAME?
HAMAL.
I'M BLUE.
BLUE?
EVER SINCE I DYED MY HAIR IN EIGHTH GRADE!
I TRY-- TRIED--TO DO A DIFFERENT SHADE EVERY YEAR.
I GUESS I'M PRETTY MUCH ALL BLUE NOW, SO IT STILL COUNTS.
MY... MINE IS A NICKNAME, TOO.
YEAH? "HAMAL." I LIKE IT.

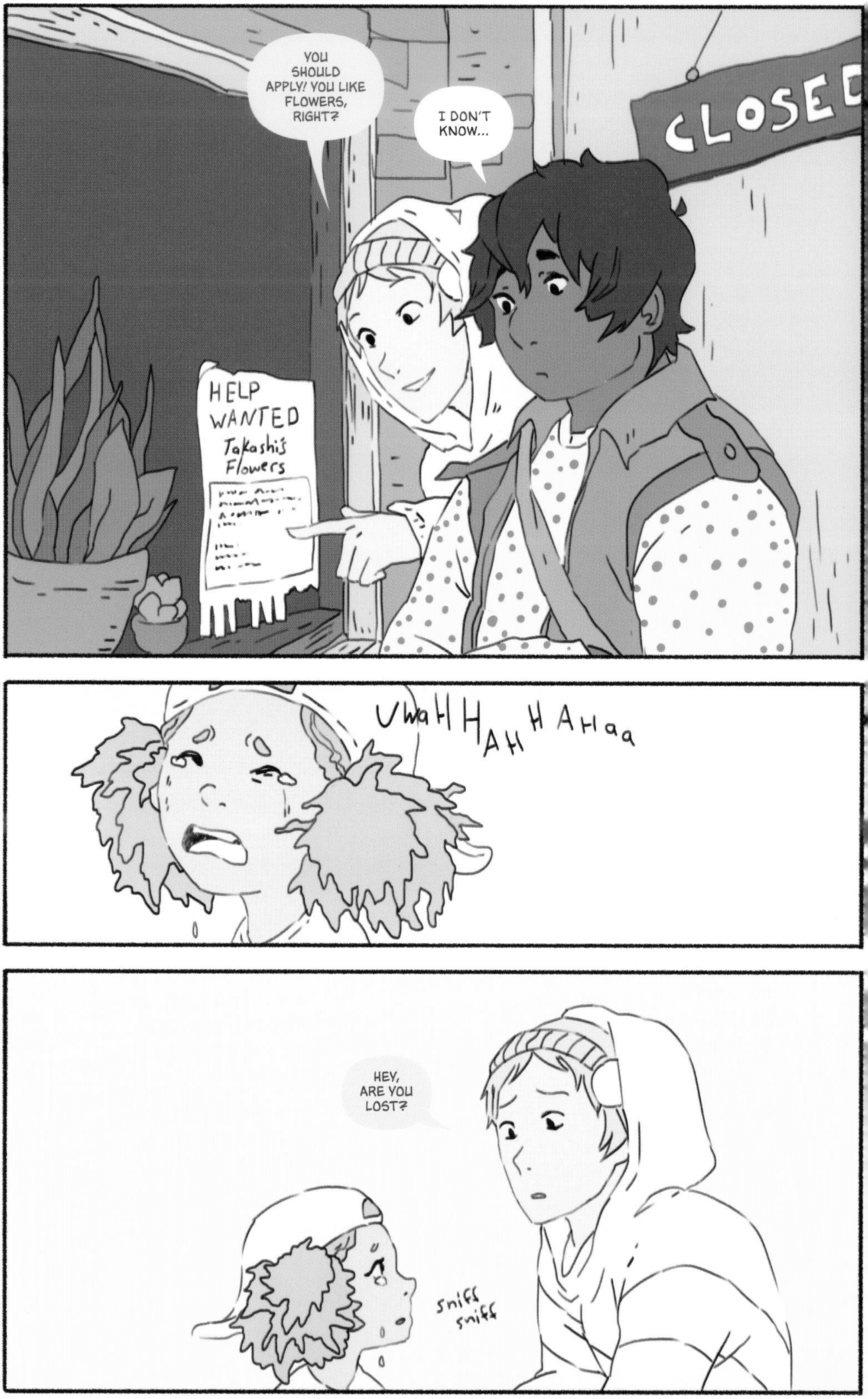
YOU SHOULD APPLY! YOU LIKE FLOWERS, RIGHT?
I DON'T KNOW...
CLOSE
HELP WANTED
Takashi's Flowers
UwaHH HAH HAHaa
HEY, ARE YOU LOST?
sniff sniff

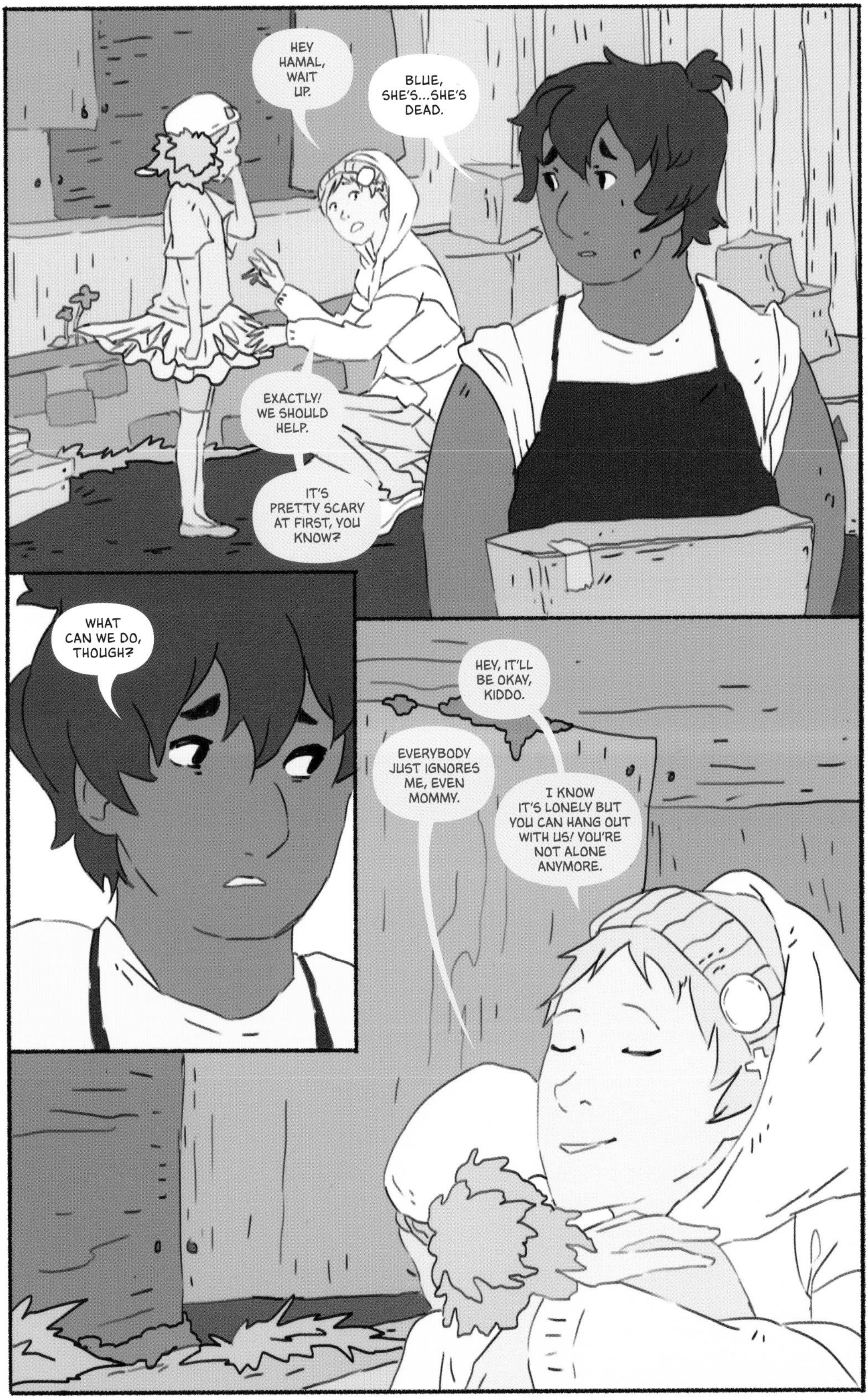
HEY HAMAL, WAIT UP.
BLUE, SHE'S...SHE'S DEAD.
EXACTLY! WE SHOULD HELP.
IT'S PRETTY SCARY AT FIRST, YOU KNOW?
WHAT CAN WE DO, THOUGH?
HEY, IT'LL BE OKAY, KIDDO.
EVERYBODY JUST IGNORES ME, EVEN MOMMY.
I KNOW IT'S LONELY BUT YOU CAN HANG OUT WITH US! YOU'RE NOT ALONE ANYMORE.

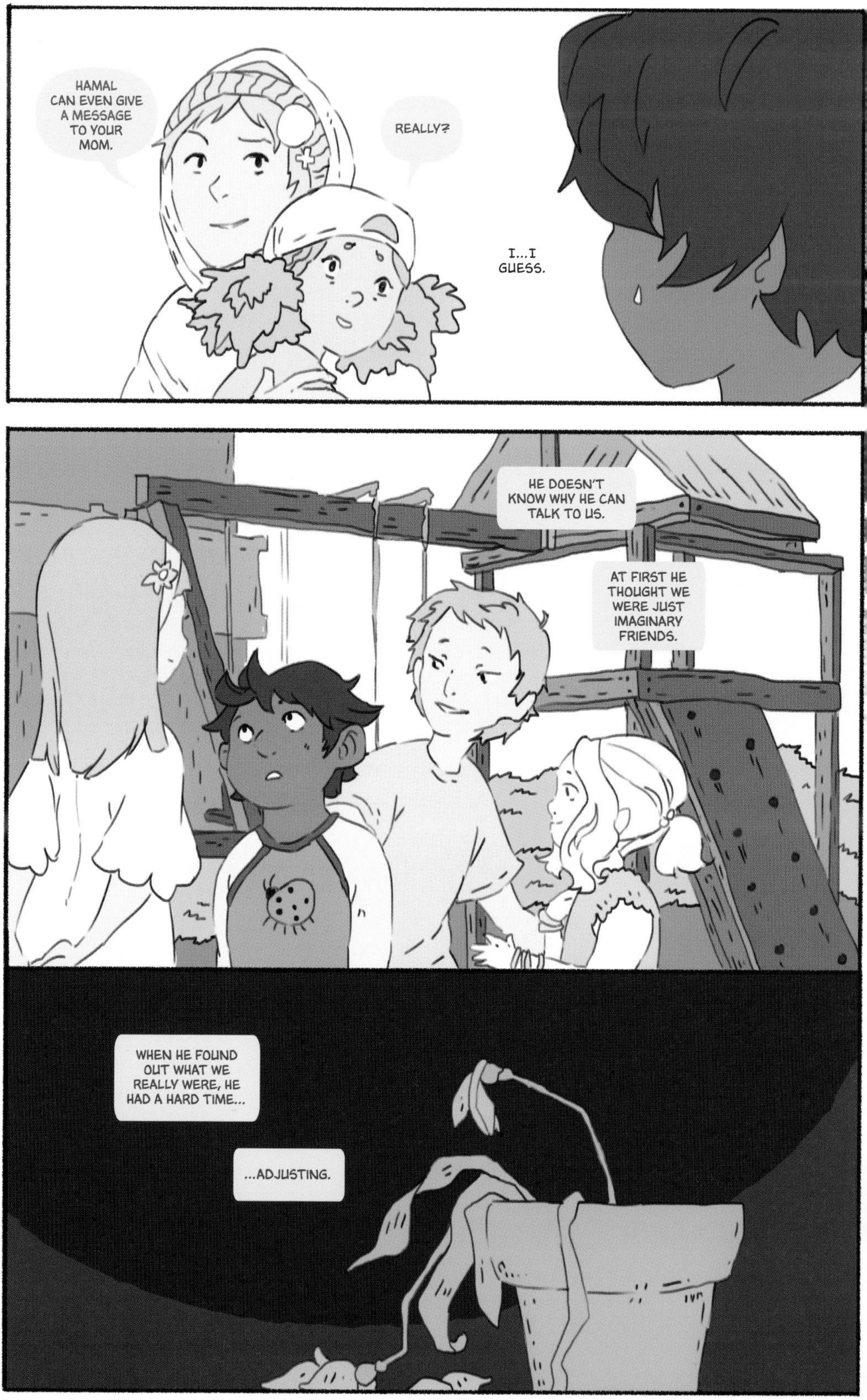
HAMAL CAN EVEN GIVE A MESSAGE TO YOUR MOM.
REALLY?
I...I GUESS.
HE DOESN'T KNOW WHY HE CAN TALK TO US.
AT FIRST HE THOUGHT WE WERE JUST IMAGINARY FRIENDS.
WHEN HE FOUND OUT WHAT WE REALLY WERE, HE HAD A HARD TIME...
...ADJUSTING.

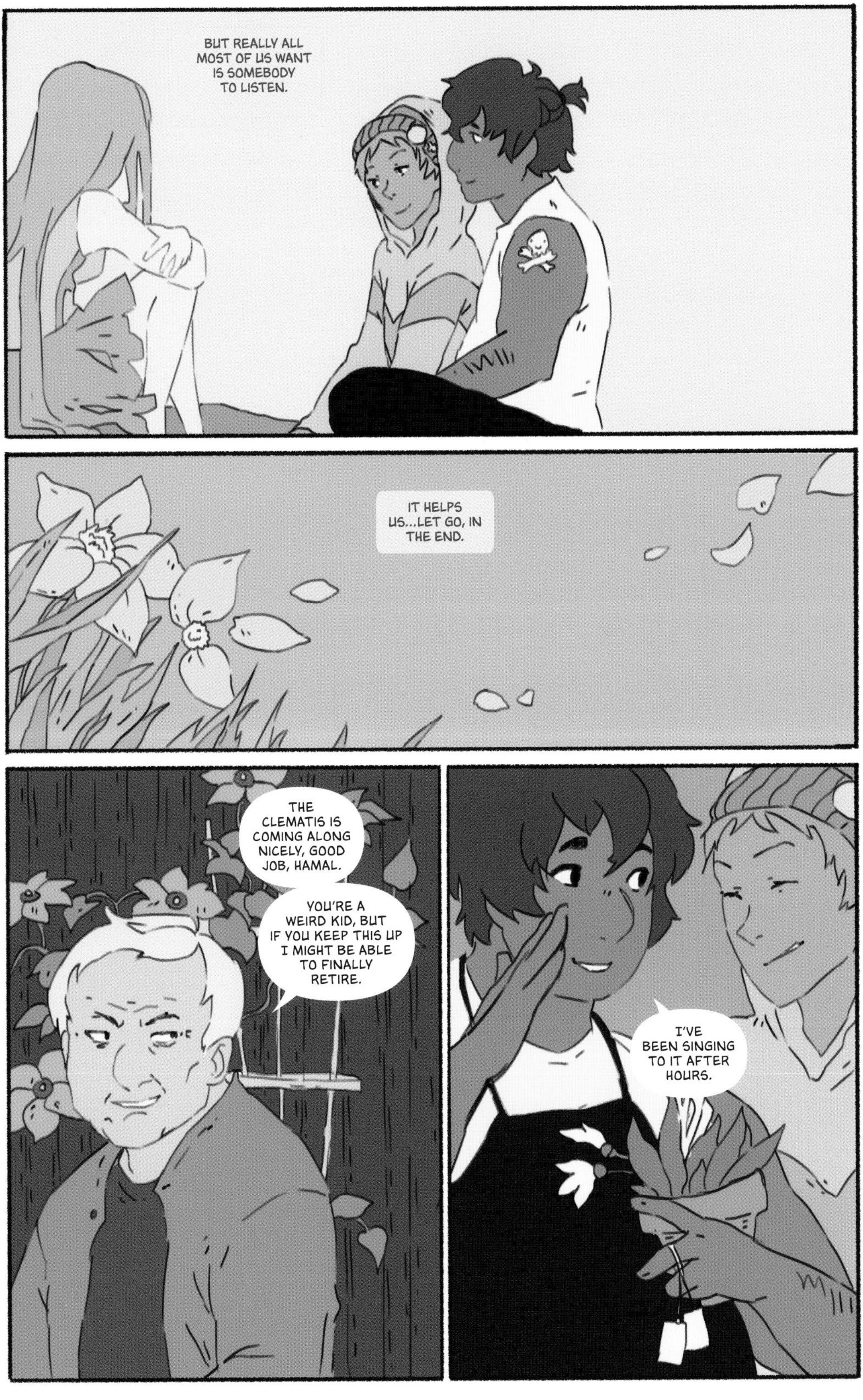
BUT REALLY ALL MOST OF US WANT IS SOMEBODY TO LISTEN.
IT HELPS US...LET GO, IN THE END.
THE CLEMATIS IS COMING ALONG NICELY, GOOD JOB, HAMAL.
YOU'RE A WEIRD KID, BUT IF YOU KEEP THIS UP I MIGHT BE ABLE TO FINALLY RETIRE.
I'VE BEEN SINGING TO IT AFTER HOURS.

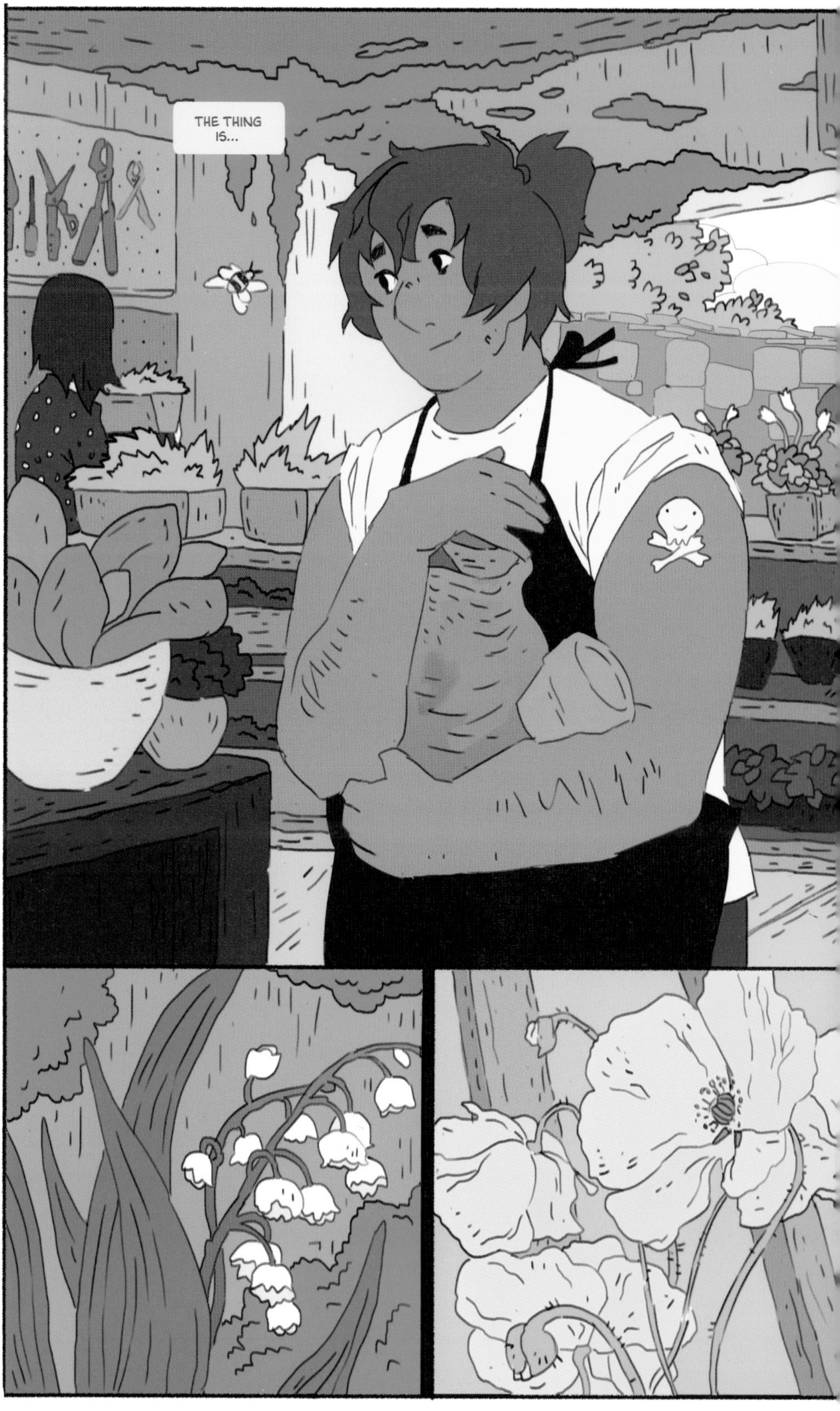
THE THING IS...

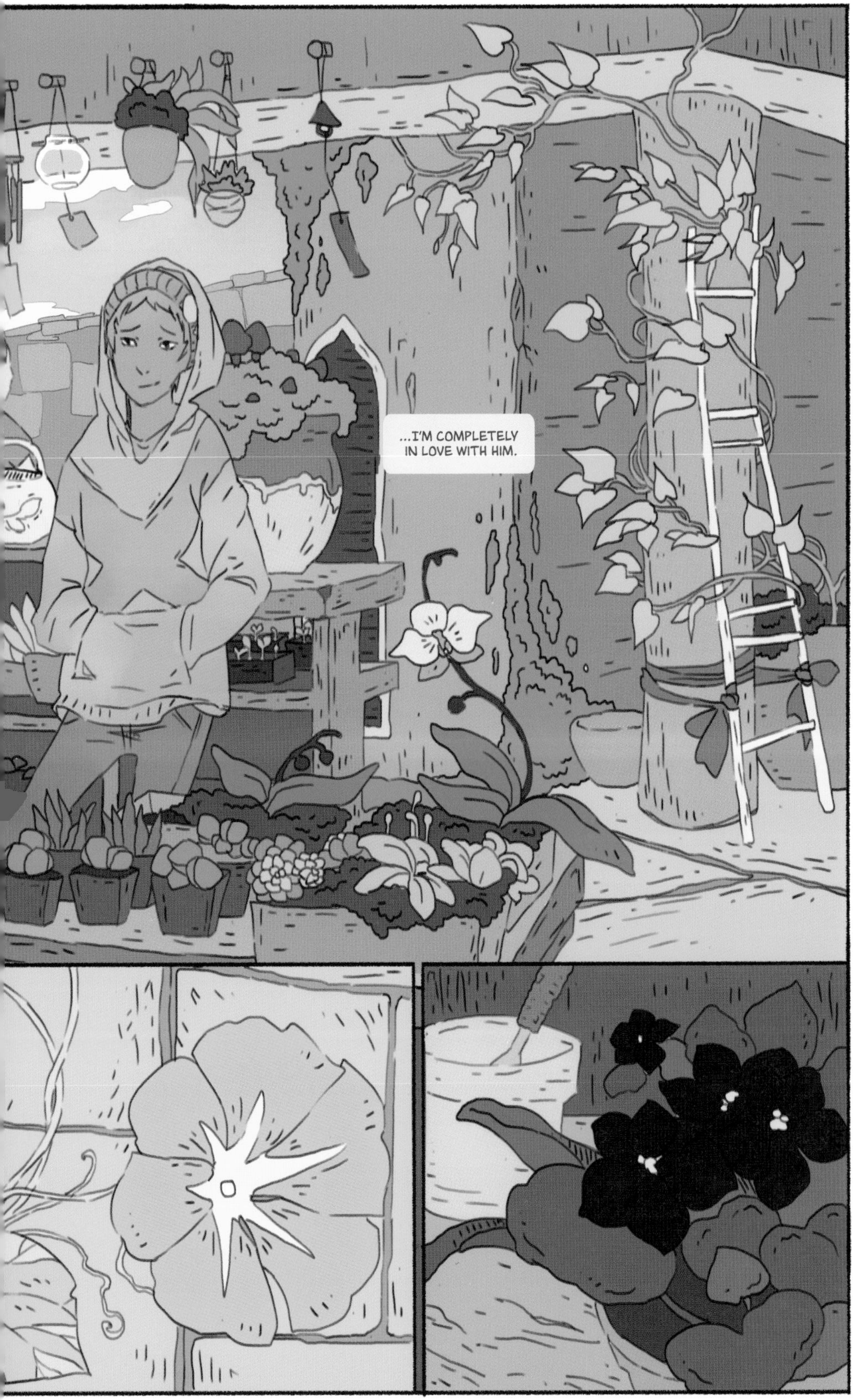
...I'M COMPLETELY IN LOVE WITH HIM.

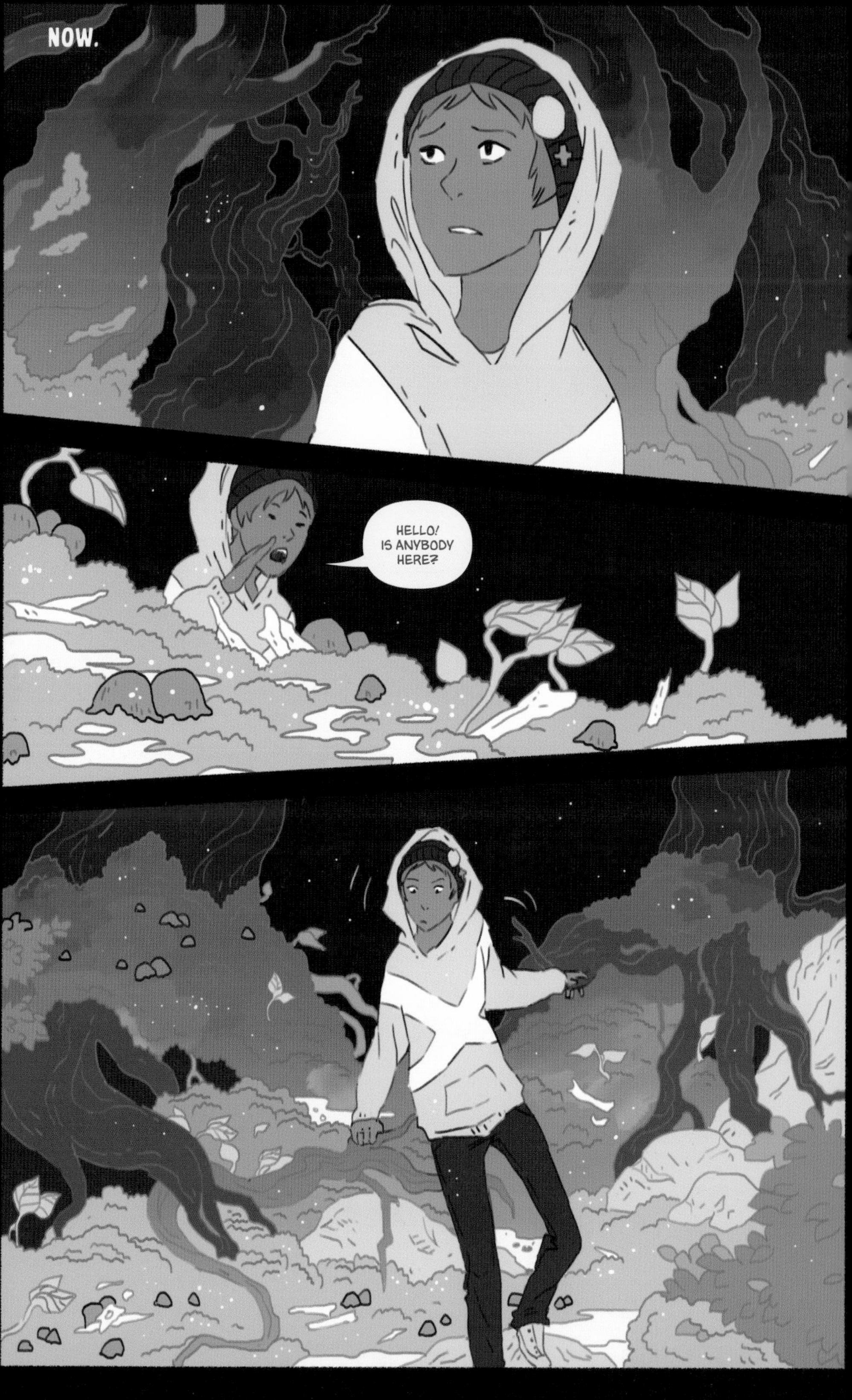
NOW.
HELLO! IS ANYBODY HERE?

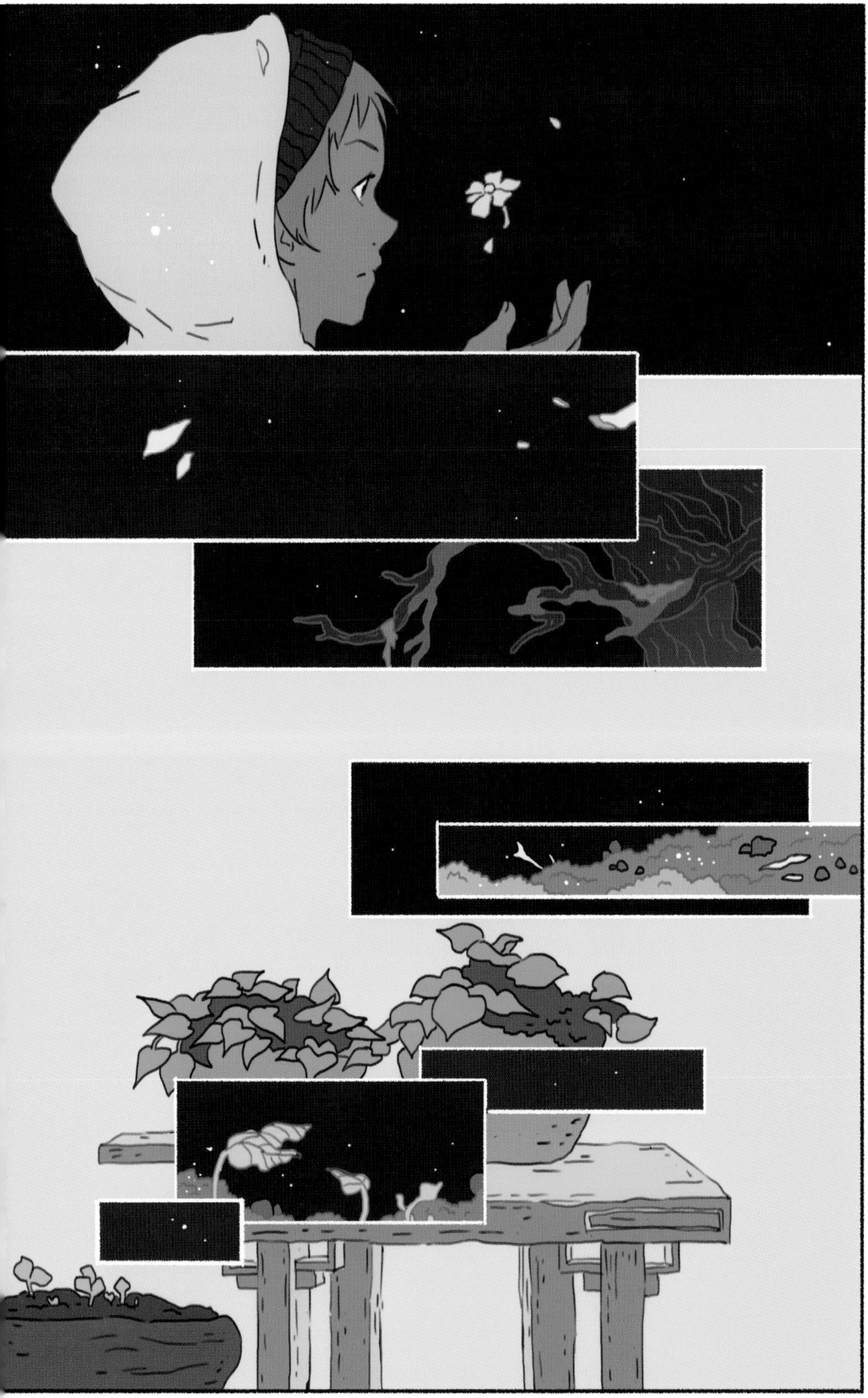

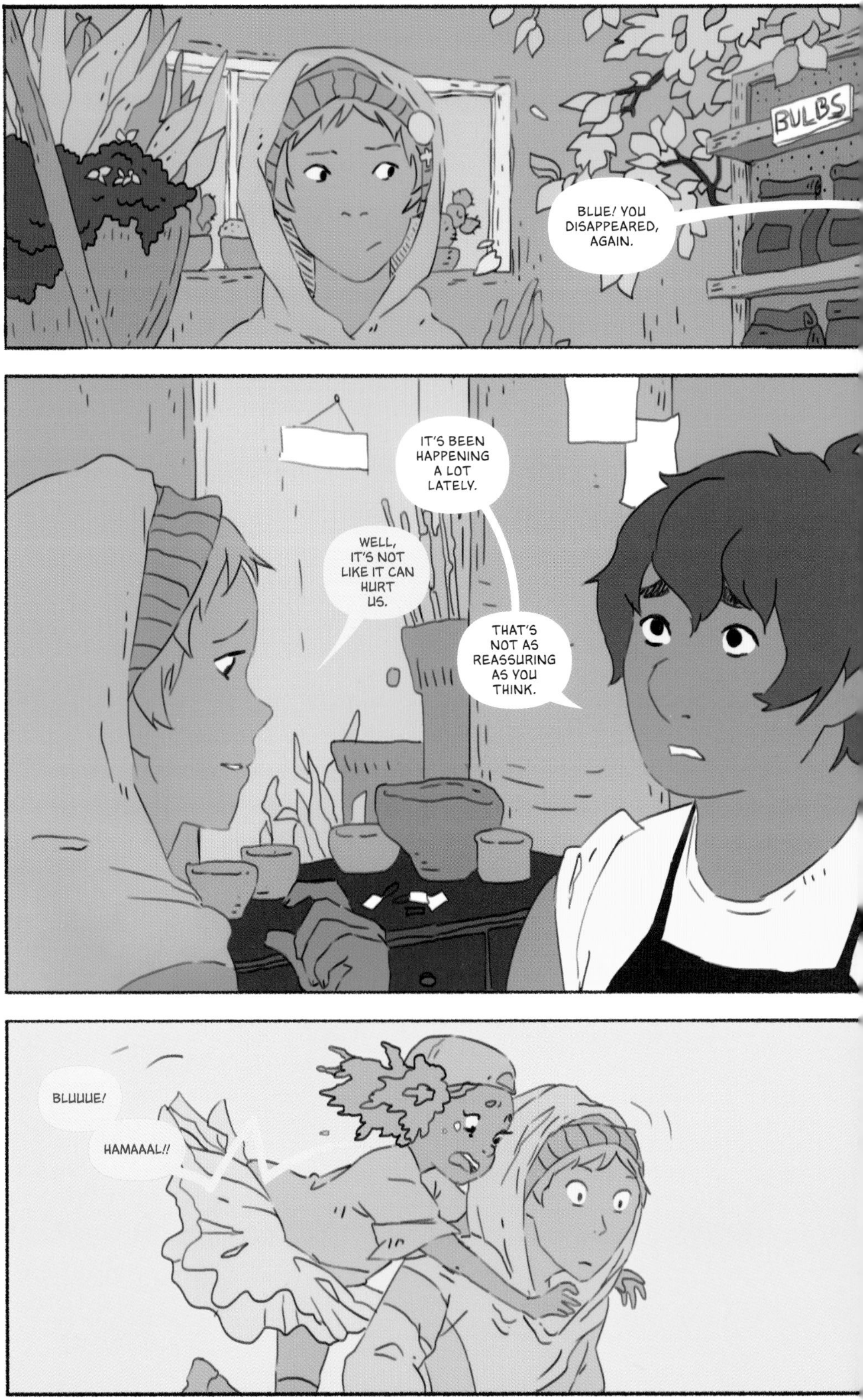
BULBS
BLUE! YOU DISAPPEARED, AGAIN.
IT'S BEEN HAPPENING A LOT LATELY.
WELL, IT'S NOT LIKE IT CAN HURT US.
THAT'S NOT AS REASSURING AS YOU THINK.
BLUUUE!
HAMAAAL!!

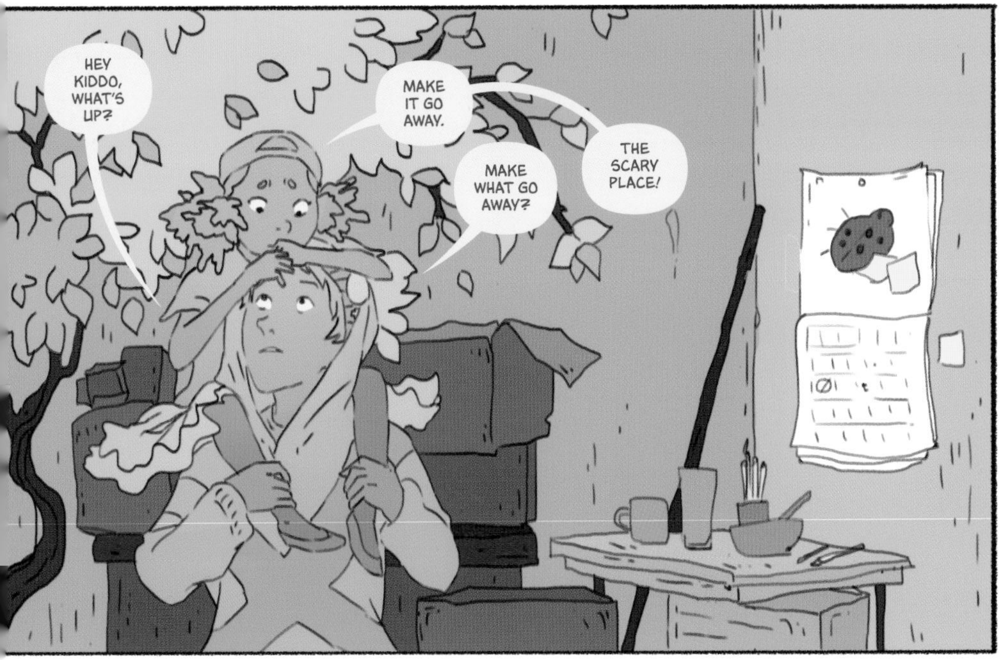
HEY KIDDO, WHAT'S UP?
MAKE IT GO AWAY.
MAKE WHAT GO AWAY?
THE SCARY PLACE!

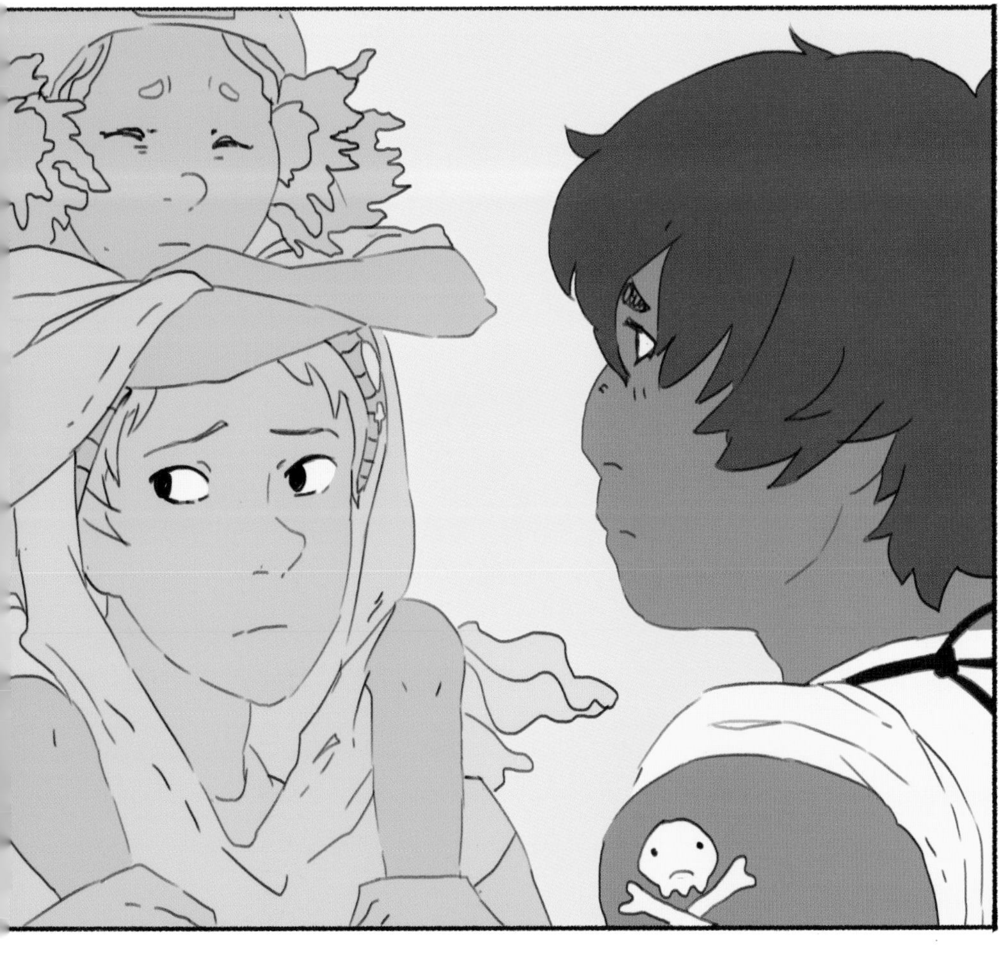

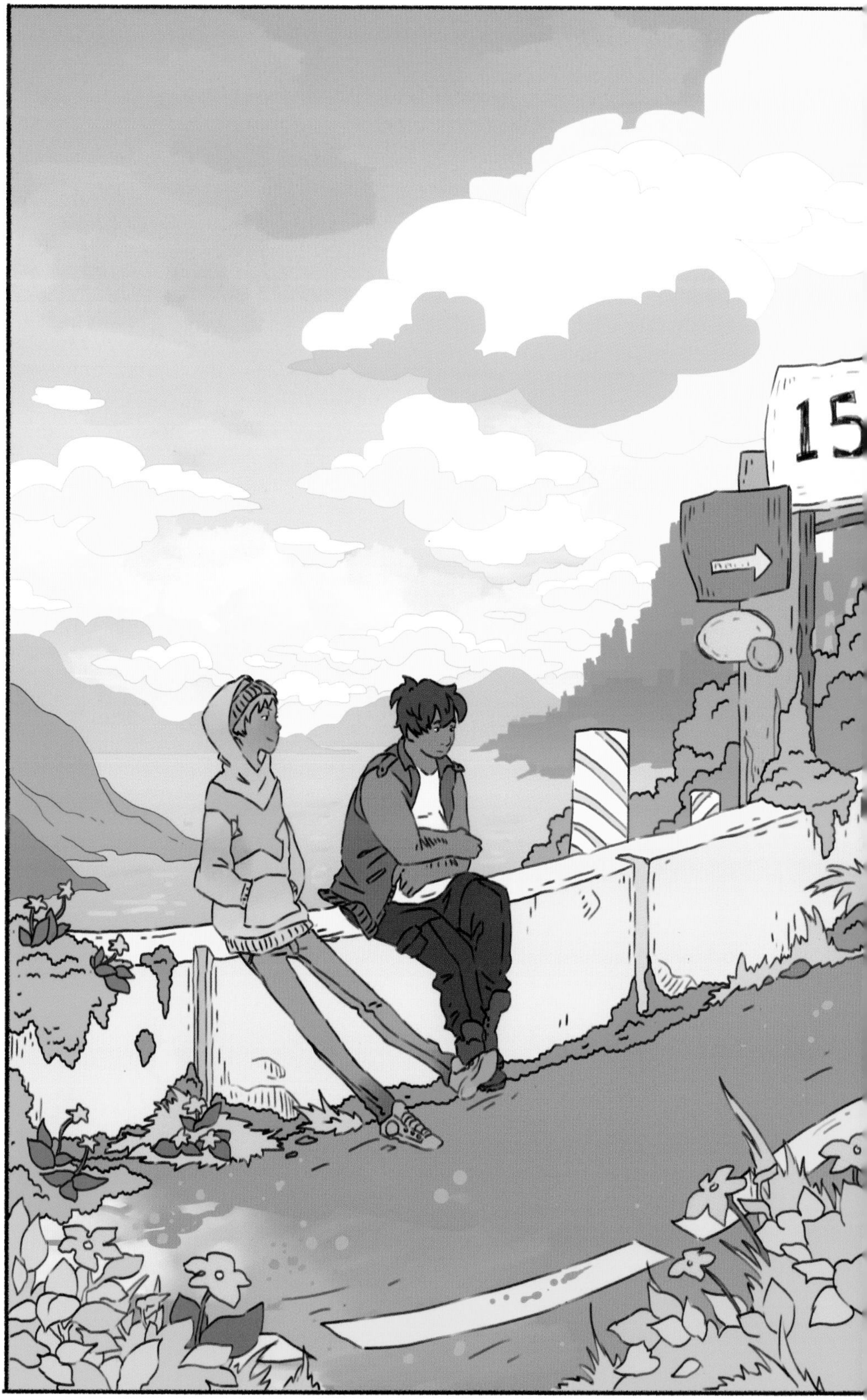
15

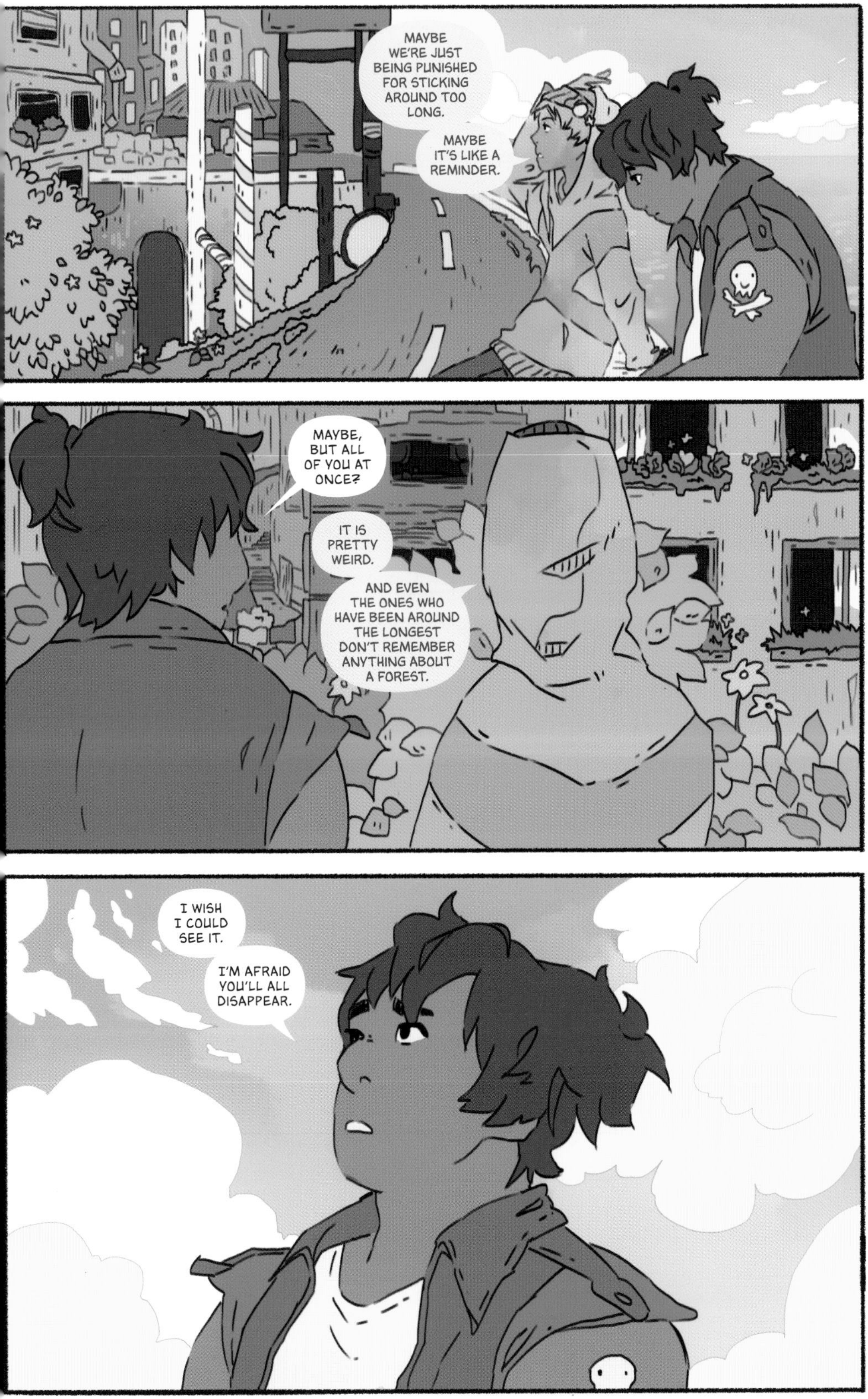

MAYBE WE'RE JUST BEING PUNISHED FOR STICKING AROUND TOO LONG.
MAYBE IT'S LIKE A REMINDER.
MAYBE, BUT ALL OF YOU AT ONCE?
IT IS PRETTY WEIRD.
AND EVEN THE ONES WHO HAVE BEEN AROUND THE LONGEST DON'T REMEMBER ANYTHING ABOUT A FOREST.
I WISH I COULD SEE IT.
I'M AFRAID YOU'LL ALL DISAPPEAR.

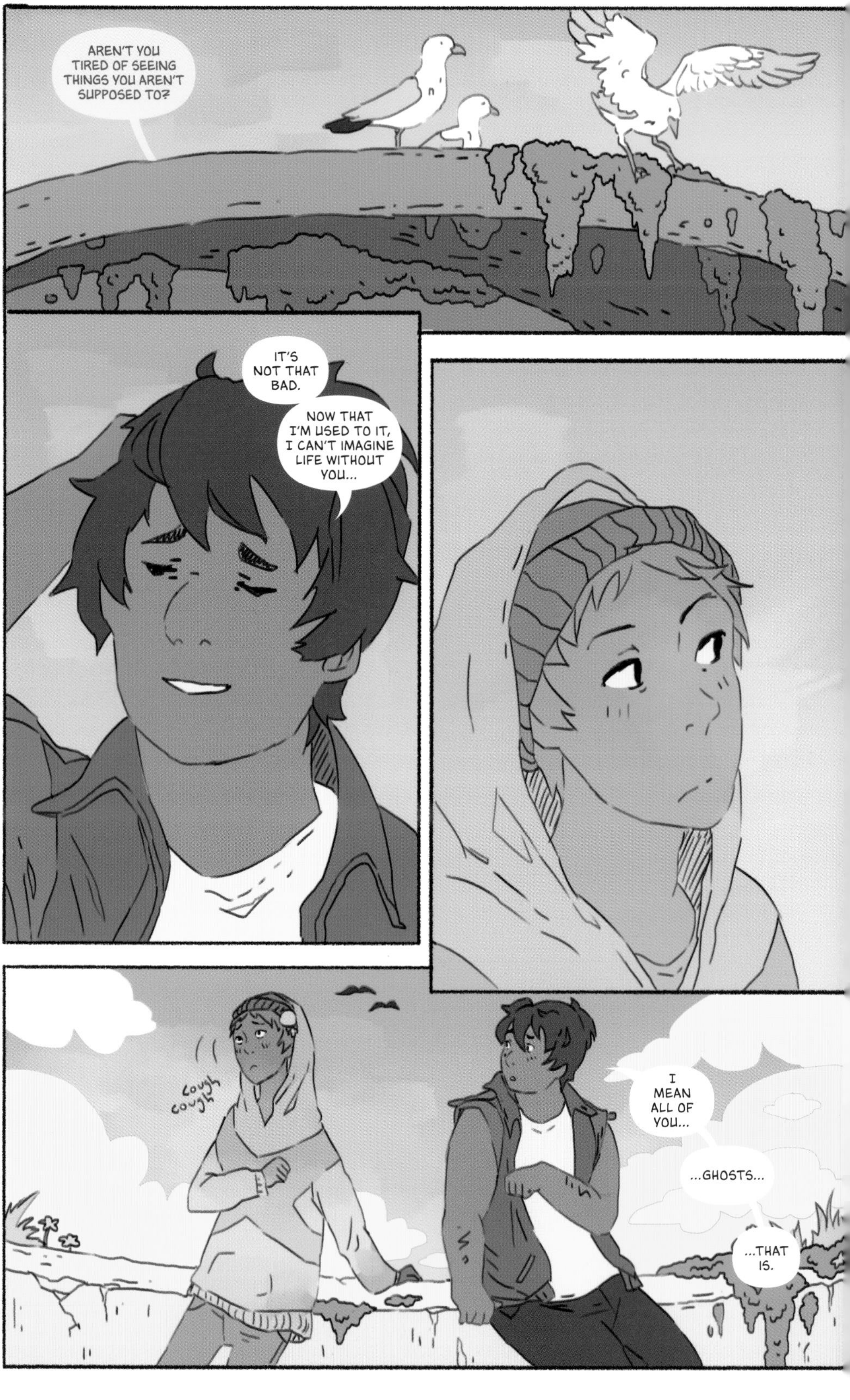
AREN'T YOU TIRED OF SEEING THINGS YOU AREN'T SUPPOSED TO?
IT'S NOT THAT BAD.
NOW THAT I'M USED TO IT, I CAN'T IMAGINE LIFE WITHOUT YOU...
cough cough
I MEAN ALL OF YOU...
...GHOSTS...
...THAT IS.

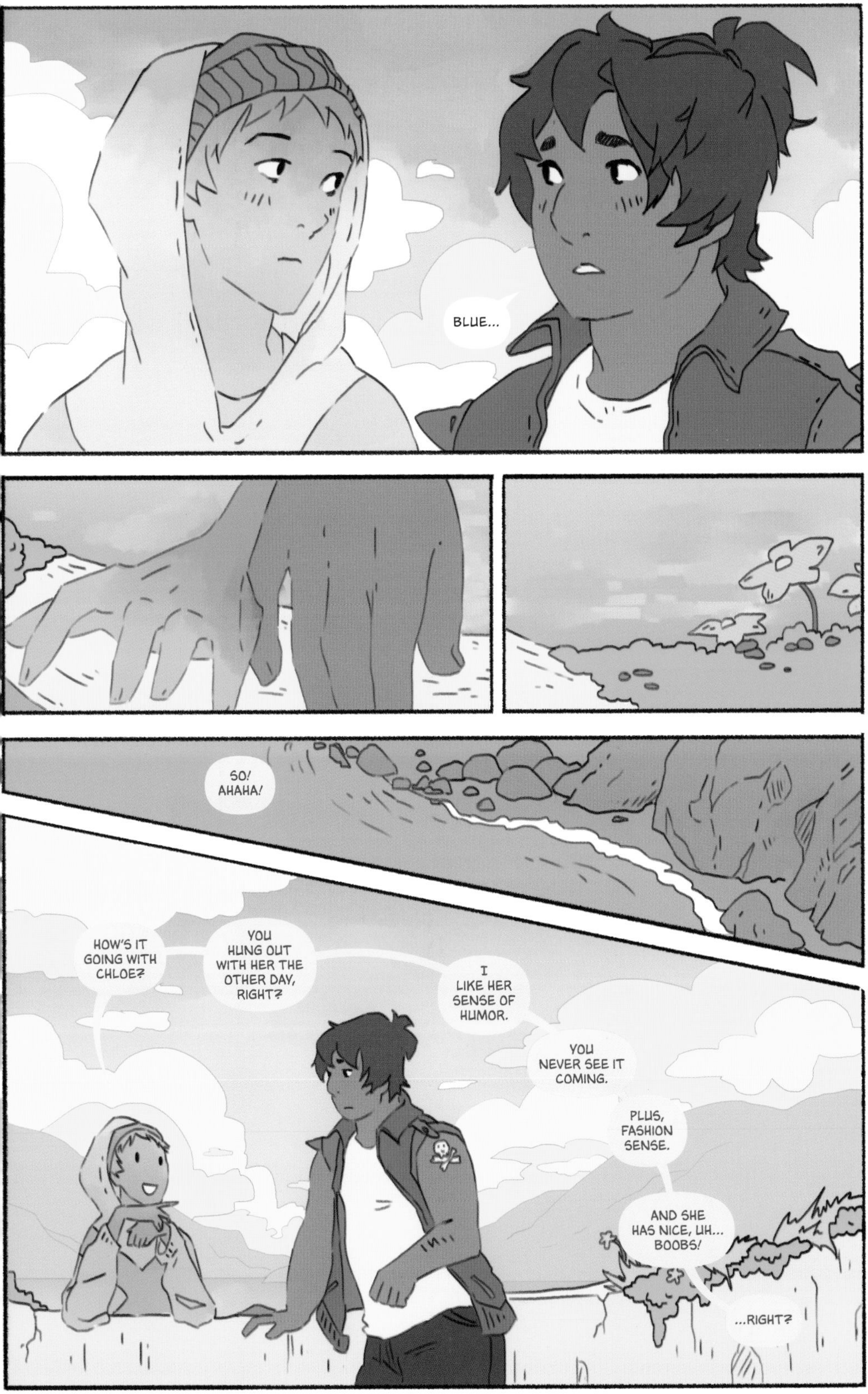
BLUE...
SO! AHAHA!
HOW'S IT GOING WITH CHLOE?
YOU HUNG OUT WITH HER THE OTHER DAY, RIGHT?
I LIKE HER SENSE OF HUMOR.
YOU NEVER SEE IT COMING.
PLUS, FASHION SENSE.
AND SHE HAS NICE, UH... BOOBS!
...RIGHT?

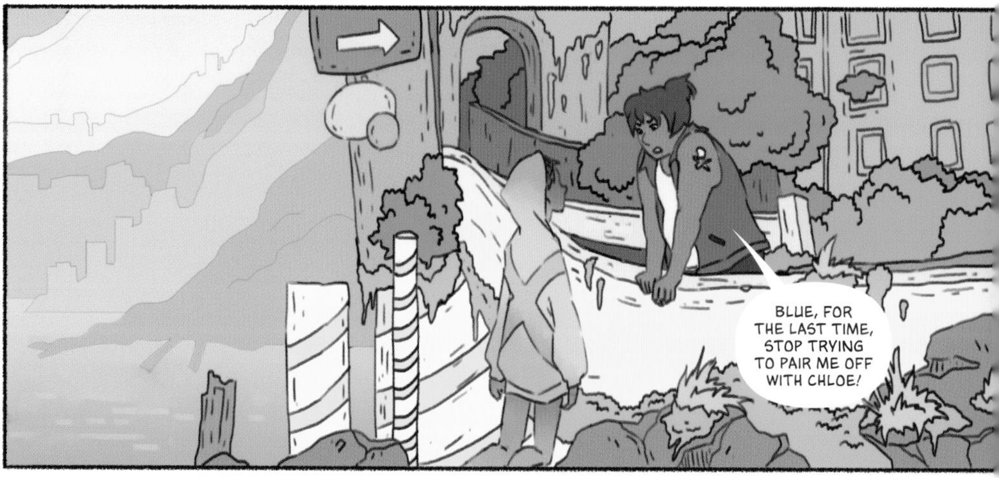
BLUE, FOR THE LAST TIME, STOP TRYING TO PAIR ME OFF WITH CHLOE!

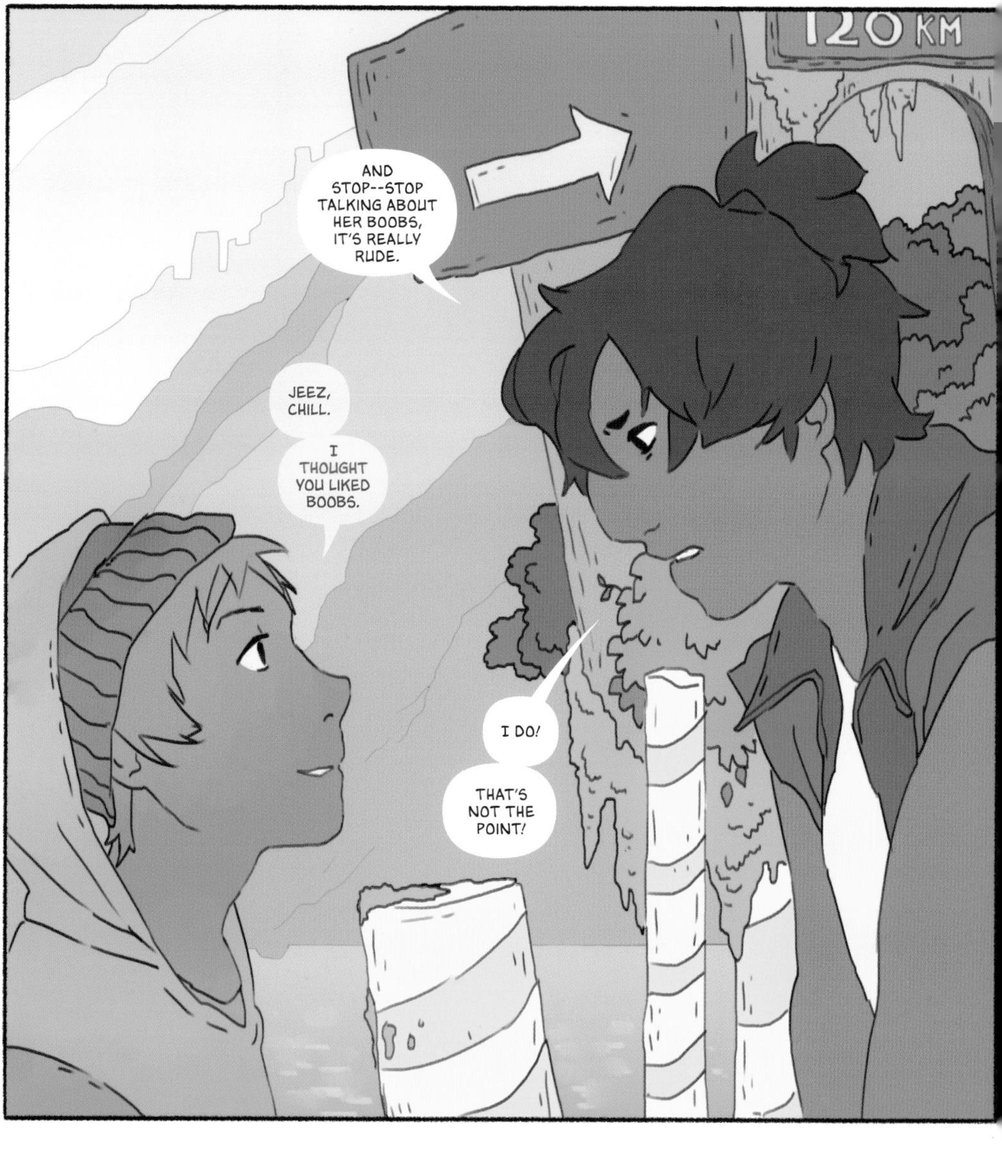
120 KM
AND STOP--STOP TALKING ABOUT HER BOOBS, IT'S REALLY RUDE.
JEEZ, CHILL.
I THOUGHT YOU LIKED BOOBS.
I DO!
THAT'S NOT THE POINT!

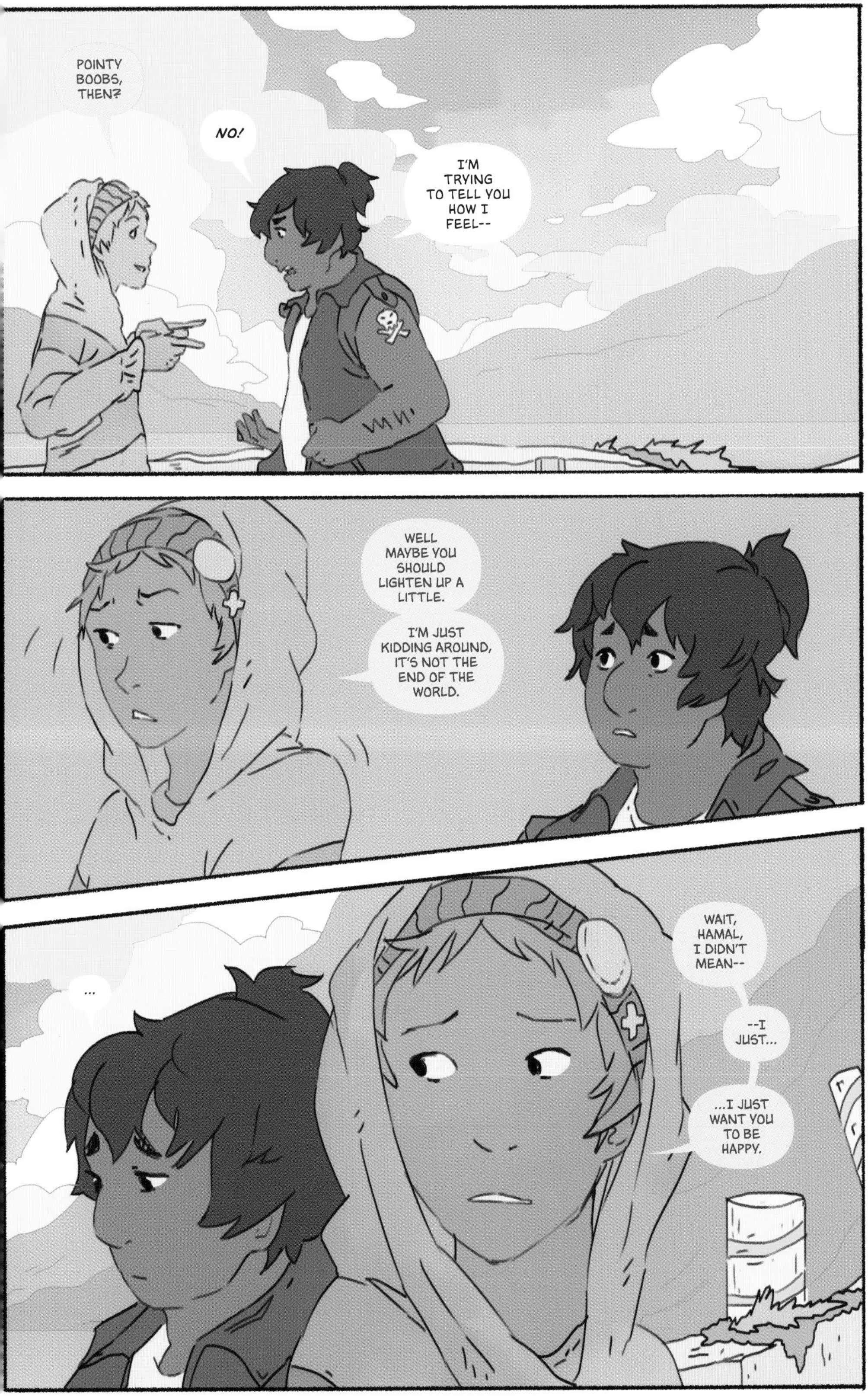
POINTY BOOBS, THEN?
NO!
I'M TRYING TO TELL YOU HOW I FEEL--
WELL MAYBE YOU SHOULD LIGHTEN UP A LITTLE.
I'M JUST KIDDING AROUND, IT'S NOT THE END OF THE WORLD.
...
WAIT, HAMAL, I DIDN'T MEAN--
--I JUST...
...I JUST WANT YOU TO BE HAPPY.

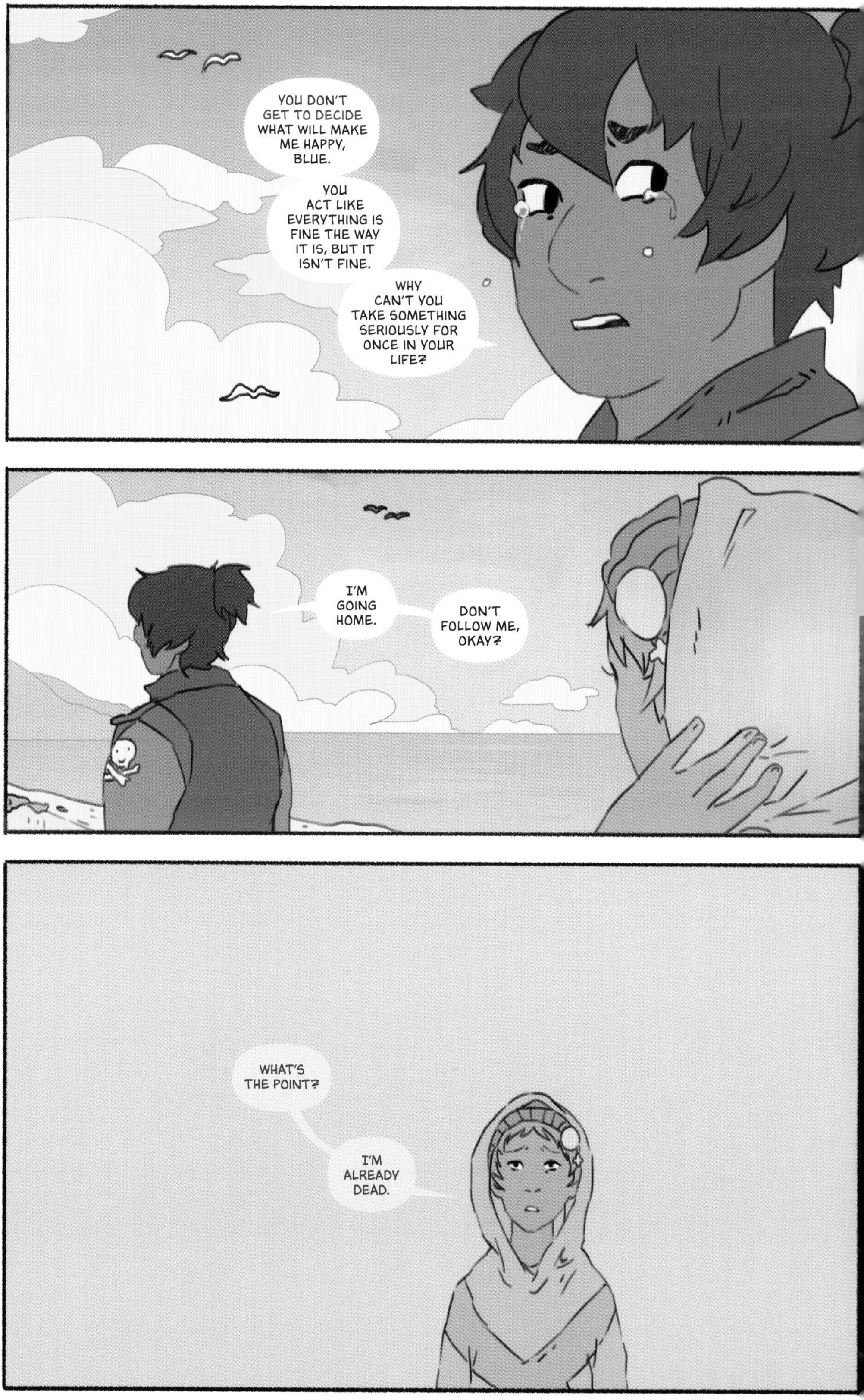
YOU DON'T GET TO DECIDE WHAT WILL MAKE ME HAPPY, BLUE.
YOU ACT LIKE EVERYTHING IS FINE THE WAY IT IS, BUT IT ISN'T FINE.
WHY CAN'T YOU TAKE SOMETHING SERIOUSLY FOR ONCE IN YOUR LIFE?
I'M GOING HOME.
DON'T FOLLOW ME, OKAY?
WHAT'S THE POINT?
I'M ALREADY DEAD.

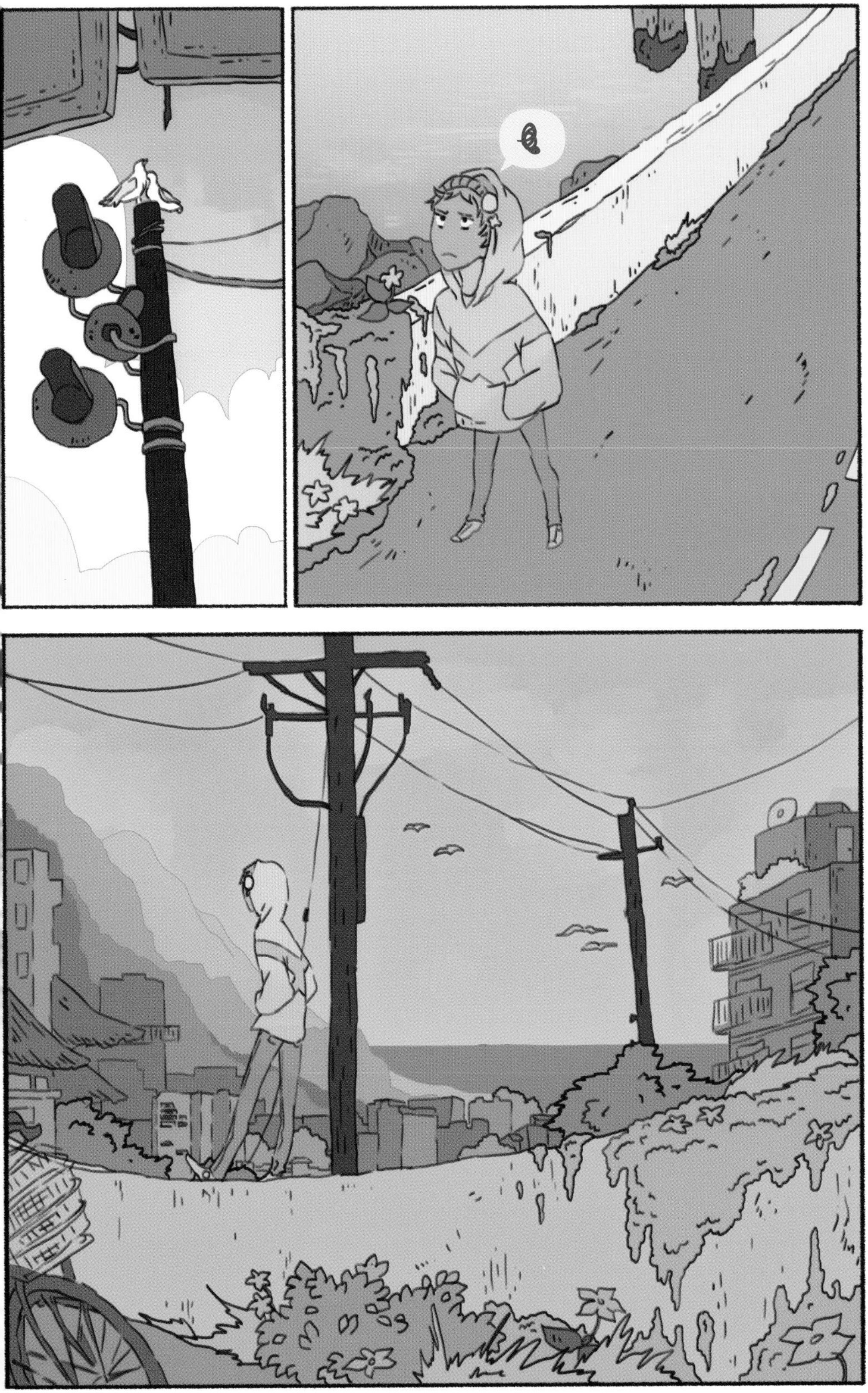

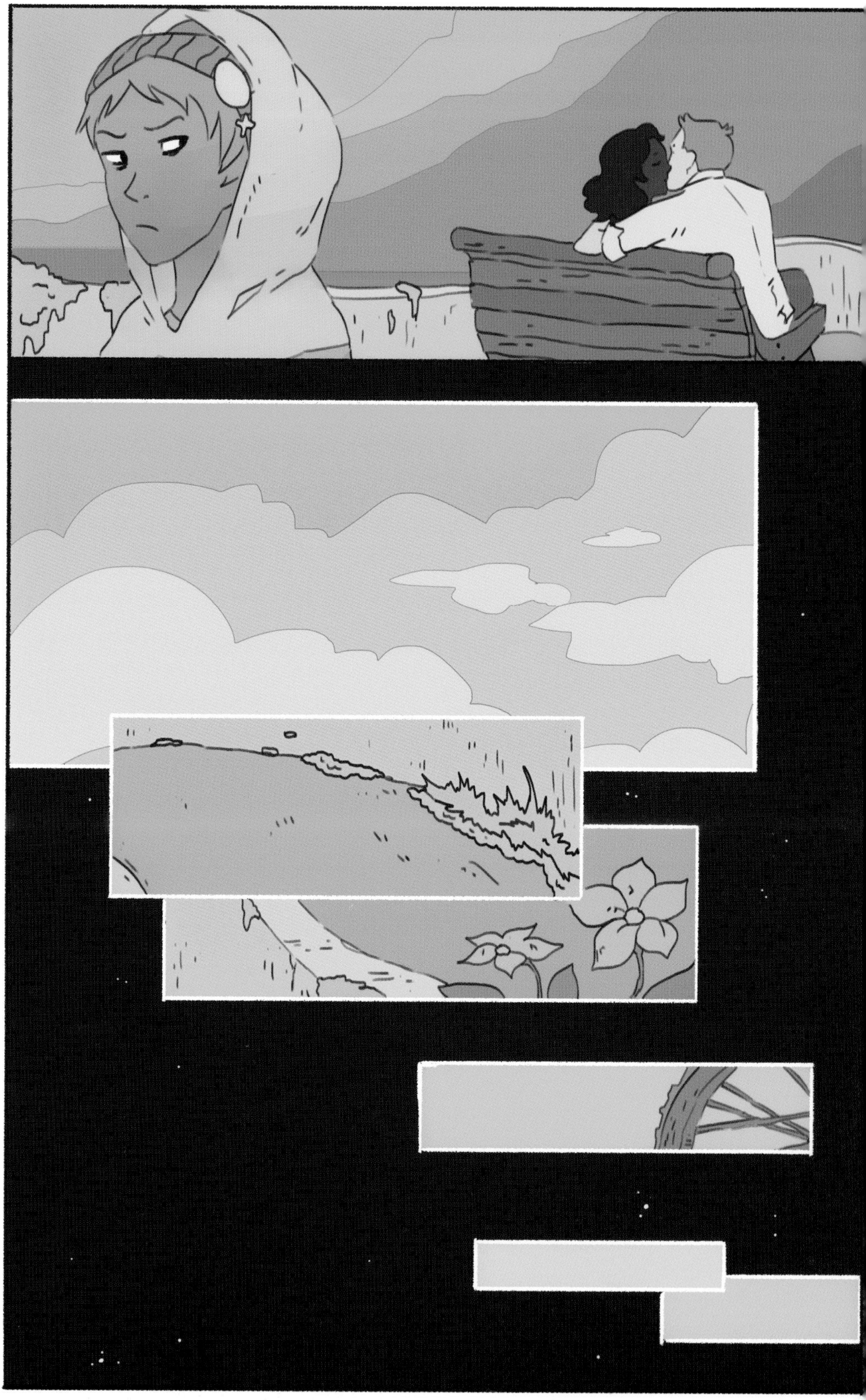

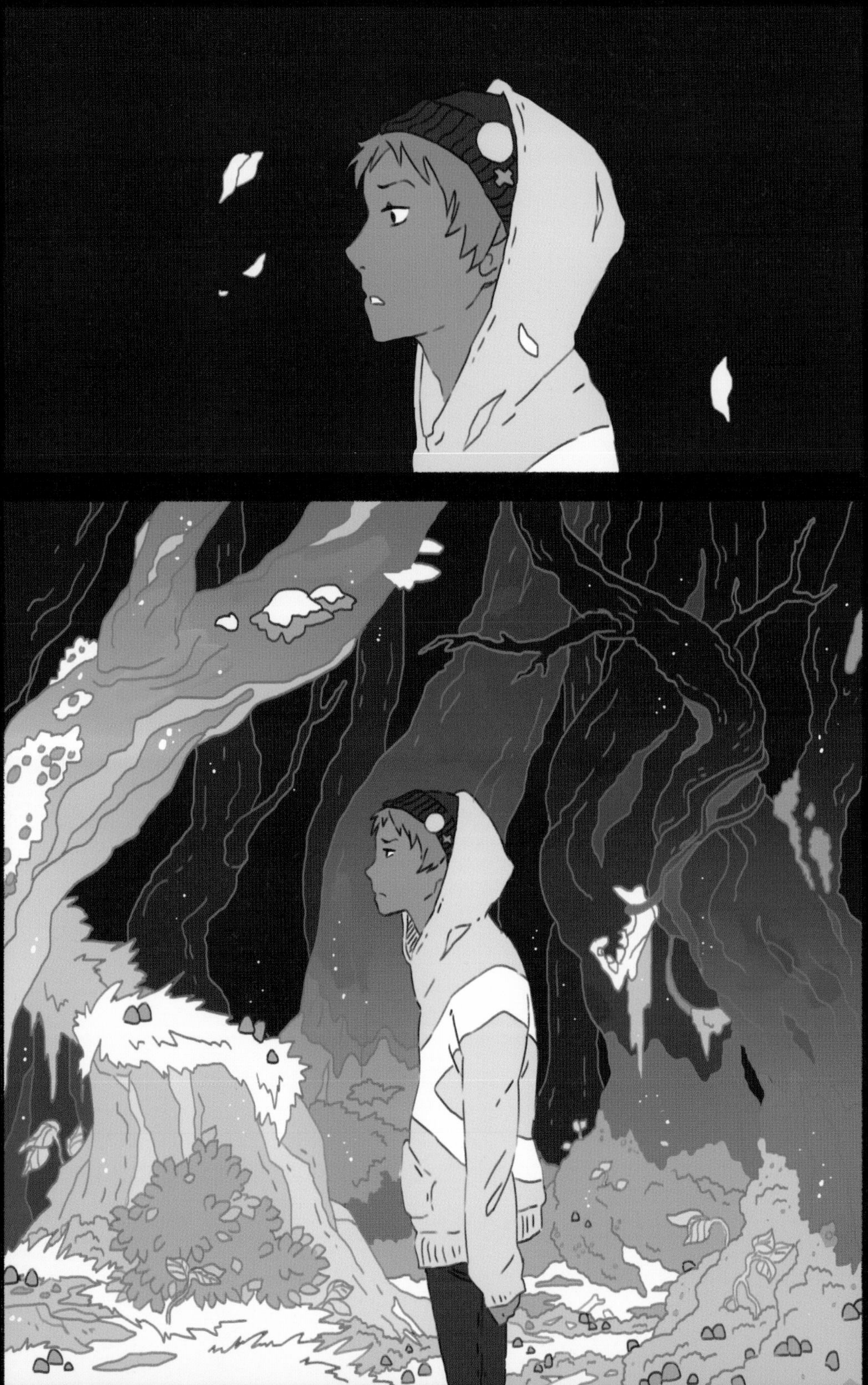

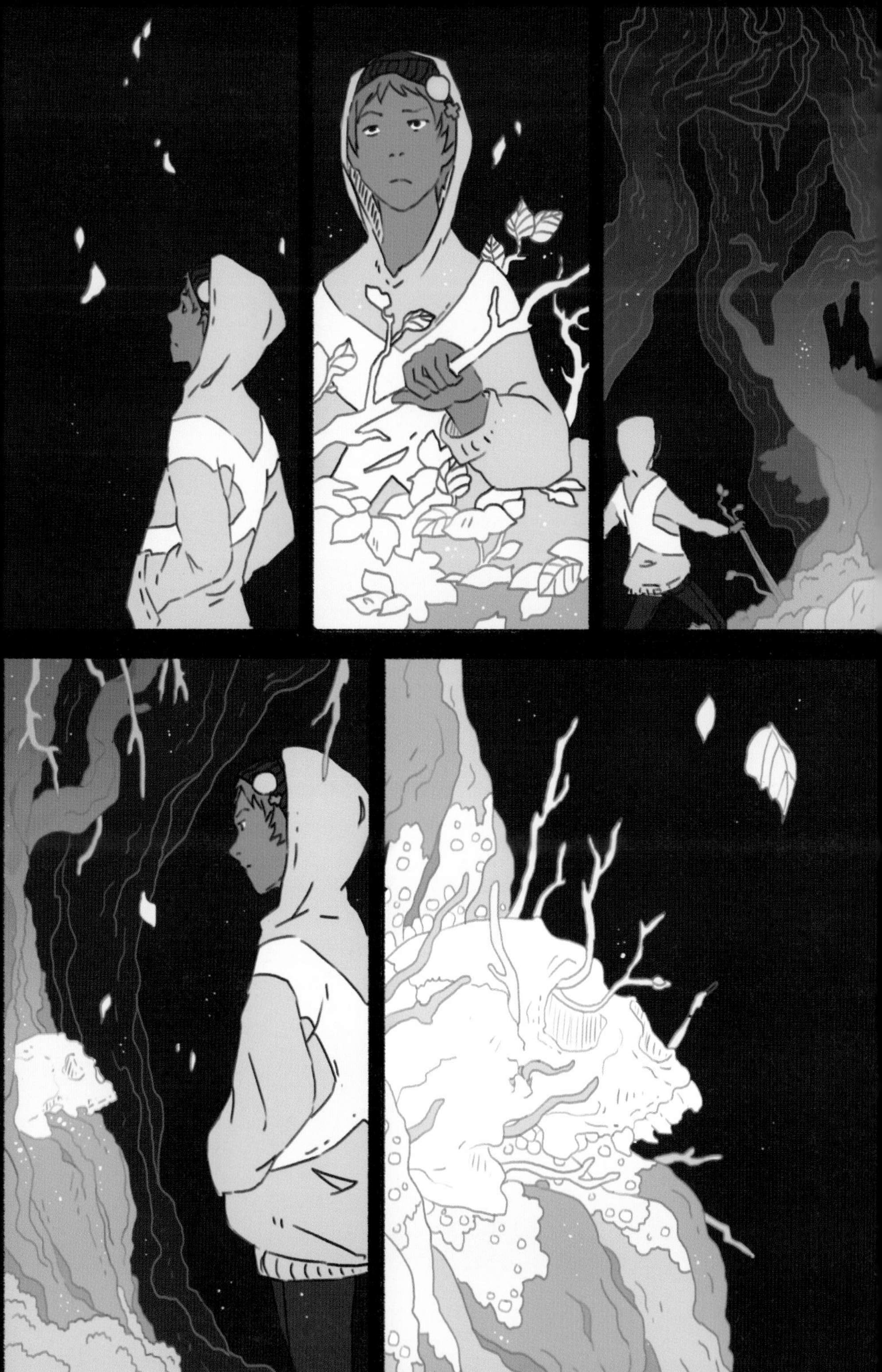

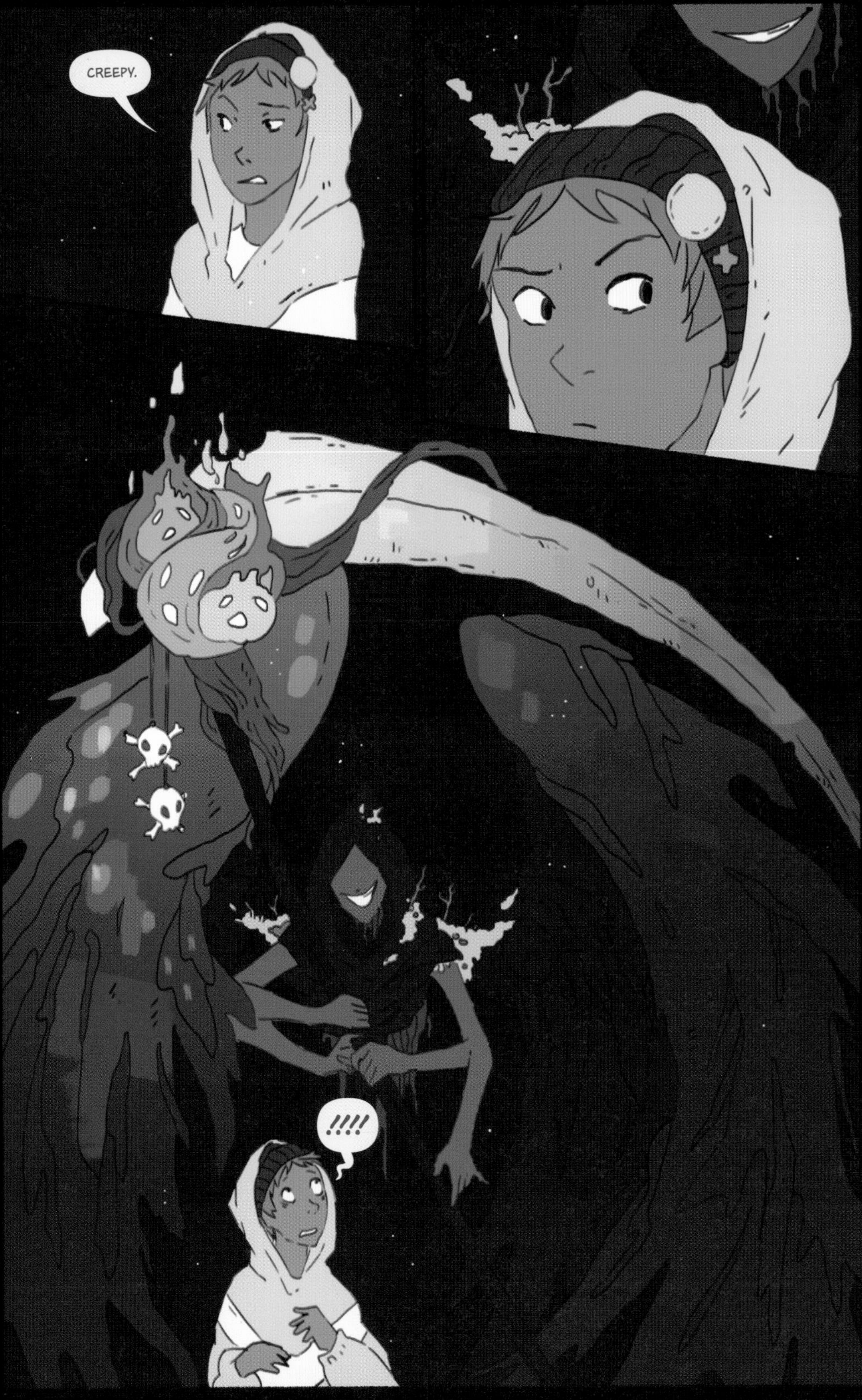
CREEPY.
!!!!

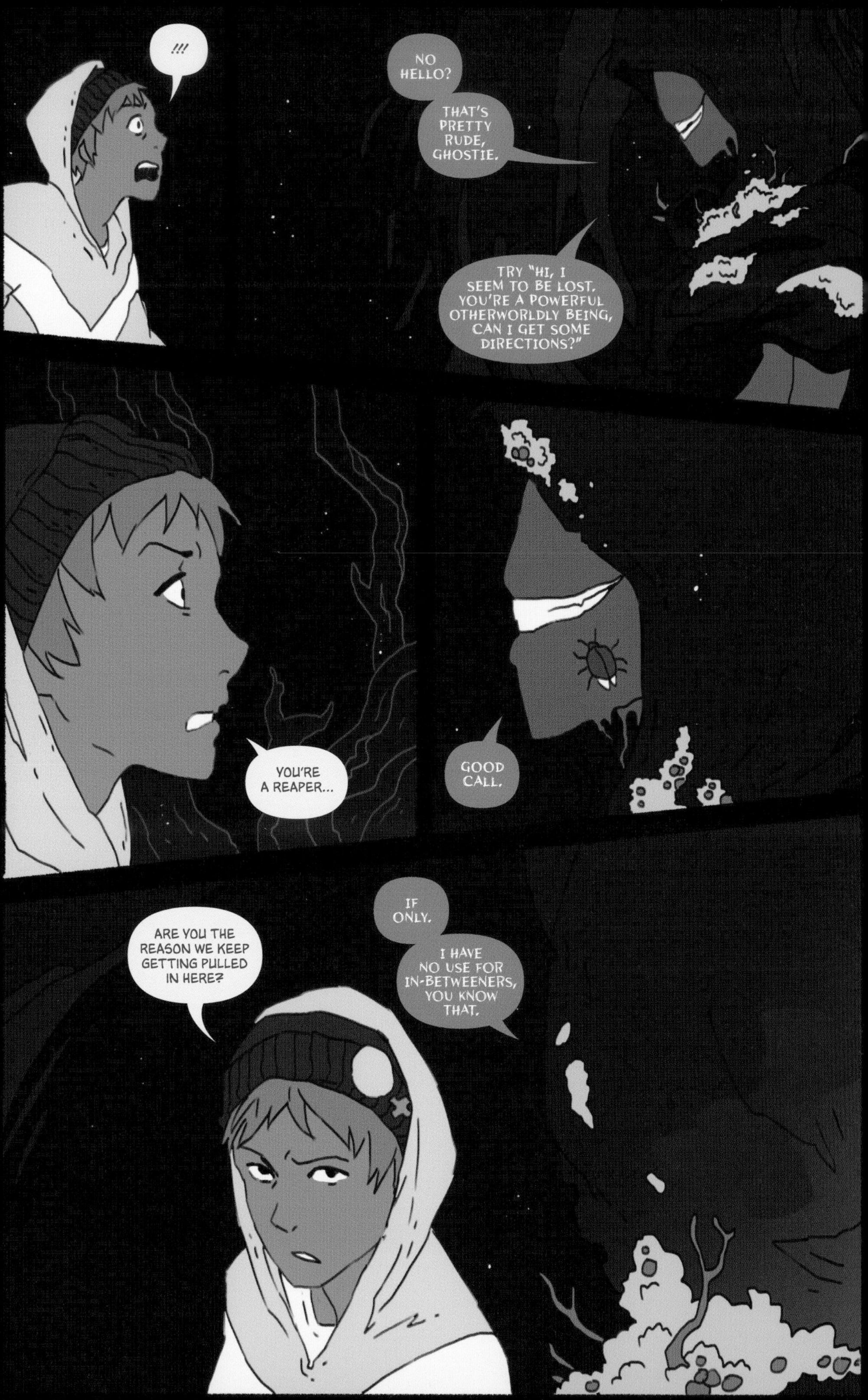
!!!
NO HELLO?
THAT'S PRETTY RUDE, GHOSTIE.
TRY "HI, I SEEM TO BE LOST. YOU'RE A POWERFUL OTHERWORLDLY BEING, CAN I GET SOME DIRECTIONS?"
YOU'RE A REAPER...
GOOD CALL.
ARE YOU THE REASON WE KEEP GETTING PULLED IN HERE?
IF ONLY.
I HAVE NO USE FOR IN-BETWEENERS, YOU KNOW THAT.

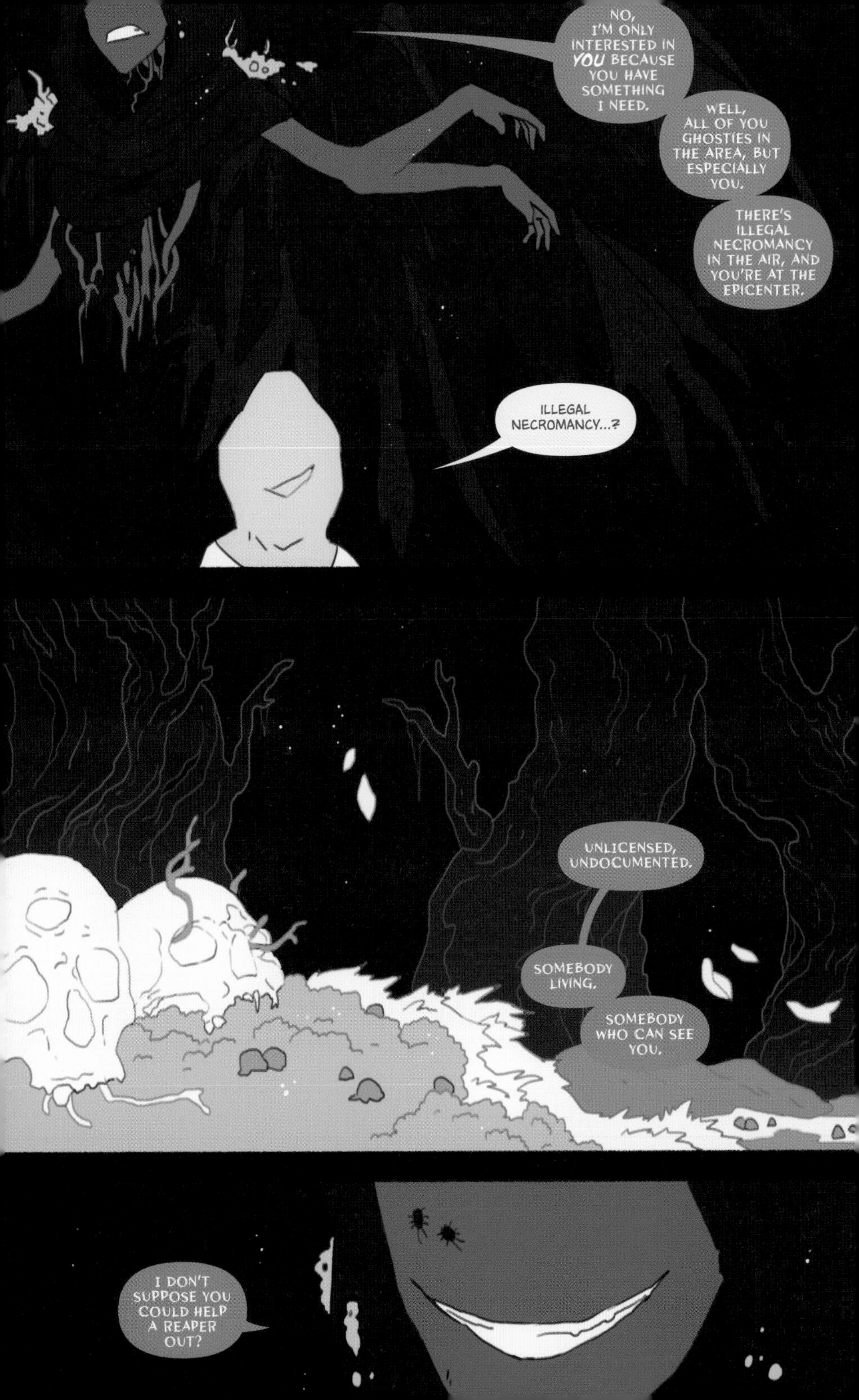
NO, I'M ONLY INTERESTED IN YOU BECAUSE YOU HAVE SOMETHING I NEED.
WELL, ALL OF YOU GHOSTIES IN THE AREA, BUT ESPECIALLY YOU.
THERE'S ILLEGAL NECROMANCY IN THE AIR, AND YOU'RE AT THE EPICENTER.
ILLEGAL NECROMANCY...?
UNLICENSED, UNDOCUMENTED.
SOMEBODY LIVING.
SOMEBODY WHO CAN SEE YOU.
I DON'T SUPPOSE YOU COULD HELP A REAPER OUT?

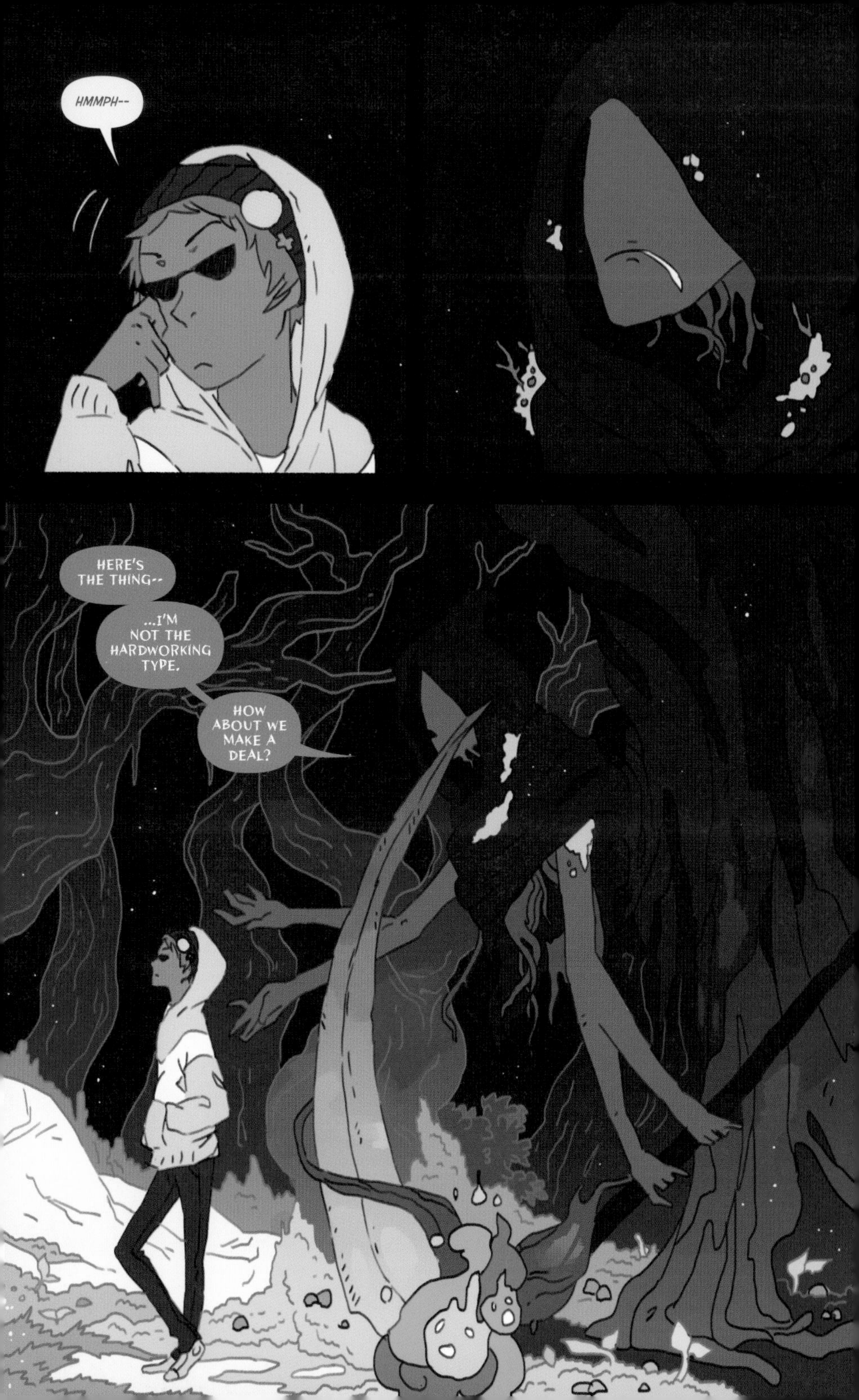
HMMPH--
HERE'S THE THING--
...I'M NOT THE HARDWORKING TYPE.
HOW ABOUT WE MAKE A DEAL?

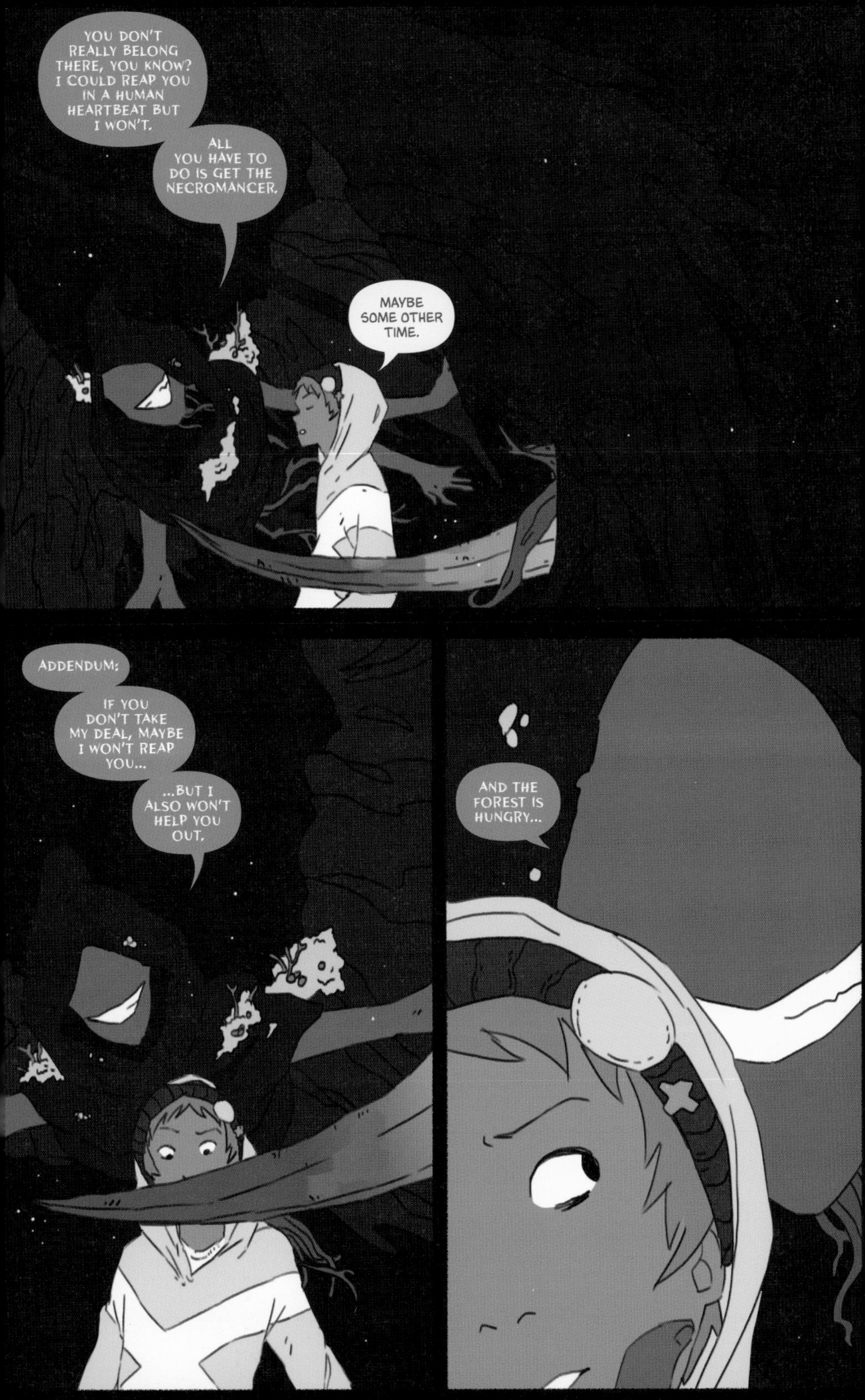
YOU DON'T REALLY BELONG THERE, YOU KNOW? I COULD REAP YOU IN A HUMAN HEARTBEAT BUT I WON'T.
ALL YOU HAVE TO DO IS GET THE NECROMANCER.
MAYBE SOME OTHER TIME.
ADDENDUM:
IF YOU DON'T TAKE MY DEAL, MAYBE I WON'T REAP YOU...
...BUT I ALSO WON'T HELP YOU OUT.
AND THE FOREST IS HUNGRY...

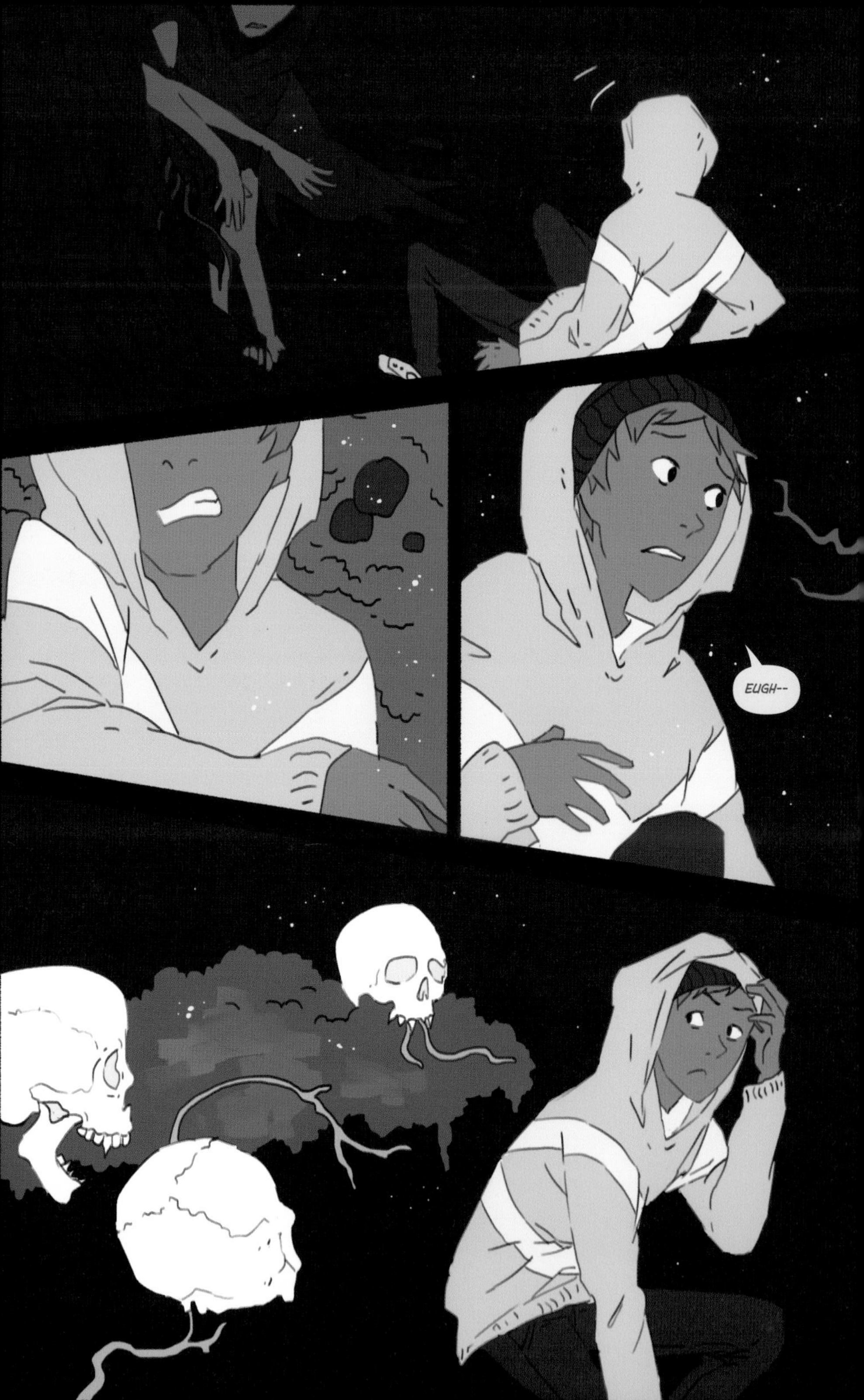
EUGH--

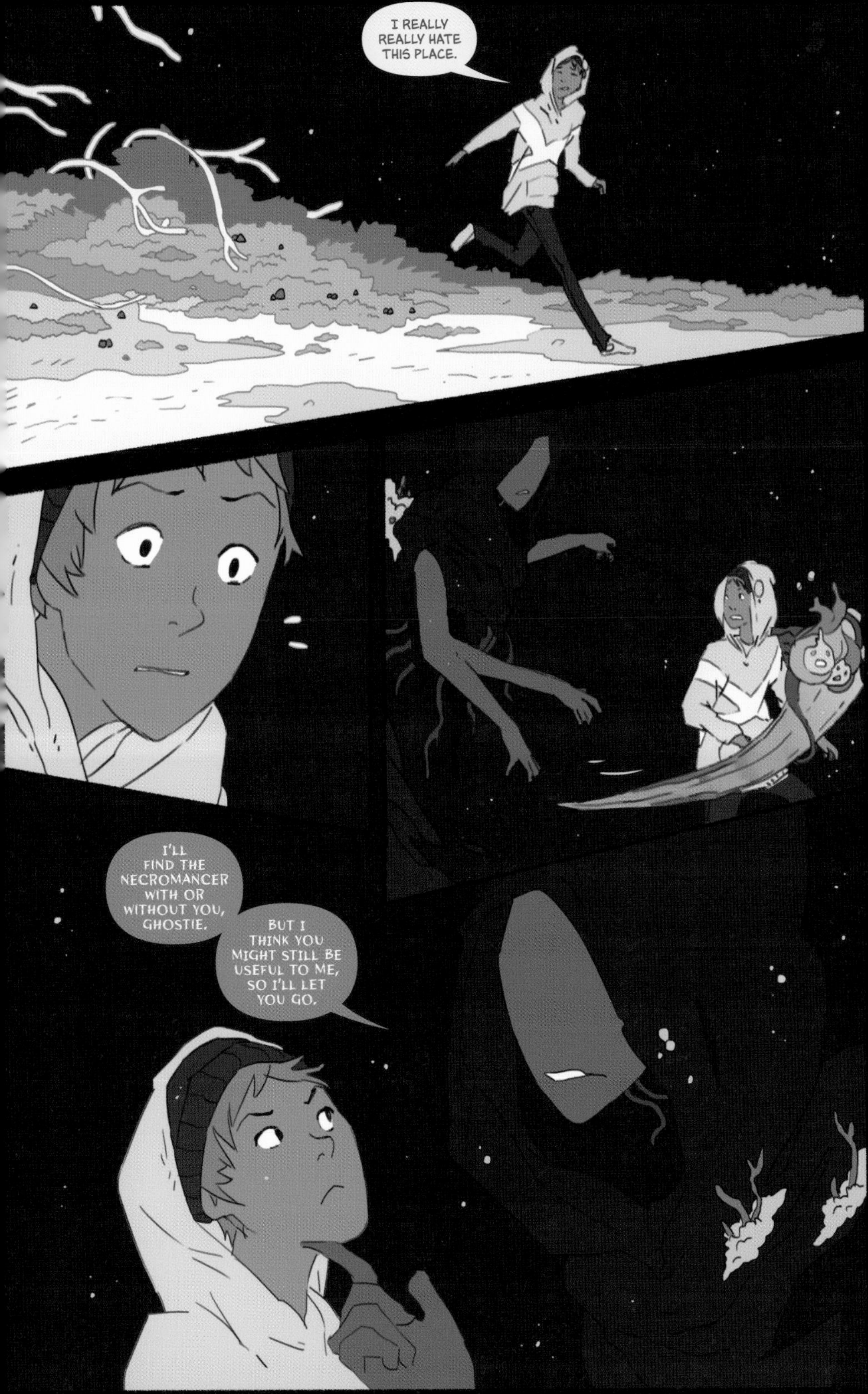
I REALLY REALLY HATE THIS PLACE.
I'LL FIND THE NECROMANCER WITH OR WITHOUT YOU, GHOSTIE.
BUT I THINK YOU MIGHT STILL BE USEFUL TO ME, SO I'LL LET YOU GO.

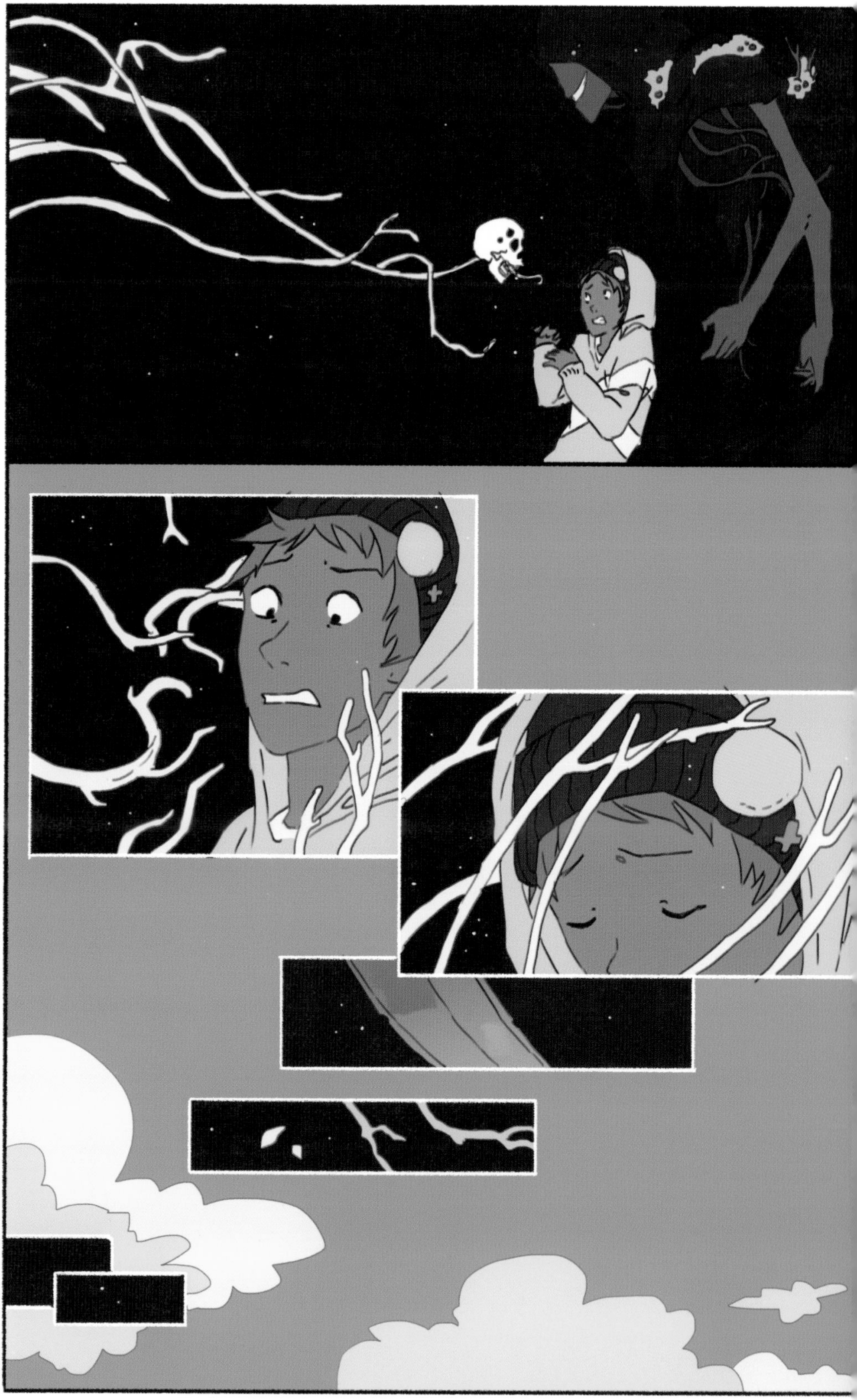

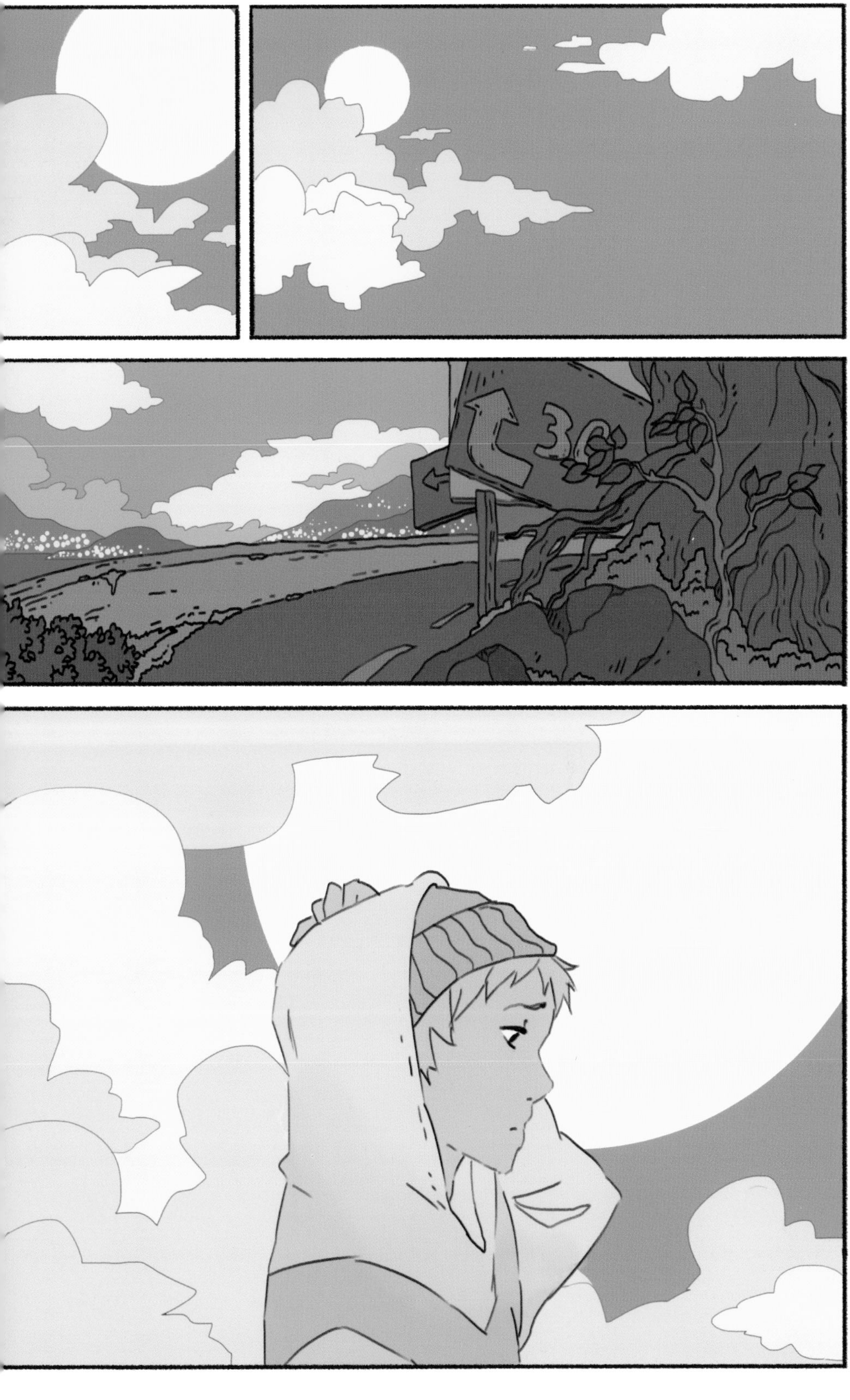

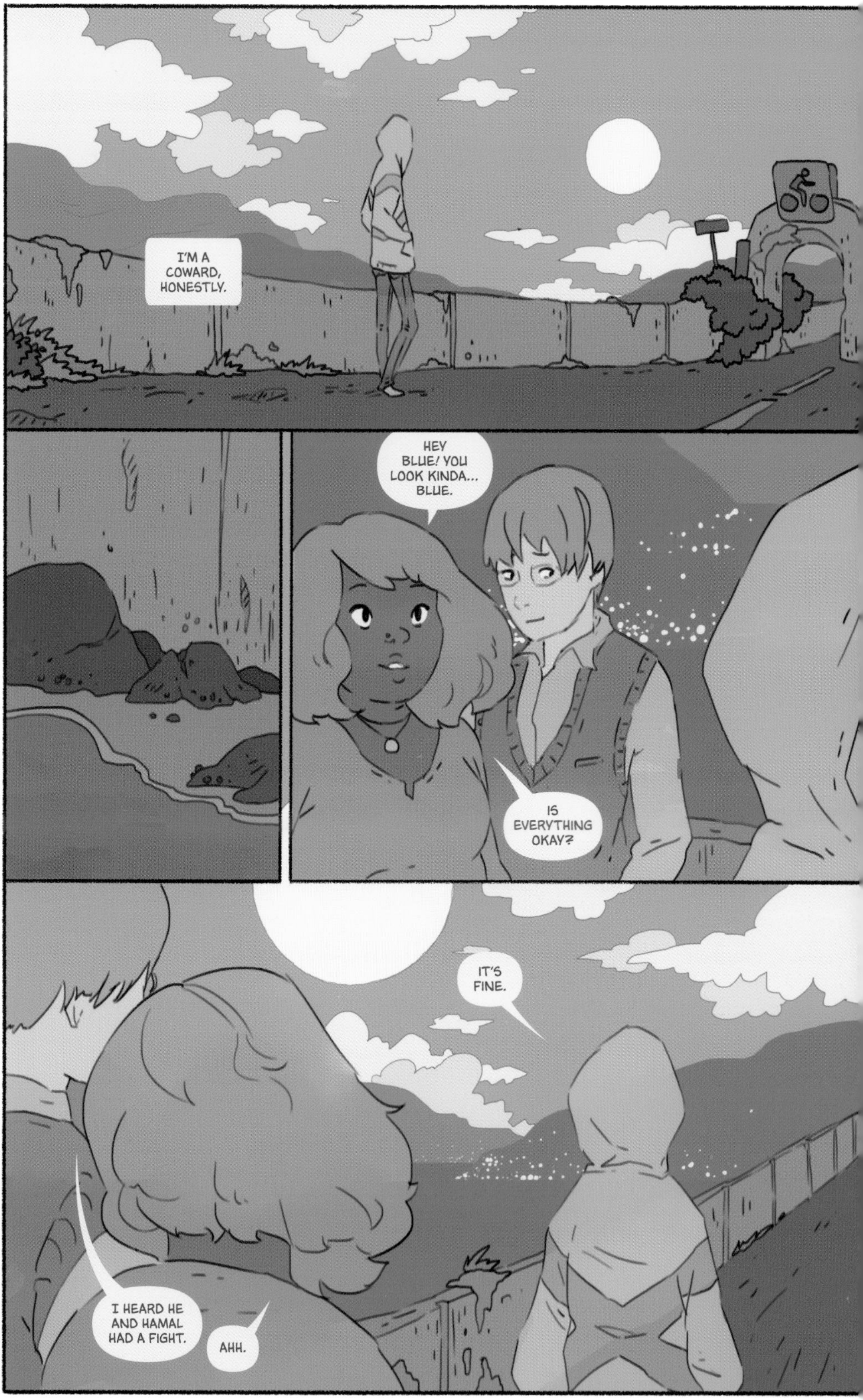
I'M A COWARD, HONESTLY.
HEY BLUE! YOU LOOK KINDA... BLUE.
IS EVERYTHING OKAY?
IT'S FINE.
I HEARD HE AND HAMAL HAD A FIGHT.
AHH.

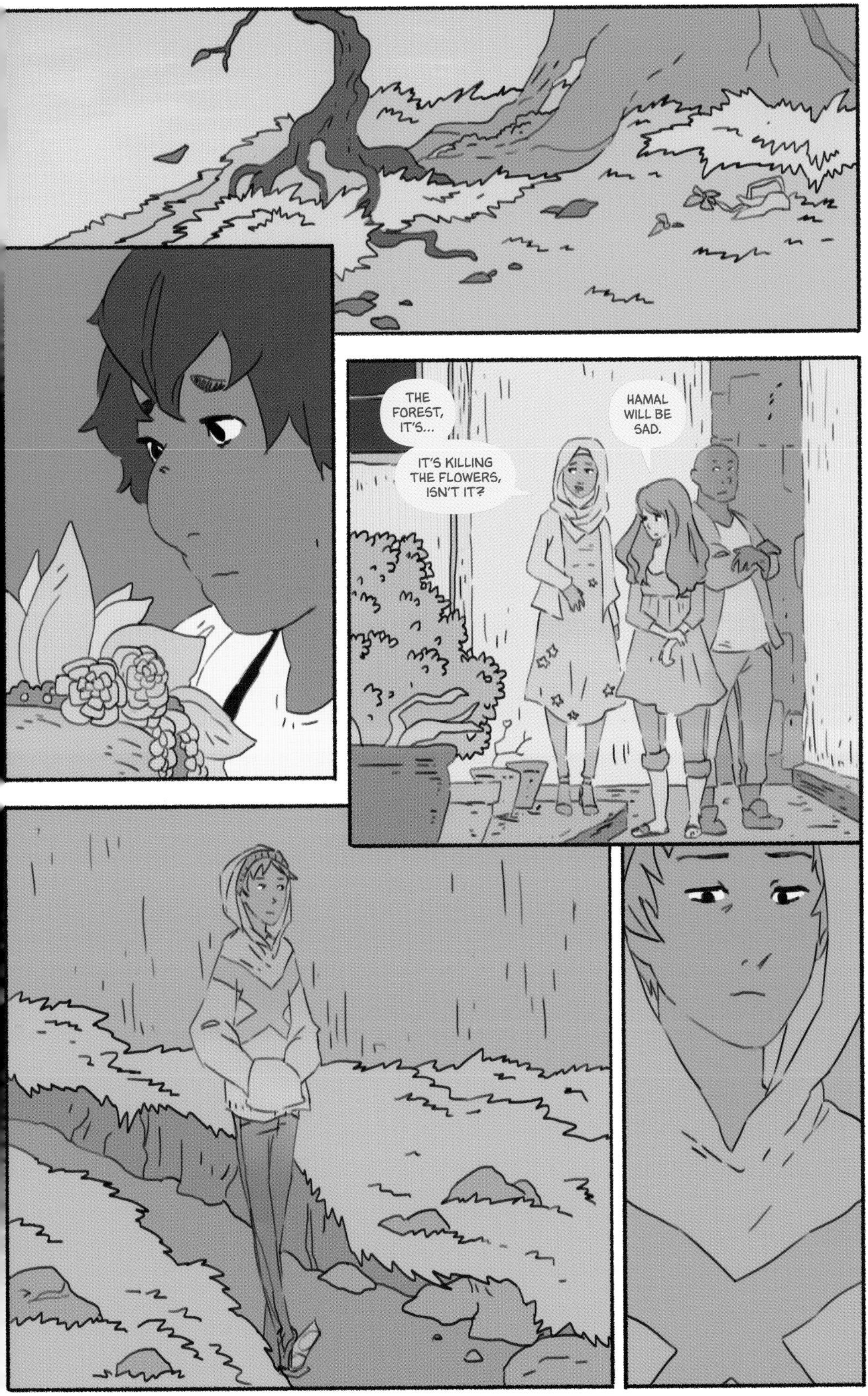
THE FOREST, IT'S...
IT'S KILLING THE FLOWERS, ISN'T IT?
HAMAL WILL BE SAD.

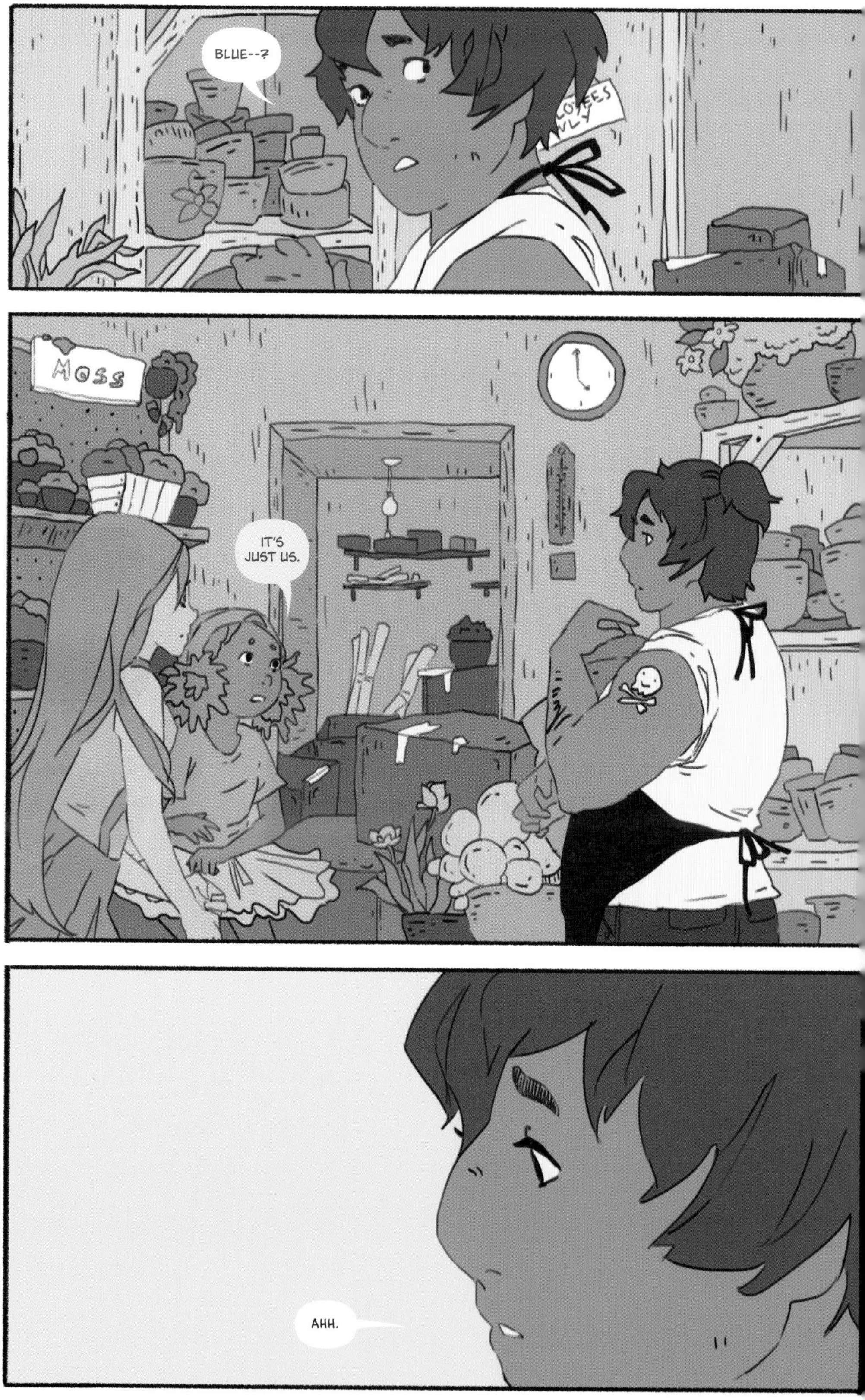
BLUE--?
MOSS
IT'S JUST US.
AHH.

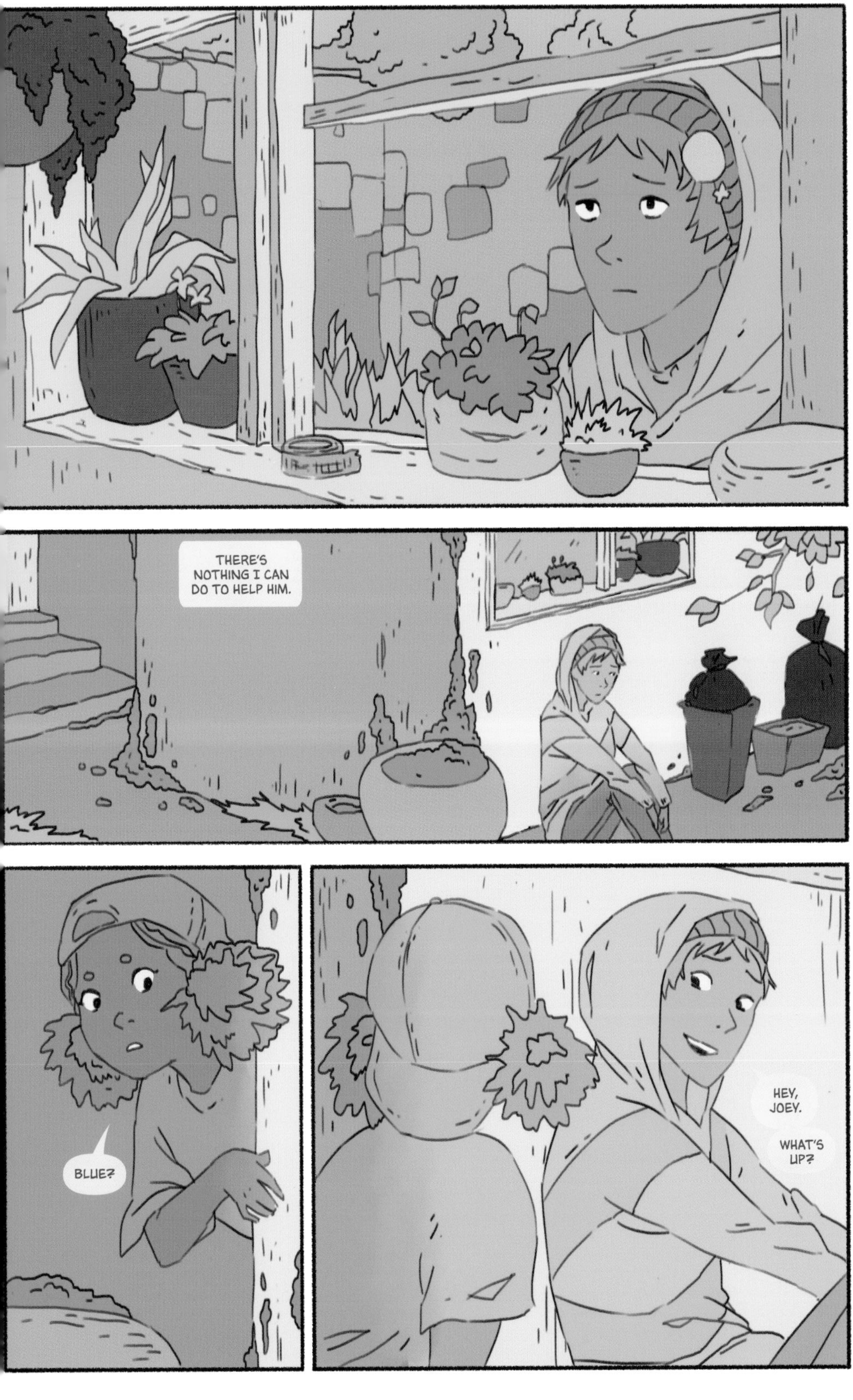
THERE'S NOTHING I CAN DO TO HELP HIM.
BLUE?
HEY, JOEY.
WHAT'S UP?

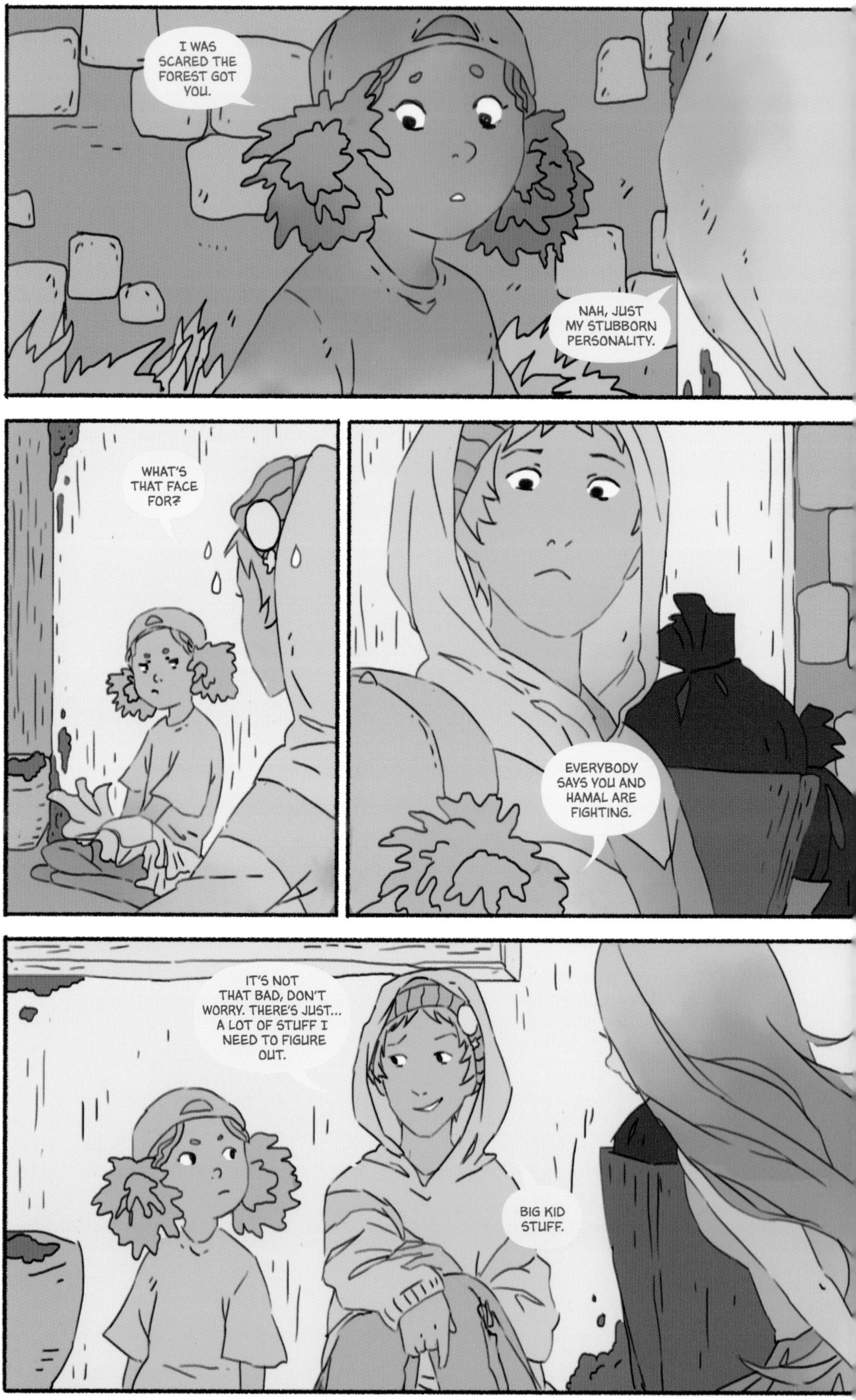
I WAS SCARED THE FOREST GOT YOU.
NAH, JUST MY STUBBORN PERSONALITY.
WHAT'S THAT FACE FOR?
EVERYBODY SAYS YOU AND HAMAL ARE FIGHTING.
IT'S NOT THAT BAD, DON'T WORRY. THERE'S JUST... A LOT OF STUFF I NEED TO FIGURE OUT.
BIG KID STUFF.

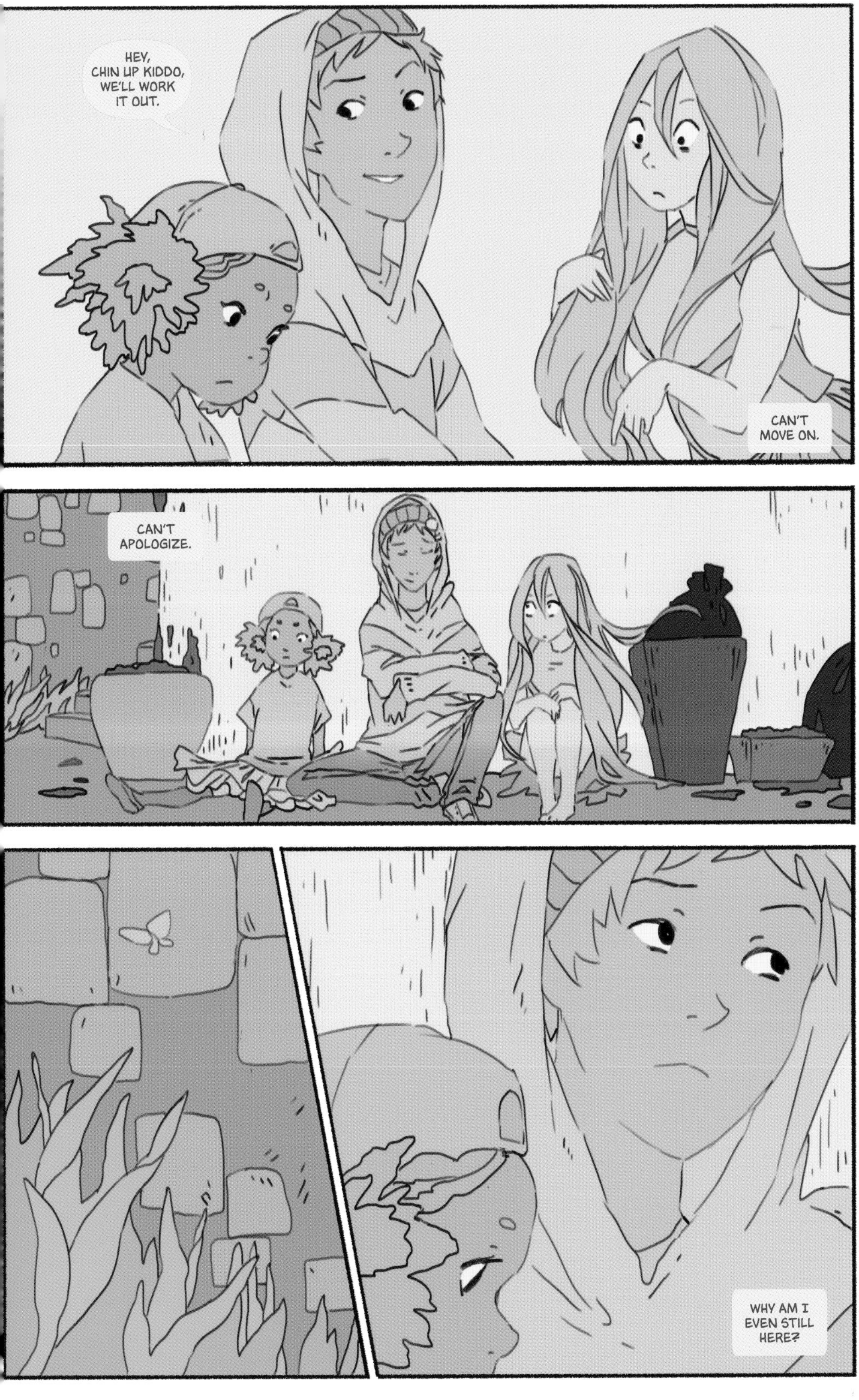
HEY, CHIN UP KIDDO, WE'LL WORK IT OUT.
CAN'T MOVE ON.
CAN'T APOLOGIZE.
WHY AM I EVEN STILL HERE?

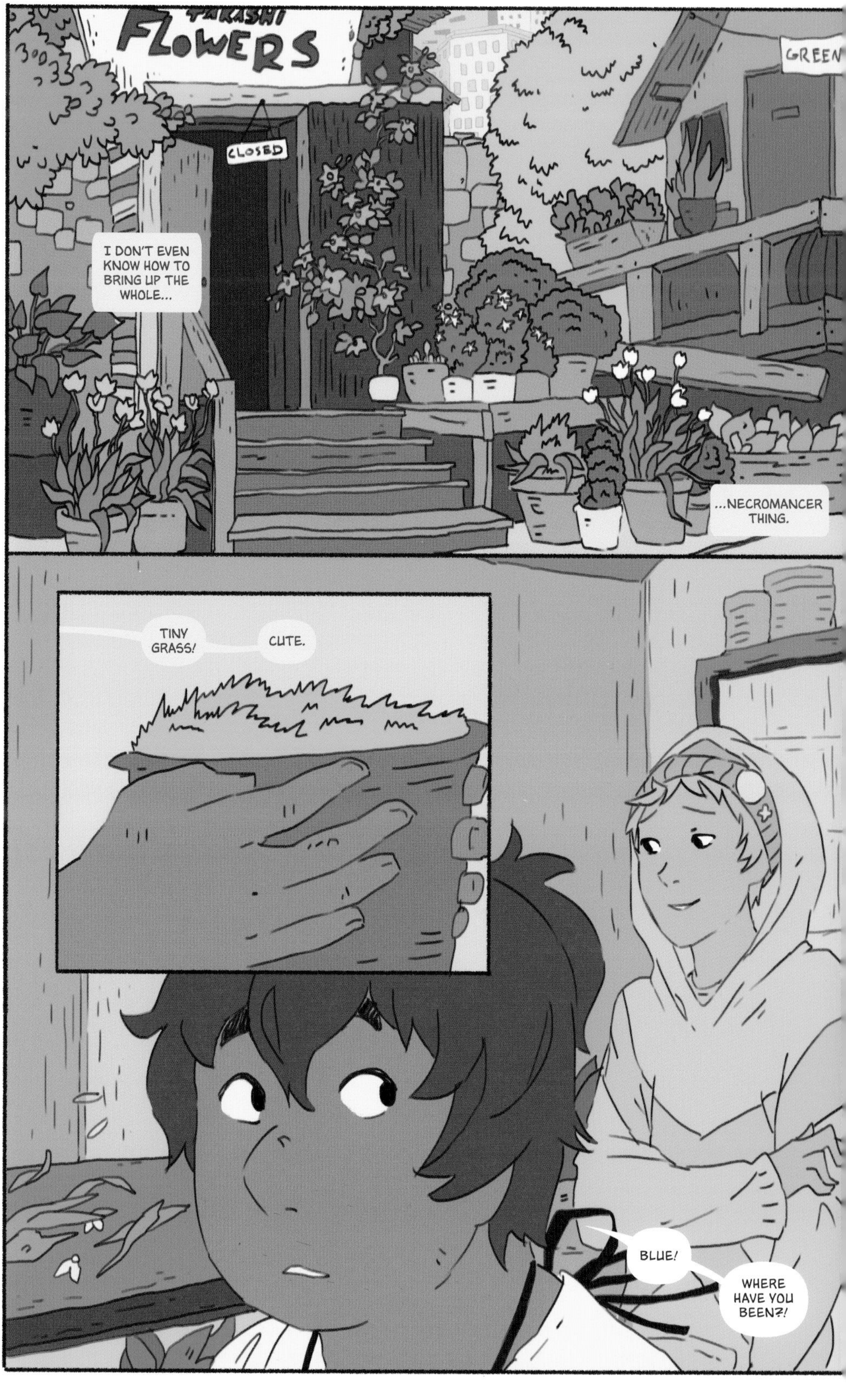
FLOWERS
CLOSED
I DON'T EVEN KNOW HOW TO BRING UP THE WHOLE...
...NECROMANCER THING.
TINY GRASS!
CUTE.
BLUE!
WHERE HAVE YOU BEEN?!

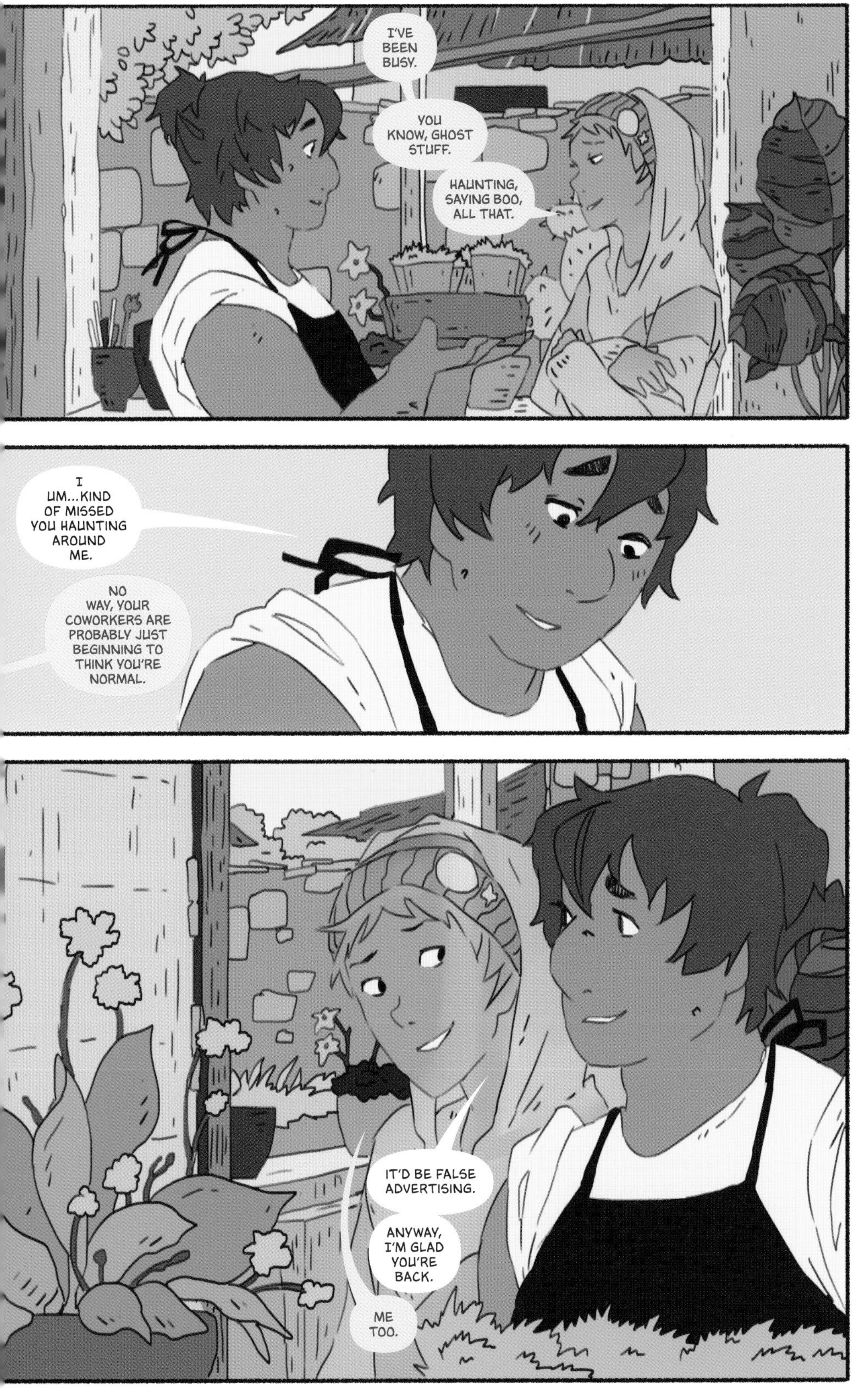
I'VE BEEN BUSY.
YOU KNOW, GHOST STUFF.
HAUNTING, SAYING BOO, ALL THAT.
I UM...KIND OF MISSED YOU HAUNTING AROUND ME.
NO WAY, YOUR COWORKERS ARE PROBABLY JUST BEGINNING TO THINK YOU'RE NORMAL.
IT'D BE FALSE ADVERTISING.
ANYWAY, I'M GLAD YOU'RE BACK.
ME TOO.

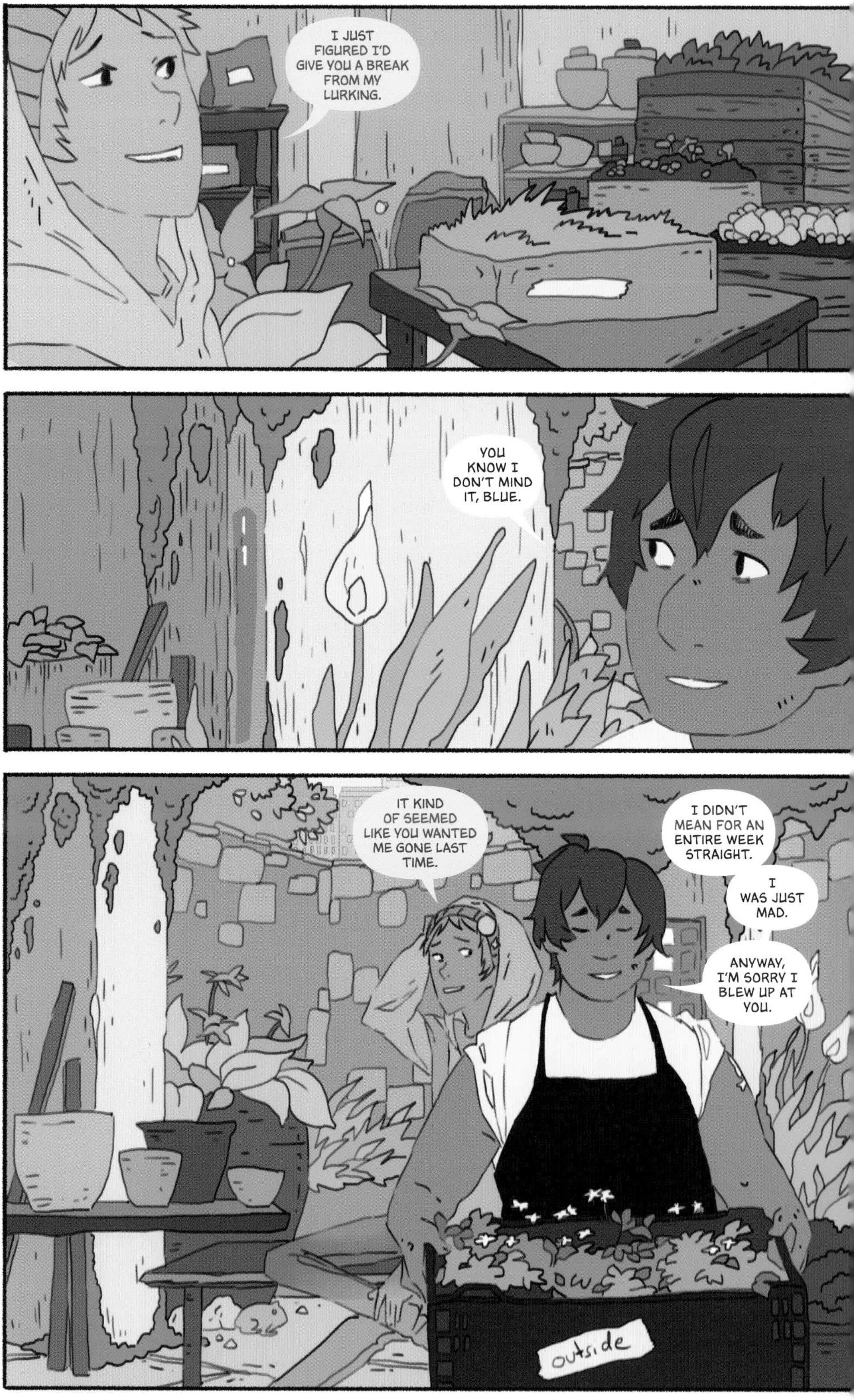
I JUST FIGURED I'D GIVE YOU A BREAK FROM MY LURKING.
YOU KNOW I DON'T MIND IT, BLUE.
IT KIND OF SEEMED LIKE YOU WANTED ME GONE LAST TIME.
I DIDN'T MEAN FOR AN ENTIRE WEEK STRAIGHT.
I WAS JUST MAD.
ANYWAY, I'M SORRY I BLEW UP AT YOU.
outside

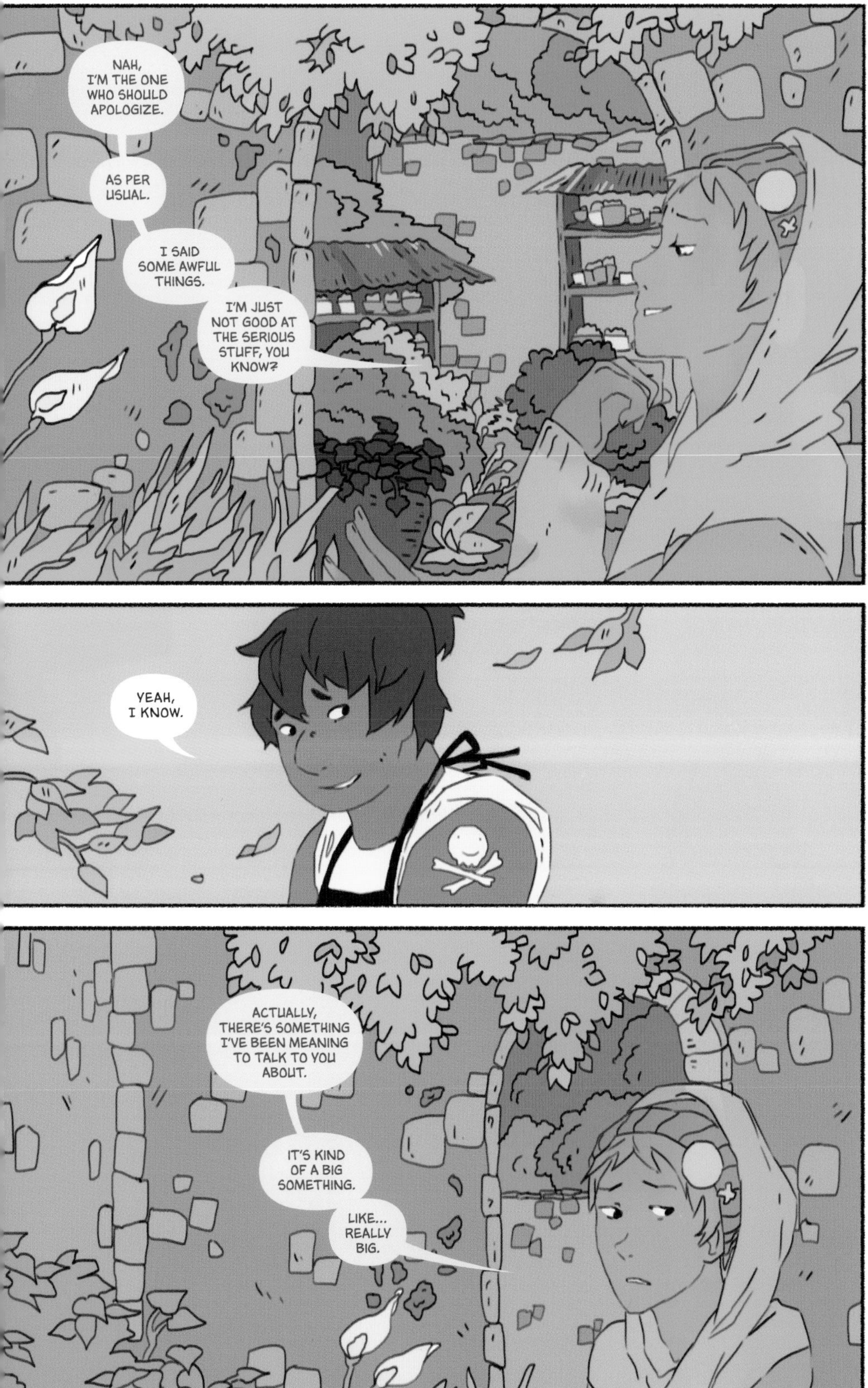
NAH, I'M THE ONE WHO SHOULD APOLOGIZE.
AS PER USUAL.
I SAID SOME AWFUL THINGS.
I'M JUST NOT GOOD AT THE SERIOUS STUFF, YOU KNOW?
YEAH, I KNOW.
ACTUALLY, THERE'S SOMETHING I'VE BEEN MEANING TO TALK TO YOU ABOUT.
IT'S KIND OF A BIG SOMETHING.
LIKE... REALLY BIG.

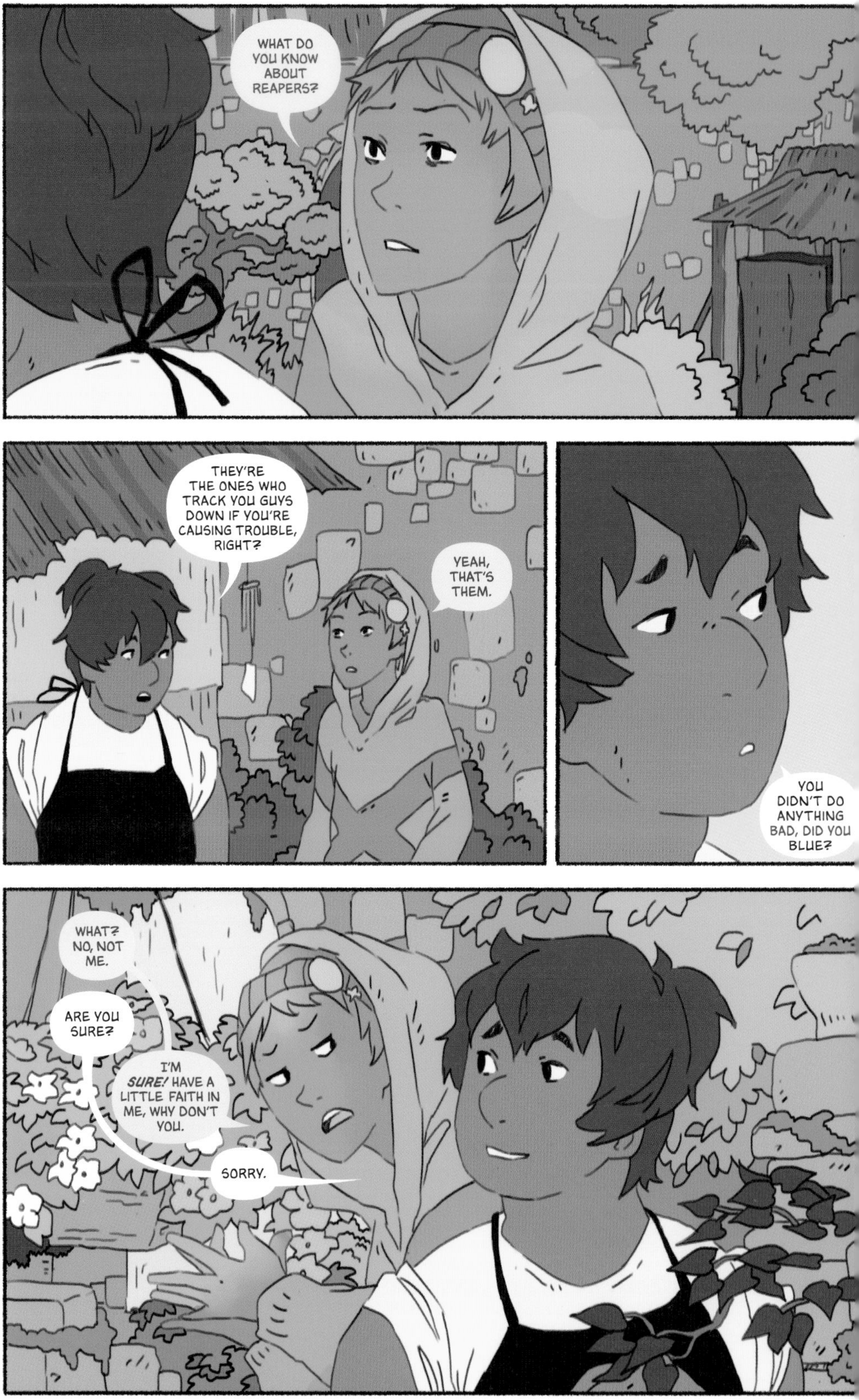
WHAT DO YOU KNOW ABOUT REAPERS?
THEY'RE THE ONES WHO TRACK YOU GUYS DOWN IF YOU'RE CAUSING TROUBLE, RIGHT?
YEAH, THAT'S THEM.
YOU DIDN'T DO ANYTHING BAD, DID YOU BLUE?
WHAT? NO, NOT ME.
ARE YOU SURE?
I'M *SURE!* HAVE A LITTLE FAITH IN ME, WHY DON'T YOU.
SORRY.

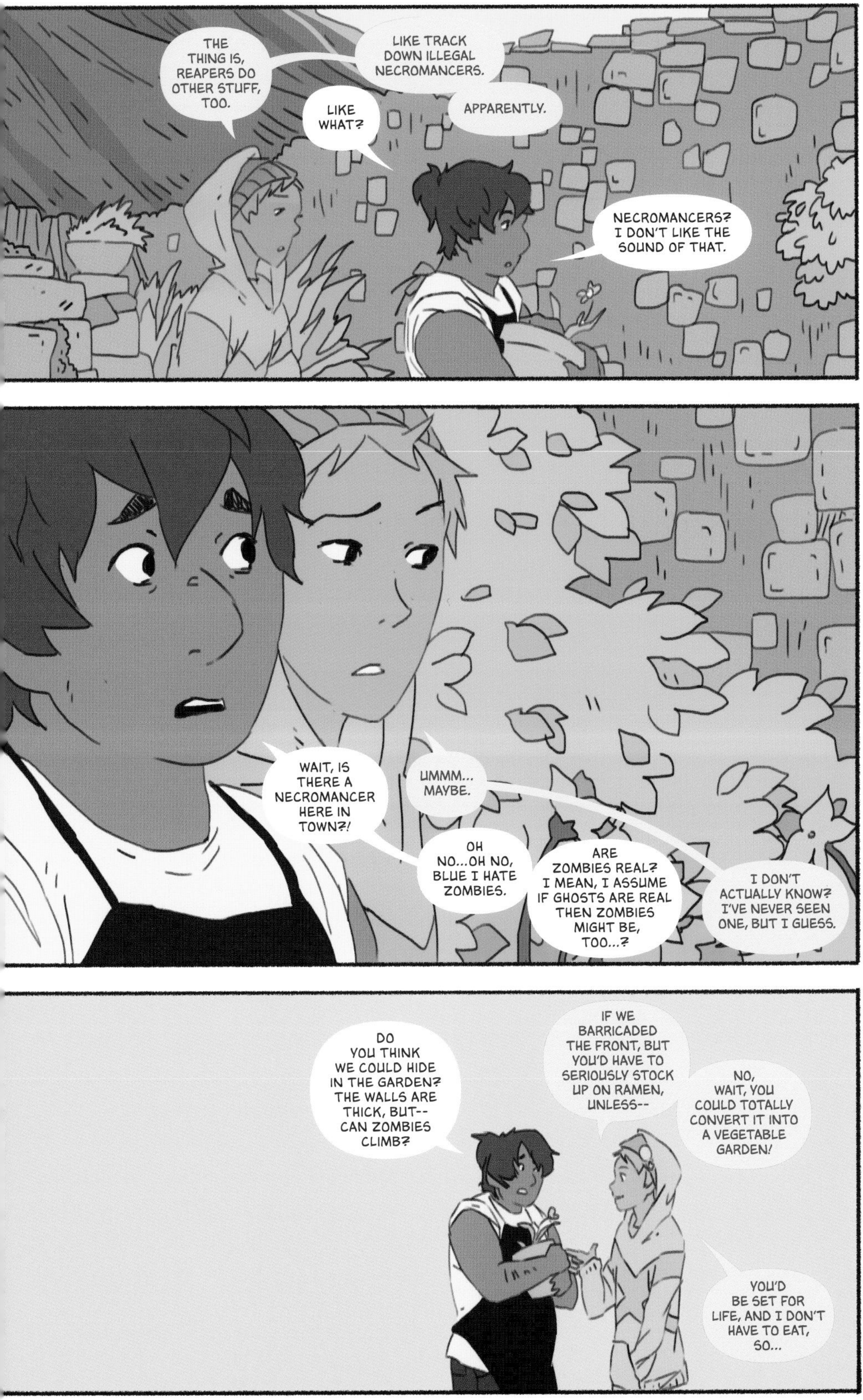

THE THING IS, REAPERS DO OTHER STUFF, TOO.
LIKE TRACK DOWN ILLEGAL NECROMANCERS.
LIKE WHAT?
APPARENTLY.
NECROMANCERS? I DON'T LIKE THE SOUND OF THAT.
WAIT, IS THERE A NECROMANCER HERE IN TOWN?!
UMMM... MAYBE.
OH NO...OH NO, BLUE I HATE ZOMBIES.
ARE ZOMBIES REAL? I MEAN, I ASSUME IF GHOSTS ARE REAL THEN ZOMBIES MIGHT BE, TOO...?
I DON'T ACTUALLY KNOW? I'VE NEVER SEEN ONE, BUT I GUESS.
DO YOU THINK WE COULD HIDE IN THE GARDEN? THE WALLS ARE THICK, BUT-- CAN ZOMBIES CLIMB?
IF WE BARRICADED THE FRONT, BUT YOU'D HAVE TO SERIOUSLY STOCK UP ON RAMEN, UNLESS--
NO, WAIT, YOU COULD TOTALLY CONVERT IT INTO A VEGETABLE GARDEN!
YOU'D BE SET FOR LIFE, AND I DON'T HAVE TO EAT, SO...

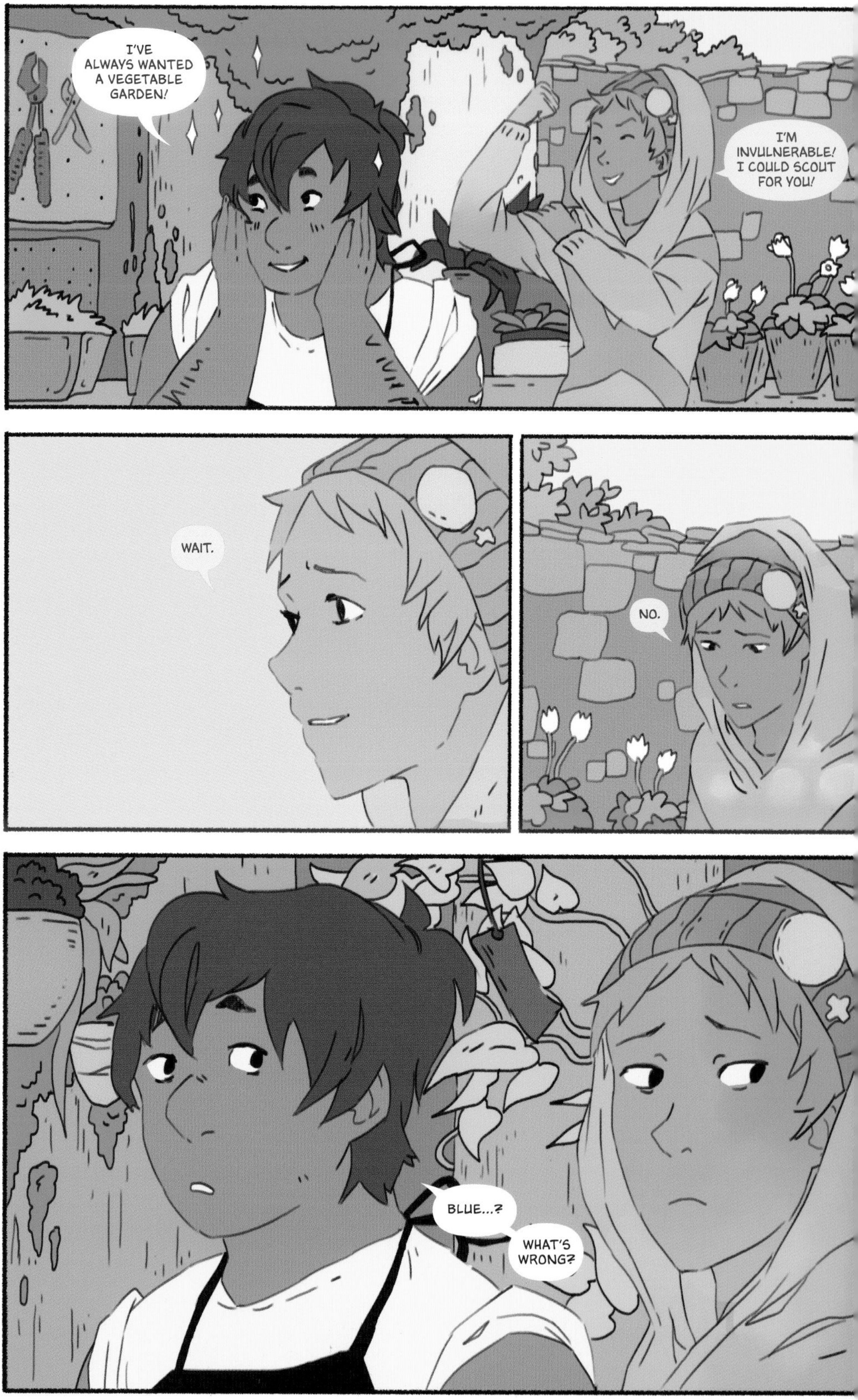
I'VE ALWAYS WANTED A VEGETABLE GARDEN!
I'M INVULNERABLE! I COULD SCOUT FOR YOU!
WAIT.
NO.
BLUE...?
WHAT'S WRONG?

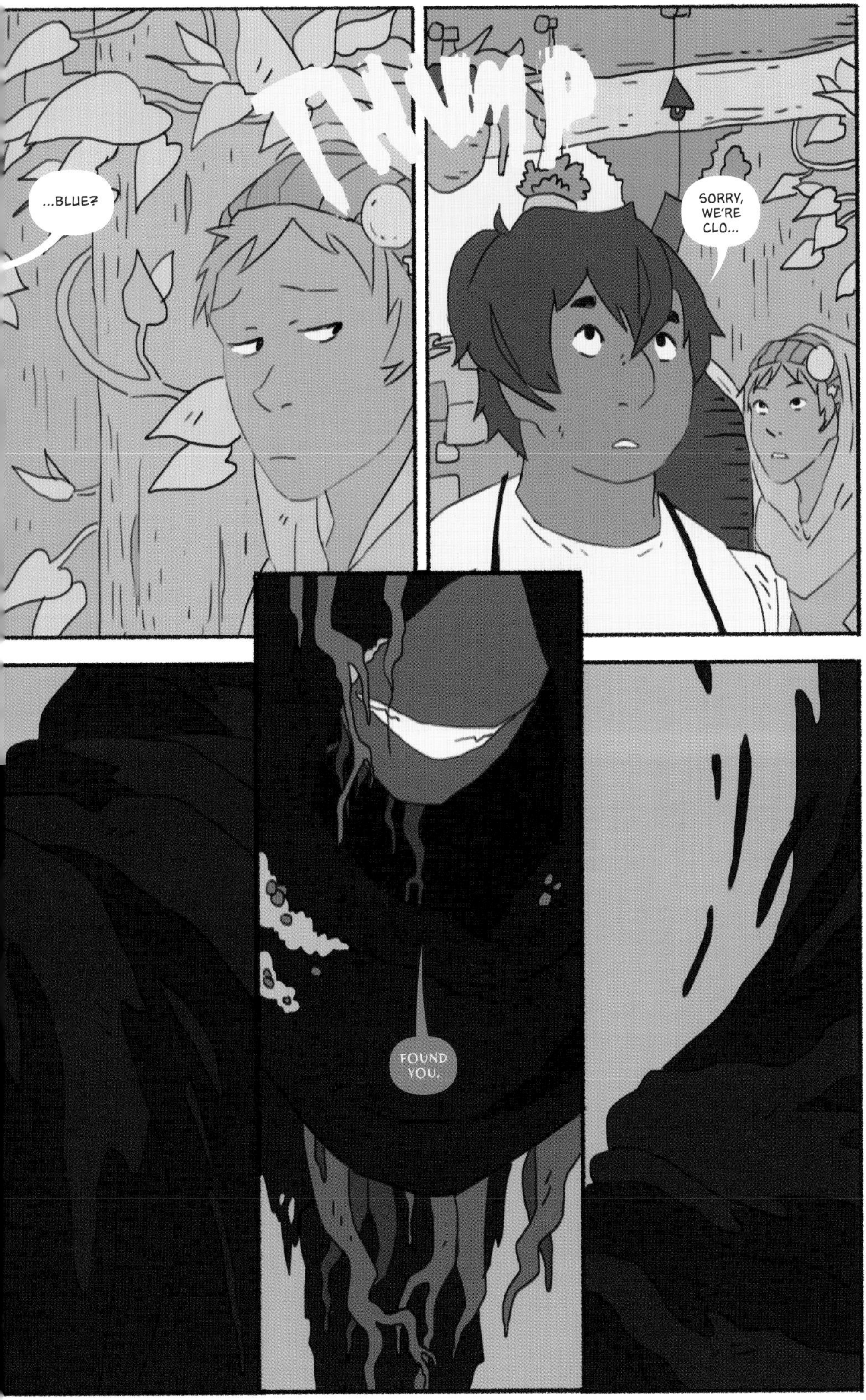
...BLUE?
THUMP
SORRY, WE'RE CLO...
FOUND YOU.

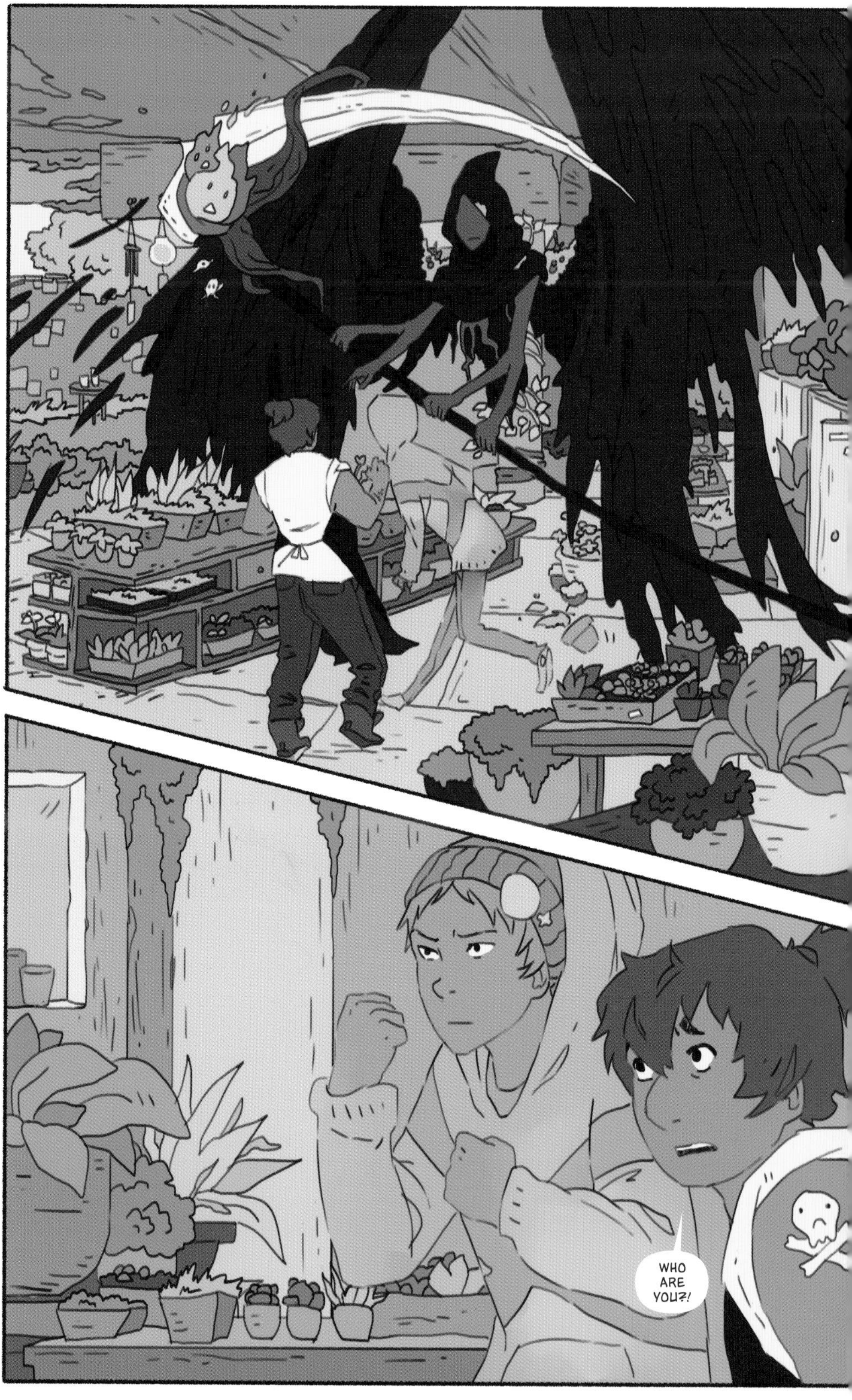
WHO
ARE
YOU?!

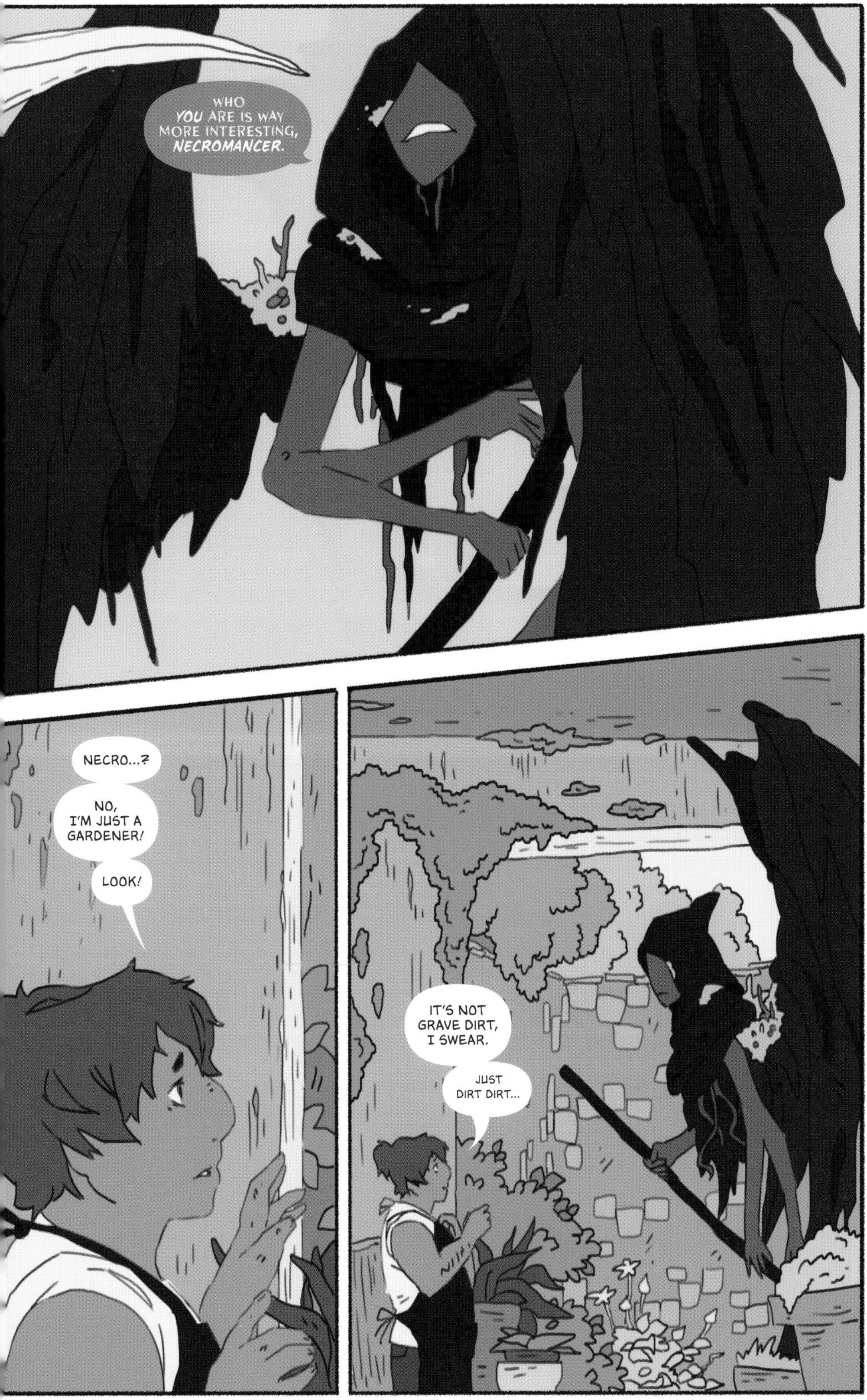
WHO *YOU* ARE IS WAY MORE INTERESTING, ***NECROMANCER.***
NECRO...?
NO, I'M JUST A GARDENER!
LOOK!
IT'S NOT GRAVE DIRT, I SWEAR.
JUST DIRT DIRT...

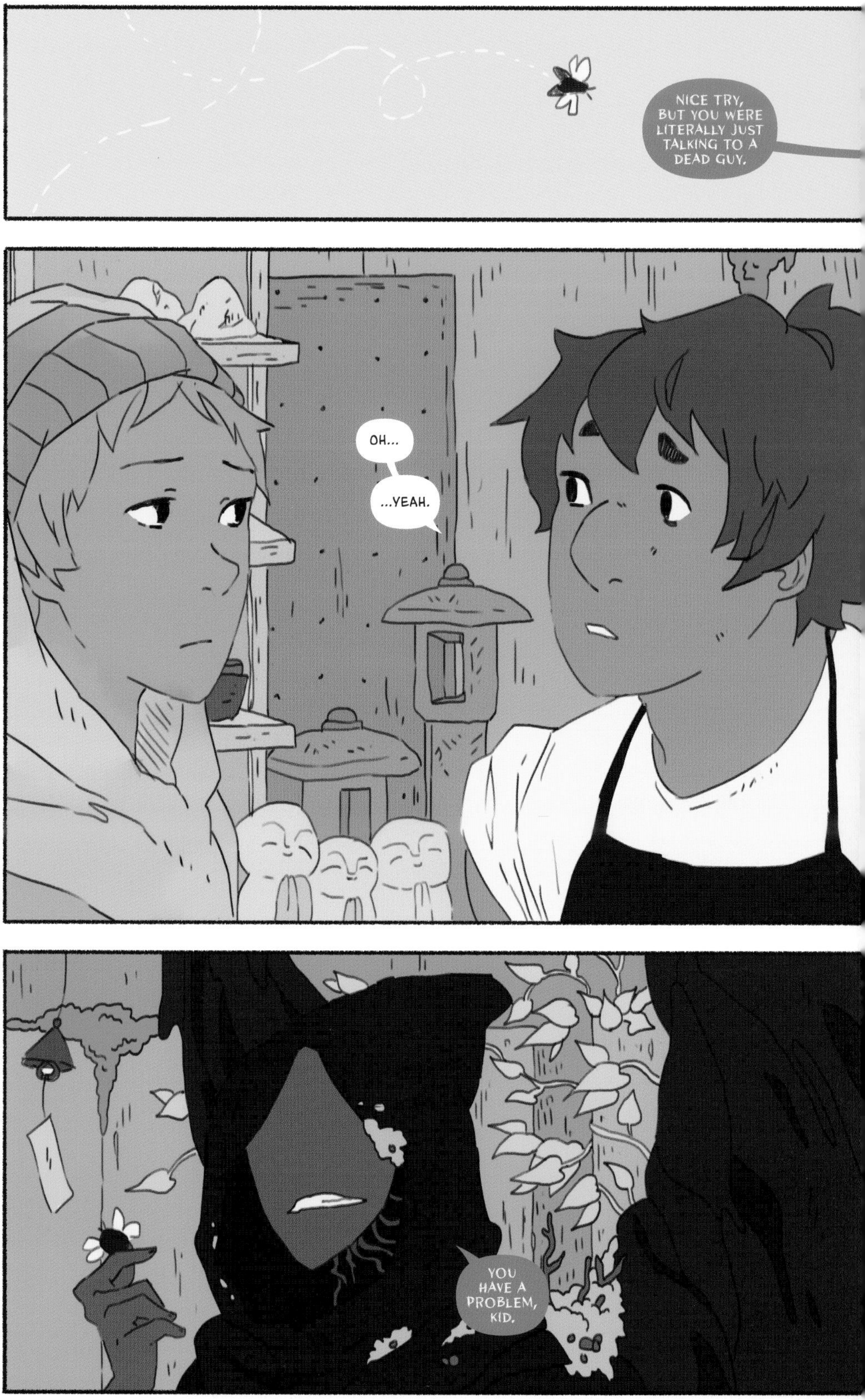
NICE TRY, BUT YOU WERE LITERALLY JUST TALKING TO A DEAD GUY.
OH...
...YEAH.
YOU HAVE A PROBLEM, KID.

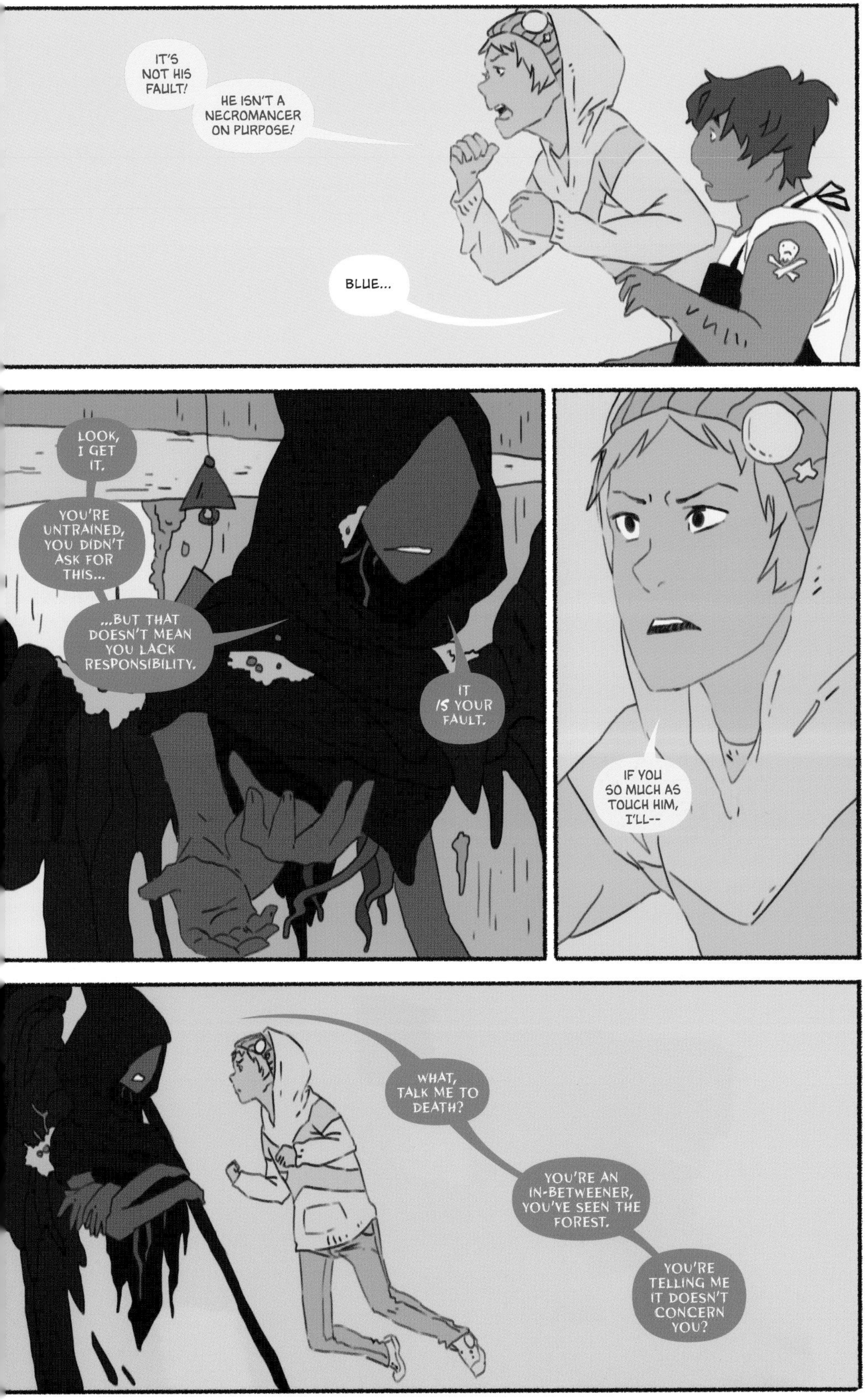
IT'S NOT HIS FAULT!
HE ISN'T A NECROMANCER ON PURPOSE!
BLUE...
LOOK, I GET IT.
YOU'RE UNTRAINED, YOU DIDN'T ASK FOR THIS...
...BUT THAT DOESN'T MEAN YOU LACK RESPONSIBILITY.
IT *IS* YOUR FAULT.
IF YOU SO MUCH AS TOUCH HIM, I'LL--
WHAT, TALK ME TO DEATH?
YOU'RE AN IN-BETWEENER, YOU'VE SEEN THE FOREST.
YOU'RE TELLING ME IT DOESN'T CONCERN YOU?

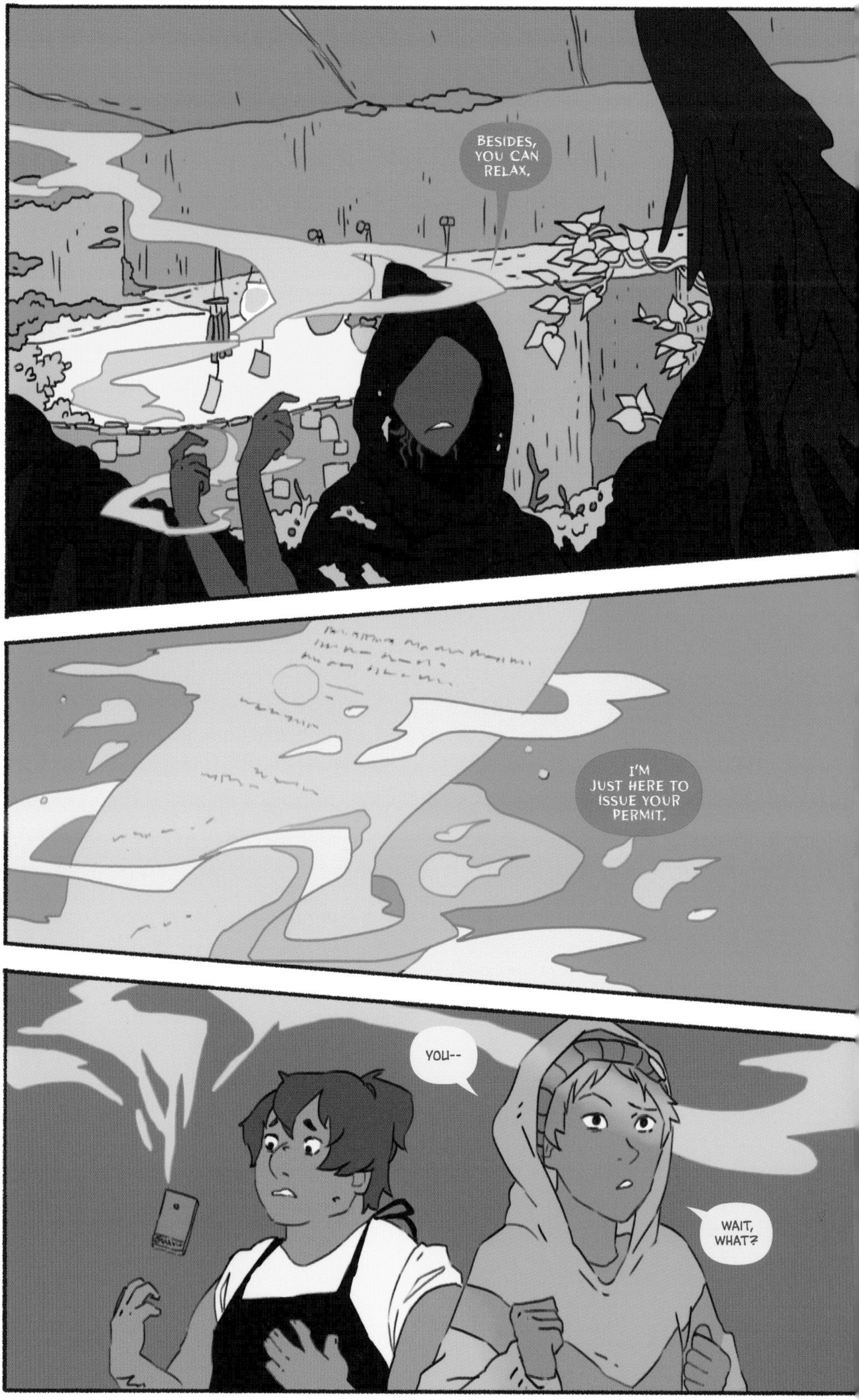
BESIDES, YOU CAN RELAX.
I'M JUST HERE TO ISSUE YOUR PERMIT.
YOU--
WAIT, WHAT?

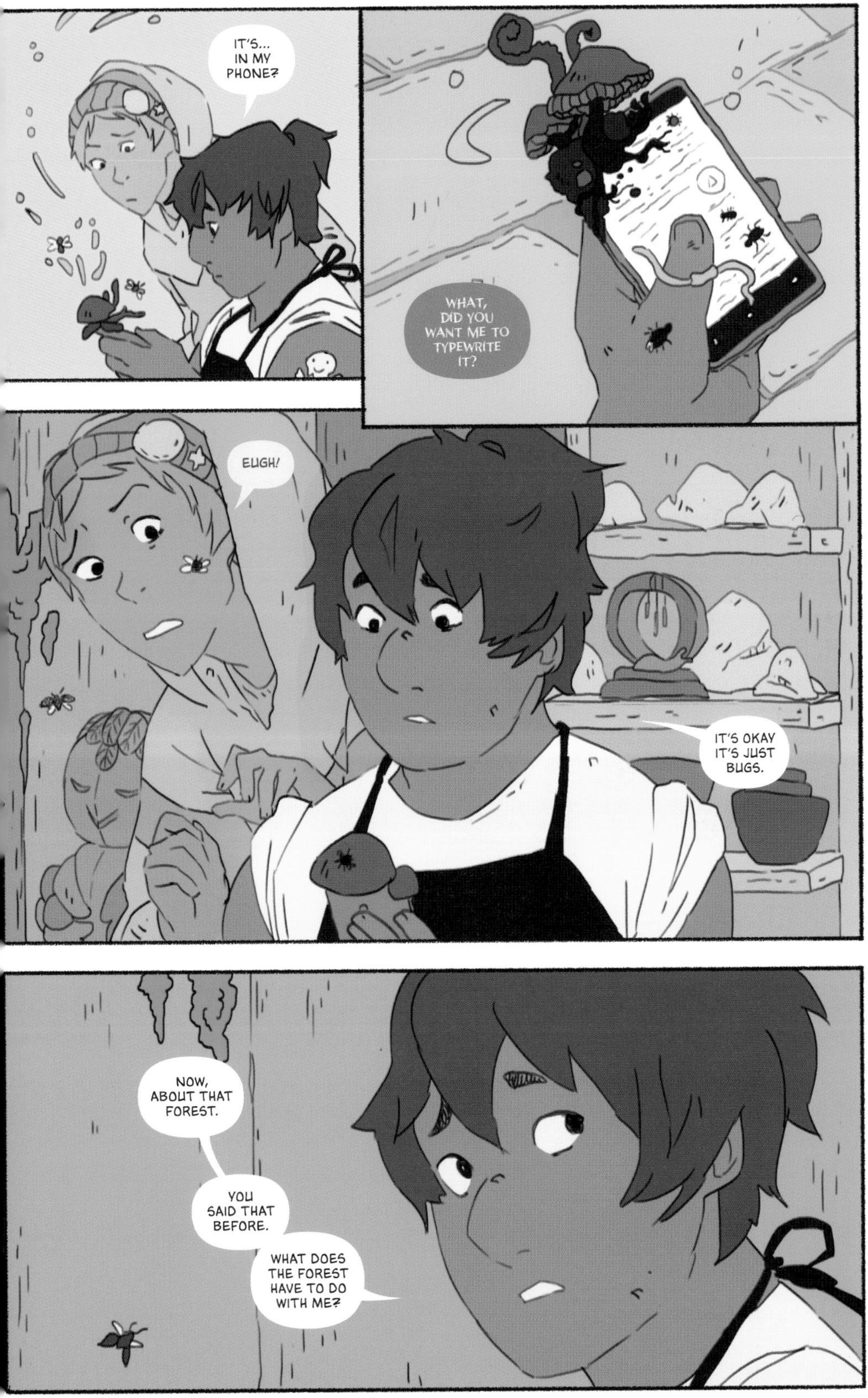

IT'S... IN MY PHONE?
WHAT, DID YOU WANT ME TO TYPEWRITE IT?
EUGH!
IT'S OKAY IT'S JUST BUGS.
NOW, ABOUT THAT FOREST.
YOU SAID THAT BEFORE.
WHAT DOES THE FOREST HAVE TO DO WITH ME?

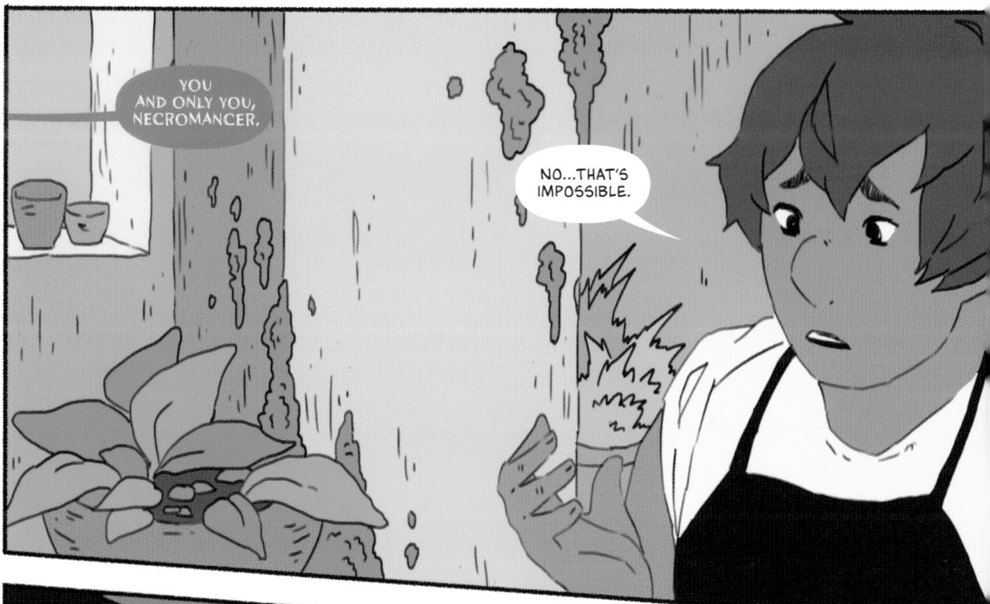
YOU AND ONLY YOU, NECROMANCER.
NO...THAT'S IMPOSSIBLE.

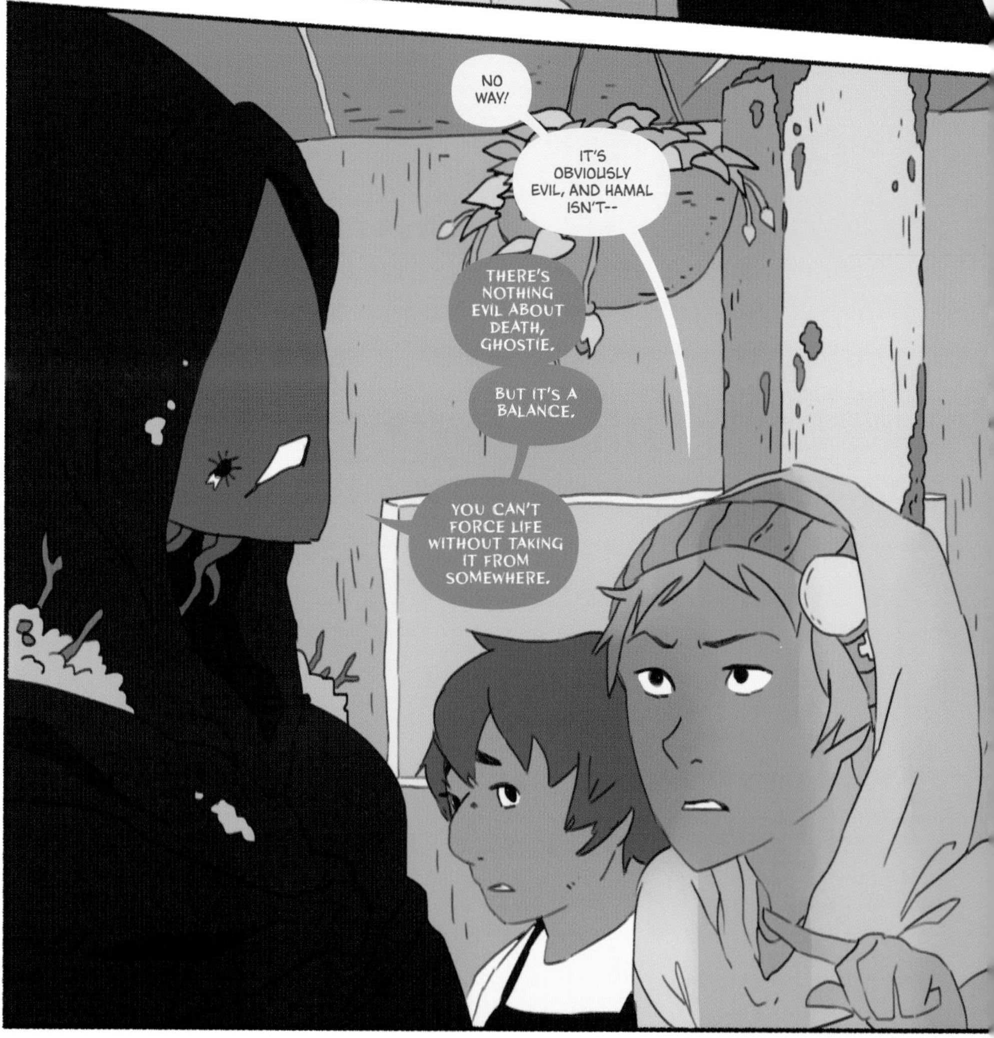
NO WAY!
IT'S OBVIOUSLY EVIL, AND HAMAL ISN'T--
THERE'S NOTHING EVIL ABOUT DEATH, GHOSTIE.
BUT IT'S A BALANCE.
YOU CAN'T FORCE LIFE WITHOUT TAKING IT FROM SOMEWHERE.

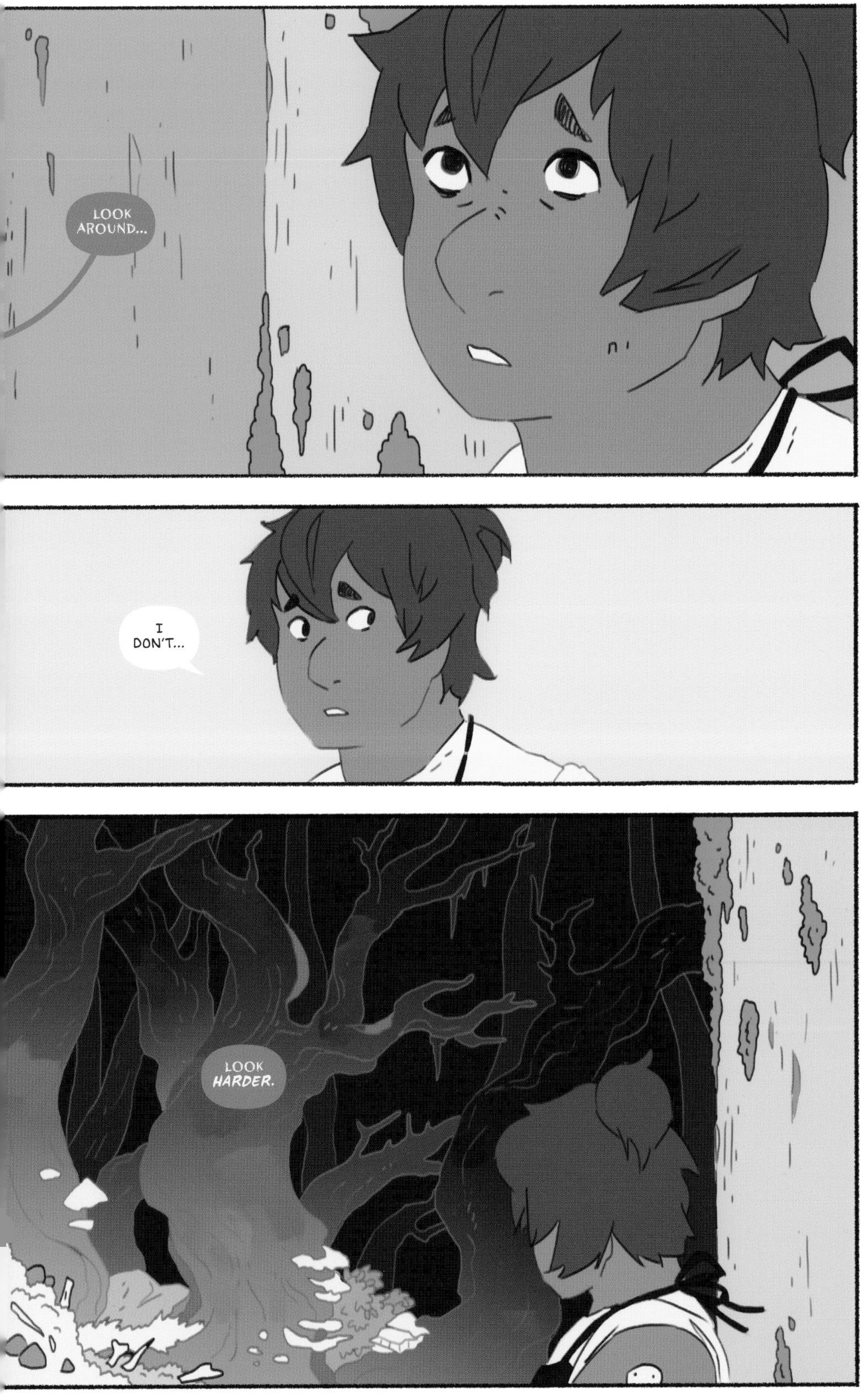
LOOK AROUND...
I DON'T...
LOOK HARDER.

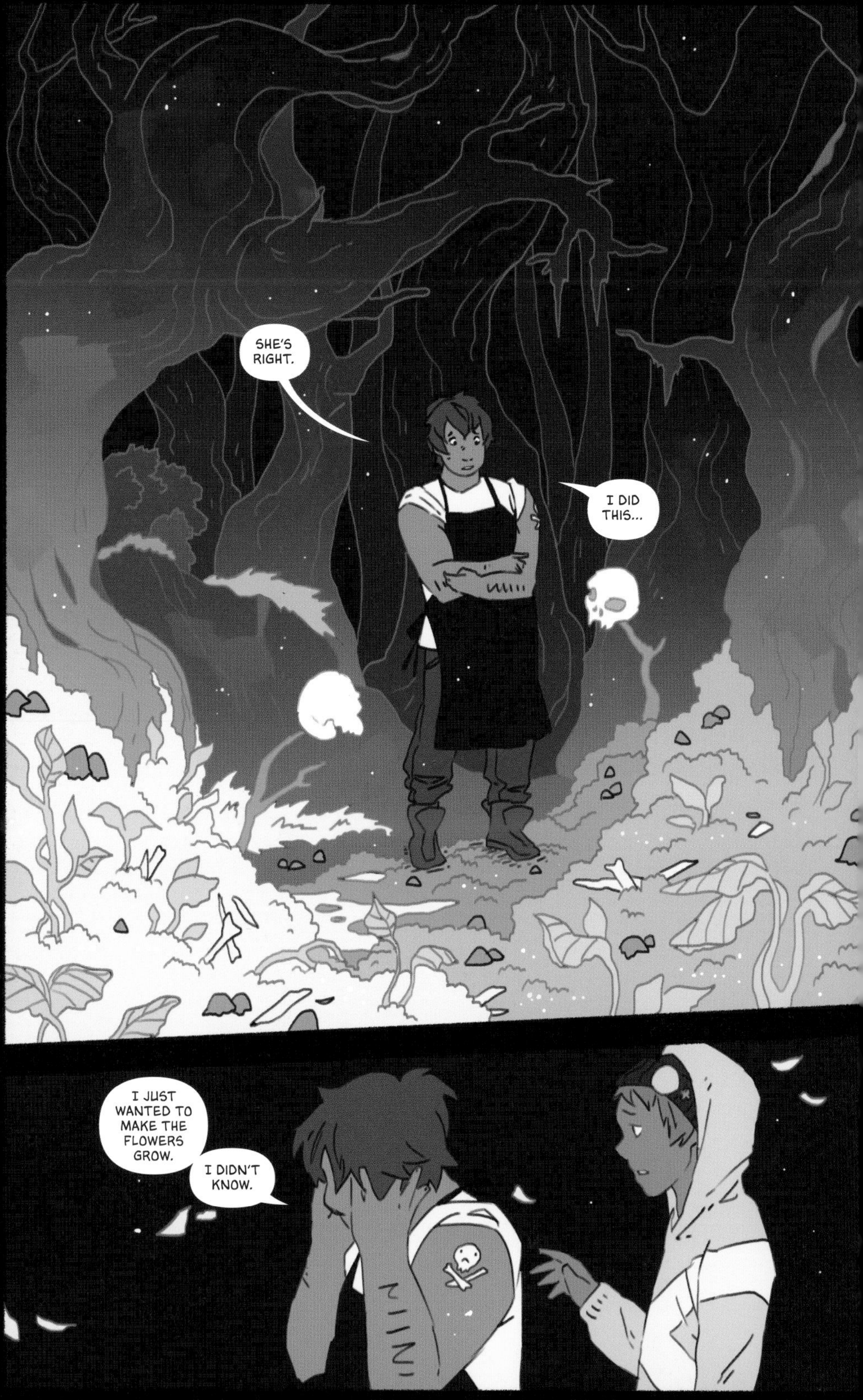
SHE'S RIGHT.
I DID THIS...
I JUST WANTED TO MAKE THE FLOWERS GROW.
I DIDN'T KNOW.

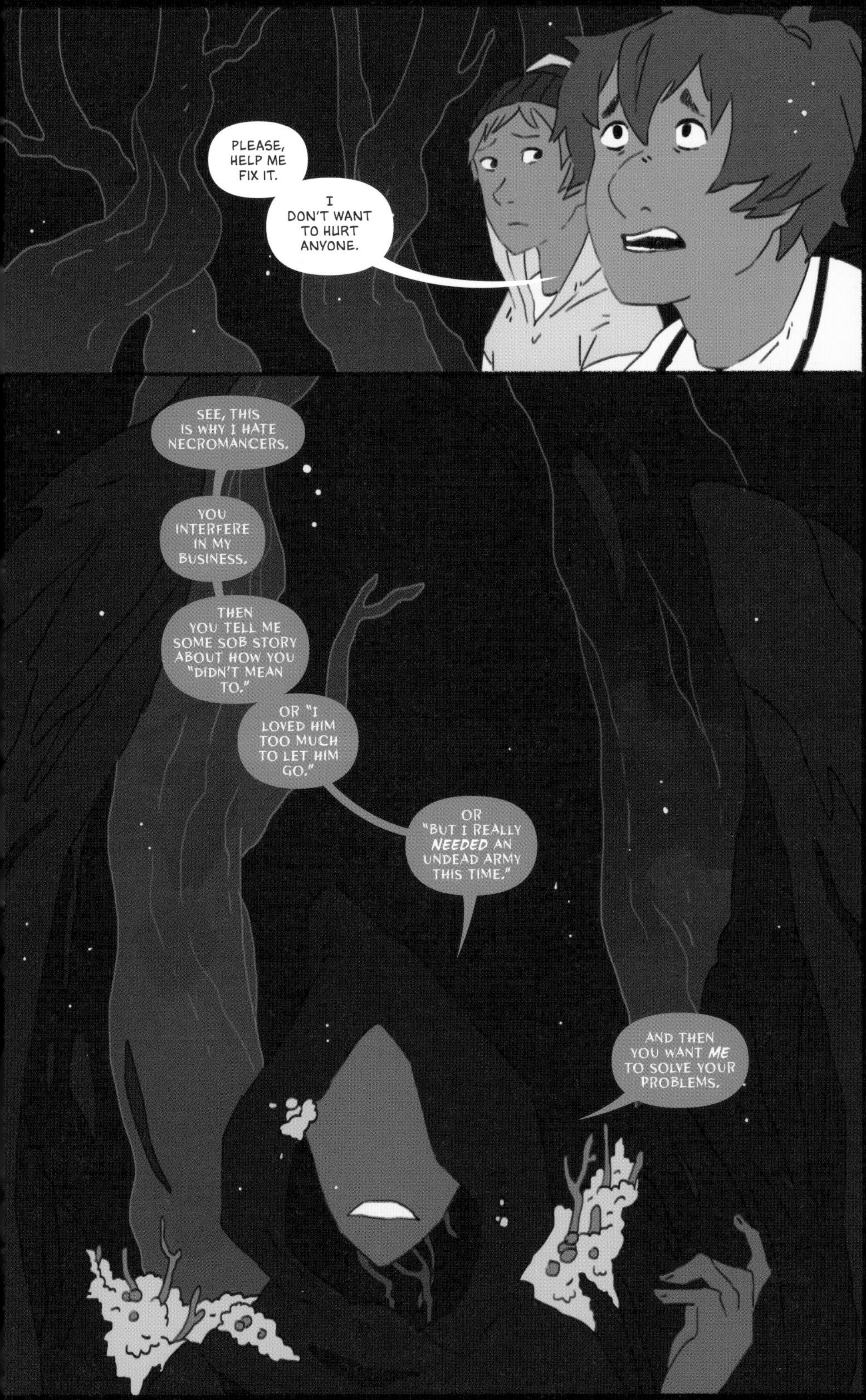
PLEASE, HELP ME FIX IT.
I DON'T WANT TO HURT ANYONE.
SEE, THIS IS WHY I HATE NECROMANCERS.
YOU INTERFERE IN MY BUSINESS.
THEN YOU TELL ME SOME SOB STORY ABOUT HOW YOU "DIDN'T MEAN TO."
OR "I LOVED HIM TOO MUCH TO LET HIM GO."
OR "BUT I REALLY *NEEDED* AN UNDEAD ARMY THIS TIME."
AND THEN YOU WANT *ME* TO SOLVE YOUR PROBLEMS.

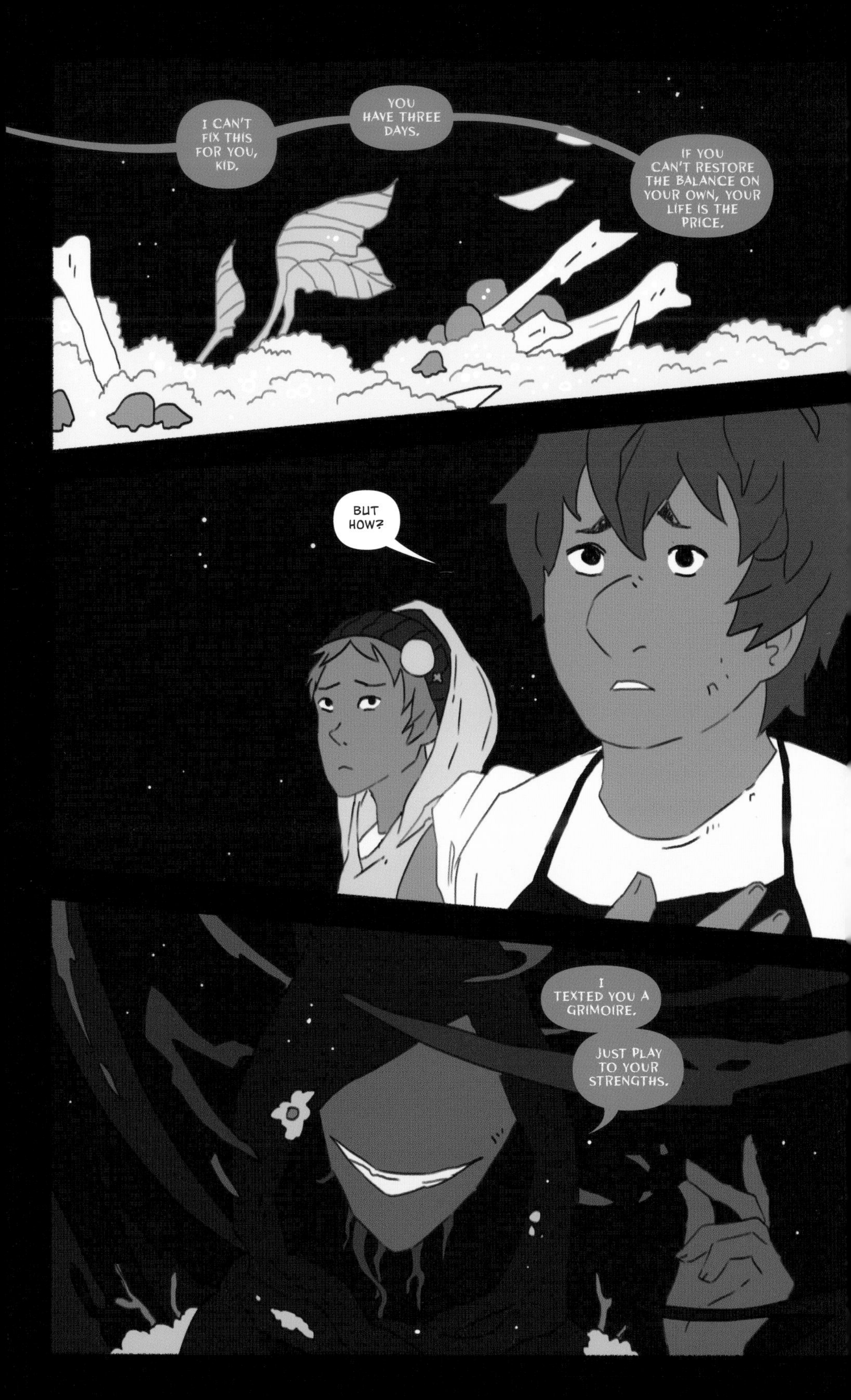
I CAN'T FIX THIS FOR YOU, KID.
YOU HAVE THREE DAYS.
IF YOU CAN'T RESTORE THE BALANCE ON YOUR OWN, YOUR LIFE IS THE PRICE.
BUT HOW?
I TEXTED YOU A GRIMOIRE.
JUST PLAY TO YOUR STRENGTHS.

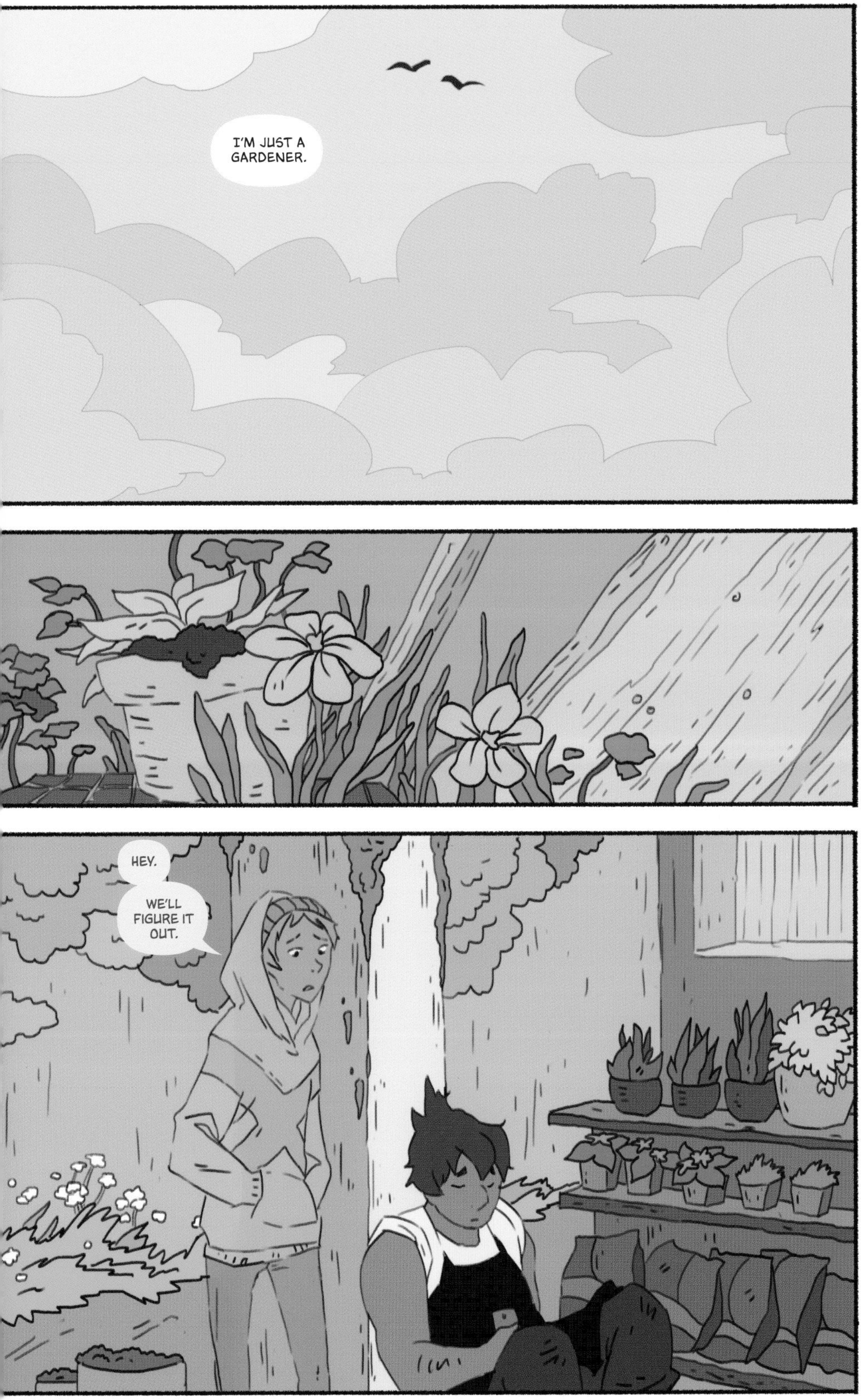
I'M JUST A GARDENER.
HEY.
WE'LL FIGURE IT OUT.

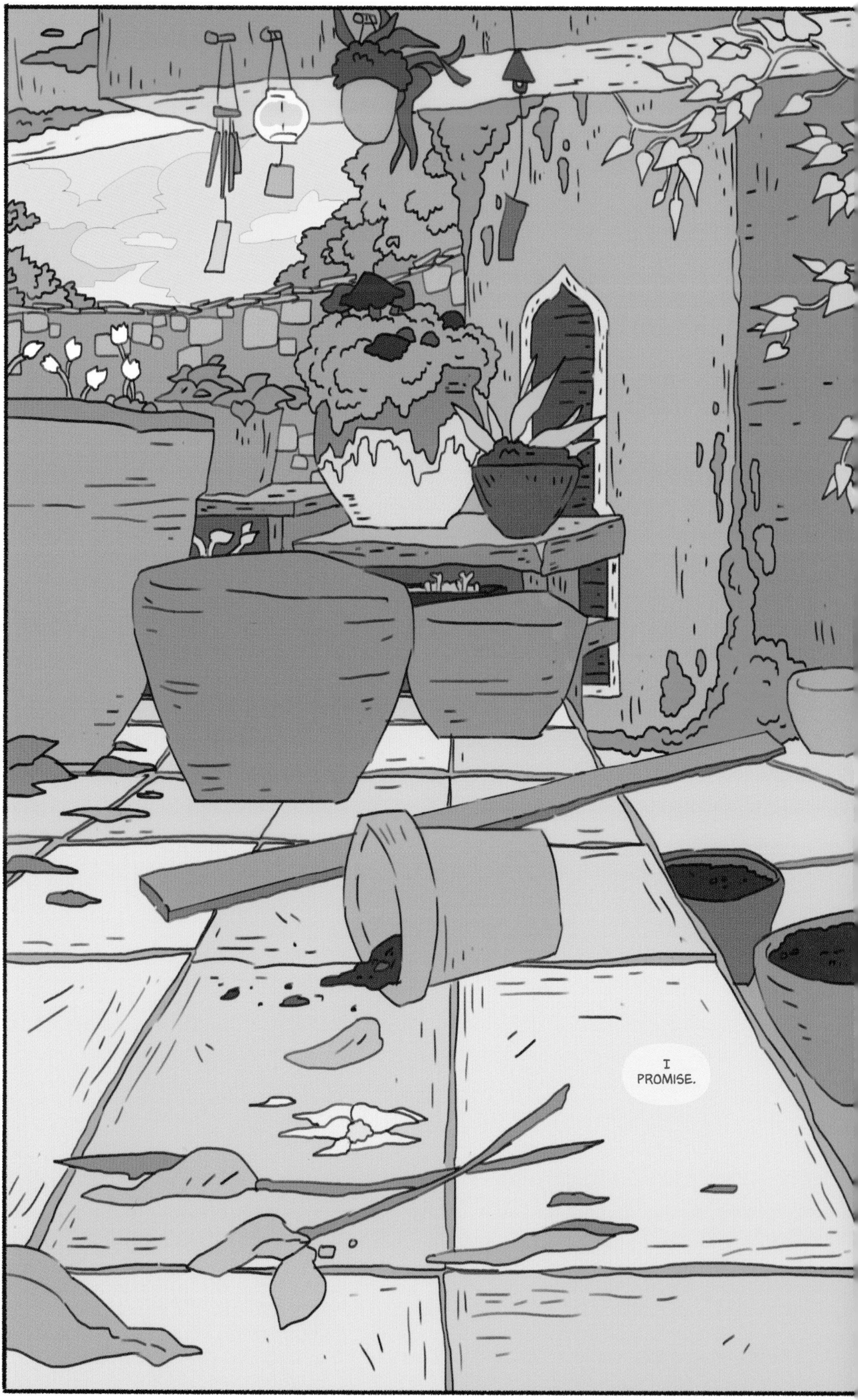
I PROMISE.

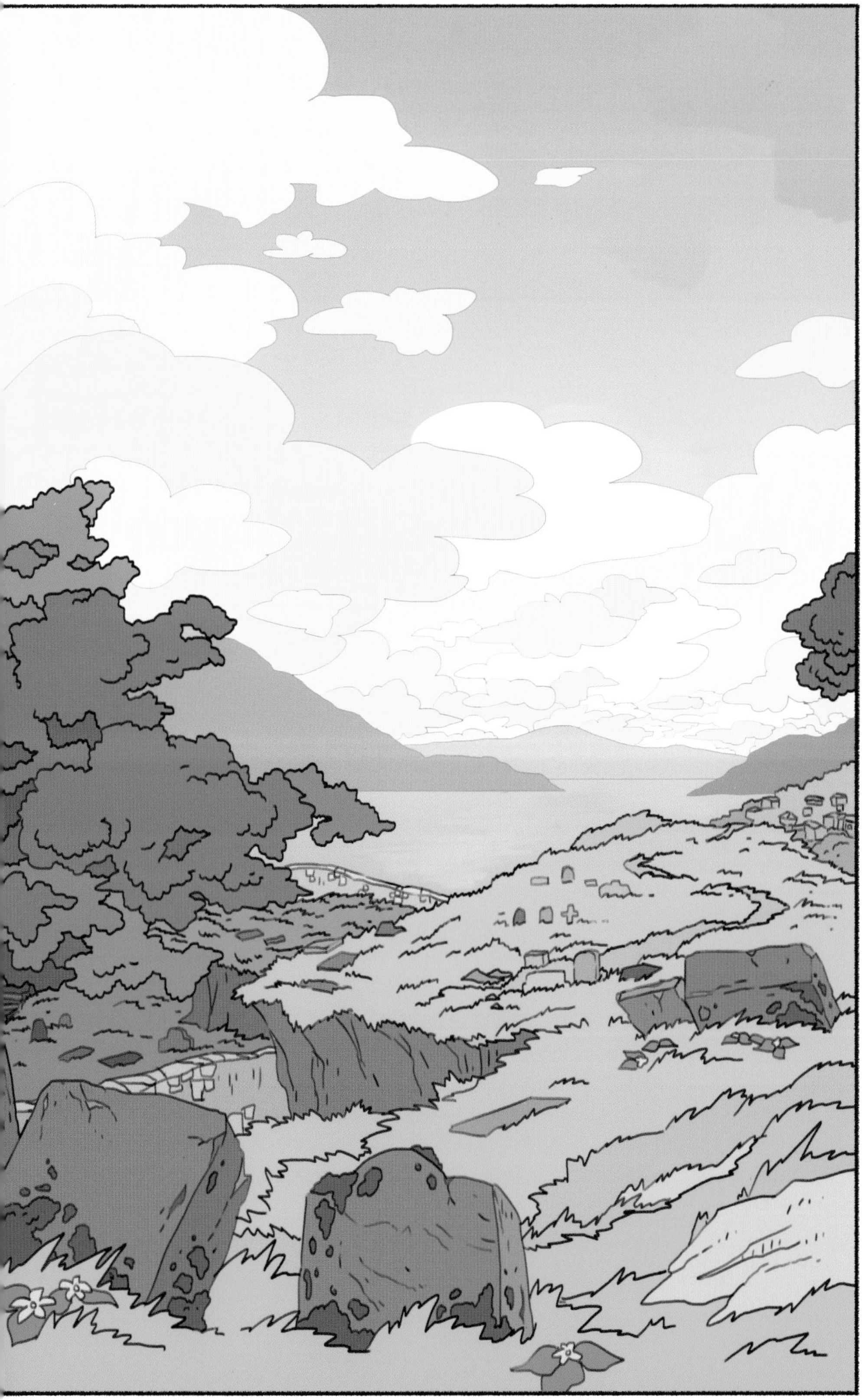

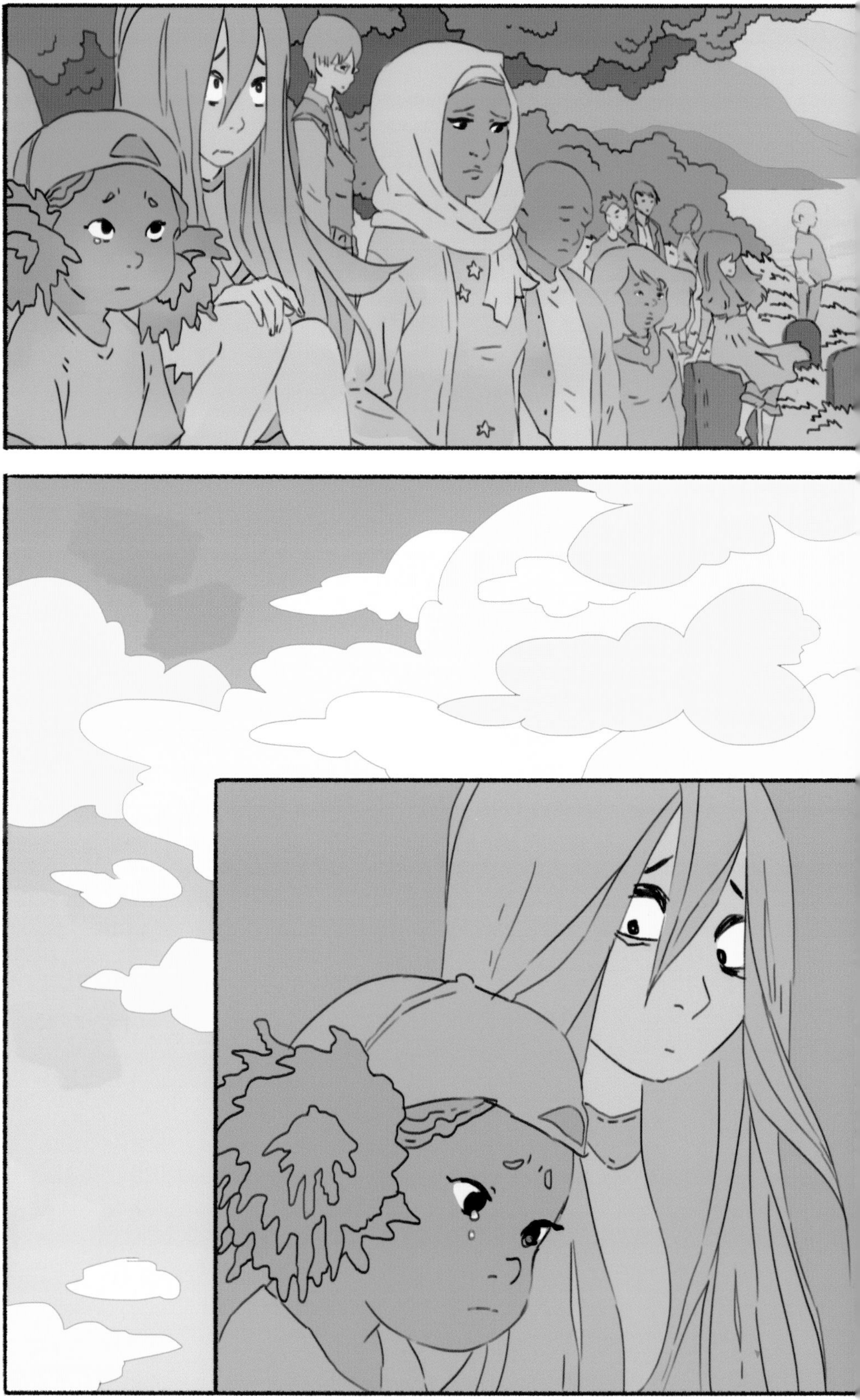

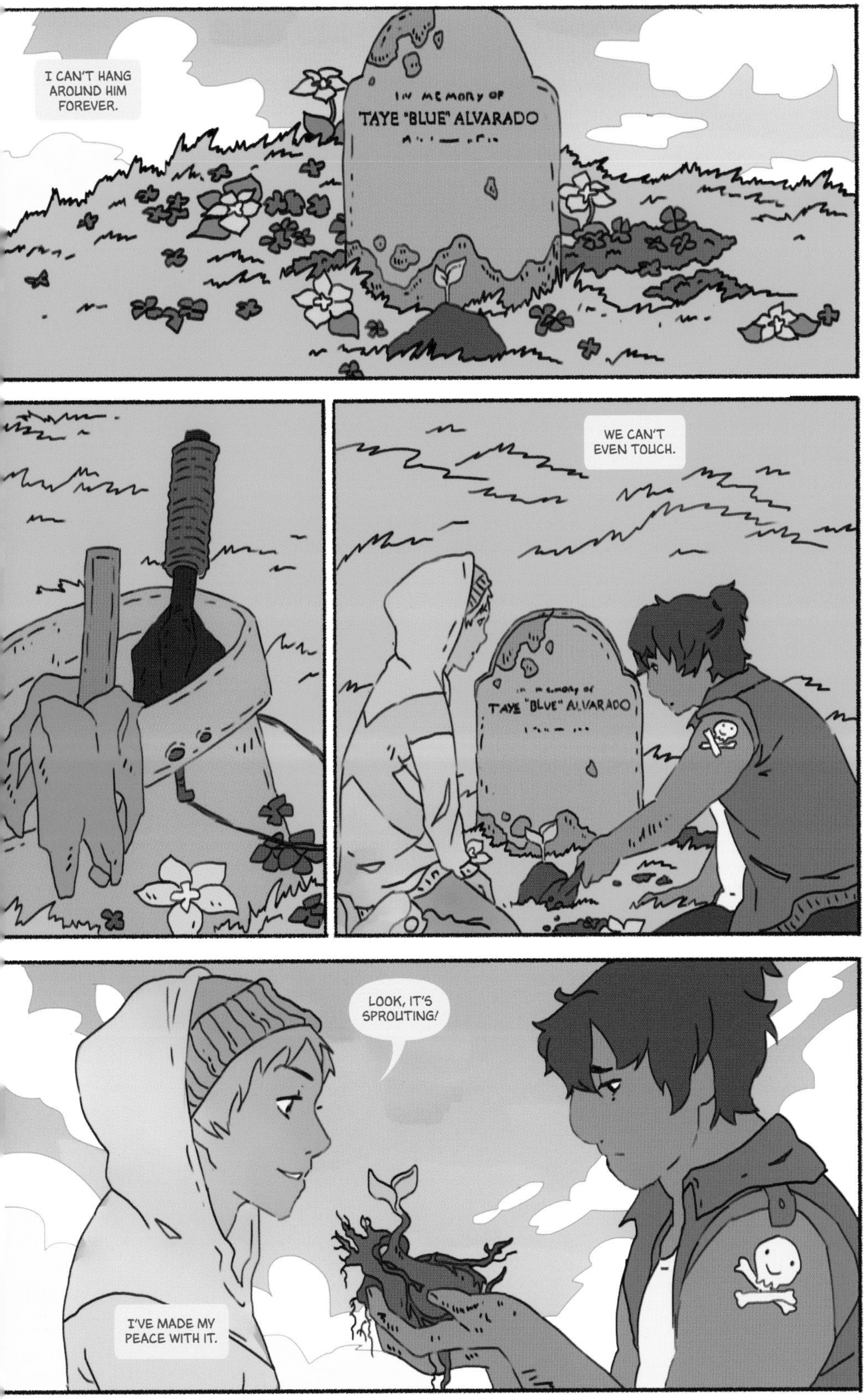
I CAN'T HANG AROUND HIM FOREVER.
IN MEMORY OF
TAYE "BLUE" ALVARADO
WE CAN'T EVEN TOUCH.
TAYE "BLUE" ALVARADO
LOOK, IT'S SPROUTING!
I'VE MADE MY PEACE WITH IT.

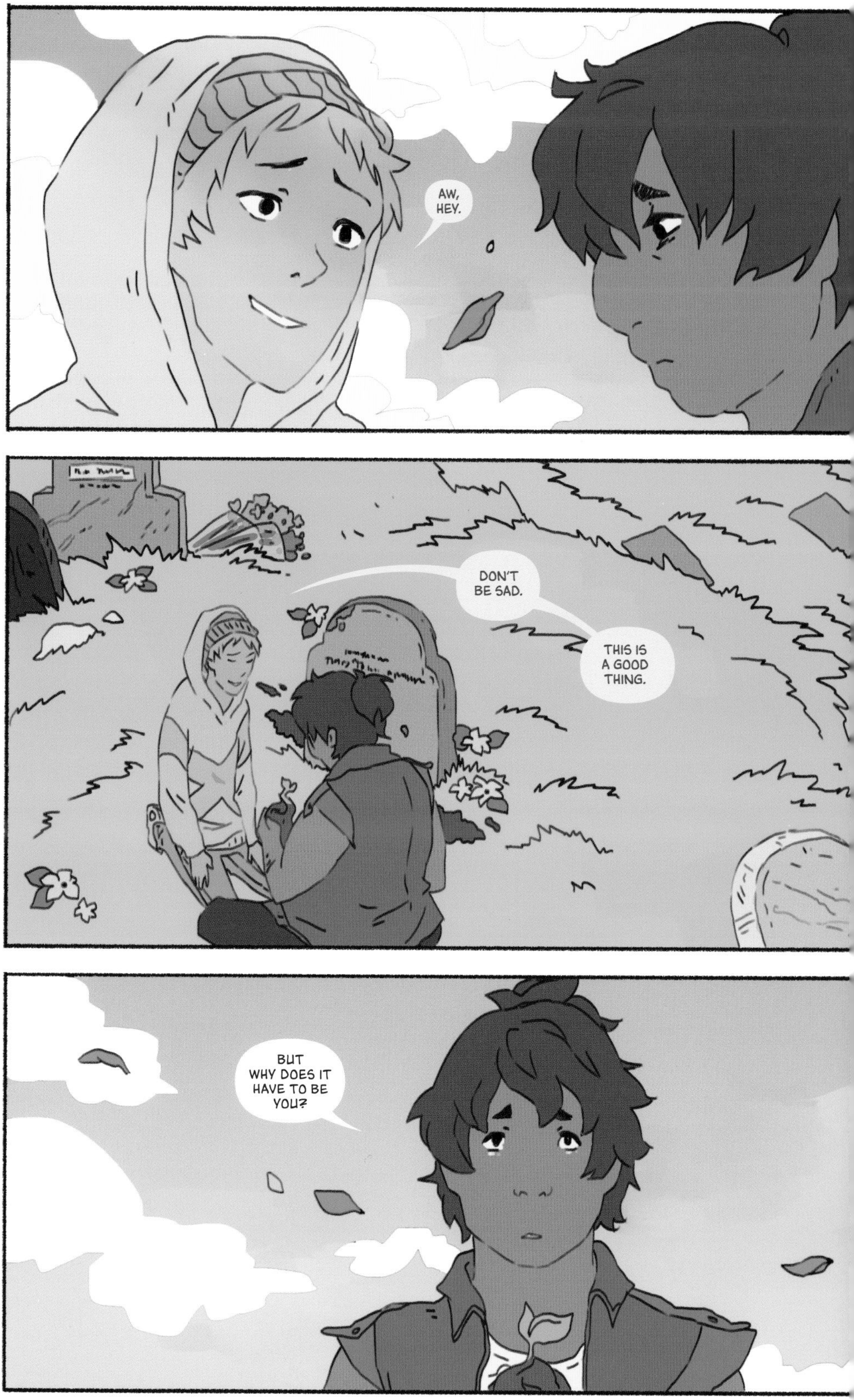
AW, HEY.
DON'T BE SAD.
THIS IS A GOOD THING.
BUT WHY DOES IT HAVE TO BE YOU?

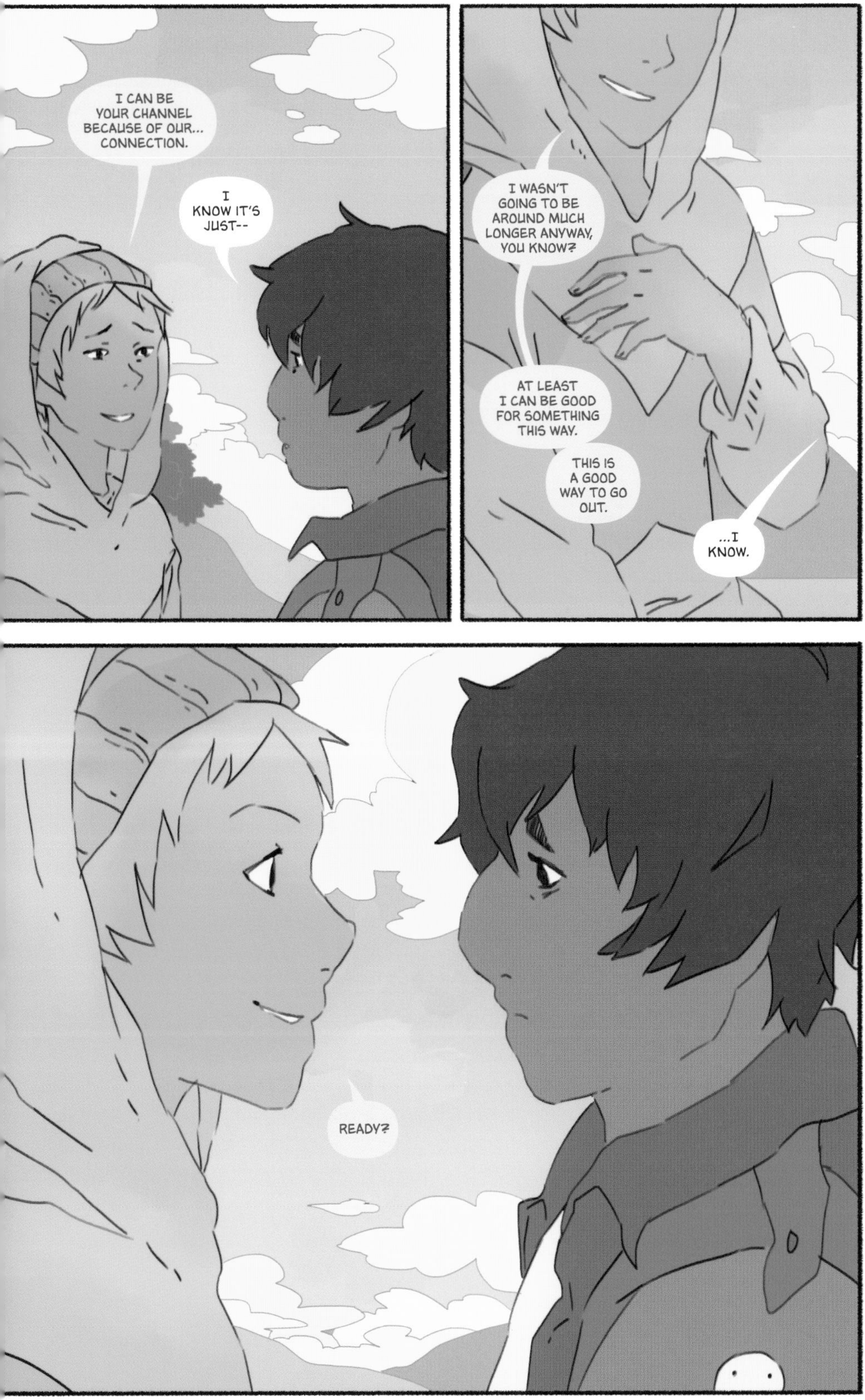
I CAN BE YOUR CHANNEL BECAUSE OF OUR... CONNECTION.
I KNOW IT'S JUST--
I WASN'T GOING TO BE AROUND MUCH LONGER ANYWAY, YOU KNOW?
AT LEAST I CAN BE GOOD FOR SOMETHING THIS WAY.
THIS IS A GOOD WAY TO GO OUT.
...I KNOW.
READY?

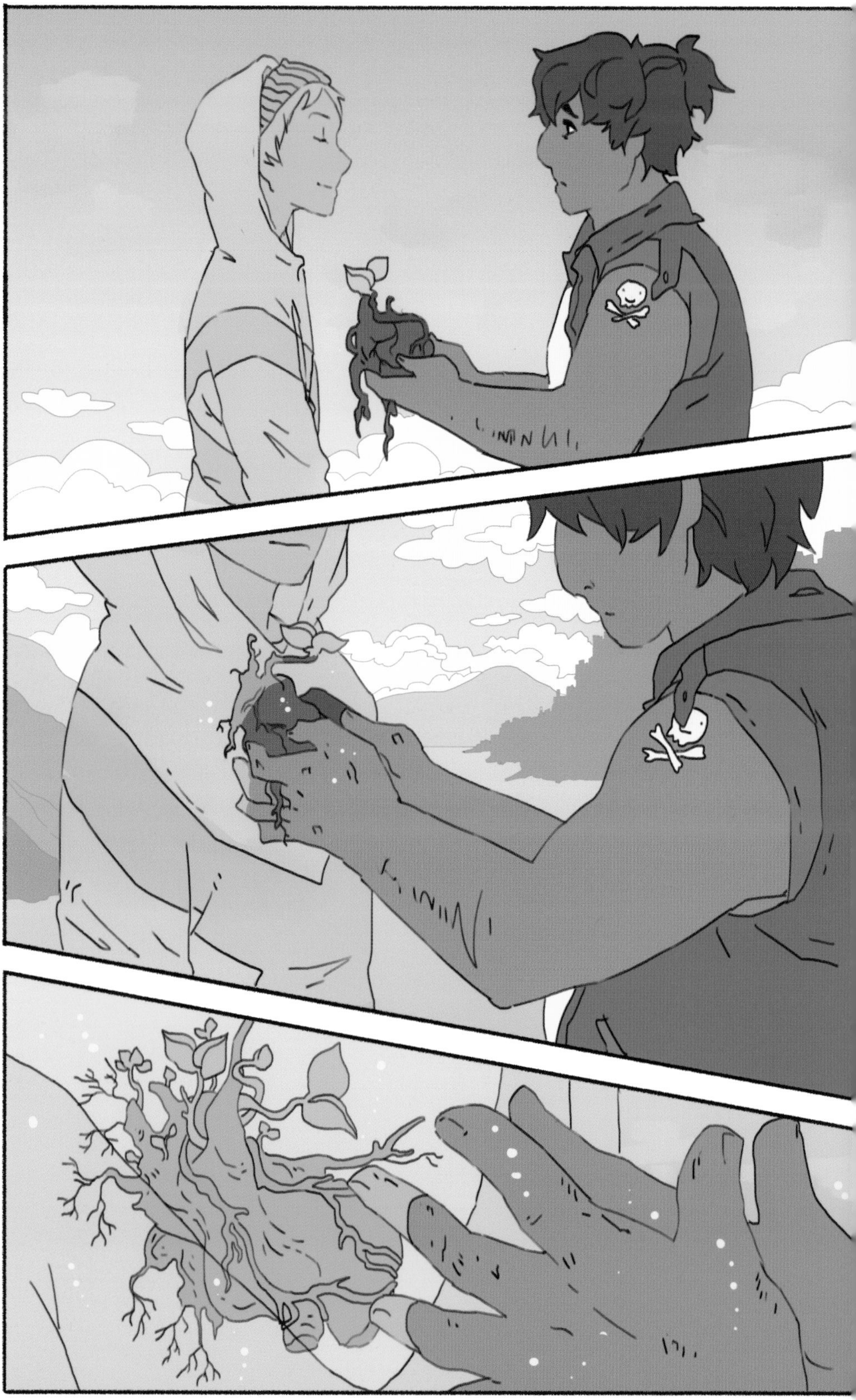

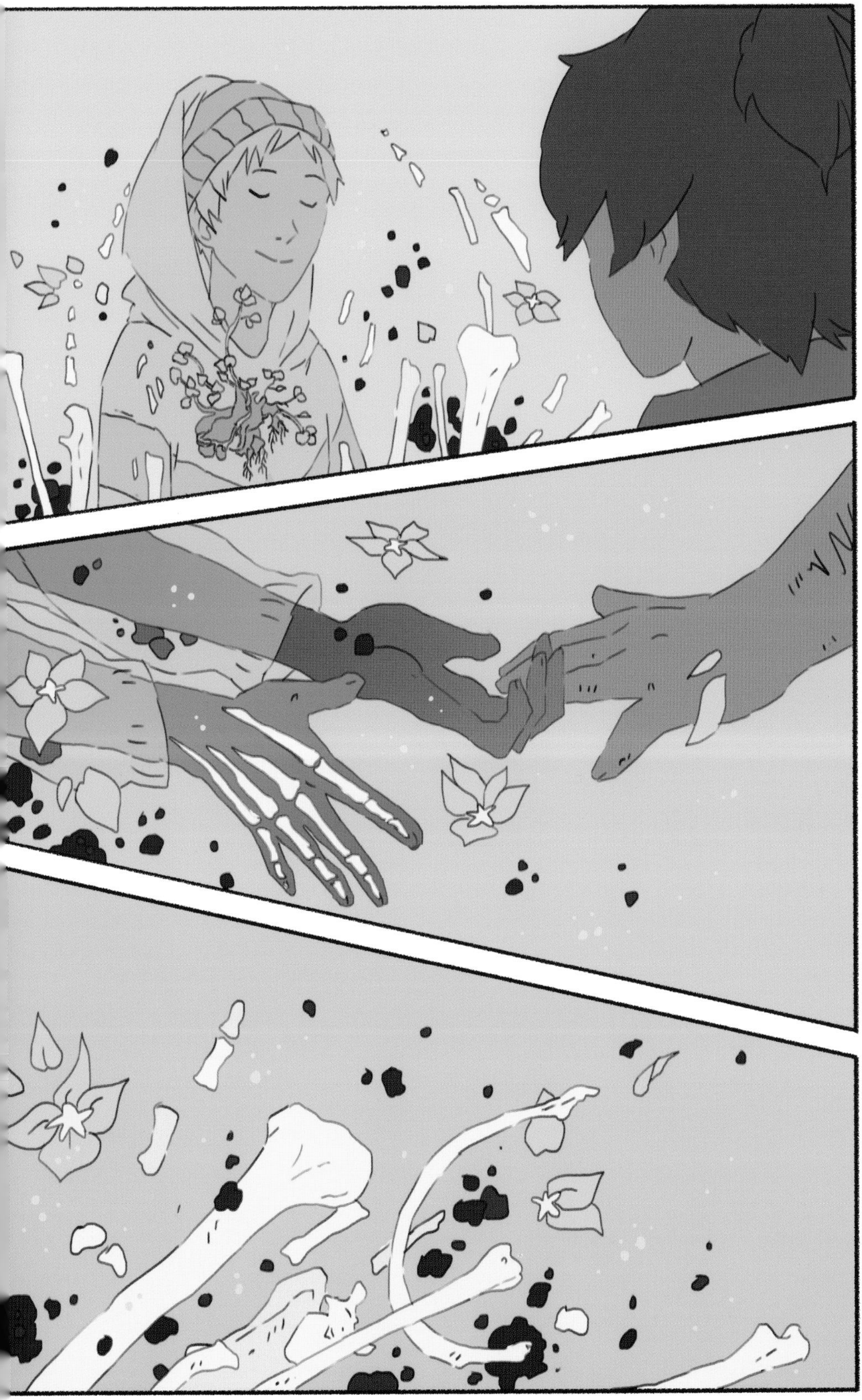

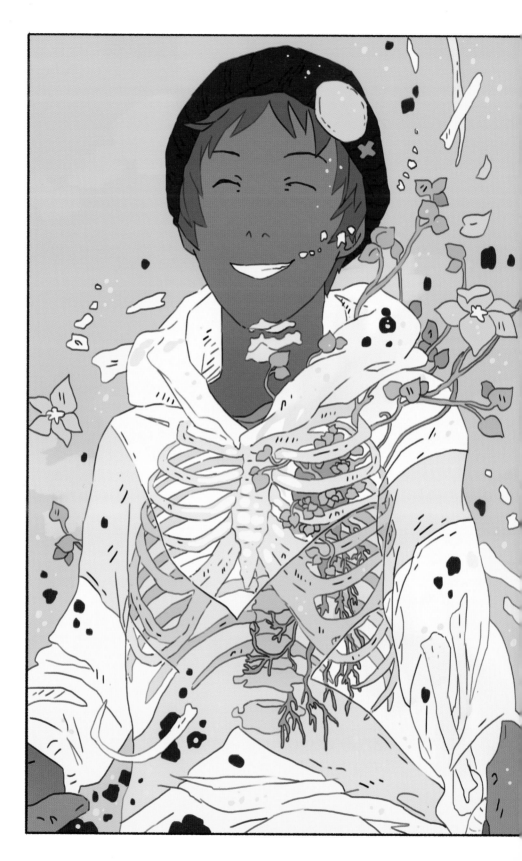

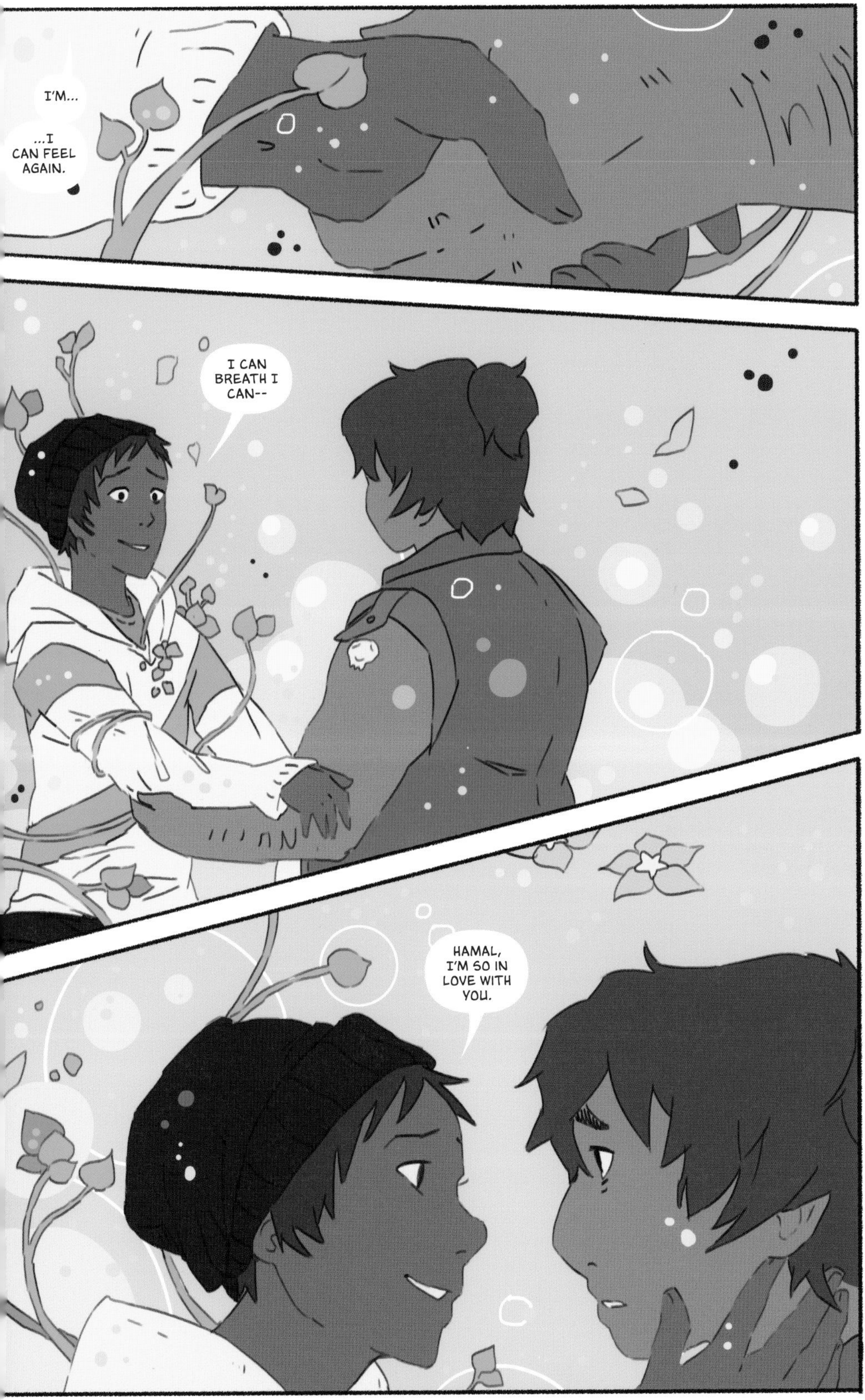
I'M...
...I CAN FEEL AGAIN.
I CAN BREATH I CAN--
HAMAL, I'M SO IN LOVE WITH YOU.

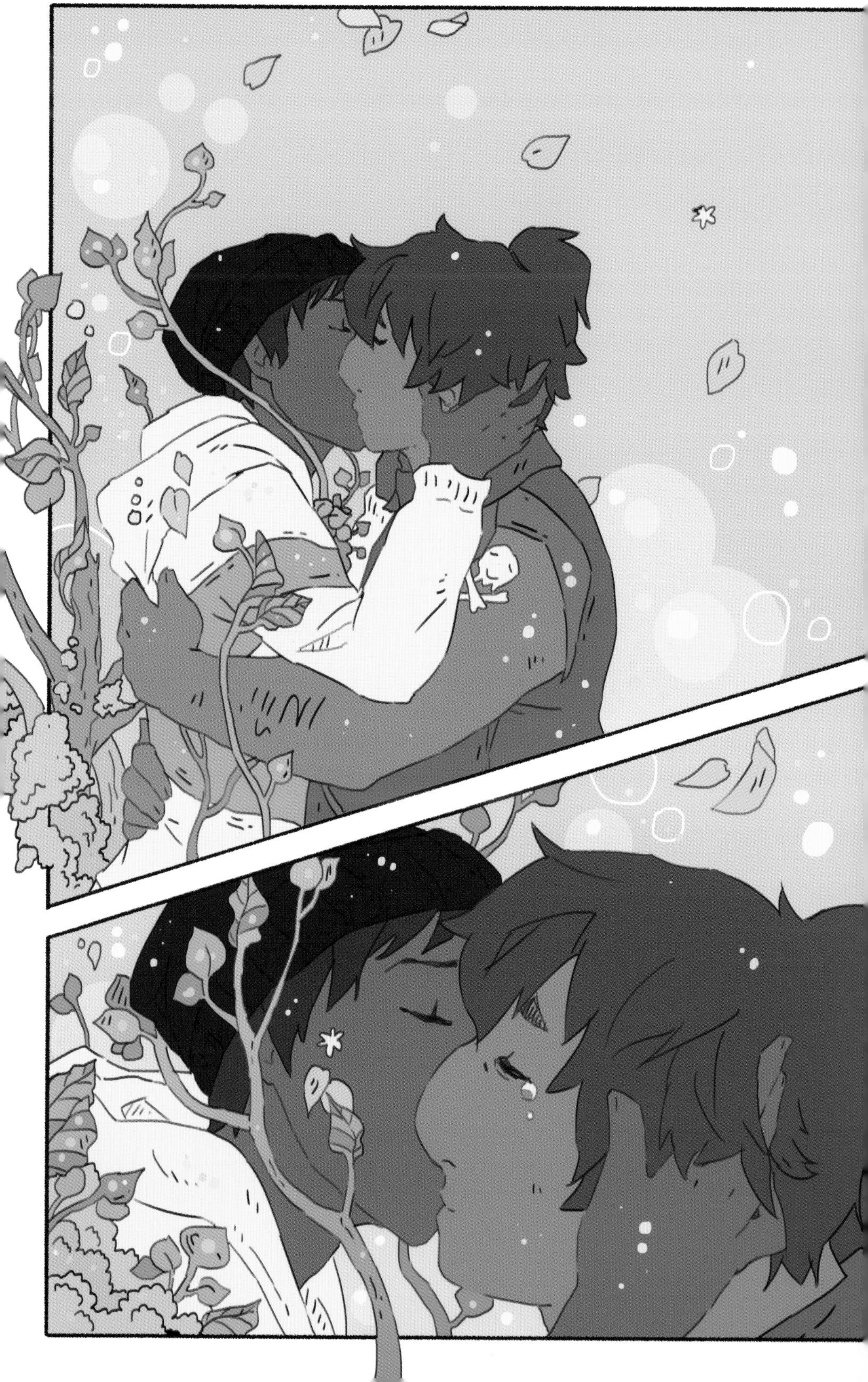

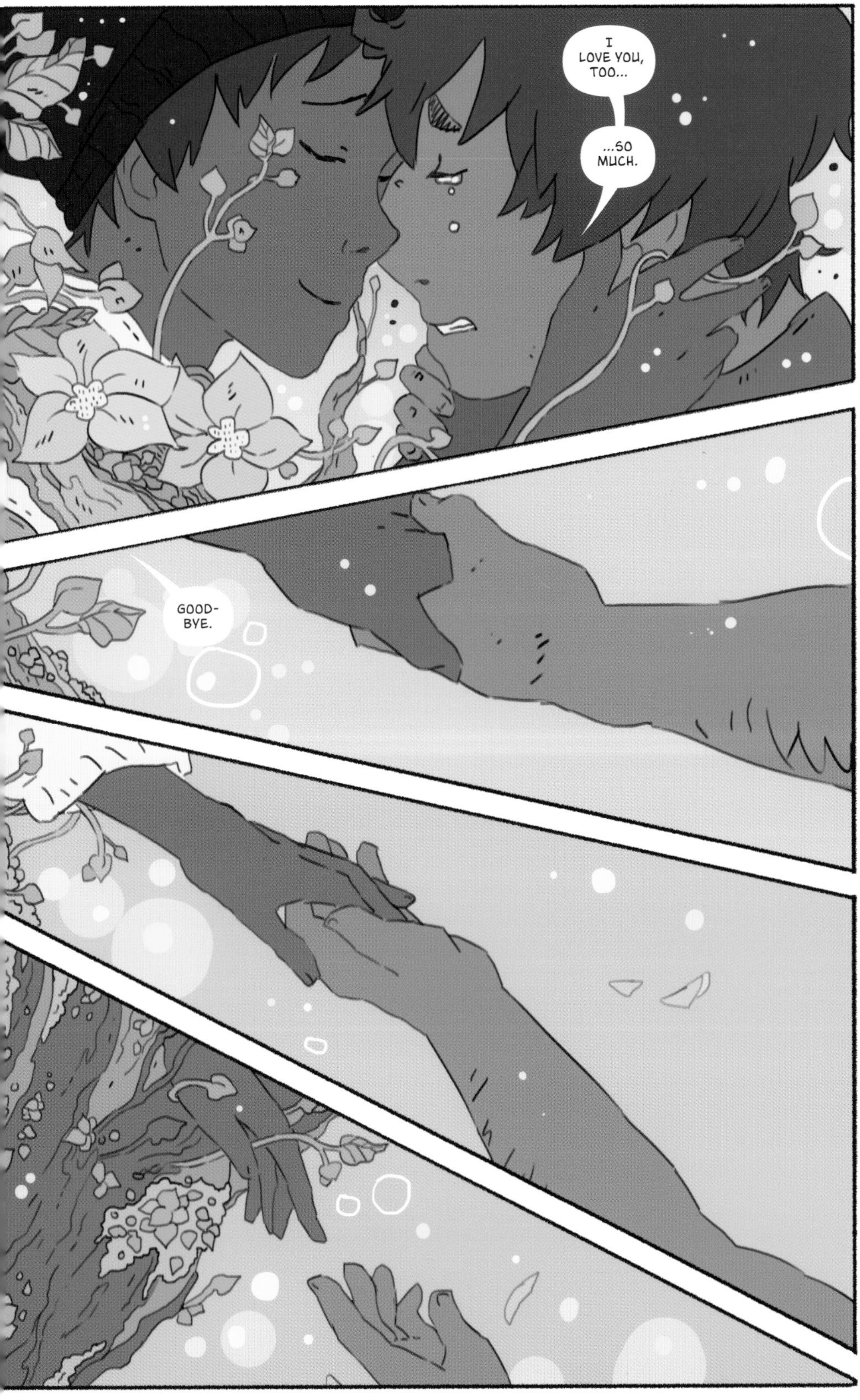

I LOVE YOU, TOO...
...SO MUCH.
GOOD-BYE.

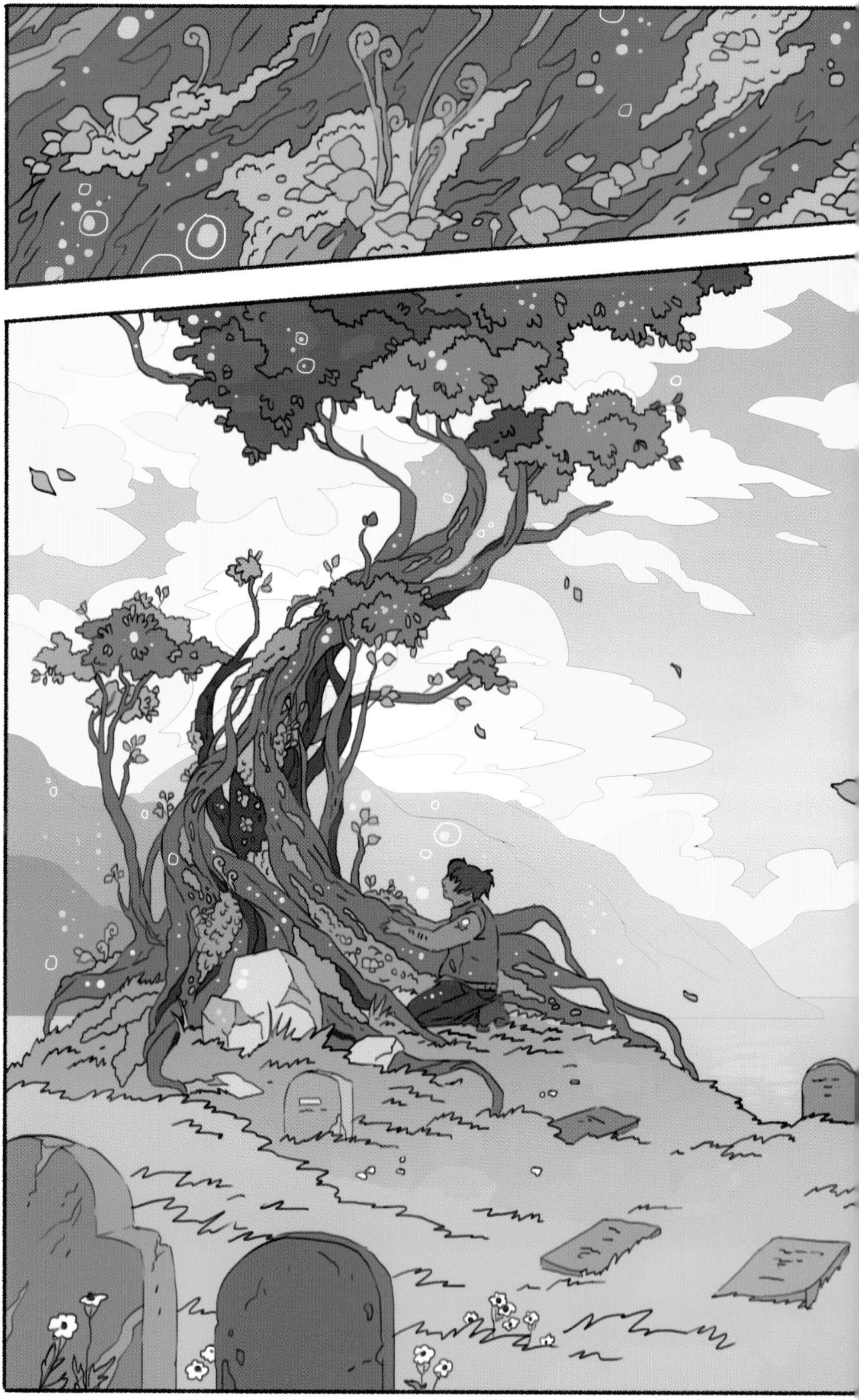

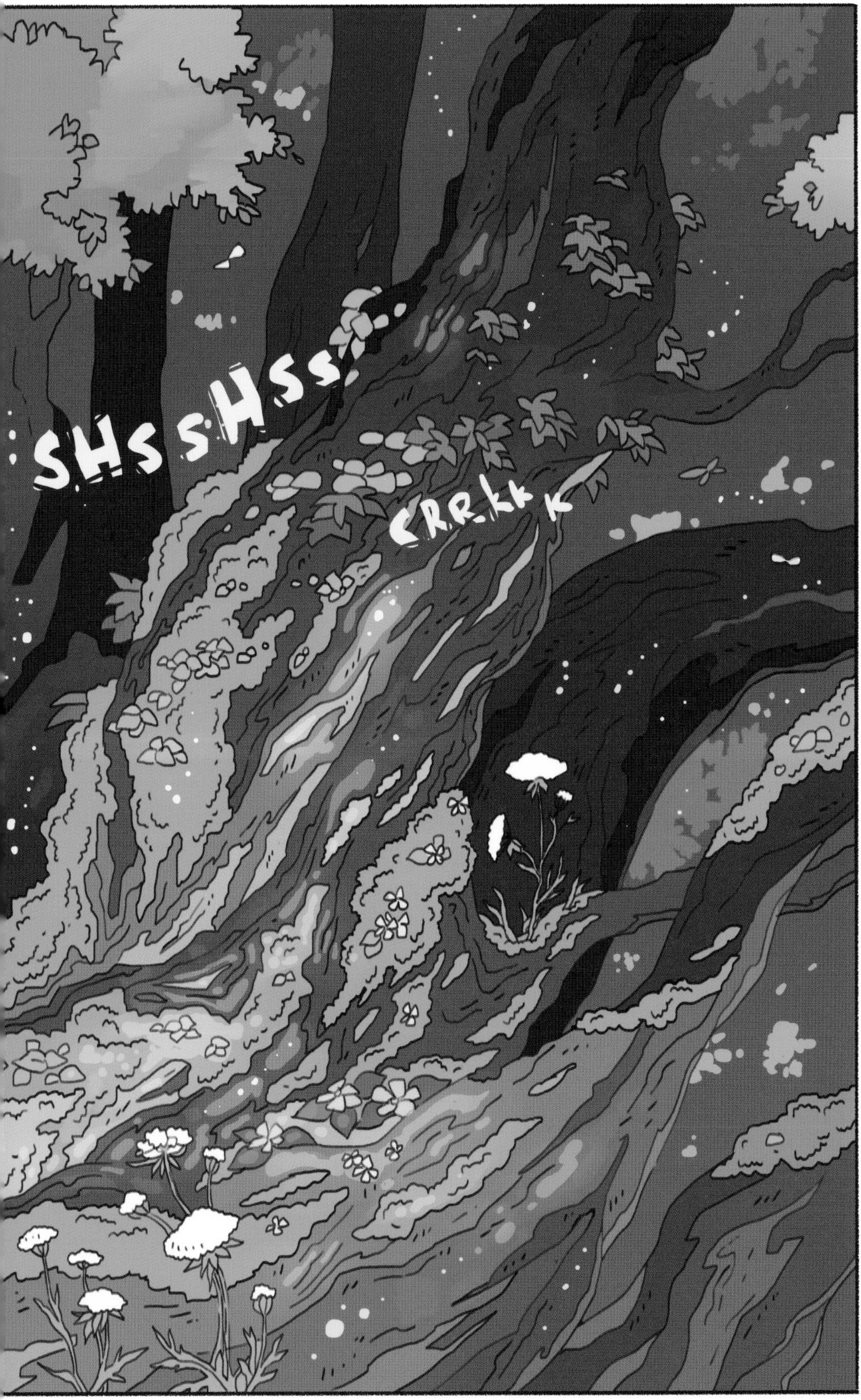
SHSSHSS
CRRKKK

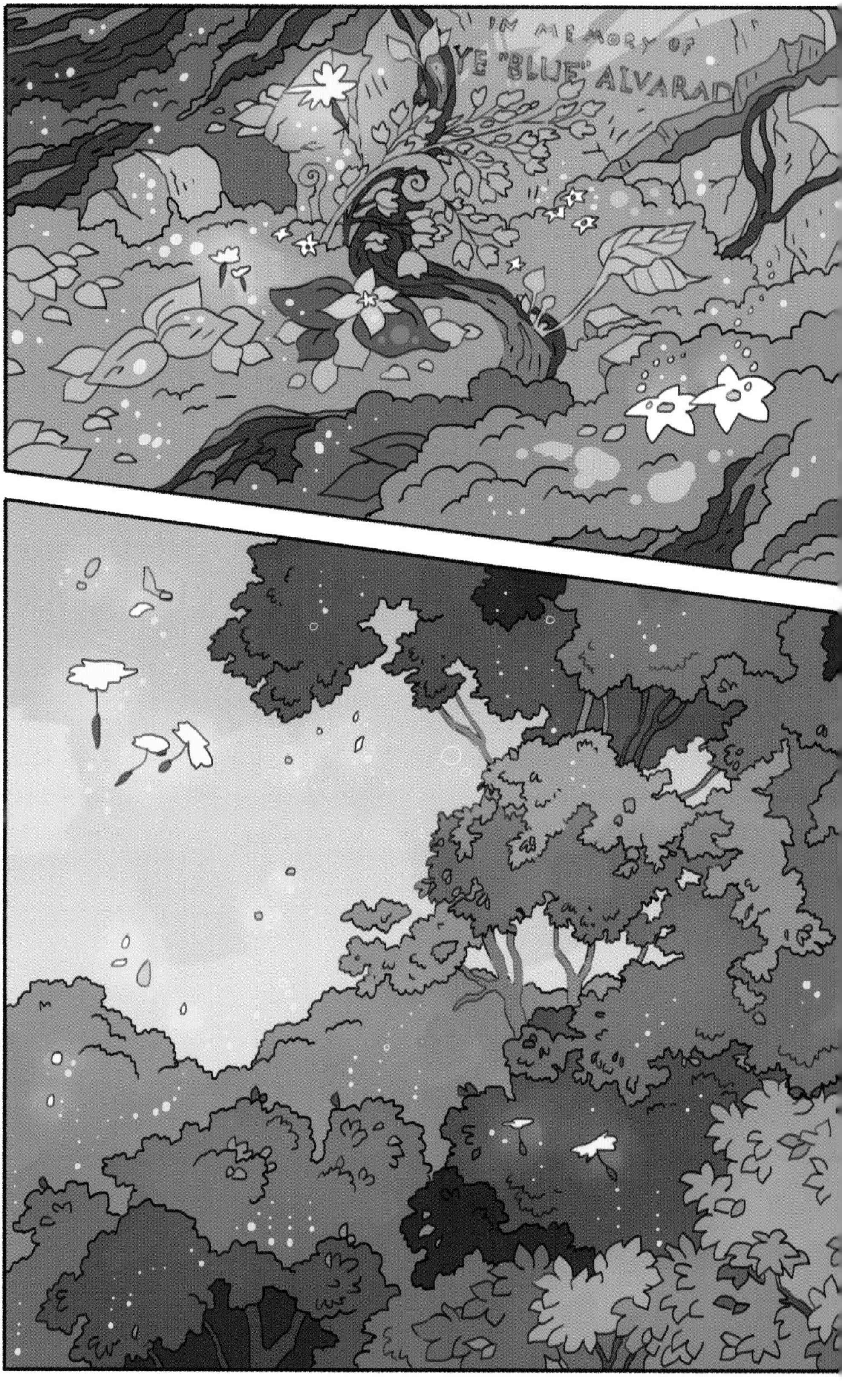
IN MEMORY OF
YE "BLUE" ALVARAD

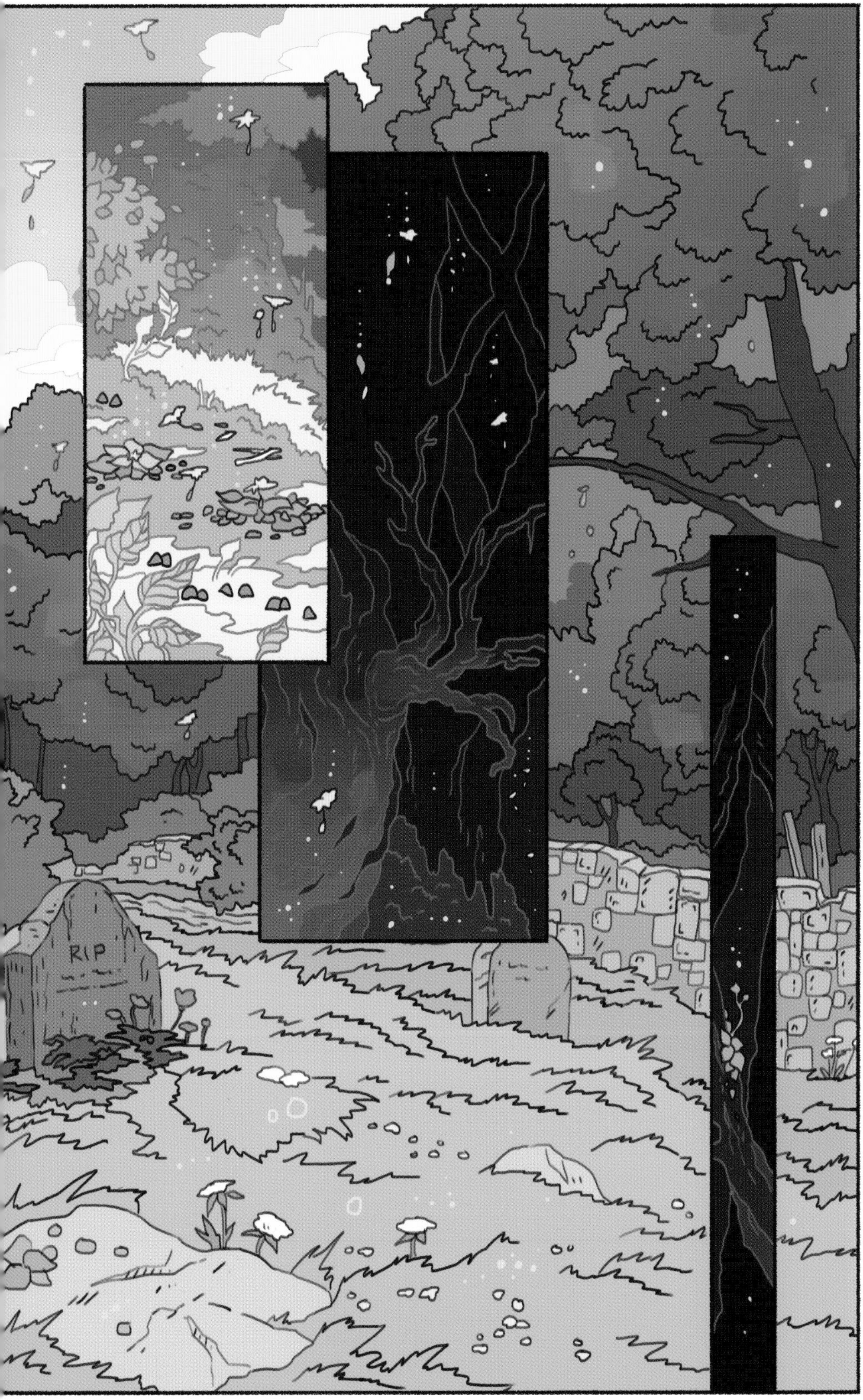
RIP

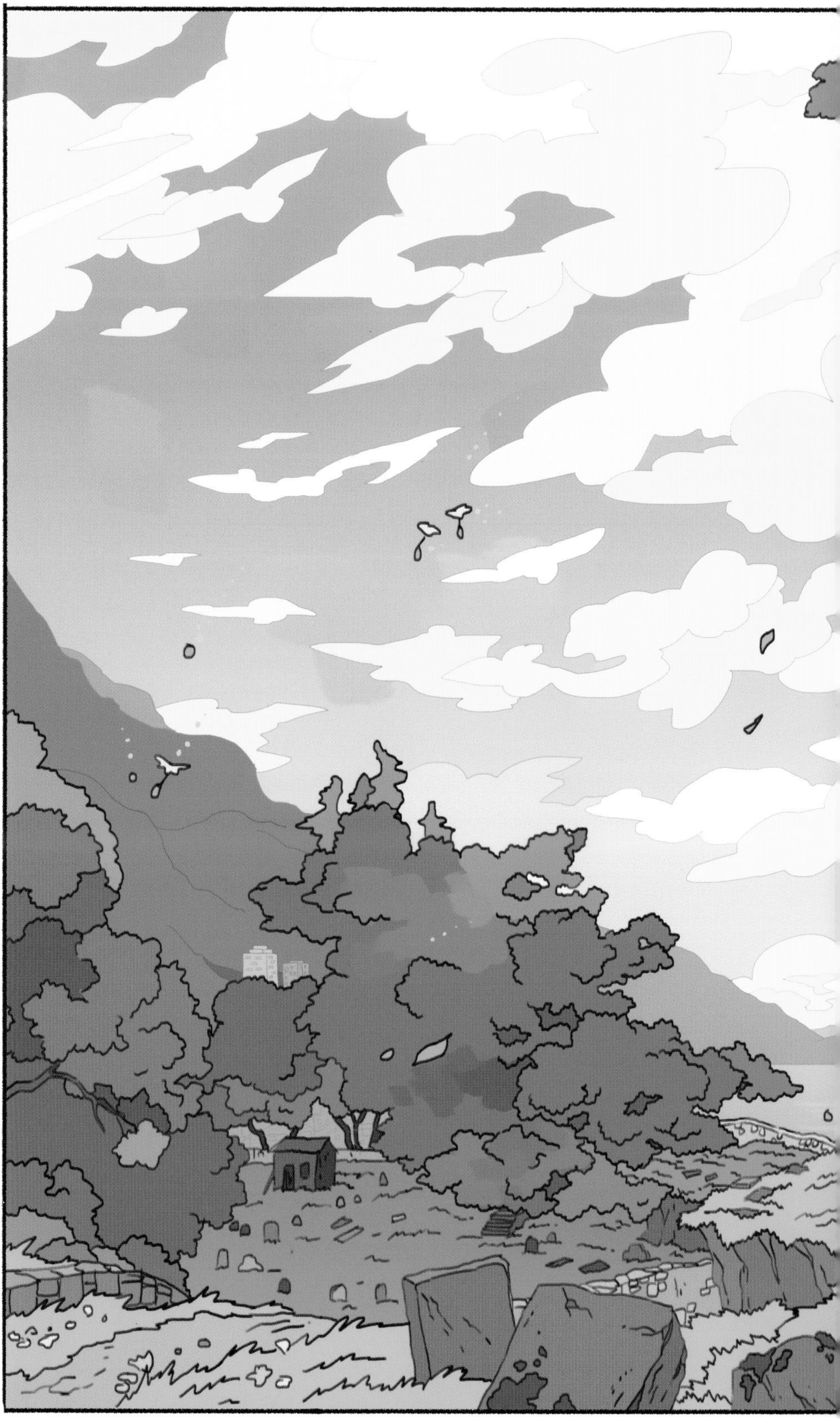

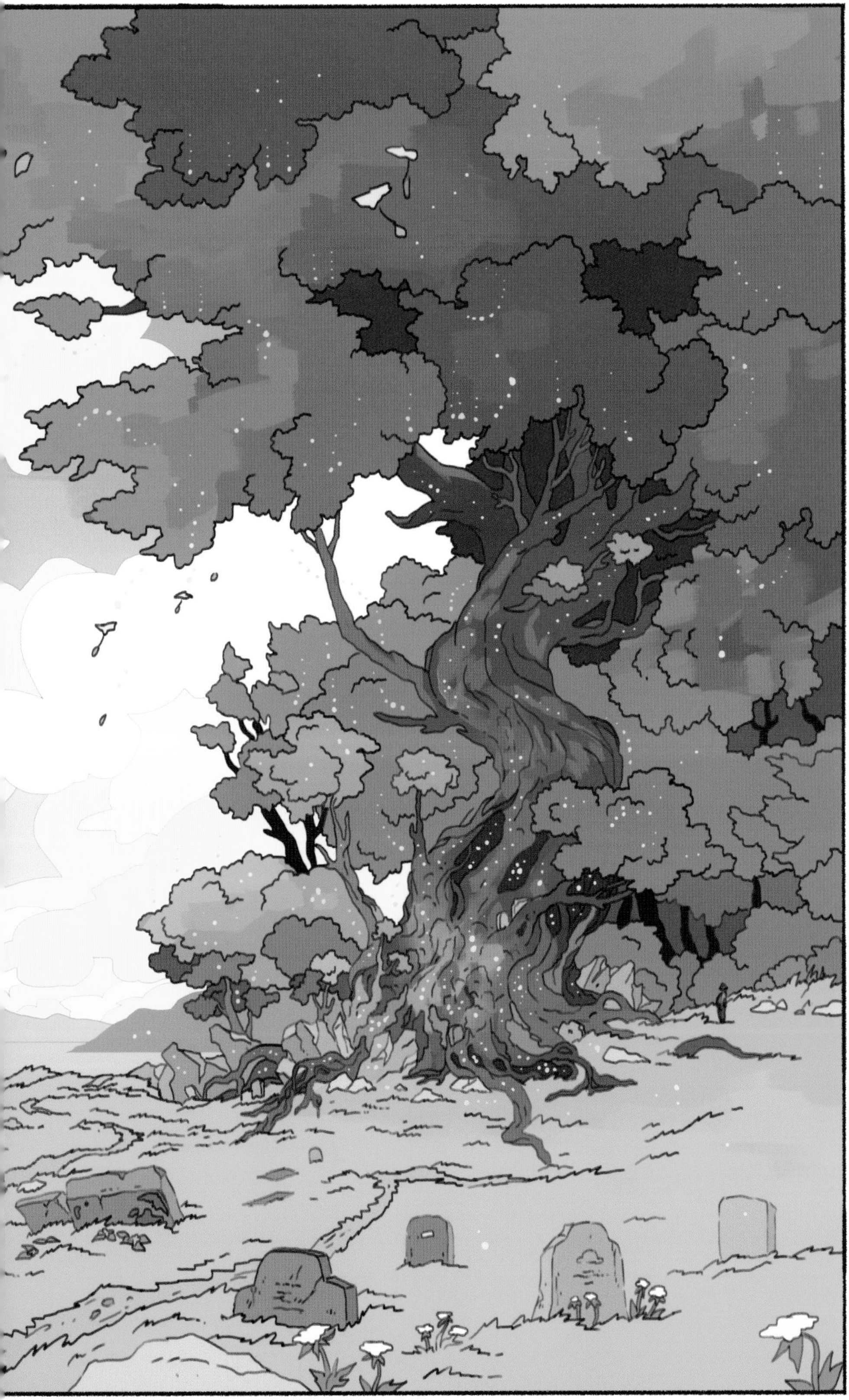

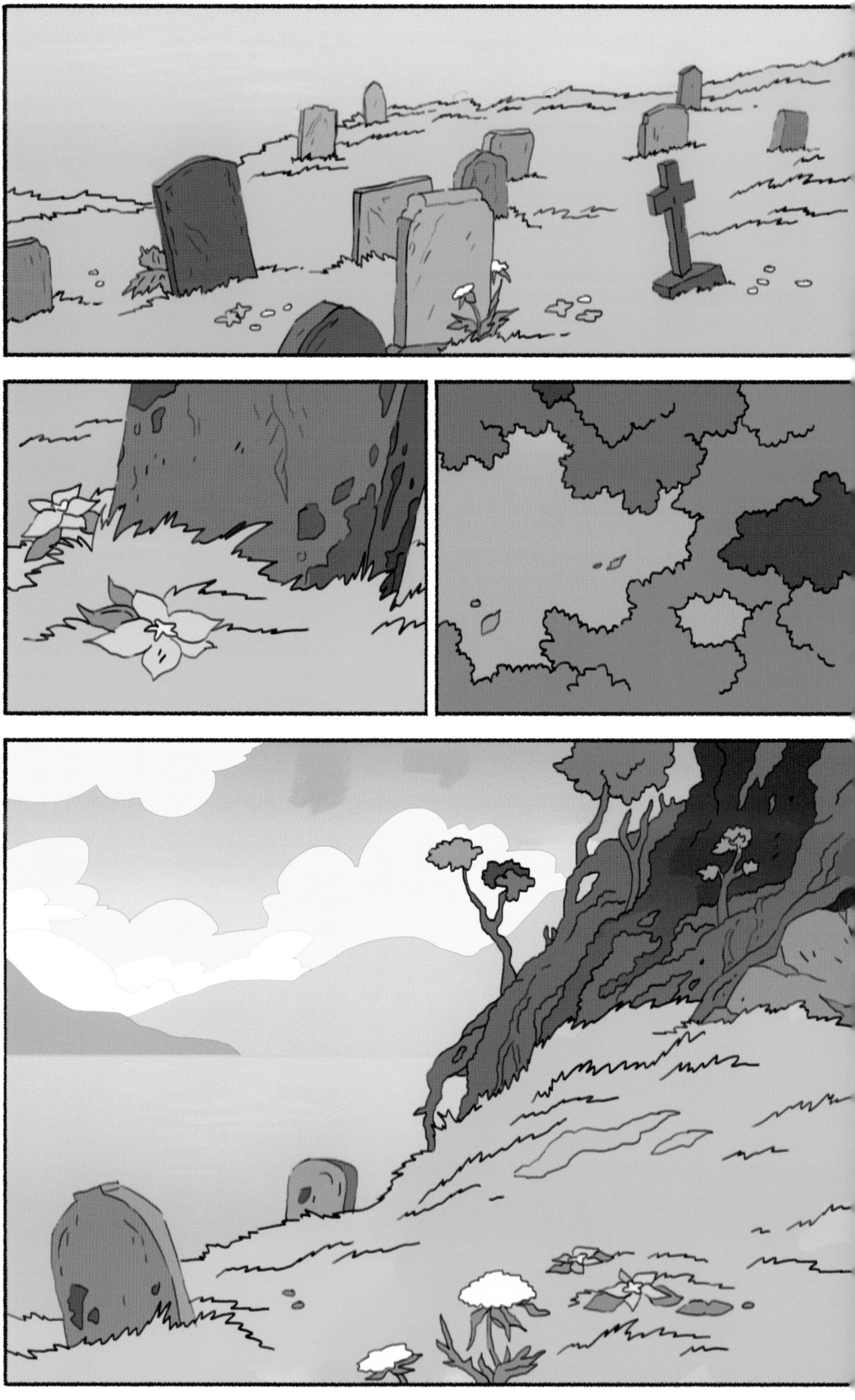

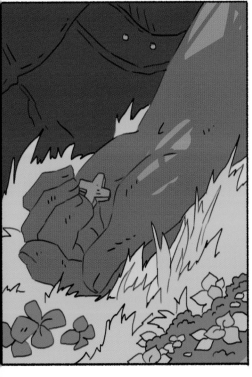

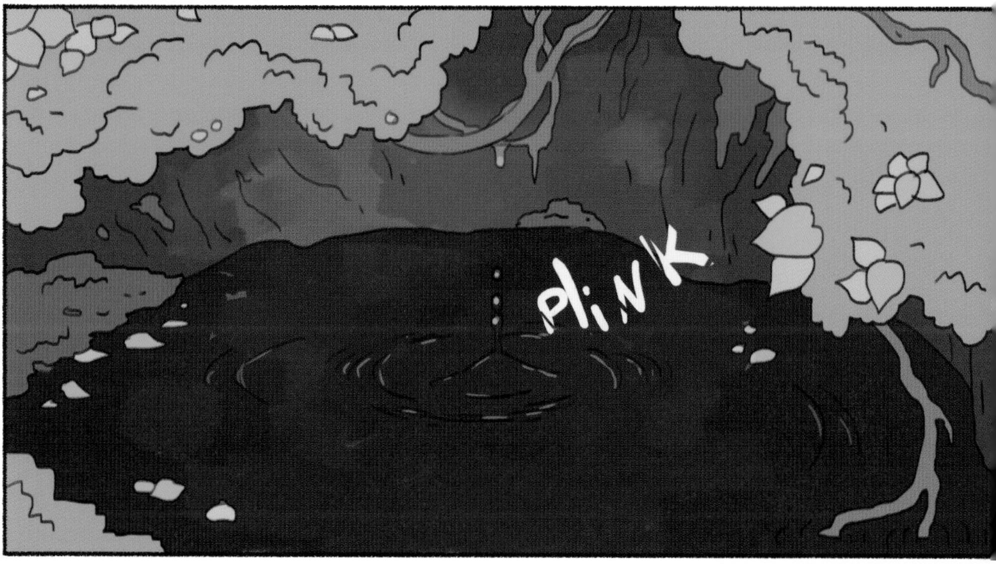
PLINK

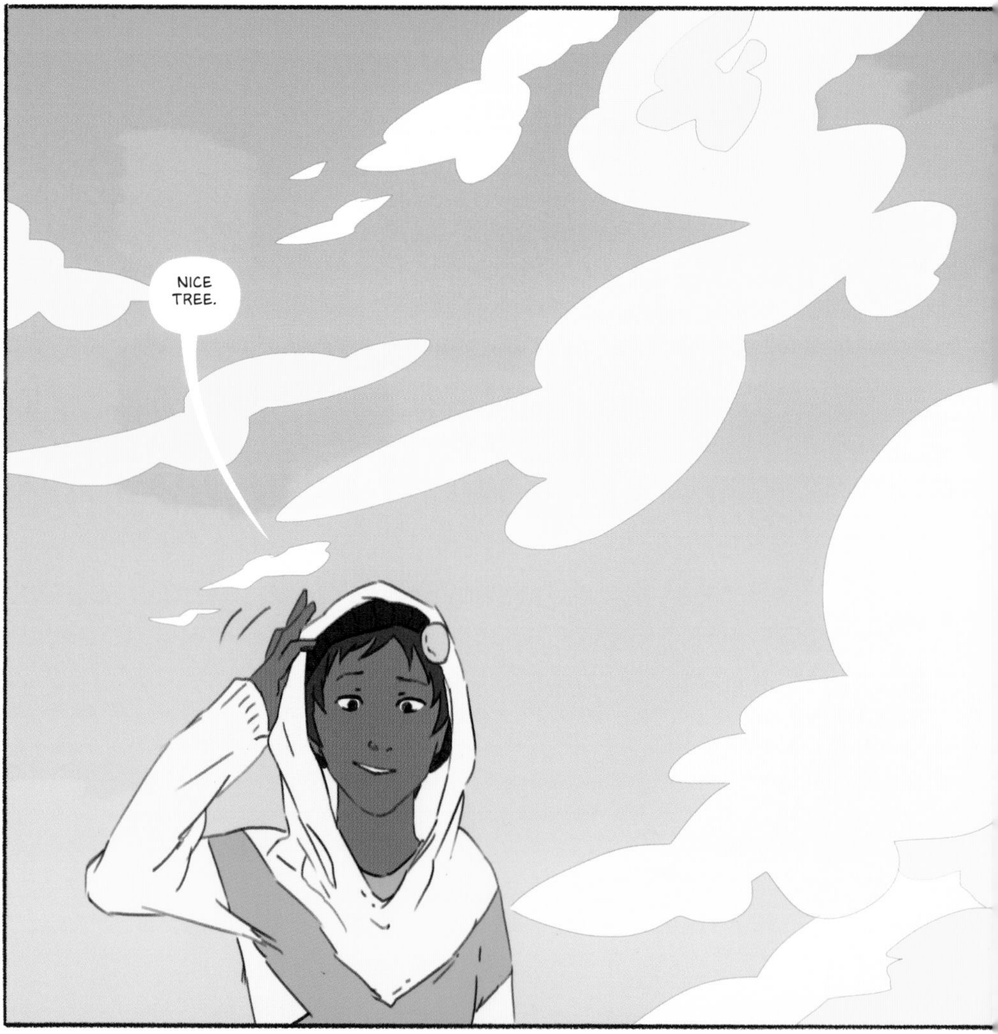
NICE TREE.

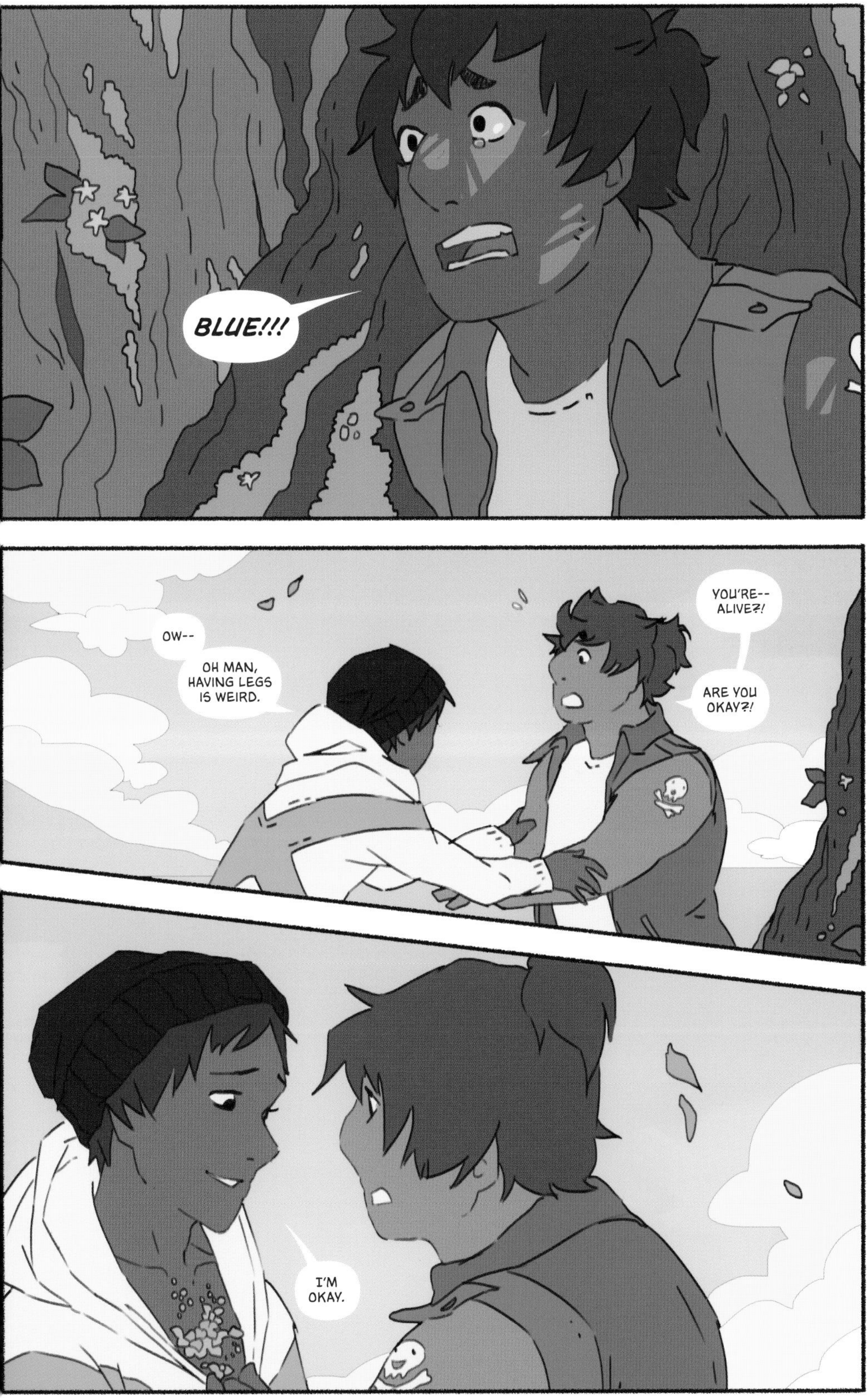
BLUE!!!
OW--
OH MAN, HAVING LEGS IS WEIRD.
YOU'RE-- ALIVE?!
ARE YOU OKAY?!
I'M OKAY.

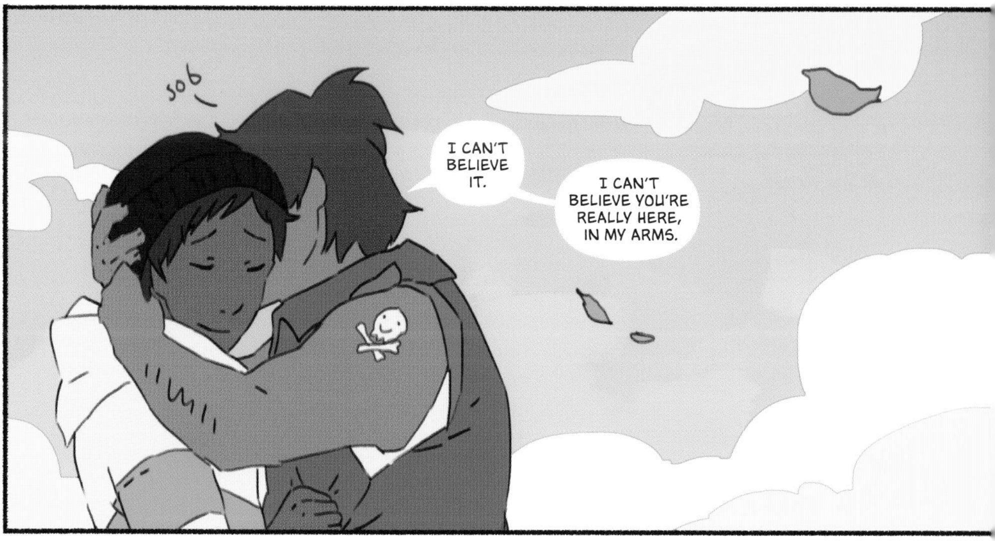
sob
I CAN'T BELIEVE IT.
I CAN'T BELIEVE YOU'RE REALLY HERE, IN MY ARMS.

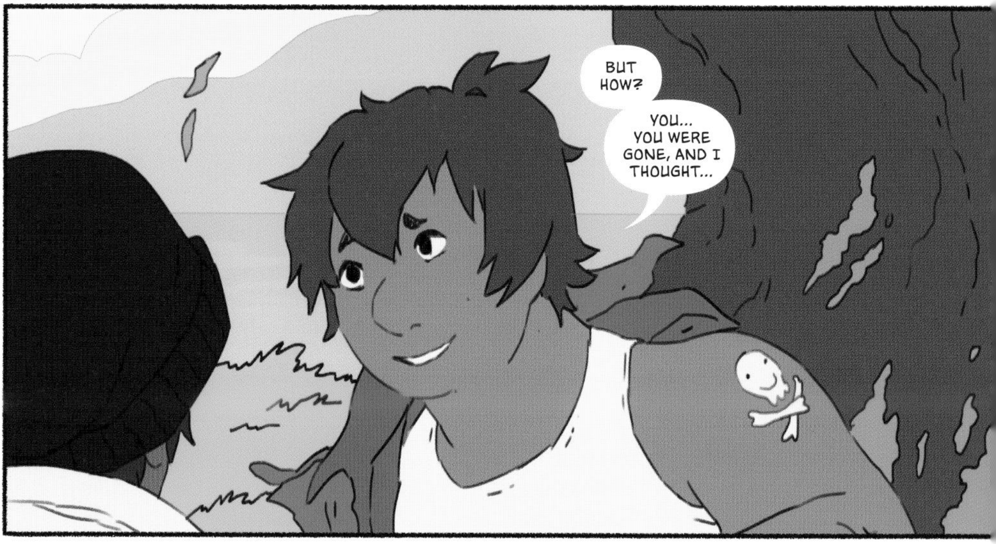
BUT HOW?
YOU... YOU WERE GONE, AND I THOUGHT...

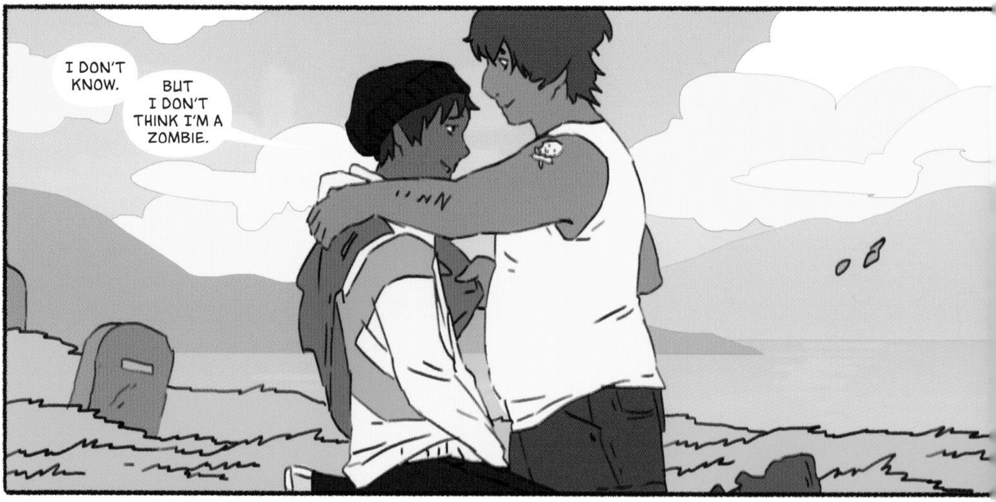
I DON'T KNOW.
BUT I DON'T THINK I'M A ZOMBIE.

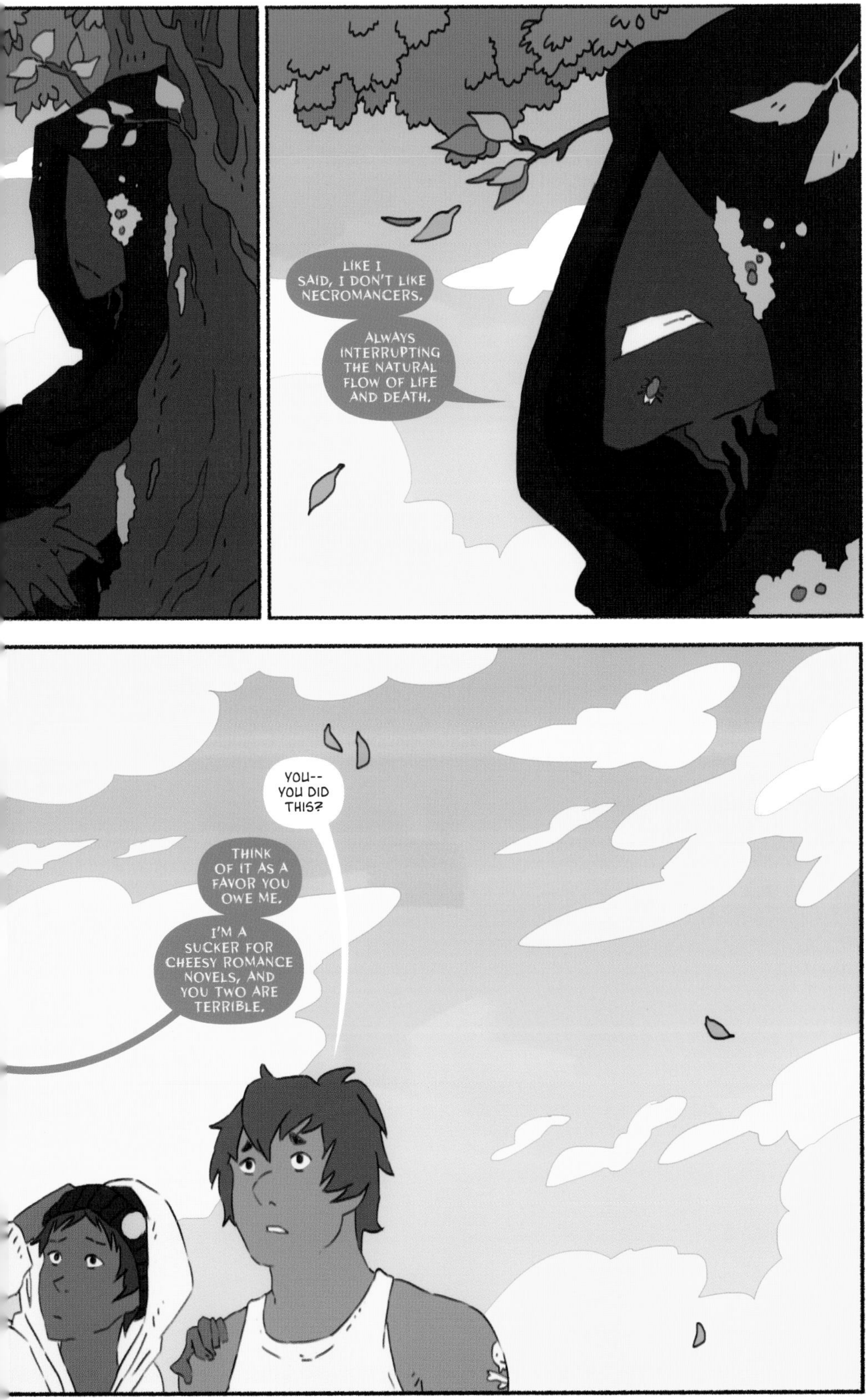
LIKE I SAID, I DON'T LIKE NECROMANCERS.
ALWAYS INTERRUPTING THE NATURAL FLOW OF LIFE AND DEATH.
YOU-- YOU DID THIS?
THINK OF IT AS A FAVOR YOU OWE ME.
I'M A SUCKER FOR CHEESY ROMANCE NOVELS, AND YOU TWO ARE TERRIBLE.

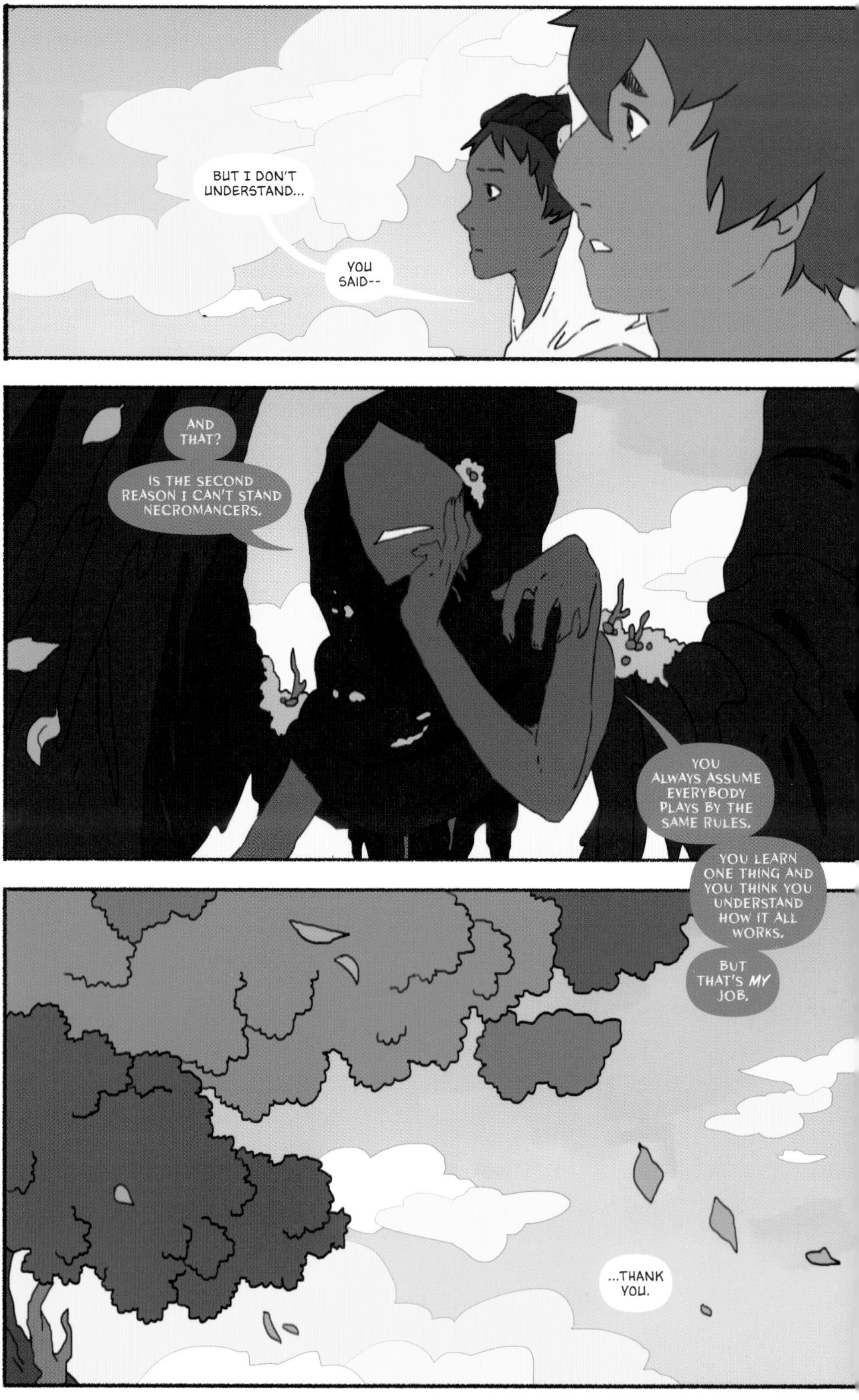
BUT I DON'T UNDERSTAND...
YOU SAID--
AND THAT?
IS THE SECOND REASON I CAN'T STAND NECROMANCERS.
YOU ALWAYS ASSUME EVERYBODY PLAYS BY THE SAME RULES.
YOU LEARN ONE THING AND YOU THINK YOU UNDERSTAND HOW IT ALL WORKS.
BUT THAT'S *MY* JOB.
...THANK YOU.

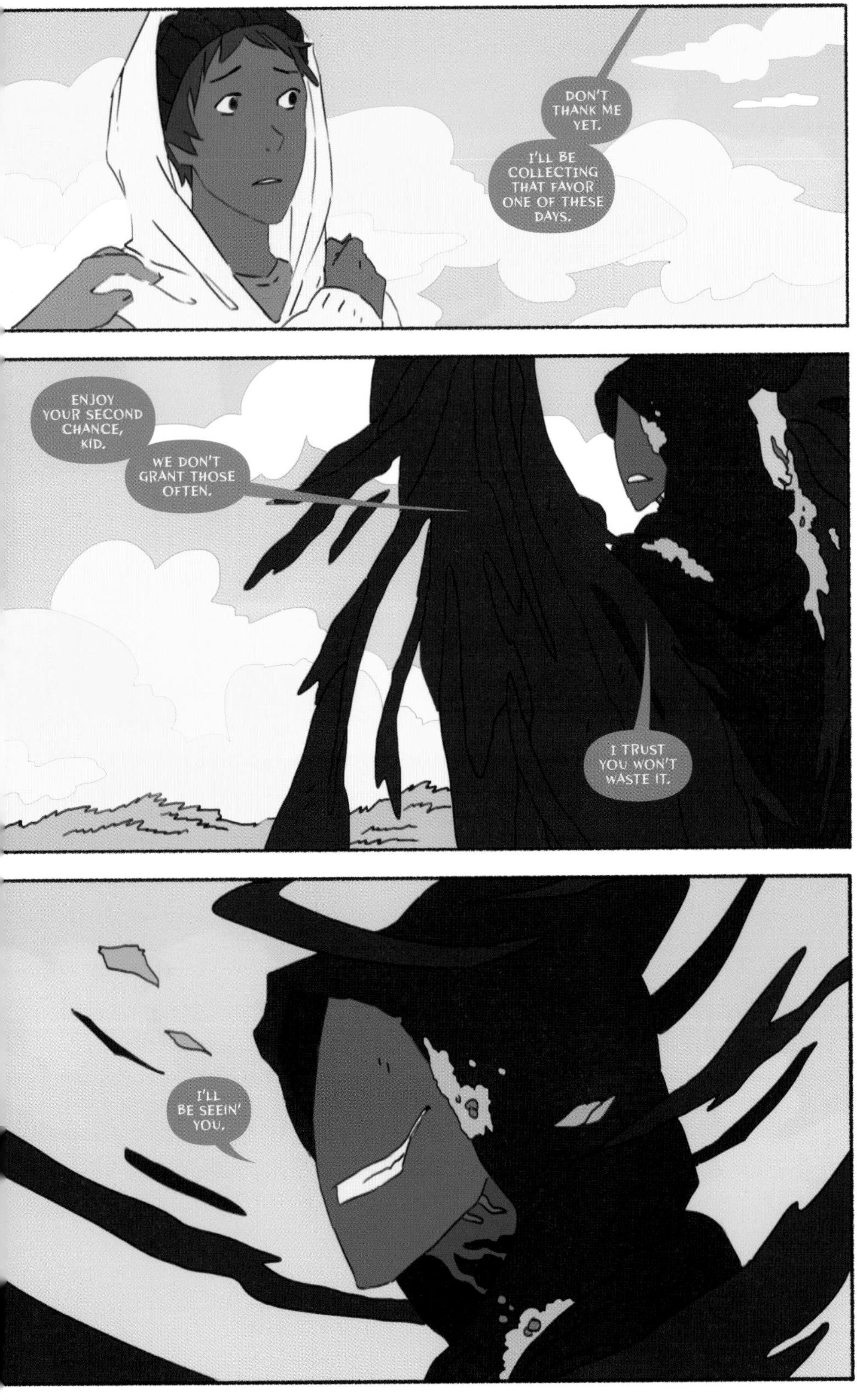
DON'T THANK ME YET.
I'LL BE COLLECTING THAT FAVOR ONE OF THESE DAYS.
ENJOY YOUR SECOND CHANCE, KID.
WE DON'T GRANT THOSE OFTEN.
I TRUST YOU WON'T WASTE IT.
I'LL BE SEEIN' YOU.

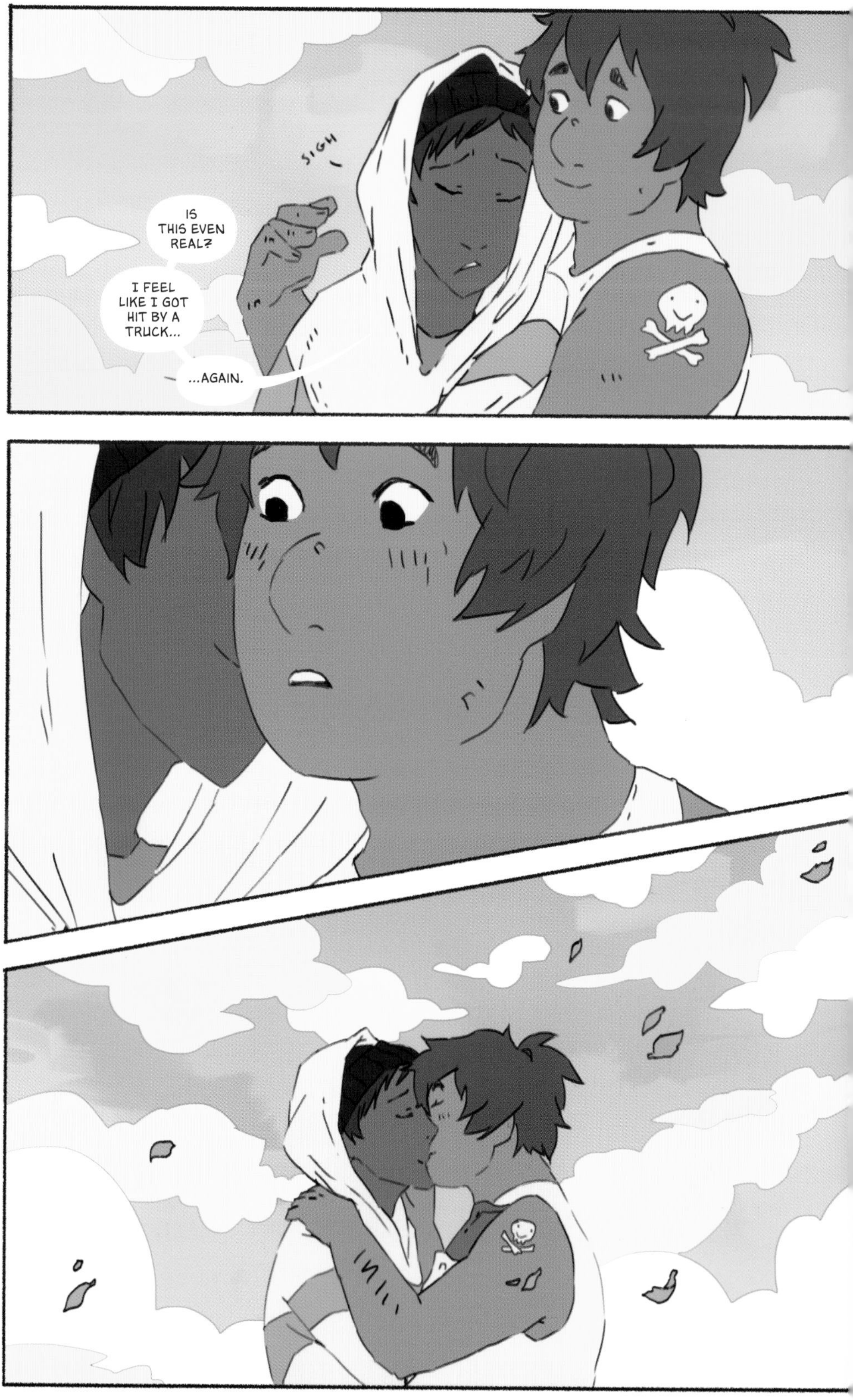
SIGH
IS THIS EVEN REAL?
I FEEL LIKE I GOT HIT BY A TRUCK...
...AGAIN.

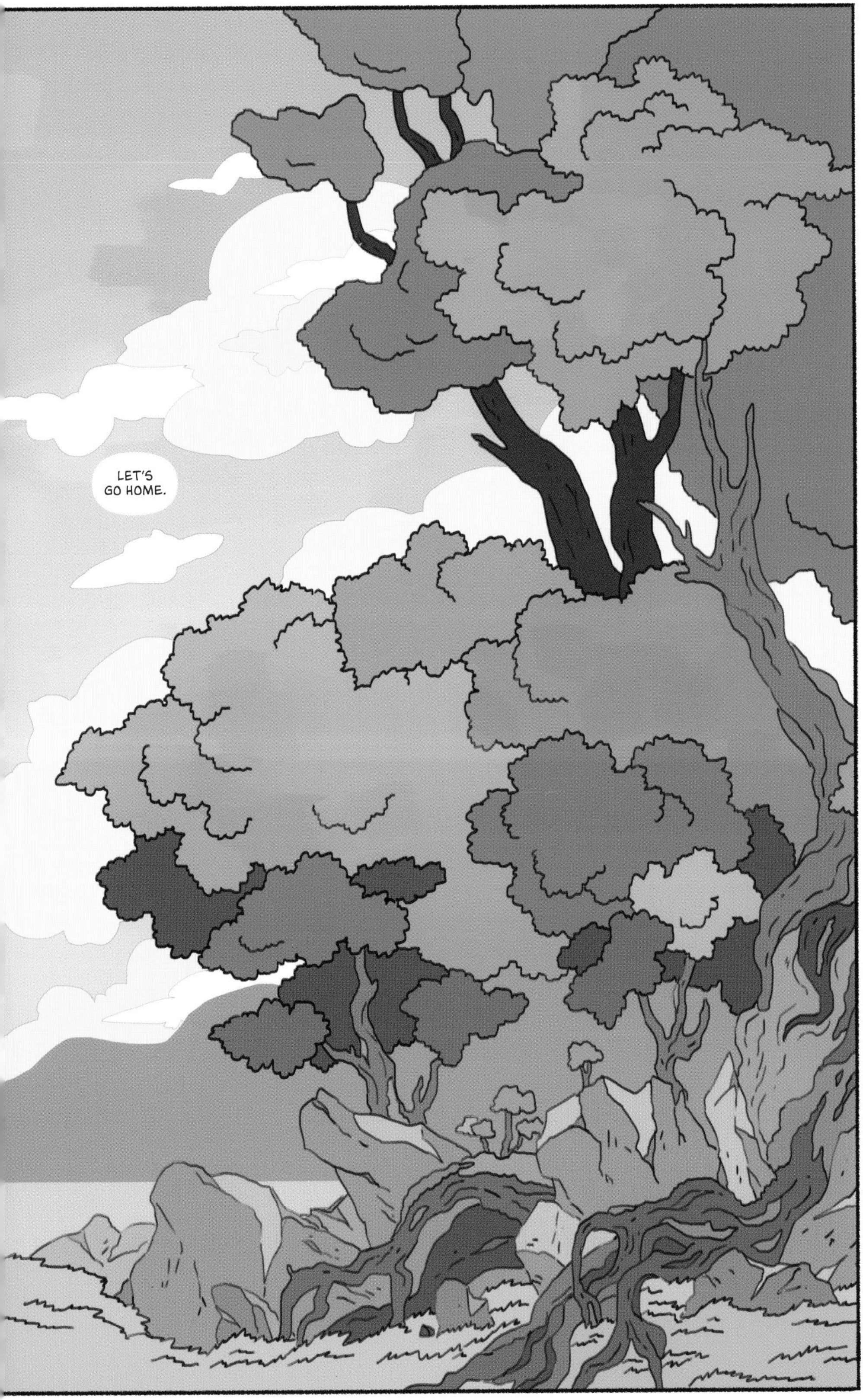
LET'S GO HOME.

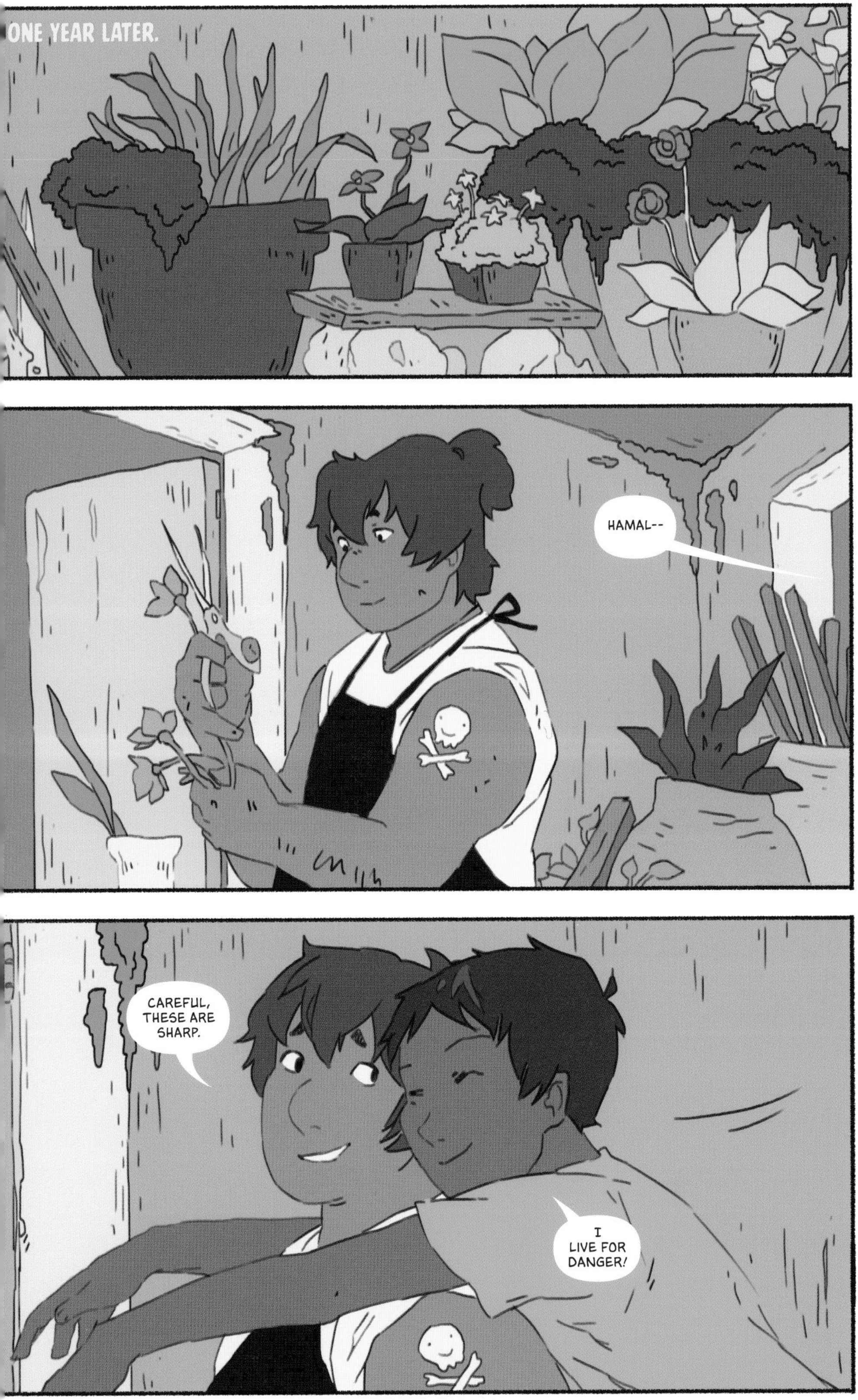
ONE YEAR LATER.
HAMAL--
CAREFUL, THESE ARE SHARP.
I LIVE FOR DANGER!

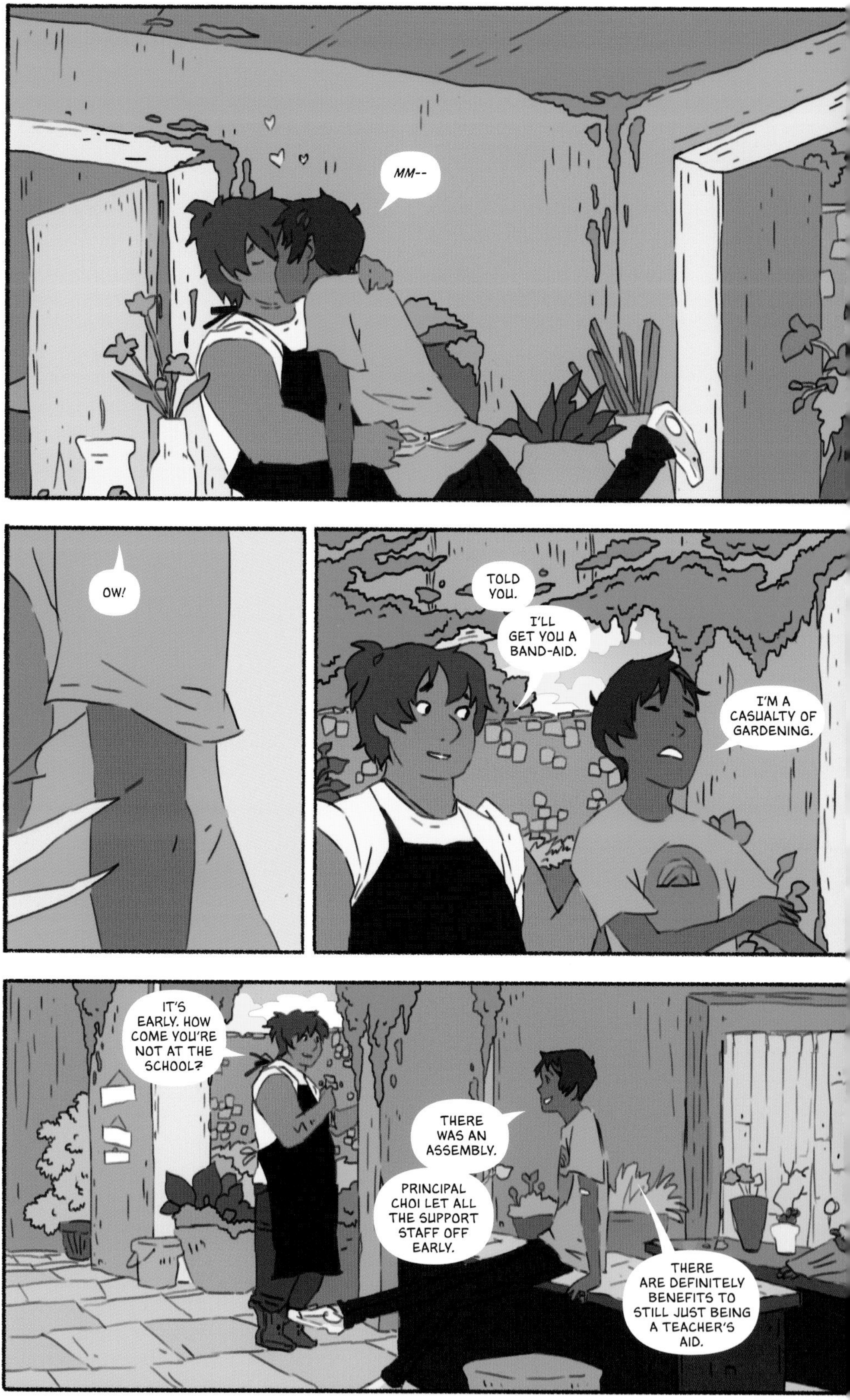
MM--
OW!
TOLD YOU.
I'LL GET YOU A BAND-AID.
I'M A CASUALTY OF GARDENING.
IT'S EARLY. HOW COME YOU'RE NOT AT THE SCHOOL?
THERE WAS AN ASSEMBLY.
PRINCIPAL CHOI LET ALL THE SUPPORT STAFF OFF EARLY.
THERE ARE DEFINITELY BENEFITS TO STILL JUST BEING A TEACHER'S AID.

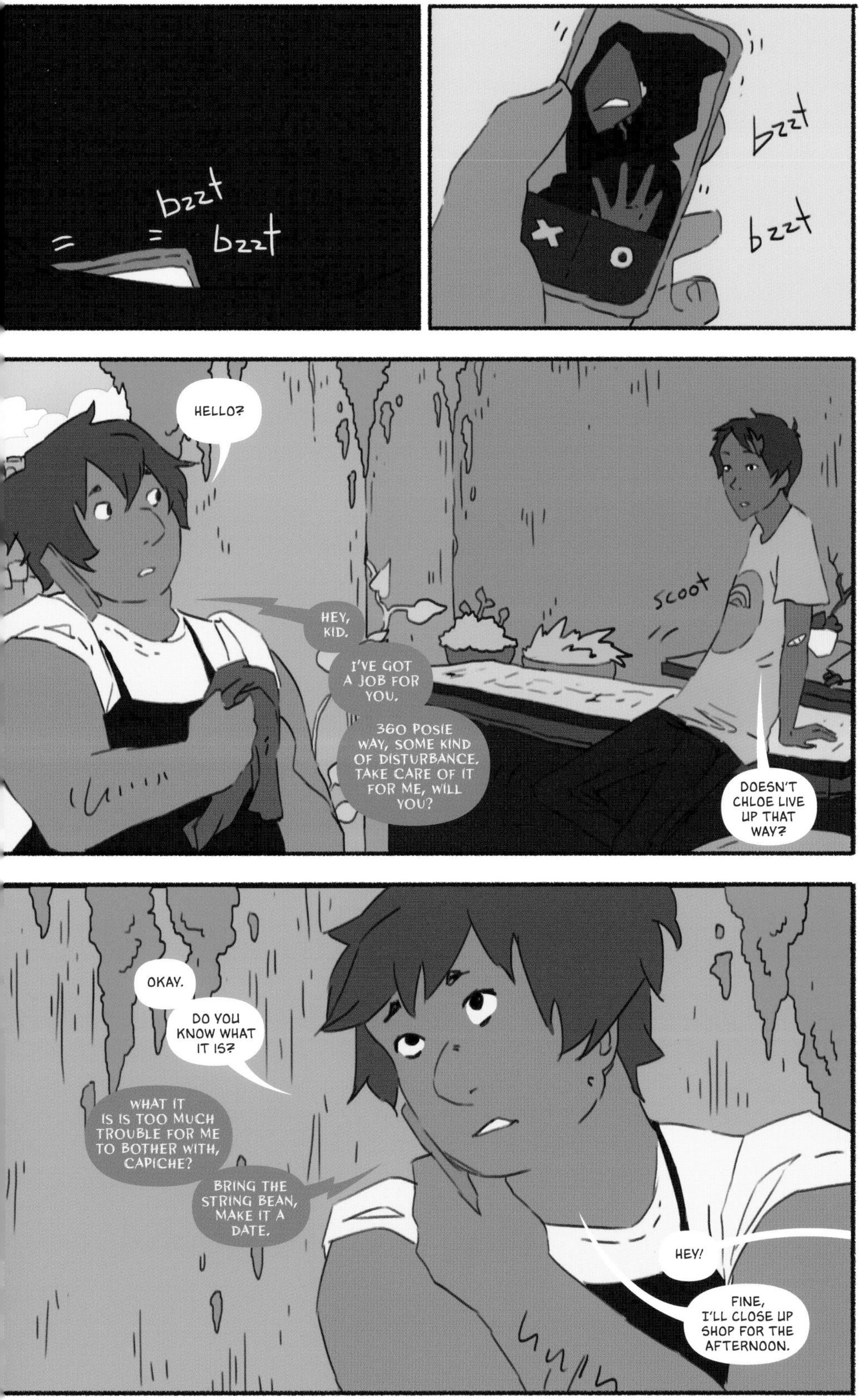
bzzt
bzzt
bzzt
bzzt
HELLO?
HEY, KID.
I'VE GOT A JOB FOR YOU.
360 POSIE WAY, SOME KIND OF DISTURBANCE. TAKE CARE OF IT FOR ME, WILL YOU?
scoot
DOESN'T CHLOE LIVE UP THAT WAY?
OKAY.
DO YOU KNOW WHAT IT IS?
WHAT IT IS IS TOO MUCH TROUBLE FOR ME TO BOTHER WITH, CAPICHE?
BRING THE STRING BEAN, MAKE IT A DATE.
HEY!
FINE, I'LL CLOSE UP SHOP FOR THE AFTERNOON.

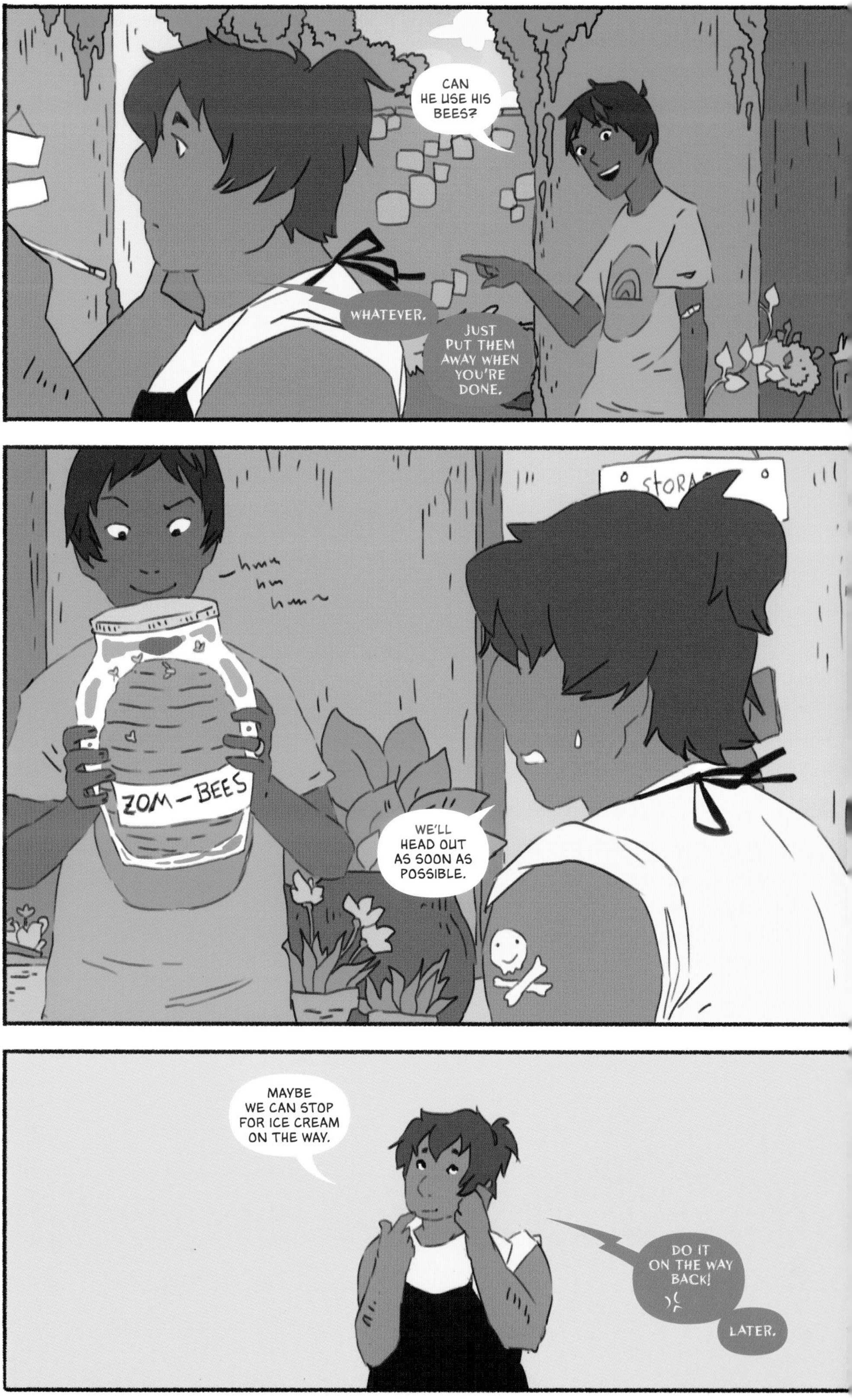
CAN HE USE HIS BEES?
WHATEVER.
JUST PUT THEM AWAY WHEN YOU'RE DONE.
hmm hm hmm~
ZOM-BEES
WE'LL HEAD OUT AS SOON AS POSSIBLE.
MAYBE WE CAN STOP FOR ICE CREAM ON THE WAY.
DO IT ON THE WAY BACK!
LATER.

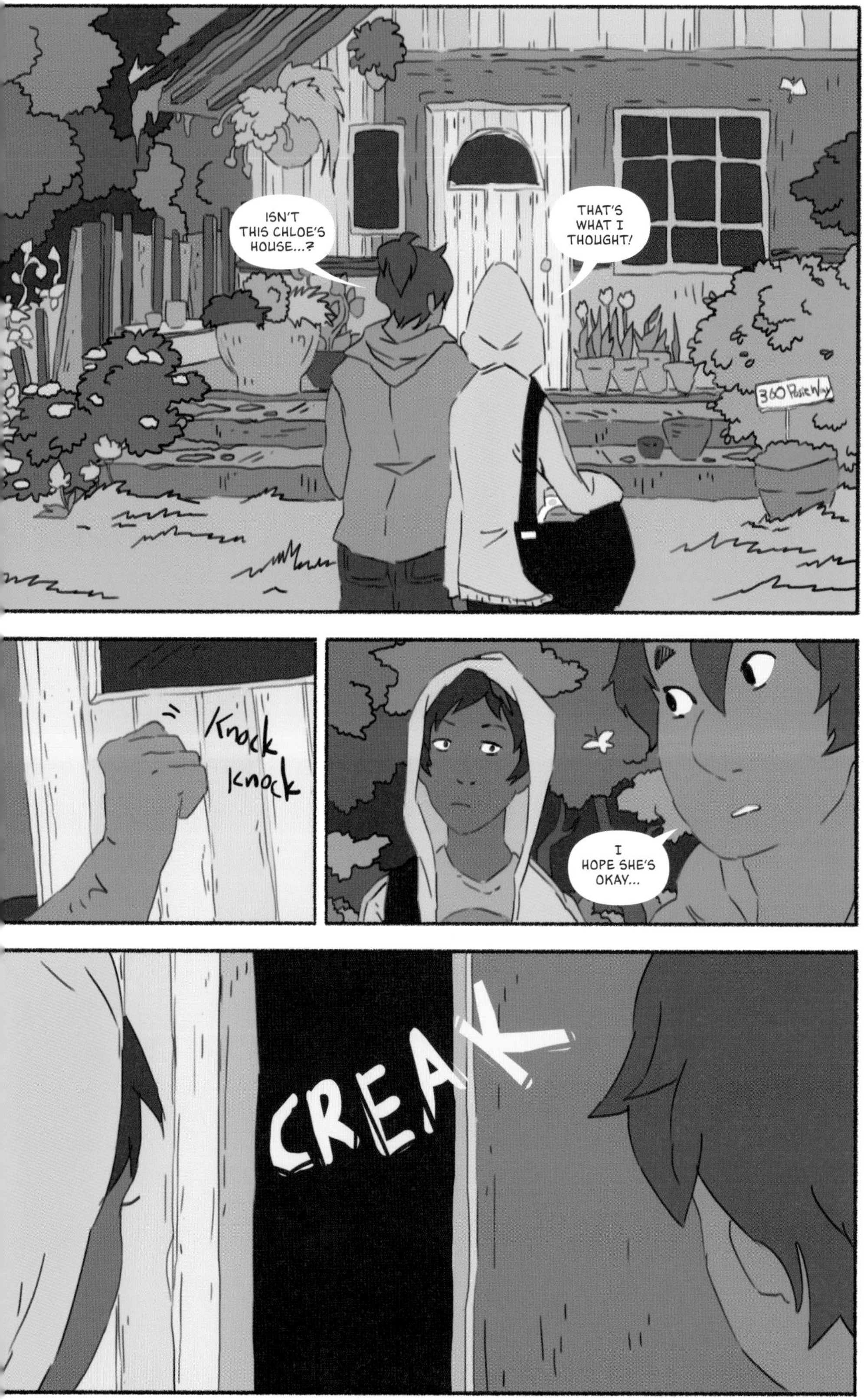
ISN'T THIS CHLOE'S HOUSE...?
THAT'S WHAT I THOUGHT!
360 Posie Way
Knock knock
I HOPE SHE'S OKAY...
CREAK

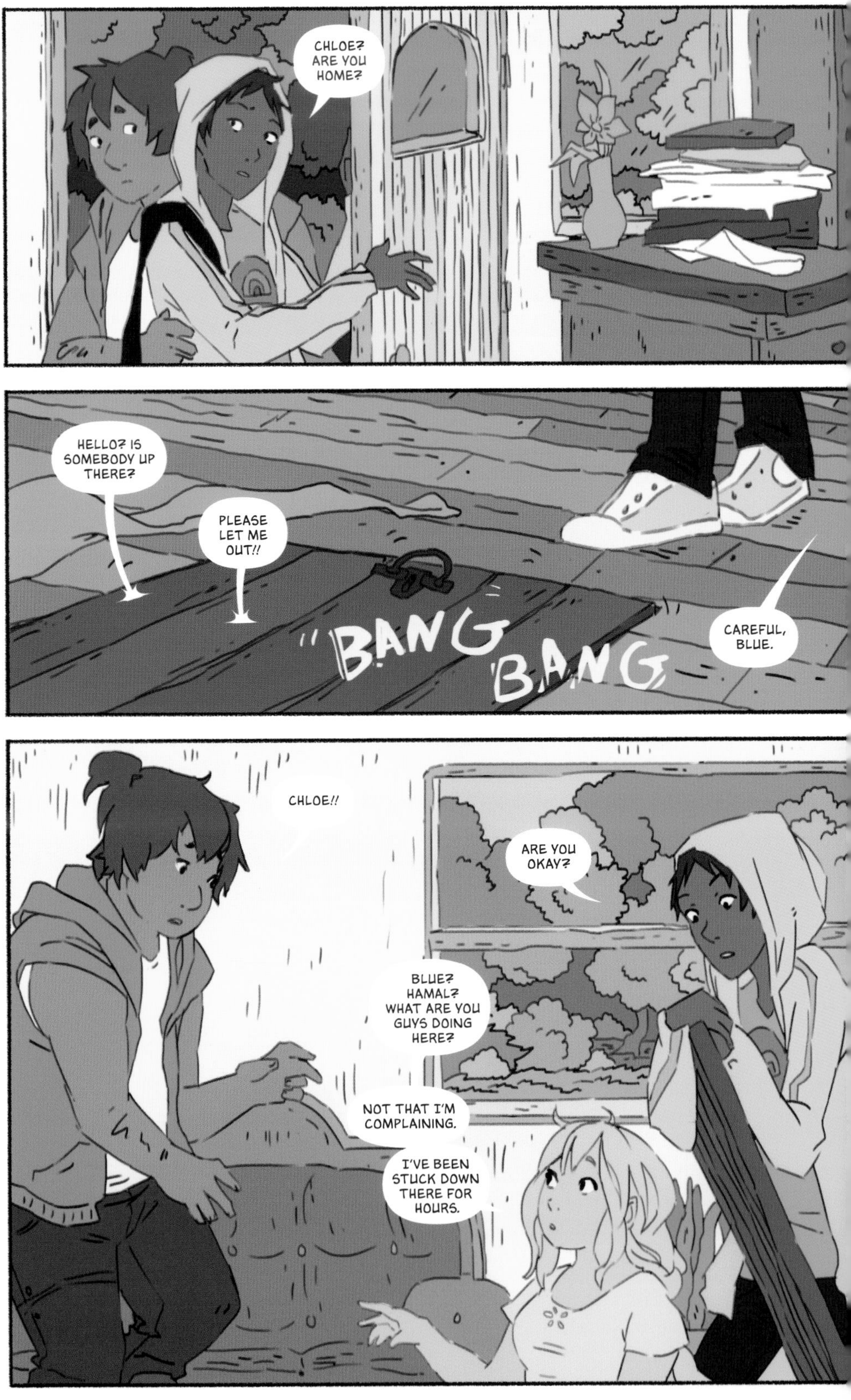
CHLOE? ARE YOU HOME?
HELLO? IS SOMEBODY UP THERE?
PLEASE LET ME OUT!!
BANG
BANG
CAREFUL, BLUE.
CHLOE!!
ARE YOU OKAY?
BLUE? HAMAL? WHAT ARE YOU GUYS DOING HERE?
NOT THAT I'M COMPLAINING.
I'VE BEEN STUCK DOWN THERE FOR HOURS.

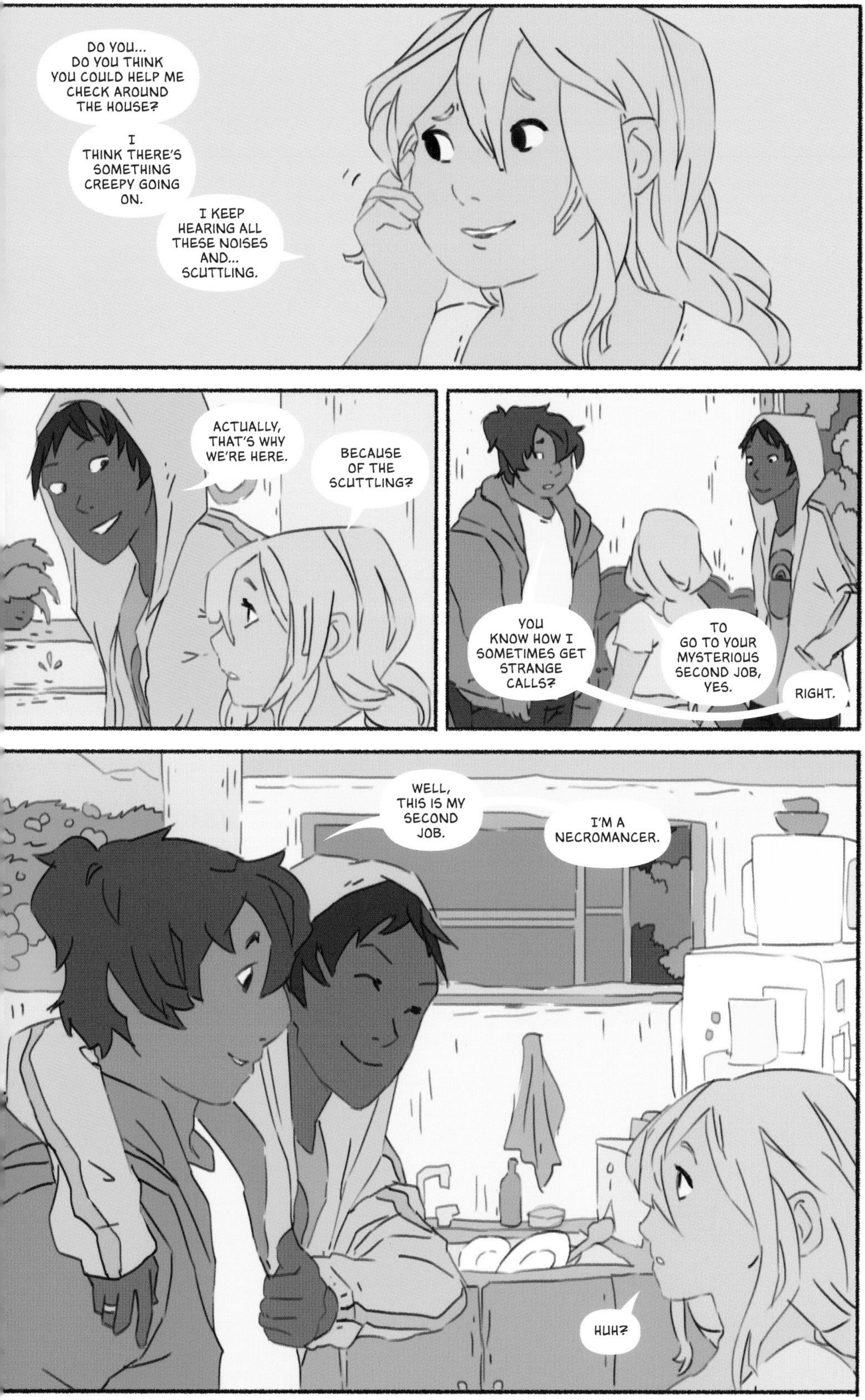
DO YOU... DO YOU THINK YOU COULD HELP ME CHECK AROUND THE HOUSE?
I THINK THERE'S SOMETHING CREEPY GOING ON.
I KEEP HEARING ALL THESE NOISES AND... SCUTTLING.
ACTUALLY, THAT'S WHY WE'RE HERE.
BECAUSE OF THE SCUTTLING?
YOU KNOW HOW I SOMETIMES GET STRANGE CALLS?
TO GO TO YOUR MYSTERIOUS SECOND JOB, YES.
RIGHT.
WELL, THIS IS MY SECOND JOB.
I'M A NECROMANCER.
HUH?

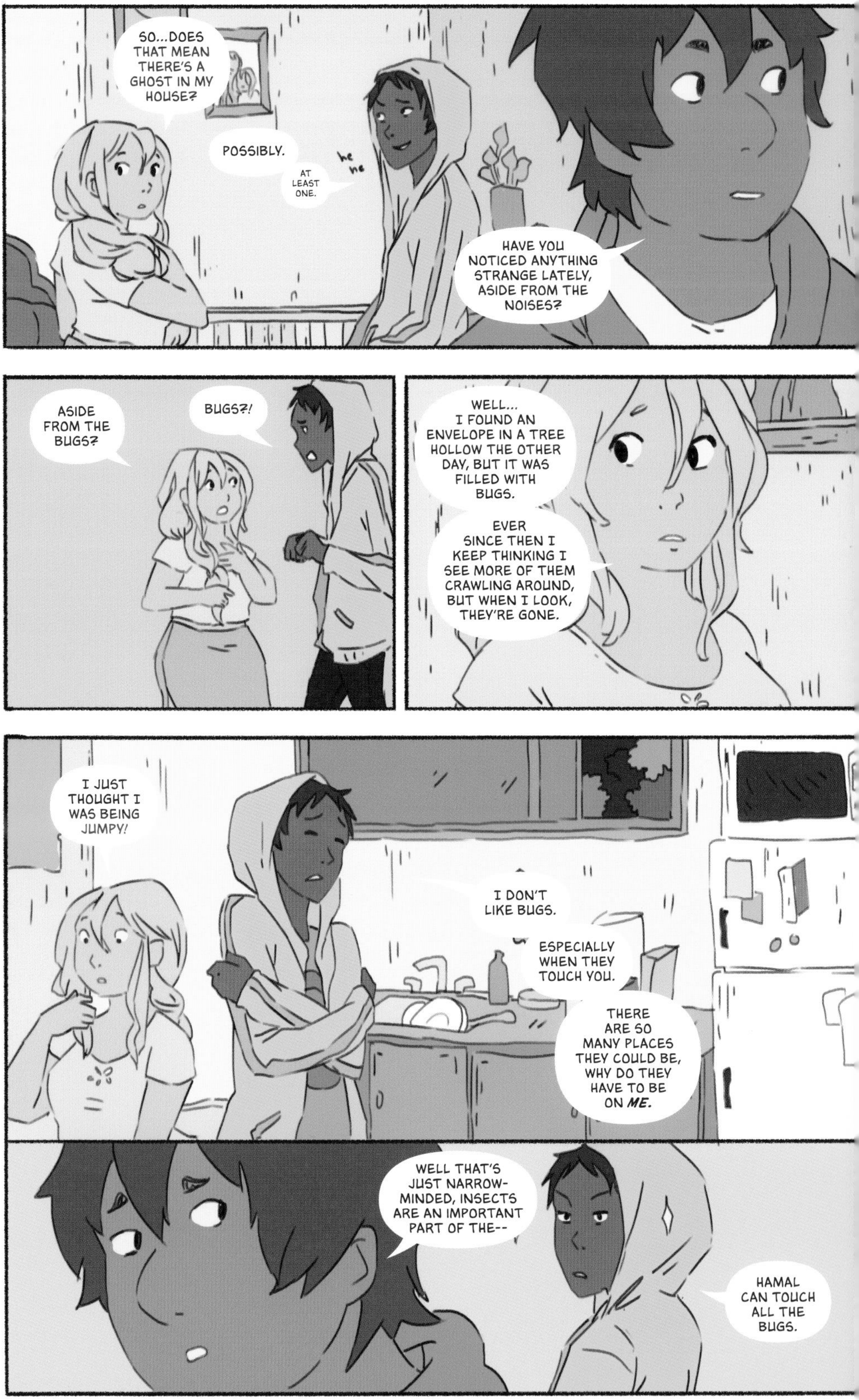
SO...DOES THAT MEAN THERE'S A GHOST IN MY HOUSE?
POSSIBLY.
AT LEAST ONE.
he he
HAVE YOU NOTICED ANYTHING STRANGE LATELY, ASIDE FROM THE NOISES?
ASIDE FROM THE BUGS?
BUGS?!
WELL... I FOUND AN ENVELOPE IN A TREE HOLLOW THE OTHER DAY, BUT IT WAS FILLED WITH BUGS.
EVER SINCE THEN I KEEP THINKING I SEE MORE OF THEM CRAWLING AROUND, BUT WHEN I LOOK, THEY'RE GONE.
I JUST THOUGHT I WAS BEING JUMPY!
I DON'T LIKE BUGS.
ESPECIALLY WHEN THEY TOUCH YOU.
THERE ARE SO MANY PLACES THEY COULD BE, WHY DO THEY HAVE TO BE ON ME.
WELL THAT'S JUST NARROW-MINDED, INSECTS ARE AN IMPORTANT PART OF THE--
HAMAL CAN TOUCH ALL THE BUGS.

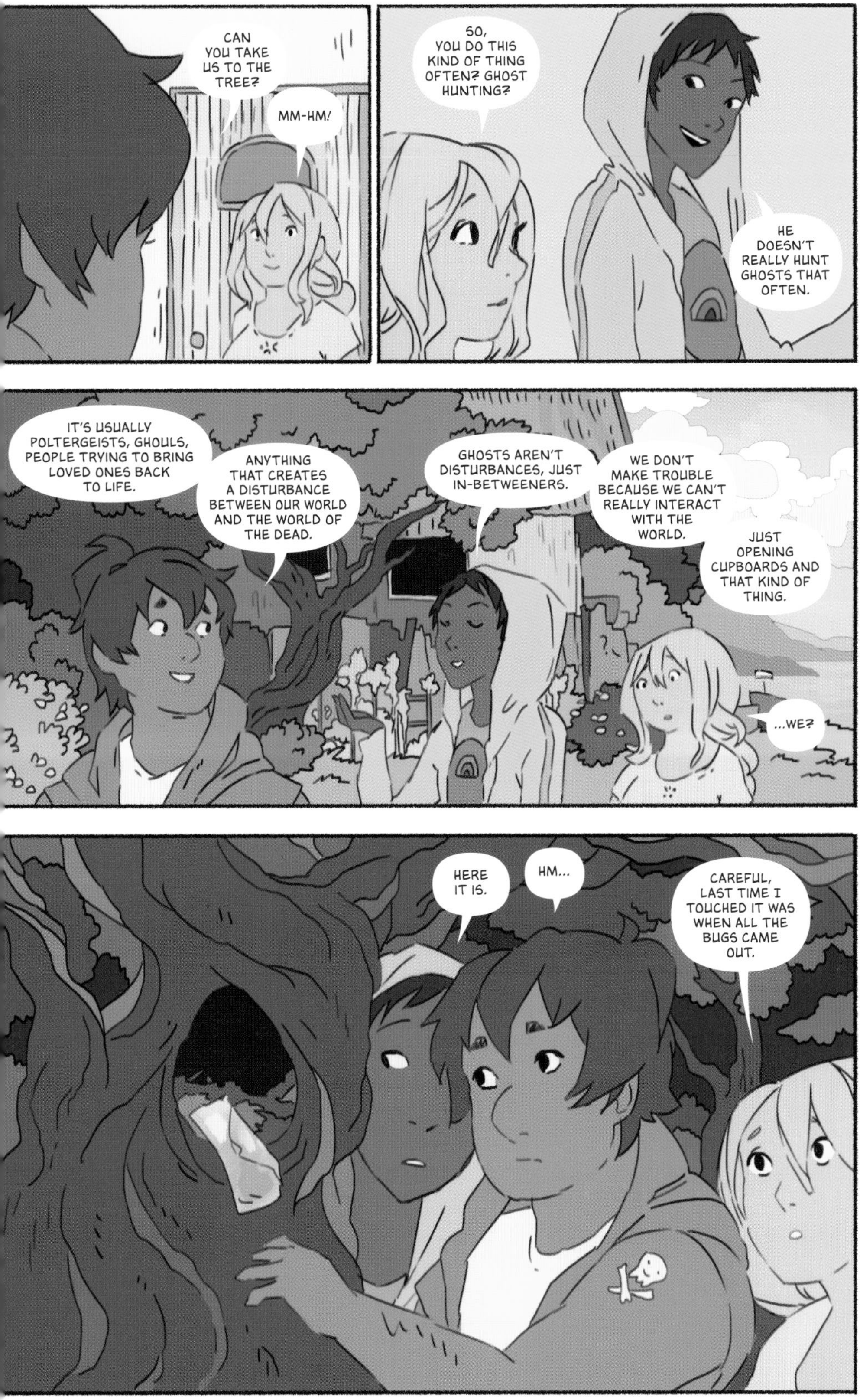
CAN YOU TAKE US TO THE TREE?
MM-HM!
SO, YOU DO THIS KIND OF THING OFTEN? GHOST HUNTING?
HE DOESN'T REALLY HUNT GHOSTS THAT OFTEN.
IT'S USUALLY POLTERGEISTS, GHOULS, PEOPLE TRYING TO BRING LOVED ONES BACK TO LIFE.
ANYTHING THAT CREATES A DISTURBANCE BETWEEN OUR WORLD AND THE WORLD OF THE DEAD.
GHOSTS AREN'T DISTURBANCES, JUST IN-BETWEENERS.
WE DON'T MAKE TROUBLE BECAUSE WE CAN'T REALLY INTERACT WITH THE WORLD.
JUST OPENING CUPBOARDS AND THAT KIND OF THING.
...WE?
HERE IT IS.
HM...
CAREFUL, LAST TIME I TOUCHED IT WAS WHEN ALL THE BUGS CAME OUT.

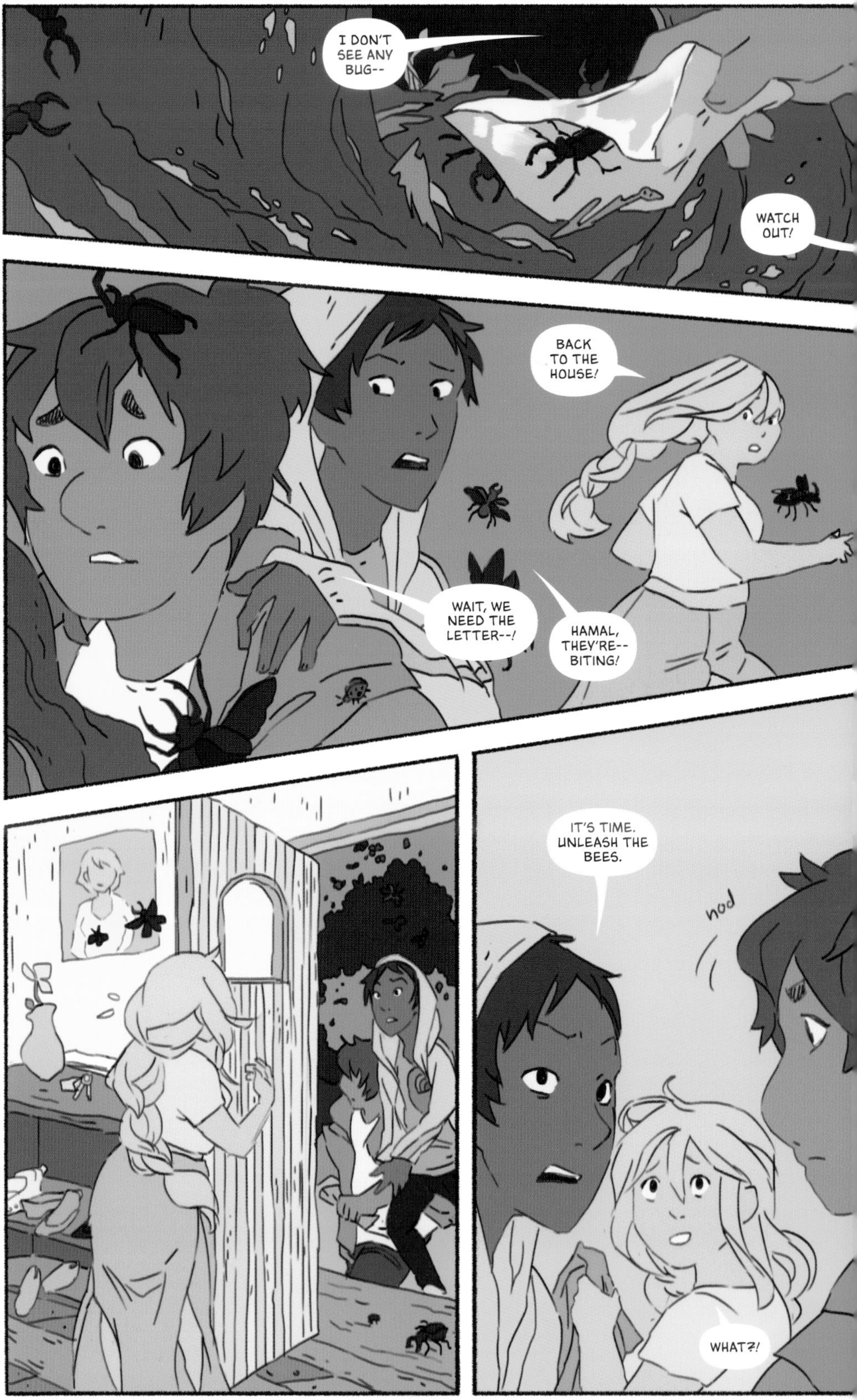
I DON'T SEE ANY BUG--
WATCH OUT!
BACK TO THE HOUSE!
WAIT, WE NEED THE LETTER--!
HAMAL, THEY'RE--BITING!
IT'S TIME. UNLEASH THE BEES.
nod
WHAT?!

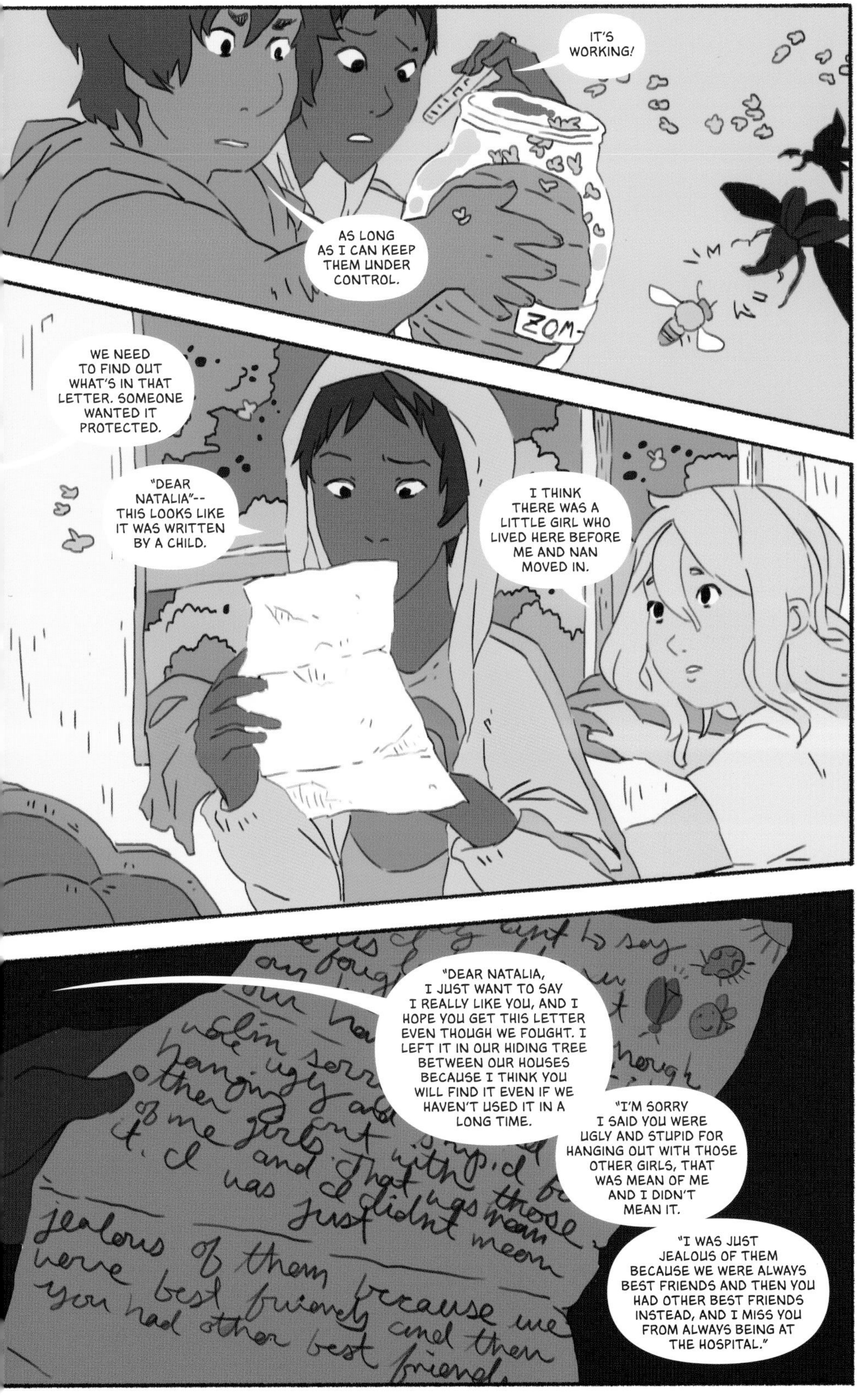
IT'S WORKING!
AS LONG AS I CAN KEEP THEM UNDER CONTROL.
ZOM-
WE NEED TO FIND OUT WHAT'S IN THAT LETTER. SOMEONE WANTED IT PROTECTED.
"DEAR NATALIA"-- THIS LOOKS LIKE IT WAS WRITTEN BY A CHILD.
I THINK THERE WAS A LITTLE GIRL WHO LIVED HERE BEFORE ME AND NAN MOVED IN.
"DEAR NATALIA, I JUST WANT TO SAY I REALLY LIKE YOU, AND I HOPE YOU GET THIS LETTER EVEN THOUGH WE FOUGHT. I LEFT IT IN OUR HIDING TREE BETWEEN OUR HOUSES BECAUSE I THINK YOU WILL FIND IT EVEN IF WE HAVEN'T USED IT IN A LONG TIME.
"I'M SORRY I SAID YOU WERE UGLY AND STUPID FOR HANGING OUT WITH THOSE OTHER GIRLS, THAT WAS MEAN OF ME AND I DIDN'T MEAN IT.
"I WAS JUST JEALOUS OF THEM BECAUSE WE WERE ALWAYS BEST FRIENDS AND THEN YOU HAD OTHER BEST FRIENDS INSTEAD, AND I MISS YOU FROM ALWAYS BEING AT THE HOSPITAL."

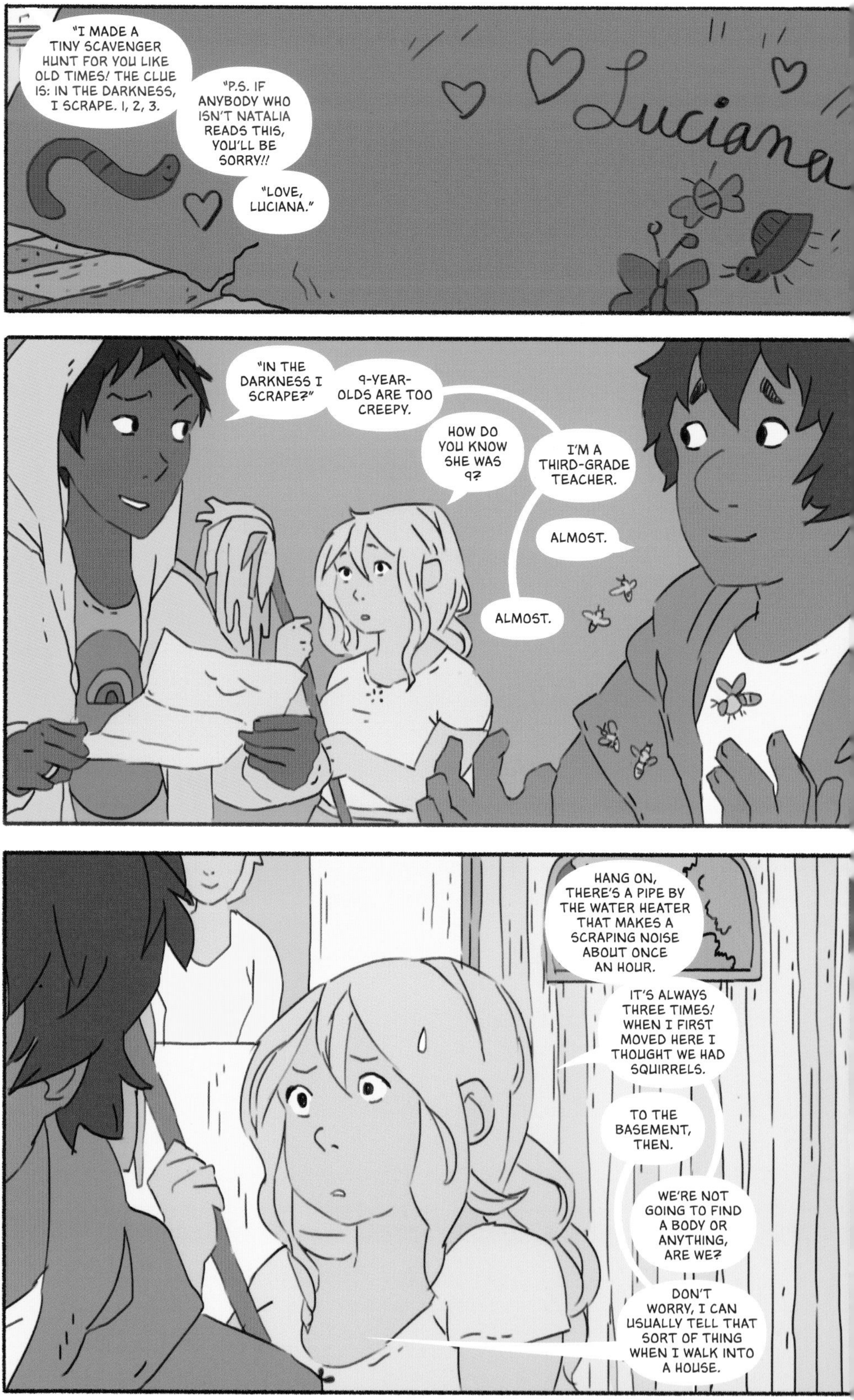
"I MADE A TINY SCAVENGER HUNT FOR YOU LIKE OLD TIMES! THE CLUE IS: IN THE DARKNESS, I SCRAPE. 1, 2, 3.
"P.S. IF ANYBODY WHO ISN'T NATALIA READS THIS, YOU'LL BE SORRY!!
"LOVE, LUCIANA."
Luciana
"IN THE DARKNESS I SCRAPE?"
9-YEAR-OLDS ARE TOO CREEPY.
HOW DO YOU KNOW SHE WAS 9?
I'M A THIRD-GRADE TEACHER.
ALMOST.
ALMOST.
HANG ON, THERE'S A PIPE BY THE WATER HEATER THAT MAKES A SCRAPING NOISE ABOUT ONCE AN HOUR.
IT'S ALWAYS THREE TIMES! WHEN I FIRST MOVED HERE I THOUGHT WE HAD SQUIRRELS.
TO THE BASEMENT, THEN.
WE'RE NOT GOING TO FIND A BODY OR ANYTHING, ARE WE?
DON'T WORRY, I CAN USUALLY TELL THAT SORT OF THING WHEN I WALK INTO A HOUSE.

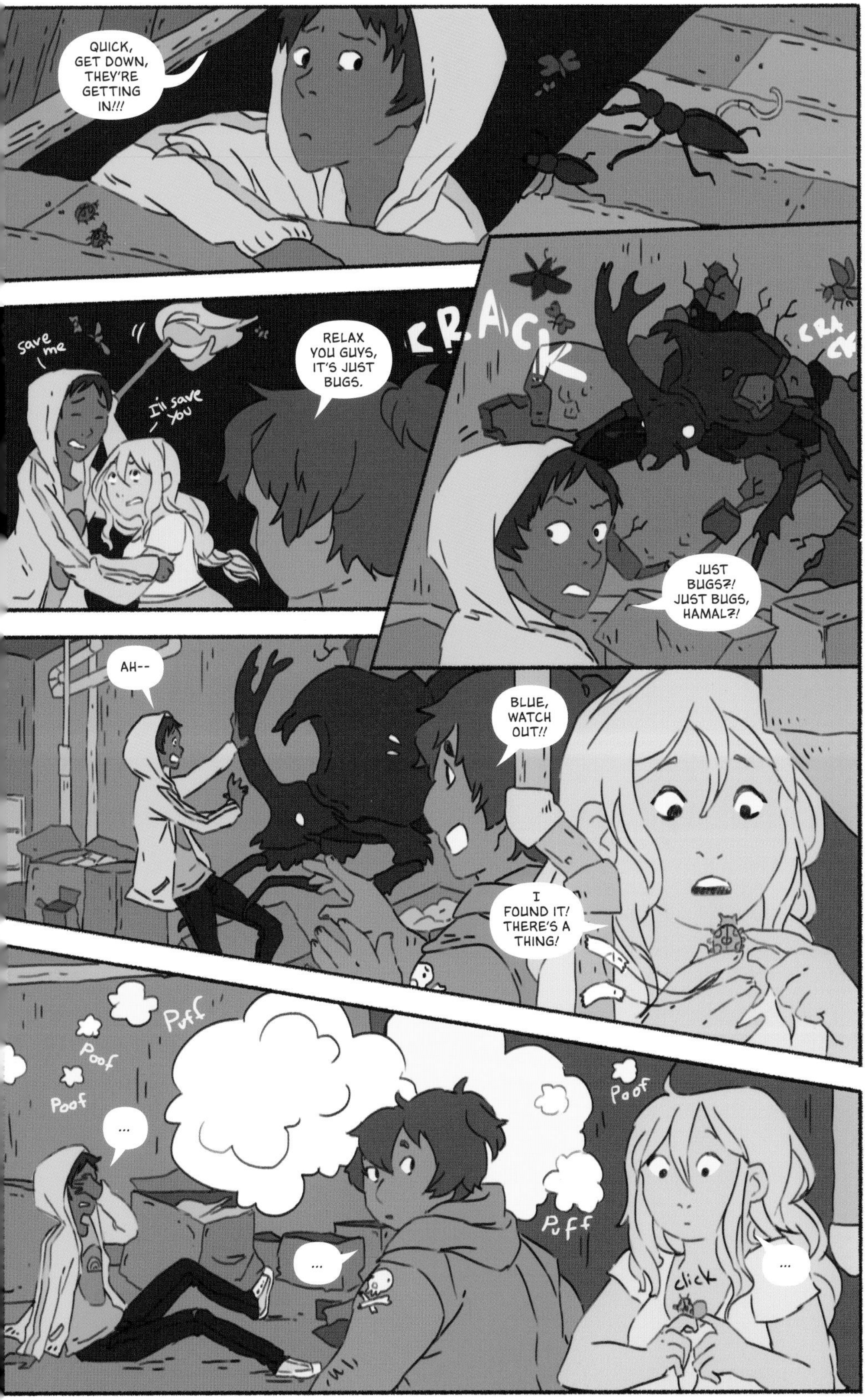

QUICK, GET DOWN, THEY'RE GETTING IN!!!
save me
I'll save you
RELAX YOU GUYS, IT'S JUST BUGS.
CRACK
CRACK
JUST BUGS?! JUST BUGS, HAMAL?!
AH--
BLUE, WATCH OUT!!
I FOUND IT! THERE'S A THING!
Puff
Poof
Poof
...
Poof
Puff
...
click
...

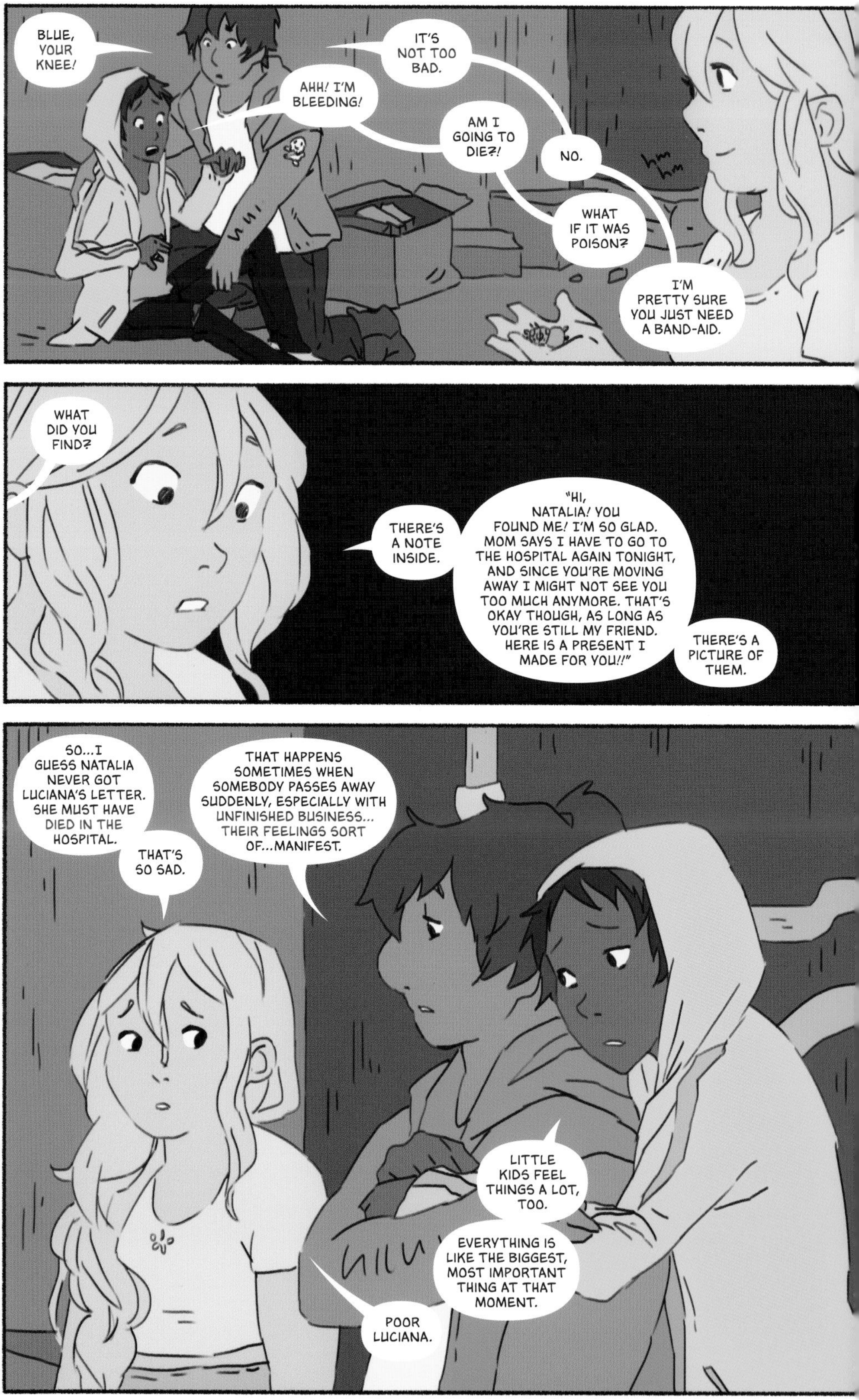
BLUE, YOUR KNEE!
IT'S NOT TOO BAD.
AHH! I'M BLEEDING!
AM I GOING TO DIE?!
NO.
hm hm
WHAT IF IT WAS POISON?
I'M PRETTY SURE YOU JUST NEED A BAND-AID.
WHAT DID YOU FIND?
THERE'S A NOTE INSIDE.
"HI, NATALIA! YOU FOUND ME! I'M SO GLAD. MOM SAYS I HAVE TO GO TO THE HOSPITAL AGAIN TONIGHT, AND SINCE YOU'RE MOVING AWAY I MIGHT NOT SEE YOU TOO MUCH ANYMORE. THAT'S OKAY THOUGH, AS LONG AS YOU'RE STILL MY FRIEND. HERE IS A PRESENT I MADE FOR YOU!!"
THERE'S A PICTURE OF THEM.
SO...I GUESS NATALIA NEVER GOT LUCIANA'S LETTER. SHE MUST HAVE DIED IN THE HOSPITAL.
THAT'S SO SAD.
THAT HAPPENS SOMETIMES WHEN SOMEBODY PASSES AWAY SUDDENLY, ESPECIALLY WITH UNFINISHED BUSINESS... THEIR FEELINGS SORT OF...MANIFEST.
LITTLE KIDS FEEL THINGS A LOT, TOO.
EVERYTHING IS LIKE THE BIGGEST, MOST IMPORTANT THING AT THAT MOMENT.
POOR LUCIANA.

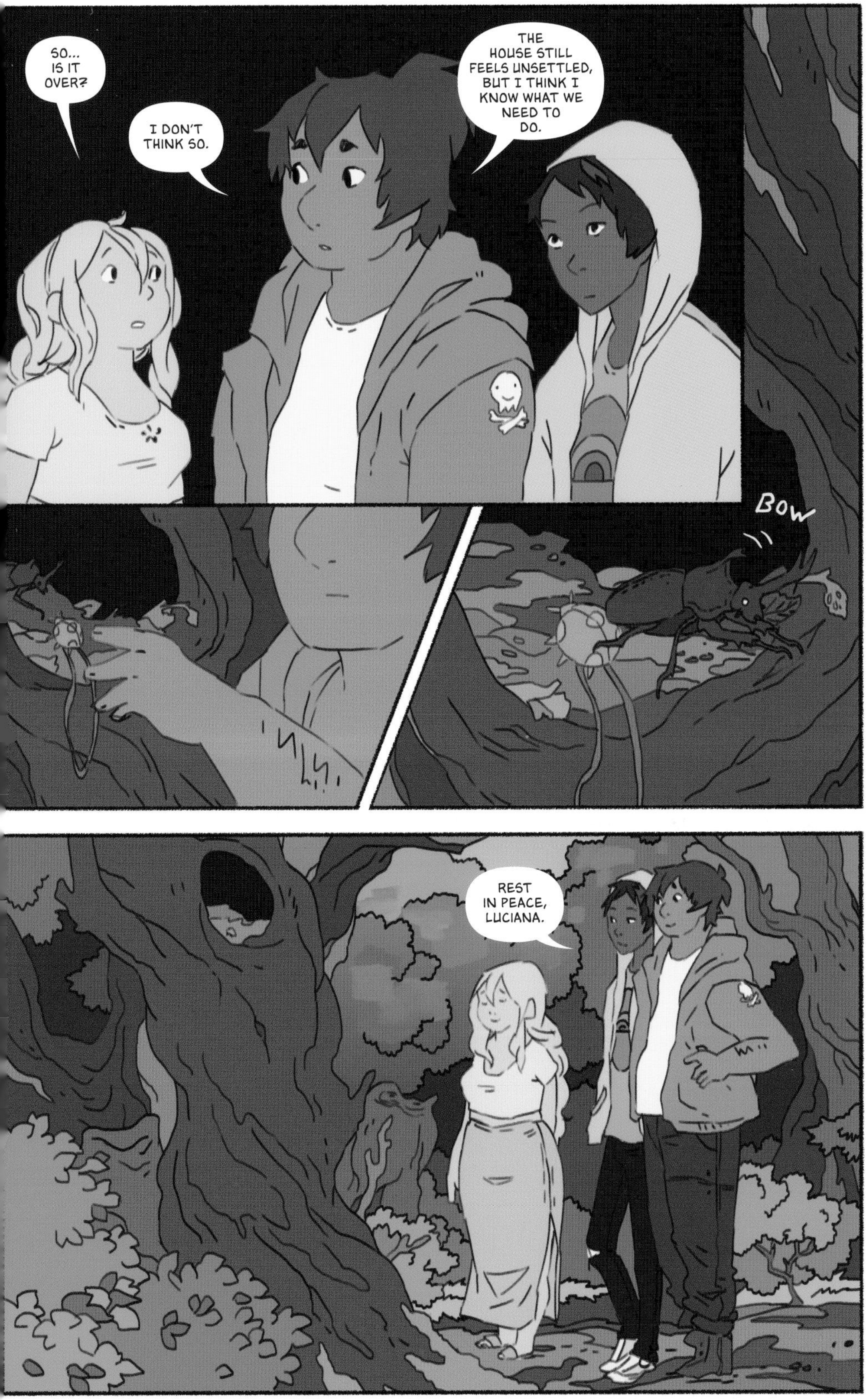
SO... IS IT OVER?
I DON'T THINK SO.
THE HOUSE STILL FEELS UNSETTLED, BUT I THINK I KNOW WHAT WE NEED TO DO.
BOW
REST IN PEACE, LUCIANA.

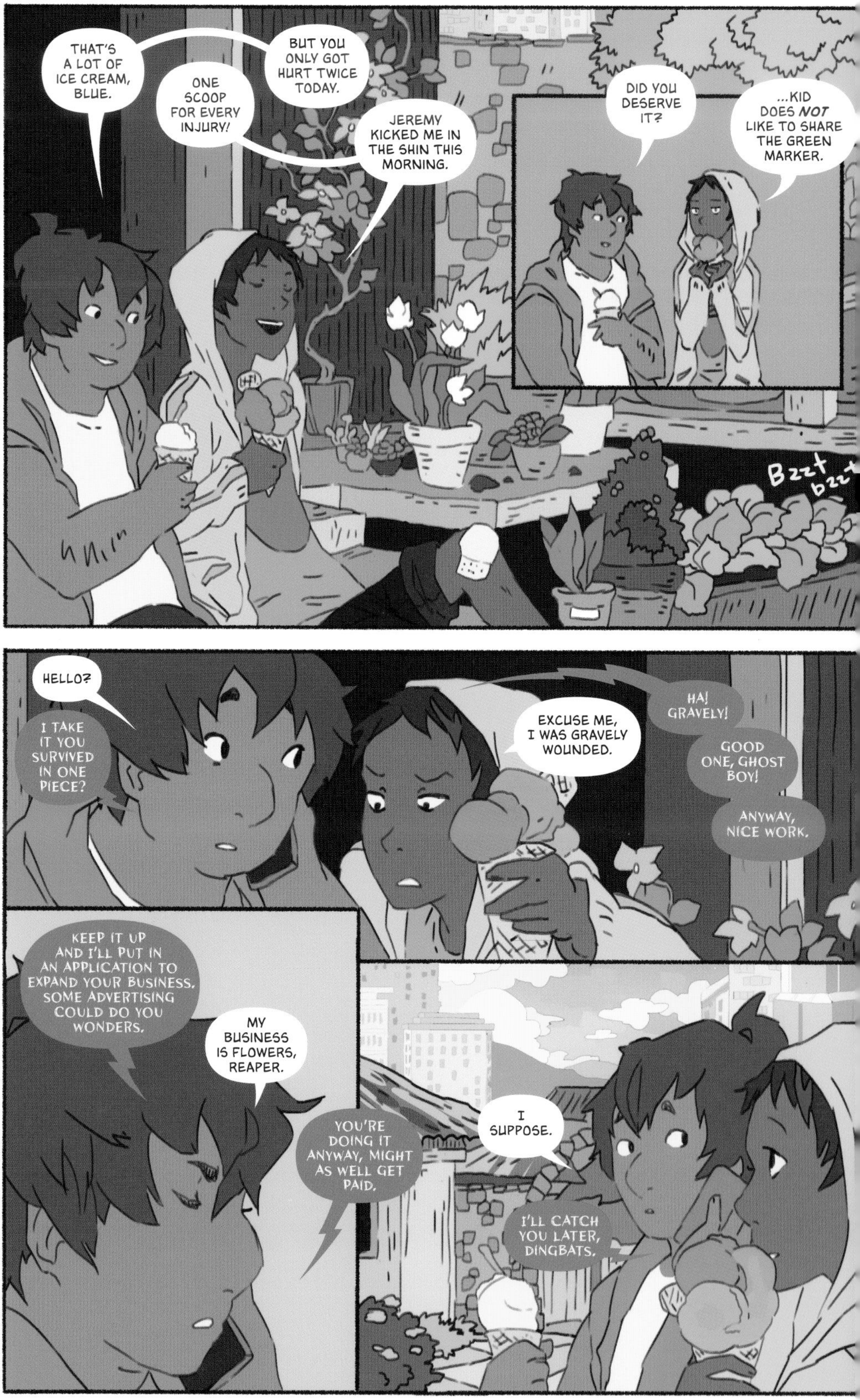
THAT'S A LOT OF ICE CREAM, BLUE.
BUT YOU ONLY GOT HURT TWICE TODAY.
ONE SCOOP FOR EVERY INJURY!
JEREMY KICKED ME IN THE SHIN THIS MORNING.
DID YOU DESERVE IT?
...KID DOES NOT LIKE TO SHARE THE GREEN MARKER.
Bzzt bzzt
HELLO?
I TAKE IT YOU SURVIVED IN ONE PIECE?
EXCUSE ME, I WAS GRAVELY WOUNDED.
HA! GRAVELY!
GOOD ONE, GHOST BOY!
ANYWAY, NICE WORK.
KEEP IT UP AND I'LL PUT IN AN APPLICATION TO EXPAND YOUR BUSINESS. SOME ADVERTISING COULD DO YOU WONDERS.
MY BUSINESS IS FLOWERS, REAPER.
YOU'RE DOING IT ANYWAY, MIGHT AS WELL GET PAID.
I SUPPOSE.
I'LL CATCH YOU LATER, DINGBATS.

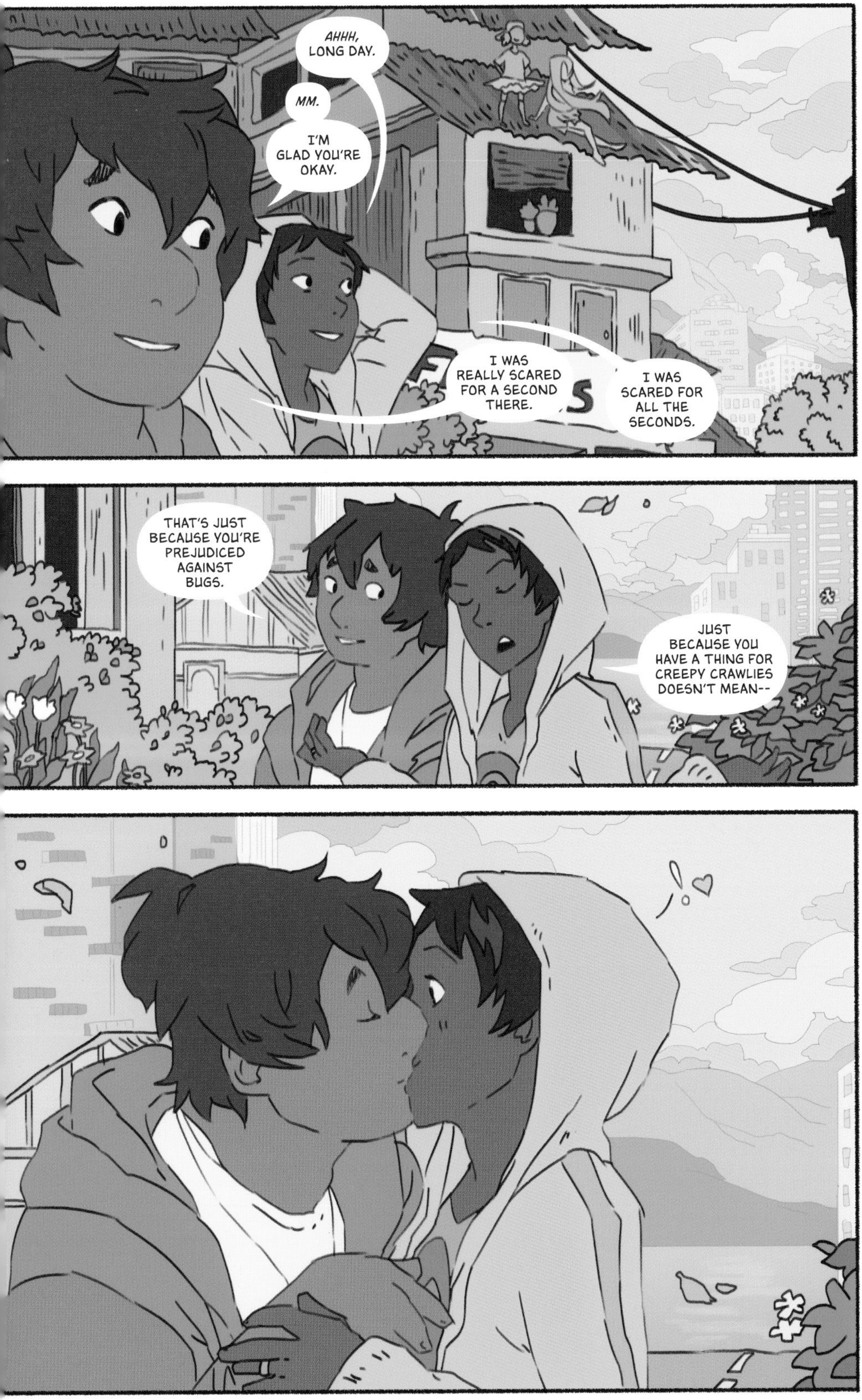
AHHH, LONG DAY.
MM.
I'M GLAD YOU'RE OKAY.
I WAS REALLY SCARED FOR A SECOND THERE.
I WAS SCARED FOR ALL THE SECONDS.
THAT'S JUST BECAUSE YOU'RE PREJUDICED AGAINST BUGS.
JUST BECAUSE YOU HAVE A THING FOR CREEPY CRAWLIES DOESN'T MEAN--

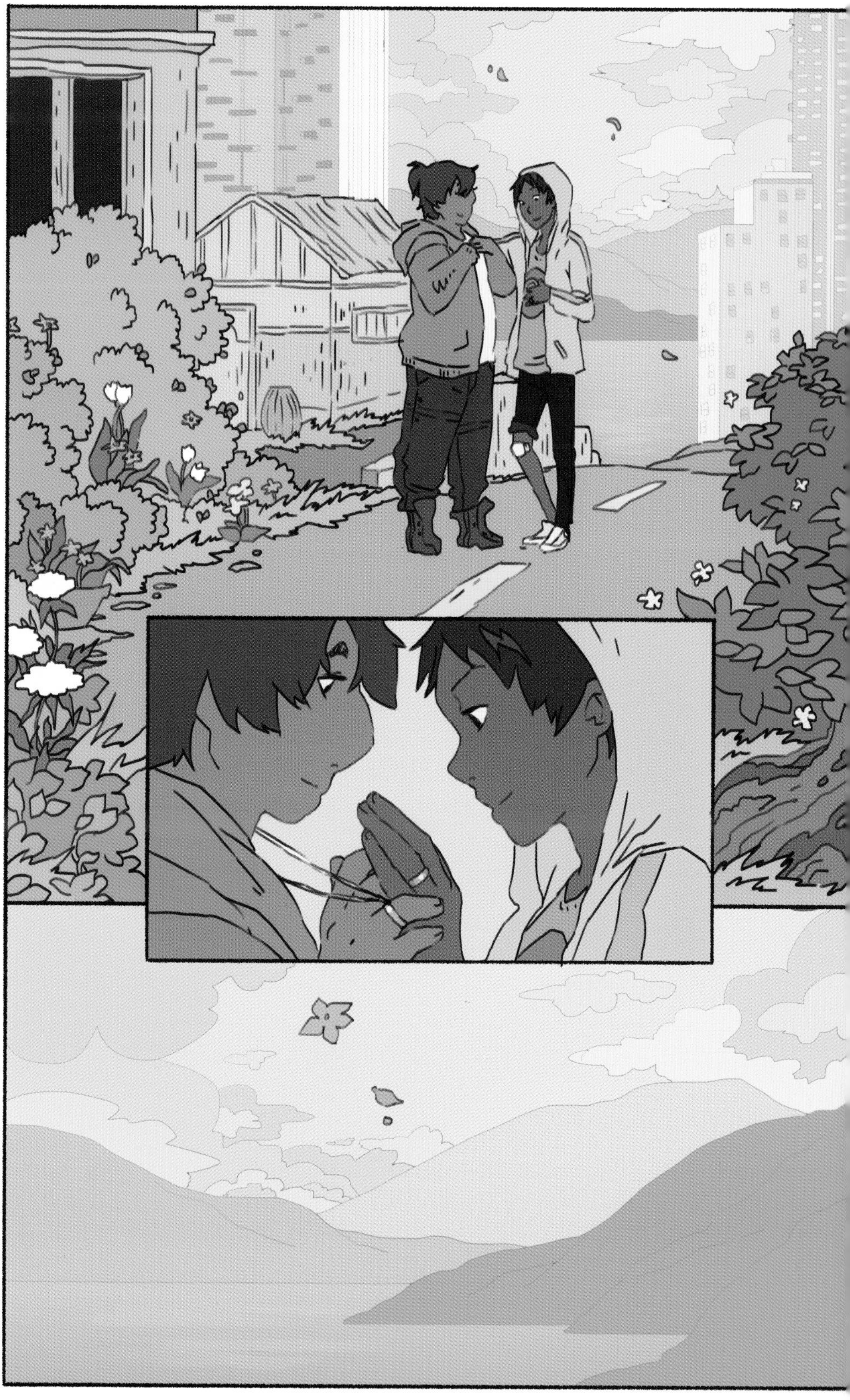

KEEZY YOUNG IS A COMIC
ARTIST BASED IN SEATTLE, WASHINGTON.
SHE DRAWS AND WRITES THE STORIES SHE
WANTED TO SEE MORE OF GROWING UP--
STORIES STARRING QUEER CHARACTERS,
BRIGHTNESS, A LITTLE CREEPINESS, AND
A LOT OF HEART. SHE NEVER FELT LIKE
SHE BELONGED IN HER FAVORITE COMICS,
AND SHE WANTS TO CHANGE THAT FOR
YOUNG PEOPLE WHO FEEL ALONE NOW BY
BRINGING SOME COLOR TO THEIR LIVES.
HER WORK USES THAT COLOR TO CREATE
WORLDS THAT ARE FAMILIAR WHILE
EMBRACING THE SUPERNATURAL.

STORY AND ART BY
KEEZY YOUNG

LETTERER: **AW'S TOM NAPOLITANO**
ASSISTANT EDITOR: **HAZEL NEWLEVANT**
EDITOR: **ANDREA COLVIN**

PUBLISHER'S CATALOGING—IN—PUBLICATION DATA

(PREPARED BY THE DONOHUE GROUP, INC.)

NAMES: YOUNG, KEEZY, AUTHOR, ILLUSTRATOR. | NAPOLITANO, TOM, LETTERER. | COLVIN, ANDREA, EDITOR. |
    NEWLEVANT, HAZEL, EDITOR.

TITLE: TAPROOT : A STORY ABOUT A GARDENER AND A GHOST / STORY AND ART BY KEEZY YOUNG ;
    LETTERER: AW'S TOM NAPOLITANO ; ASSISTANT EDITOR: HAZEL NEWLEVANT ; EDITOR: ANDREA COLVIN.

DESCRIPTION: [ST. LOUIS, MISSOURI] : THE LION FORGE, LLC, 2017. | "BASED ON THE WEB COMIC CREATED BY
    KEEZY YOUNG."

IDENTIFIERS: ISBN 978-1-941302-46-0

SUBJECTS: LCSH: GARDENERS--COMIC BOOKS, STRIPS, ETC. | GHOSTS--COMIC BOOKS, STRIPS, ETC. |
    EXTRASENSORY PERCEPTION--COMIC BOOKS, STRIPS, ETC. | LCGFT: GRAPHIC NOVELS.

CLASSIFICATION: LCC PN6728.T37 Y68 2017 | DDC 741.5973--DC23